MW01132734

Nominated by: The State Library of South Australia, Adelaide
Publisher of nominated edition: HarperCollins Australia
The Claimant by Janette Turner Hospital
Nomination Citation: A dark and delicious tale which begins as a complex riddle of identity and class divisions in wonderfully drawn settings in France, Australia and Manhattan. The story never becomes too cryptic though. Our panel highly recommended this novel.

Australian reviews of THE CLAIMANT
Here is one of the most unusual fictional postscripts to Australia's involvement in Vietnam, besides being a vivid, ambivalent snapshot of American politics of the 1960s as galvanized by the war.... Hospital combines psychological acuity with command of a range of settings, from luxurious to grunge, that will tempt those who might wish to bring the novel to the screen. In the meantime, readers have a big book to enjoy.

Sydney Morning Herald

The Claimant shares its vibrantly beating heart with the implications and intricacies of privilege, the iron grip of lineage, the complexities of naming and identity...and the persistence of the essential self.... Janette Turner Hospital is a splendid prose stylist in command of her art, and amazingly confident in exploring and testing its possibilities – now a lush sensuousness, now a sort of electric sparking precision and, and not least of all her armoury, a free-ranging referencing of literature and art... *The Claimant* is a genuine page-turner.

Australian Book Review

The Claimant is a book about spies and collaborators, about art and religion, and its focus is a fictional court case in the late 20th century over a family fortune and the search for a lost heir. Its concern is the way our identities change, even in the simplest ways, depending on the stages of our lives, who we are with, what the expectations are of us – our class, our politics, our nationalities. Told in an intricate and complex way, *The Claimant* is ...a mystery thriller. It's a feat of plotting, and I imagined Janette Turner Hospital holding all the plot points and identities like a huge hand of cards.

Australian Broadcasting Commission: National Book Program
[Interview with Romona Koval, who selected The Claimant for nationwide discussion]

THE
CLAIMANT

For Sissy

Janette Turner Hospital
4·19·17

By the same author

The Ivory Swing
The Tiger in the Tiger Pit
Borderline
Dislocations
Charades
Isobars
The Last Magician
Collected Stories
Oyster
North of Nowhere, South of Loss
Due Preparations for the Plague
Orpheus Lost
Forecast: Turbulence

THE
CLAIMANT

JANETTE
⬥TURNER⬥
HOSPITAL

BIBLIOTHECA
BOADICEA

Published by

Bibliotheca Boadicea

ISBN: 978-1533448415

First American Edition
First published by HarperCollins Australia in 2014

The author may be contacted via her literary agents:
New York: Deborah Schneider @ Gelfman Schneider/ICM Partners
   Email: deborah@gelfmanschneider.com
Sydney: Barbara Mobbs Literary Agency
   Email: beemobbs@bigpond.com.au

Cover design by Jane Evelynne Higgins

Printed in the United States of America

For Cliff
my first and best reader
my toughest and most astute critic

Contents

You're born, you know, the wrong names, wrong parents.
I mean, that happens. You call yourself what you want to call
yourself. This is the land of the free.

Singer/songwriter Bob Dylan,
Born Shabtai ben Zisel Avraham Zimmerman

Now if a man's subject is deception, you are deceived if you think
you grasp his meaning...

Hilary Mantel

Prince Wen Hui's cook was cutting up an ox.
'Good work!' the Prince exclaimed. 'Your method is faultless.'
'What I follow is Tao,' the cook said.
'My cleaver finds its own way. I cut through no joint, chop no bone.
A good cook needs a new chopper once a year—he cuts.
A poor cook needs a new one every month— he hacks!
I have used this same cleaver nineteen years...'

Prince Wen Hui said, 'My cook has shown me
How I ought to live my own life.'

Chuang Tzu; trans. Thomas Merton

THE
CLAIMANT

BOOK I
MARLOWE

1.

During the week of the sequestering of the jury Marlowe places bets and makes confessions in bars all over Manhattan. The trial of the Vanderbilt claimant consumes him. He admits this to total strangers but they share his fixation. Sometimes they raise the odds, sometimes they toss a coin before deciding. Bartenders keep unofficial books.

Status updates on the claimant flash in bright white lights in Times Square. *Is he or isn't he? Jury to decide.* Heated opinions fog the subway system and eddy up into the streets. At Columbus Circle, where so many lines converge, musicians find that a handmade sign on a guitar case—**Go Claimant!**—increases both donations and fights. Assorted experts—psychiatrists, psychologists, clergy—deem the covert gambling obsessive.

Marlowe's confessional maunderings are equally obsessive but never drunken, never *actually* drunken. He is meticulous. No sliver of data is too small or too insignificant for scooping up.

He scribbles something—*Master of the Game*—on the back of a coaster, flips it over (so that the promotional *logo* faces up) and slides it along the bar to the nearest elbow. He cannot resist this kind of snide secret joke. He flirts compulsively with exposure. "Name's Marlowe," he says, speech slightly slurred. "What's your take on this Vanderbilt thing?"

On the matter of the Vanderbilt claimant, everyone has an

opinion, usually vehement.

Marlowe listens with reverential attention. He nods thoughtfully. "You're right. I think he must be the real thing. But for the sake of argument, and because I'm a gambling man, I give you five to one he's a fraud."

Alternatively, he says: "I agree. Absolutely. The claimant's as phony as a two-dollar bill. But for the sake of argument..."

Marlowe himself, as avid a reader of the *New York Times* as of the tabloids, is a consummate sounding board. He affirms whatever the speaker believes and offers buttery endorsements from the most impressive of sources. He quotes Shakespeare and Plato. The speaker is flattered and buys the next round of drinks. People are drawn to Marlowe. They are eager to confide in him and he is more than willing to absorb. He is like blotting paper. He is charming, unfailingly warm and witty, always courteous. In addition, he has a talent for picking up the significant tips of conversation from neighboring barstools and booths, a skill crucial to both of his careers. He gathers intelligence.

He has been present in court every day since the trial began, attentive to prosecution and defense, focused on detail, scrutinizing faces, searching for one in particular.

Will she show up?

Does she believe that the Vanderbilt claimant is the heir?

Can she possibly—in this third week of October 1996—still believe that the heir is alive?

Everywhere Marlowe smells her perfume. He hallucinates. He turns often, sure she is on the barstool beside him. *I knew you'd show up,* he almost says. His sensory memory is acute and can be disorienting but he never loses track of what is real and what is not. Or so he believes.

He is turning a coaster over and over between his fingers like a coin, somewhat awkwardly because of the stiffness of the cardboard. The reverse side rests on the back of his knuckles. *Master of the Game,* his scrawl announces to the ceiling in ballpoint ink.

Still a narcissist, he imagines her accusing. He can hear her voice, tinged with disdain. *Still flirting with being caught. Can't resist the rush, can you?*

Still haunted? he snaps back. *Still in denial after all these years?*

In the week of the sequestering of the jury, Marlowe cannot go anywhere in Manhattan without hearing burning opinions, pro and con. The Vanderbilts—according to those betting heavily in favor of the claimant—cannot believe that a man who works for a living—actually *works*—could be a member of their upper-crust clan, especially not a man who breeds cattle and butchers them.

"This is not the kind of activity in which the Vanderbilt family has ever been engaged," a family lawyer announces to the press. "The only animals that have ever been of interest to the Vanderbilts are racehorses, Preakness and Belmont Stakes winners, Kentucky Derby contenders."

"And yet," a reporter needles, "aren't cattle herds, dairy and beef, bred at the Biltmore Estate which the Vanderbilts own?"

"Tourism," the family lawyer says dismissively. "Token herds. Re-enactment of farming in the chateaux and great landed estates of Europe. Part of the family heritage and family business."

"Is there any truth to the rumors that the trial is nothing but a publicity stunt—?"

"No," the lawyer says, though many believe one of his tasks is to drum up national attention and free promotion for the Vanderbilt chateau— the Biltmore Estate—in North Carolina.

Polls show that half the population thinks the claimant is the Vanderbilts'w own straw man, a family invention, put together by lawyers either for publicity reasons (Biltmore tourism) or for the sole purpose of preempting any dispersal of assets or any future challenges to the will. Thousands are betting that the claimant is a fraud but a family-sponsored fraud.

There are media rumors of bitter factions within the Vanderbilt family: one side inventing and sponsoring the claimant in order to defraud the other side; or, possibly, for similar reasons, one side finding and coaching a claimant with massive kickback promises if he wins.

Everyone concurs that the Vanderbilts have always been notorious for interfamilial litigation of the most astonishingly vicious sort—between parent and child, between spouse and ex, between siblings—and much anecdotal evidence and embroidered memories are wittily exchanged as proof.

Marlowe listens. He blends in. Though his eagle eye and scavenger's ear have been focused on the claimant from the first bizarre hint of his existence, the trial had actually been muddling along for a year without attracting much notice beyond the upper social circles of New York, but that changed overnight. The claimant's testimony in court in March 1996—eight months before the closeting of the jury—triggered an explosion of curiosity and investigative media zeal. When the countess (mother of the heir) died a mere six weeks after the claimant's appearance, the line-graph of public attention shot up like a fly ball and hovered there, suspended high in the air for week after week as the legal arguments dragged on, until the final updraft (the sequestering of the jury) blew it out of the stadium.

The countess (a Vanderbilt widow, recently deceased) was insistent that the claimant was her long lost son; the rest of the extensive Vanderbilt family and its lawyers were and are equally insistent that he is not.

The core questions, all over Manhattan, are the same.

Is the claimant a fraud?

Is he a hoax?

Does he even exist apart from a single brief video-interview that was shown in court and partially reproduced in stills in newspapers? Is there any kind of proof that the speaker in the video is actually the claimant, let alone any proof that the claimant is the actual heir?

The man in the video is good-looking and muscular. He is wearing an Akubra hat (the Australian version, though rather more stylish, of the cowboy's Stetson), a denim shirt and faded jeans. Behind him: green pasture and cattle, a loop of river. He wears riding boots and is leaning against his horse, the reins loose in his hands. Any actor could have been paid by the countess or by her lawyers to act the part. He certainly bears no resemblance to the Harvard graduation photograph of Gwynne Patrice Vanderbilt.

If the claimant does exist, and if—as the Vanderbilt widow and her lawyers have claimed—he is (was?) her long lost son and heir, then had he somehow metamorphosed into likable blue-collar hunk or was he—is he—a brilliant con man?

The lawyers for the Vanderbilt family have sought to demonstrate that the claimant is uneducated, a butcher by trade, currently raising cattle on rural flatlands vaguely north of nowhere on the coastal downs of Queensland, Australia. They have argued that he can in no way be the refined and reserved intellectual son of the late Lawrence Gwynne Vanderbilt whose only child (or rather, whose only acknowledged and legitimate child), a Harvard graduate *summa cum laude*, had been tragically lost in Vietnam.

On the other hand, even the family lawyers are at a loss to explain why the heir, an activist anti-war protestor of the 60's, had suddenly and inexplicably enlisted in the infantry and been shipped to Vietnam in '69.

Court testimony has provided further confusion. Witnesses for the defense swore they had known the claimant at Harvard. "We were same year, class of '68," one witness declared. "What I mean is, Gwynne Vanderbilt, the real one, was in my year, and I recognize something about the claimant's eyes that doesn't completely rule out the possibility... Also he was a wicked mimic—he could do professors, LBJ, Johnny Carson—so, you know, that Australian accent doesn't throw me. It's within his range.

"He certainly never preened as one of *those* Vanderbilts, and I never thought of him that way, especially since no family showed up for his graduation. Only his girlfriend came. There was a history of family acrimony made all the worse by the total impossibility of divorce. His mother was Catholic, he said. Devout to the Nth degree."

"He always had this gaunt haunted look," another Harvard alumnus, class of '68, testified under oath. "We figured he was one of us, back then. You know, keeping ourselves going on nothing except what we inhaled, worrying about the draft and about dying. Would we go or would we march? I know Vanderbilt went and never came back. Well, at least, we believed he never came back. He was officially declared Missing in Action but I do think it's possible—or at least not *impossible*—that the claimant could be him."

"Physically, I wouldn't have recognized him," another witness said, "but hey, you wouldn't know me from my college yearbook photo either. I took a course he was teaching in Fall '68 when I was an undergrad at Boston College. We knew him as McVie but there was talk that he was really a Vanderbilt who'd legally changed his name as some sort of political penance. The rumor was that he was studying to become a priest. Speaking for myself, I never believed the Vanderbilt rumor. It was certainly my opinion at that time that he was blue-collar Boston Irish, like me, like all of us at Boston College, and as proud of it as we were. In fact, I know he was working a couple of days a week at a butcher shop in Somerville... you know, the kind of down-market Catholic neighborhood that I grew up in. We knew he had a Harvard degree, so

I figured he must have got in on a scholarship, which is the sort of thing that would mark you an outsider at Harvard. I really have no significant evidence one way or the other as to whether or not McVie was a Vanderbilt, but I do think the claimant on the video is McVie. Or *could be* McVie. So my point is simply that he's not uneducated. Not by a long shot."

Someone who had been at prep school and at Harvard with the young Gwynne Vanderbilt—and had known him as such—testified that his former fellow-student had gone off the rails in the late sixties. "There was both a Vanderbilt and a McVie in my year at prep school, I can swear to that. McVie was a scholarship student from inner Boston, one of those rough Irish-mob areas. He was a complete outsider at Dryden Academy. As you'd expect, none of us knew him and we didn't associate with him. In fact, in our yearbook, there isn't even a photograph of McVie, just a silhouette outline. God only knows what that means. But he and Vanderbilt became friends, no one understood why. McVie was killed in Vietnam and the word was that Vanderbilt was unhinged by his death. He joined marches and demos. We parted company in all senses because I never had any time for that anti-war flag-burning stuff, but Vanderbilt, he got high on the rabble. It was a phase, you know, with quite a few of my friends, preppies slumming it, getting arrested, big thrill. It was the trendy thing to do back then.

"Some of them fell by the wayside, fried their brains on dope and never climbed back out, but most of us had no intention of losing our student deferment. No way we planned close encounters of the terminal kind with the Vietcong and we all sobered up as soon as we went on the market. We were just as patriotic as the guys drafted into Vietcong fodder, but there are different ways of being patriotic, and keeping the economy firing on all cylinders is one of those.

"To be honest, I have colleagues on Wall Street who keep posters of Che Guevara in their pool-table rooms. They joke about it, but they can still get maudlin after a few martinis."

Other Dryden alumni were called to the witness stand. Definitely, they confirmed, they had known both a Vanderbilt and a McVie at prep school but everyone's memories of the latter were vague. No one was surprised, assorted Dryden alumni testified, that after graduation McVie dropped out of sight. Someone thought he remembered that McVie had been accepted at Harvard but had never shown up. Someone thought he heard McVie had been drafted. Someone surmised that McVie had been killed in Vietnam. Someone else remembered that in senior year at Harvard Vanderbilt moved off campus. There were rumors he was trying to pass himself off as blue-collar instead of blue-blood.

The claimant was supposedly born in New York to one of the richest and most powerful Protestant families in America, but he was French and Catholic on his mother's side and of aristocratic lineage, offspring of a line of erotic and sumptuous extra-marital beddings that stretched back to Louis XIV. He grew up in a village in France—in the chateau that dominated the cluster of vineyards and houses—and was fluent in French.

No. He could barely speak broken French. He was Australian and sounded Australian. When he opened his mouth, the muddy diphthongs of Crocodile Dundee oozed out, sluggish as the chocolate custard left behind by a river after floods.

No. He was blue-collar American. He enlisted in December 1968, just before Christmas—infantry, Charlie Company—was promptly shipped off to basic training at Fort Bragg, North Carolina, then to a short advanced training stint in California, and then to Vietnam, after which he was either killed, or was Missing in Action, or was tended and protected by South Vietnamese villagers who became boat people and eventually made their way to Australia, or he was evacuated to the Philippines after the fall of

Saigon in 1975 after which he made his way to Australia, perhaps with the dog tags and ID of a fallen Aussie soldier whom he may perhaps have tried to save or may have killed.

Of the few things known for certain, one is that having been purportedly located by the lawyers of la Comtesse de la Vallière Vanderbilt, mother of the heir, the claimant is a cattleman and a butcher in a small town in Queensland, Australia. He has been there since the mid '70's and is accepted by locals as prototypical Irish-Australian.

Will the real claimant please stand up? tabloid headlines demand. *Which persona is the actual fake?*

Is it just possible, some op-ed writers surmise (and Marlowe, under assorted pseudonyms, has been some of them) that the claimant is the genuine article, an authentic offshoot of the vast and branchy Vanderbilt tree, so many of whose saplings have sprouted from serial nuptials and rogue dalliances? When Vanderbilt sowers go forth to sow, they have a history of scattering their seed as lavishly as they scatter their fortunes. If even the family cannot keep track, how can the lawyers?

In short: Will the jury award a lavish penthouse on Fifth Avenue with a view of Central Park, a mansion on Long Island (a mansion in need of repairs and under a certain degree of duress from several banks and a mortgage company), a lifetime annuity, title to the Vanderbilt widow's derelict chateau in the Loire Valley, and legal entitlement to the name and rank of *le vicomte*?

Or will they send the claimant to jail?

Will DNA settle the issue? Can the judge mandate it?

This question is of burning interest to Marlowe. He has chatted up lawyers and law-school professors. Why does the claimant refuse to be tested if he does not have something—the blood-print of his actual paternity—to hide?

Not necessarily so, he is informed by law professors at NYU.

The paternity test is not absolutely conclusive, but depends on the number of chromosomal locations investigated. The statistics generated with too few locations are not definitive and in some cases can result in wrong conclusions, such as the father being excluded when, in fact, he is the true father.

The claimant's lawyers will want to rule out the possibility of a false negative being introduced in court, they explain. They write op-ed pieces for the *New York Times*. Marlowe himself, on artfully forged stationery, writes an essay that is published in the Week in Review. The byline identifies him as senior partner of a law firm specializing in fraud—detection and prosecution—and he raises questions that grab public notice.

Could *le Vicomte* Gwynne Patrice de la Vallière Vanderbilt—as the claimant is styled by the Vanderbilt widow's lawyers in court documents—actually be a direct descendent of Alfred Gwynne Vanderbilt, great-grandson of Cornelius, the so-called Commodore, the original nineteenth-century steamship and railroad robber-baron, the first mega-millionaire? Alfred Gwynne was a dandy and a horse-racing man and a high-stakes gambler who inherited one fortune, made another one, married into a third one (which divorced him on the grounds of adulterous goings-on that did not even try to be discreet), then married again into a fourth one. He had houses in Newport, London, and New York.

He was a lucky man.

He had actually booked passage on the Titanic but changed his plans on the eve of the trip. He did sail three years later on the equally ill-fated Lusitania and went down with the ship in the best possible way, immortalized as a hero, calm, charming, cool to the last, giving up his life-jacket to a woman from a second-class berth. He'd had time before the Lusitania sailed to run through his two marriages, various affairs, and one particularly high-profile and scandalous liaison staged in transit and in luxury on his private railroad car. The woman was the wife of the Cuban attaché in Washington, D.C. and the tabloid publicity was such that she killed herself one year later. Alfred Gwynne had by then floated on, unscathed, to other attachments. He had three legitimate sons from his two marriages. The number born on the wrong side of the sheets was unknown.

Could the claimant be the carrier of so much genetic *brio?* asks the Week in Review. Could Alfred Gwynne Vanderbilt possibly have been the claimant's great-grandfather?

Marlowe (via his pseudonym in the Week in Review) generates a torrent of reader responses.

That Australian cowboy? A Vanderbilt? Please.

Historians weigh in to remind the public that Cornelius Vanderbilt, the original maker of the fortune, was a brutish, foulmouthed, ruthless thug of a man, rigidly harsh with his own children and utterly devoid of social graces; that the next generation and the one after that were equally disreputable, equally despicable, equally inclined to vicious family litigation, though massively more mega-rich.

Not relevant, an editorial rebuked. Fortunes made in the nineteenth century should be judged in context and the art of becoming civilized usually takes three generations.

Scratch a Vanderbilt and the Commodore bleeds out, counters Marlowe, playing devil's advocate in a pseudonymously-signed letter to the *Times.*

The claimant never actually appeared in court but was represented in surrogate form by his mother—that is to say, by *la comtesse,* Lawrence Gwynne Vanderbilt's widow—who swore that the claimant was indeed her son. Thus his image and personality were constructed from the jigsaw pieces of many conflicting memories and from lawyers' briefs and from that single sensational video interview and from gossip and rumor and from Marlowe's busy seedlings of disinformation, all of which grew rank as weeds and are still growing, dense, luxuriant, unstoppable. They are coiling themselves into the minds of comedians on late-night TV. Jerry Seinfeld makes mock phone calls to Australia and the calls are answered, unintelligibly, by someone who sounds like a drunken Crocodile Dundee.

Are you the real McCoy or the fake one? Jerry Seinfeld asks.

The trial has been a bonanza for stand-up comedy and for professional eavesdroppers alike. Marlowe thinks of himself that way—as *professional eavesdropper*—both literally and ironically. Intelligence gathering is the essence of his dual careers. He is writing a memoir. He does intend eventually, possibly, to publish it, but under what name?

Perhaps *Chameleon*?

He can, after all, take on local coloration wherever he is without even thinking about it. This is an aspect of intelligence not sufficiently examined, he thinks, and he would like to make up for the omission. He is constantly writing drafts in his head.

2.

The Autobiography of a Master of the Game is what Marlowe will call his memoir.

I was born and I grew up south of the Mason-Dixon line...

He can visualize the first published page. He can see the cover. The author photograph is one-quarter profile, in shadow, and shows the back of a man's head against a vista of live-oaks and a plantation house with white columns. Marlowe will note that the domestic help arrived before breakfast every day because his mother never liked to have them live in—too great an invasion of privacy—but he will also make clear that he was closer to his black nanny than to his own mother. He was intimate with both sides. *You may make of that what you will,* he writes; he intends to write.

Summers, it was his family's black domestics and their men folk who cared for him. He raced cars with them on country roads. He was free to kick over the traces. His father subjected him to many stern and sorrowing speeches, but never failed to post bail or pay his fines. Boys will be boys, was what he always said to his wife.

Later he said: It's time to stop sowing wild oats. Boys will be boys, he said, but if they don't respect family honor, they deserve to be pistol-whipped. God gave them the intelligence to be discreet and to be gainfully occupied.

Marlowe himself has always been gainfully occupied and he

does not mean this purely or only in the personal financial sense. When he was busy dropping out of prep schools and the Ivy League, his parents had not the slightest notion of his lucrative parallel career as an investment broker—a business he began as a student, hiding under his first corporate name, a witty one, that was shelved with some regret after his first bankruptcy—but they were deeply uneasy about his official c.v. School counselors and psychiatrists (the latter privately hired) reassured them of his sky-high I.Q. His father, devastated by his expulsions (which he felt now exceeded the leeway of Boys will be boys) believed that his natural talents could be put to patriotic use. He arranged an interview and an offer. Marlowe signed on. He honestly cannot recall the name he was to use at the time—there have been too many of them—but for the sake of convenience let us say he was Lucifer then. *Lucifer Investments: For returns that are fiendishly fine.*

Marlowe likes to imagine how readers will react to his memoir on the far side of the afterlife that he has begun to acknowledge to himself may, after all, be inevitable.

You know it's inevitable, whispers the voice, *her* voice, from the barstool beside him. *You don't want to be caught but you can't stop daring them to catch you. And you will be caught.*

"I won't," he says aloud.

"Sorry?" The bartender raises his eyebrows.

"I won't be caught." Marlowe believes this. He insists on be-lieving. He is simply too clever.

How did you do it? his future readers will want to know. *How did you herd us over your cliff like lemmings?* They will not be able to suppress a secret desire to meet him one more time in a wine bar or at a black-tie gallery opening. Isn't that the way it always began? With champagne? This time, his future readers will convince themselves, Marlowe will be on their radar and the out-come will be utterly different.

The outcome, Marlowe knows, will not be different, will never be different.

That is his genius. He is one of the true Masters of the Game.

And here is the crux of the matter. It takes one to know one, and they recognize one another, the master players, the charmers who never get caught. They have a sixth sense, an intuitive awareness of other chameleons who have changed their names or sloughed off earlier selves or filed other editions of themselves under tabs such as: *To be shredded* or *To be resumed between midnight and dawn* or *To be revisited later.*

Maybe it is pheromones, but whatever the reason, Marlowe has known from the start. He recognized the Vanderbilt heir (the real one, the actual heir, long deceased) and the shape-shifting name-changing woman with whom he has played cat and mouse for so many years. He recognized them as members of his tribe before he knew who they were.

Gwynne Vanderbilt was McVie when Marlowe first met him, but McVie did not look like the claimant or act like him, a detail that Marlowe knows is neither here nor there. All those front-page and evening news photographs that the entire nation became so tired of seeing (Vanderbilt heir as slightly-built Harvard nerd side-by-side with claimant as muscle-man Australian jackaroo), they mean absolutely nothing in the long run. Body type, Marlowe knows, is as changeable as dyeing one's hair or switching the color of one's eyes with contact lenses. He knows the literature on this subject. He has *written* some of the literature on this subject. He has published an article about an anorexic teenager who ate her way through depression, ballooned up to 250 pounds, was kindly treated by a documentary filmmaker and ended up in her late 20s as a willowy model in love with the man behind the camera.

He knows that bodily metamorphosis means nothing.

He has a different source of evidence altogether for knowing that the claimant is a fraud. *Once an imposter, always an imposter,* he reminds the invisible woman beside him. *As though you don't know,* he adds. He is constantly drafting and redrafting the memoir, editing his past and future selves.

The practice of deception, he has written in one of his drafts, *requires acute and constant mental agility and is addictive. The rush of getting away with fraud is like crack, but greater and greater risk is required to get the same high. The need can break out whenever temptation takes it, and temptations are endless. People are so desperate to trust in saviors, so ravenous to believe in magic and in instant wealth. You cannot overestimate gullibility, but the gullible love to find someone to blame.*

Marlowe has already published a paper on the psychological need of the duped to exonerate themselves. It appeared in a scholarly journal under the initials E.E. There is that other side of Marlowe, one of his many other sides, the academic side, the side that somewhat embarrasses him, the side that interested Langley and the other intelligence agencies for whom he gathers and passes on data. (He knows very well that his memoir, even if published pseudonymously or posthumously, will be heavily redacted. There will be much use of black felt markers.)

But how exactly, his future readers will want to know, did they meet: the real Vanderbilt heir, Marlowe, and the woman who held both men in thrall?

Answer: by happenstance, the way all of life comes.

Well, perhaps not completely by happenstance, since Marlowe saw himself as already deployed in the fields where subversive weeds were cropping up. For the record: They met in a Harvard Extension class in the late sixties, summer school 1968 to be precise, the "Sociology of Power," a course they all aced. After the class, they'd go drinking in Harvard Square and talk until they'd solved the world's problems.

You may remember—Marlowe has completed a draft or two lest crucial detail slip from recall —that 1968 was a turbulent year, that summer school began shortly after the assassinations of Martin Luther King and Bobby Kennedy and shortly before the violent Democratic Convention in Chicago that August. The Australian naval vessel *HMAS Hobart* in Da Nang Harbor, supporting the American cause, had come under "friendly fire" from US pilots in June with the result that Australians were killed and wounded by their allies.

The death toll of American troops in Vietnam had risen to 30,000.

The heir was calling himself Patrick McVie at the time; his girlfriend was calling herself Lilith Jardine; and I can't remember for certain what I was required to call myself on that detail. We drank too much and confessed to each other that we did not know where we were headed or even where we wanted to go. I remember (with embarrassment) rambling on about how I had caused anguish to my father. I'd hated my prep schools—first Dryden, then Philips Exeter—had been kicked out, was transferred a couple of times, dropped out of Yale my first year, was finagled into West Point by my father, then finagled out in the nick of time.

The other two made more guarded confessions, even when drunk (even when *apparently* drunk) which was one of those early warning signals that caused my antennae to vibrate. There were several things I intuited very quickly: that if Lilith had official transcripts they were not under the name of Lilith Jardine; that McVie had not been born into a Boston Irish family as he claimed, had not been an altar boy at St. Ann's, did not have a father who ran a butcher shop in Somerville, Mass. On the other hand, McVie was definitely an adjunct professor on several campuses (Boston College, Regis College, those solid and respectable private Catholic institutions of higher education) and he was taking the summer school course because the topic interested him. So he said. McVie was a puzzle I had yet to solve.

Lilith was another puzzle. She had an unpaid internship at the Boston Museum of Fine Arts, and she also worked several hours per week at Harvard's Fogg Art Museum, for which she was paid the usual low internship rates.

We all claimed to be Democrats. We all claimed to be against the Vietnam War.

To be honest, I didn't care one way or the other about the war. I knew there was no risk I would ever be drafted (my dropping out of Yale and West Point and the loss of my student deferment notwithstanding) and besides, I had already been recruited for a loftier cause. Keeping my eye on the people who enrolled in Harvard Extension was one of my tasks.

We all distinguished ourselves in that course. Lilith and McVie were both overachieving polymaths, which is another way of saying they were preeminently equipped to be first-class con artists. McVie's focus was moral philosophy, of all the pointlessly dead-end trails, going back to St Augustine and the theory of the Just War, blah blah blah, which is why, for a while, we called him Sir Gawain. Well, I called him Sir Gawain. He had that air about him, the air of a pure knight and true, not self-righteous exactly, in fact not at all, which made his earnestness all the more irritating to me. Contemplative, I suppose would be the word. An introvert. Anxious. Always fearing himself to be morally in the wrong (which is, I've come to realize, a condition genetically inherited by Catholics.) You can imagine how this drove a Southern Protestant like myself up the wall at the same time as it made me extremely watchful. He had the air of someone thinking about the priesthood, which, at that time and place, was something to keep an eye on. There were priests treating the burning of draft cards as sacred obligation. There were priests who broke into local draft boards and poured blood on the files. You've probably either forgotten all this, or never known about it, but I can assure you that a white dog-collar put you on the watch list back then. Remember the Berrigan brothers, Daniel and Philip, both priests? They were arrested. They served time.

McVie and Lilith and I were all straight-A students. To be more precise, two of us were, and I was whenever I bothered to turn in a paper or take an exam. I never completed a degree, not even an undergraduate one, because I had too much contempt for jumping through other peoples' hoops. I was never sure if the other two had genuine degrees. McVie did have part-time employment as an adjunct professor at Boston College, which suggests some Harvard post-graduate credits, but there are ways of scamming that.

Lilith claimed to have majored in Art History at NYU, but if she did so, she graduated under a different name. Following her internship at the Boston Museum of Fine Arts, she was offered exchange-semesters in London and Paris. She did not accept but I made photocopies of her invitations. A contact of mine—a genius in graphic design—made some delicate changes which have proved useful. All this happened decades ago. Even so, and even now, you have no idea how rarely reference letters are checked out, provided the letterhead is impressive and the original signature real. Or even if not. Believe me.

Make me a dare and I will find my way into any academic or financial institution you care to name. It's a skill set with which I was born, I don't know why.

Marlowe believes there is a serendipitous intersection of an intensity-hungry gene and an advantage-taking gene and a genius gene. One gene is *grafted* on to the other, so to speak, and the ensuing hybrid is destined to leave a mark on history. *Graft*, now there's an interesting word, he thinks.

He reads biographies of other members of the tribe. He reads the prison confession (later retracted) of a nineteenth-century Master of the Game and quotes (from faulty memory, no doubt) this shape-shifting forebear in his memoir: *There are men with an abundance of money and no brains; and there are other men with an abundance of brains and no money. Surely the men with a surplus of money and no brains were made for men with a surplus of brains and no money.*

You probably do not recognize the "confession"— sic transit gloria—but the Tichborne Claimant was the most famous defendant in the most protracted case in the British courts in the late nineteenth century, a case still not settled by DNA, a case for whose ultimate posthumous verdict we are still waiting.

This was one of numerous topics on which I wrote a scholarly paper, published under the pseudonym E.E. My scholarly self—I call him *Erasmus Erratorum*—pops up from time to time like the ghost of Hamlet's father. I can't quite keep him locked in the cellarage. He is a bit of an embarrassment to me, given that I have two other reputations to maintain and E.E. would not earn me any cachet in either of those other fields of combat. E.E. is compiling data for a history of dazzling con men and con women, an anthology of essays, some published already and some not-yet-written. Tentative title: **Masters of the Game.**

We three masters (McVie, the woman who drove us both crazy, and myself) we belong at that intersection of intensity, genius, cunning. Lilith would probably swear that she and McVie were never after ill-gotten gains. I've never believed her, and I'm honest enough to admit that I was, not that I believe such gains are ill-gotten. It's a high and dangerous calling, to live by one's wits, and every penny is well-earned. But we are all pathological liars. It's the sine qua non of survival in the shape-shifting trade.

The thing is: we were drawn to each other from that first Harvard class. Well, let me be blunt for posterity: I do not know if they felt the same way about me, but I do know I experienced them as amphetamines. I am still trying to account for the attraction and for its intensity. One (Lilith, naturally) was sexual. The other? I think it was the fact that I sensed prey. It turned me on.

I remember that I had a dream in which I reached across a bistro table in Harvard Square to touch McVie's arm, merely to get his attention, and I saw, with some fascination, that my fingers had turned into ragged claws and that my mouth was a long hooked beak. I tore McVie apart and I ate him. This gave me the most incredible rush. I awoke from this dream very happy. But I also recognized the dream as wish fulfillment. I knew there were ancestral reasons that linked us and bound us.

There is this curious fact about identity-switchers: the ancestors of all of us, in the nineteenth century or earlier, changed countries of residence, names, spouses, professions. It was a shape-shifting time. All our forebears, doubtless for good and urgent reasons, abandoned existing families and assorted locations in Europe for the New World: America, Australia, New Zealand, South Africa, any place where they had no past. They passed on their survivor gene and their self-reinvention gene. Speaking of self-reinvention...

Call me Marlowe, which was my name at the time of trial, if memory serves.

Or call me Chameleon.

3.

Marlowe intends in his memoir to tell the truth, the whole truth, and nothing but the truth, except for such small embellishments as he believes will be essential for good narrative structure and for filling in gaps that would otherwise exasperate his future readers.

To begin then: Marlowe knows—or once knew—Gwynne Patrice Vanderbilt, (aka Patrick McVie, the name by which Marlowe first knew him.) He knew and knows Lilith by several names. He learned that her original name, her childhood name, was Capucine, a name bestowed by her father, Christophe le Jardinier, Christopher the Gardener, who was manager, steward, gardener, *viticulteur*, and general factotum of the chateau owned by *la comtesse*, mother of the Vanderbilt heir. Capucine, Cap for short, was her father's little nasturtium, his little flower, but the name by which Marlowe first knew her was Lilith Jardine.

He wishes he could say *he knew Lilith* in the Biblical sense and he is tempted to claim that he did, because there were intimations, there were directions they might have taken, and there were certainly possible nights and there was that almost-weekend in New York. But what restrains him is her habit of mocking in an exquisitely courteous way and of always speaking the cutting truth, which is a curious thing to say about a professional dissembler. Above all, if he publishes posthumously, he fears (if she outlives him) that she will rebut his account acerbically and ruinously when he is beyond all possibility of spin control.

In the eleventh-hour interest of full disclosure—though who can predict the eleventh hour? By the actual eleventh hour, or by what Marlowe deems to be a few minutes short of that penultimate hour, he may delete anything that he has already placed on the record. Nevertheless. In his hypothetical eleventh-hour confession he will remind his reader—he will not be able to resist this reminder—that he is a master of disinformation, that verbal spin has been essential to his dual professions, that he can gut a reputation or a politician's career in a week.

Caveat lector.

But also remember this: He knows things that no one else knows.

In bars in Harvard Square in the sixties, late into the night, drinking beer, smoking pot, inhaling past and future selves, the three of them heard each other's sob stories and confessions and redactions. They signed off on each other's retractions. They allowed almost infinite leeway. They permitted variations on each theme. Everything was oral, evanescent as the smoke from their weed. That, at least, is how Marlowe saw things.

We are fabulists, he explains in his memoir (first draft, which he will probably revise). *We are story tellers. We create beautiful lies that will save our skins in the blink of an eye. Later we retract our confessions. You will never be able to pin us down.*

A few of us, however, perhaps for reasons of vestigial religious superstition inculcated in childhood, perhaps owing to primal and universal moral instincts to which we do not consciously subscribe, a few of us feel the need to set down—at least once—the unadorned truth. We leave sealed instructions for our lawyers: Not to be published until after my demise.

Consider his current version:

While the jury in the trial of the Vanderbilt claimant is seques-
tered, a man named Marlowe walks into the Oyster Bar in that
underground murk of the terminal at Grand Central Station (a
vast edifice that is the hub of the original Vanderbilt's railroad empire.) Something compelling draws Marlowe. He has been present
each day at the trial, scanning the public gallery as closely as he
keeps an eye on the witness stand though the claimant himself
has never actually appeared in court, at least not in the corporeal
sense. Marlowe is watching for someone. He is reasonably certain
she will appear. He believes she will have a compulsion to find
out if the jury is convinced that the Vanderbilt heir—against all
probability—is still alive. He thinks he may have caught a glimpse
of her in the gallery. She was definitely there eight months back
when the trial was in its early stages and the video of the claimant
was shown. He has not seen her since then but has kept track of
her moves. He once met her—decades ago—in the Oyster Bar for
an assignation that did not go as planned and he has an intense
premonition that he might find her there again.

The bar is crowded but he feels a beam of heat on the back
of his neck. It has the force of a punch. He turns. On the far side
of the room is a mirror and in the mirror he sees the woman he
once spent time with day after day, week after week. Then they
lost contact. They lost contact in the normal sense of that word
though he has usually been able to monitor her whereabouts when
he wanted to. He makes a signal, a small movement of his hand,
beckoning her reflection. The woman in the mirror raises a champagne flute and smiles a half smile and something cold and smooth
touches Marlowe's cheek.

Holy shit! he murmurs, an involuntary expression of shock. He
swivels on his bar stool and there she is beside him, just as she so
often is in his fantasies, the tube of glass in her hand, effervescent,
resting lightly against his face. "Lilith!"

"Lucifer himself," she says calmly. "Still in the business, I see."

"Meaning what?"

"We both know what I mean, Lucifer."

"I discarded that name thirty years ago. Name's Marlowe at present. I heard you were in Australia these days."

"Did you indeed?"

"I did. I have contacts at Sotheby's, you know. We're talking observable traces. I keep my eye on you."

"Should I be flattered that I'm still on your radar?"

"Sotheby's assigned you to Sydney. And yet here you are, back in New York in the very week that the Vanderbilt trial is wrapping up."

"That's Sotheby's for you. More travel than I realized I'd signed up for."

"I saw you when the video was shown. You were in the gallery but you managed a vanishing trick before I reached you. I thought the prospect of the jury verdict would bring you back. It's making quite a splash in the Australian press, I see."

"Ah." Lilith raises her eyebrows. "So you keep up with the Australian press."

"I keep up with media all over the world. It's part of my job."

"Which of your jobs would that be?"

"Both of them, naturally," Marlowe says.

"Financial finagling and the seeding of disinformation."

"I do know where to draw the line when it comes to risk, which is clearly something you *don't* know, given your unofficial activities. Are you en route to somewhere else?"

"Would I tell you?"

"You don't need to. I have access to airline reservations whenever I want them, remember. You keep traipsing all over the world. Ostensibly for Sotheby's."

"For Sotheby's, yes. But you're out of date, Lucifer. I've been more or less retired for over a year, though I still accept occasional assignments. I'm flattered that you pretend you can keep track."

Marlowe is flustered but he covers well. He has, it is true, lost focus. Stung, he might have offered, by way of extenuation: *I'm less involved with surveillance than I used to be. My financial affairs, these days, gobble up the lion's share of my time. Risk is my thing, yes, and I manage it well, but for the moment—to be perfectly honest—I'm floundering in very choppy waters. My house of cards is coming down. It's only a matter of time, although I'm sure I'll find a way out.* Instead he says smoothly: "So. On to the Middle East from here?"

"Not this time."

"Though," Marlowe says, improvising rapidly, "that's where the high end of the art market is."

"True. The high end of the art market is there."

"I do happen to have seen records," Marlowe says—and this is partly true, used to be true—"of your business encounters with Saudi princes, army generals, assorted dictators, even African ones. Kenya, Zimbabwe, Guinea. I still can't quite get my mind around the fact of the President of Equatorial Guinea owning a Degas and two Monets."

"Weird, isn't it? What a pity you squander so much intelligence access."

"When you meet with these mega-rich thugs," Marlowe, genuinely curious, asks, "what do you do? What do you talk about?"

"We drink champagne and we talk about art. They all spend vast sums of money buying paintings and re-selling them and trading them up. Sotheby's is the appraiser of choice."

"And you're the field worker of choice? Even though you're supposedly retired?"

"Often works out that way."

Marlowe raises his glass. "To your global status. Quite

a compliment."

"Not really," Lilith shrugs. "We all have a narrow focus of expertise. As I'm sure you remember, mine is French painting and furniture, seventeenth and eighteenth centuries, not a crowded field. After that, it's more a case of my being willing to travel at short notice, especially to places considered unwise, places where other appraisers in our limited field won't go."

"But you will. Because you're addicted to risk."

"Not how I would put it."

"How would you put it?"

"I'd say I can't let myself off the hook."

"Bullshit. You want to go out as a martyr, one more fake halo. That's why you can't keep away from the Middle East." Lilith refuses to break eye contact. After several seconds, intense ones, Marlowe looks away. He looks into the mirror that reflects the mirror behind the bar. "Fuck," he says, swiping several glasses from the counter with a sweep of his arm. The sound effects are shattering. "No one travels there for legitimate reasons. Not these days. Not as often as you do."

"Let's not pretend, Lucifer, that you have a clue anymore as to how often I go or don't go to the Middle East or to anywhere else. But I do still travel wherever I'm asked to go when the need is acute. Wherever art needs to be appraised." To the barman she says: "I'm so sorry. It's my fault. I've upset him. I'll pay for this."

"And wherever you go in the Middle East," Marlowe prods, "or Bosnia, Serbia, wherever, we have eyes. We know you have secret meetings on the side."

"I'm sure your kind does know."

"Your meetings are being recorded." Marlowe does have former colleagues who do this, and he can call in occasional IOU's, but he is ad-libbing, free-wheeling, embarrassed, angry. "Your destinations trigger attention. You must know that."

"I know your kind keeps track. If only I scored as often as I trigger attention. In reality, it's a lottery. The president of Equatorial Guinea, for example, or rather his son, keeps all his paintings in his *pied-a-terre* in Paris and does all his art trading there. So sadly I don't hit pay-dirt nearly as often as I'd wish. I'm not telling you anything your kind doesn't already know."

"You never declare your pay-dirt at Customs."

"What is there to declare?" Lilith asks. "What am I carrying? Words. Letters and photographs. It's not contraband."

"It's considered contraband by the countries you visit. Don't pretend you're not smuggling dynamite."

"Most of it I carry in here." She taps her forehead. "And they can't run that through the scanner. But believe me, I have a few unpleasant souvenirs of border detentions."

"I know. I've seen reports. You're risk-addicted."

"And you're not? But I've got a lucky gene too. Generally speaking, the people buying or selling the artworks have the power to arrange smooth passage. There's the beauty of it. They don't lose a blink of sleep over torture but they have a passionate love of fine art. Or at least a passionate love of being *perceived* as lovers of fine art. Or at least a passionate love of being able to buy fine art as an investment and then trade it up and it never seems to enter their heads that I don't share their views."

"How do you explain your sudden disappearances into the scruffier parts of their cities?"

"I don't try. I'm a tourist. They love tourists. Hell, even a Hitler-wannabe like Mugabe pushes tourism in Zimbabwe. I publish travel articles on the side and mail copies back to my hosts. I'm a photo-journalist. I always include a spread of the warlord in his palace gardens. He has me sign them and has them framed. I would have thought you knew all this. You should check in with your kind more often."

"I wanted to hear your version. We have a collection of every travel article you've published," Marlowe lies smoothly. "It's a useful tracking device. You know you're a source of serious concern. You're causing us dangerous complications with governments we need to keep on our side."

"That's your problem," Lilith says. "By the same token, the fact that our government pays lip-service to human rights but gives no backup... that creates problems for me."

"Have you the slightest idea how often I've intervened to save your skin?"

"Are you claiming you have a conscience, Lucifer?"

"Who are you at present?" Marlowe asks.

"What a question."

"If you're here on business with your New York office, why are you in the Oyster Bar right now?"

"Interesting point. I was invited. Most mysteriously. Or summonsed, you could say. Or subpoenaed."

"By whom?" Marlowe asks.

"That is the question, isn't it? Naturally I assumed by you. Though I know it's possible—just—that neither of us knows the answer to that conundrum." She smiles. "Air tickets supplied and sent by international courier to Sotheby's office in Sydney, signature required, sender identified by nine-digit number. Same courier brought my hotel reservation confirmation. They weren't sent by Sotheby's New York. I checked. Could be a wealthy private collector, I realize that. They like to remain anonymous, especially if they're buying or selling stolen art. The summons specified a meeting time here at the Oyster Bar. I wasn't sure if I'd be meeting you or Celise or some other person unknown, some buyer or seller of stolen art, but for some reason I suspected you would be the one to show up. So I'd ask why you came here. And I'd ask if Celise knows you are here and if she sent you. And I'd ask what exactly

Celise is hoping she'll get out of all this, not that I care very much."

"Celise didn't send me, and she hasn't the faintest idea where I am. As for her plans for the future, that's Martian territory to me. But I don't wish to discuss my wife."

"I'm sure you don't. I assume you do know that she buys stolen art, presumably with your money, but that's your affair. She fences it in the Middle East." A tremor afflicts Marlowe's hands which he clenches tightly, keeping them below the intricate molded overhang of the bar. He projects his inscrutable look. "But I would like to know why you expected to find me here," Lilith says.

"I got a Fedex-delivered message," Marlowe says slowly, "sender unknown, suggesting you'd be waiting for me in the Oyster Bar. And I came because, well, I wanted it to be true."

"How touching."

"I was hoping you'd think so. Did you send it?"

"Sorry. No."

"Ah. Well... I came because I hoped you did, and because this is where... Remember?"

Lilith meets his gaze without blinking. "Remember what?"

Marlowe closes his eyes and sighs. "Okay," he says. "Postscript received. Permit me to indulge in a possibly self-deluding romantic memory for a minute or so. I want to believe that things might have gone differently. I want to believe that you thought so too. They could have, couldn't they? Gone differently?"

Lilith studies her champagne flute. "This is ancient history," she sighs.

Marlowe watches her succumb to nostalgia and the soft backwash laps at him too and takes them both by surprise: the sixties, that sweet brief moment between the pill and AIDS, when sex was as thick in the air as mold spores and risk-free, or so they all thought. They all believed they could end a war and change the world.

31

"We were so naïve," Lilith says.

"So young," Marlowe says. "So happy. And we could have, couldn't we? Become involved?"

"There might have been brief moments," she confesses. "That summer. You're brilliantly devious and intelligent, and intelligence has always turned me on. The mind is the sexiest organ and yours was seductive. So was your style."

"Indulge me. What exactly about my style?"

"Your elegance. I suppose it comes with your Southern Old-Money genes. Your absolute certainty that you only had to crook your little finger and the world would fall over itself to do your bidding."

Marlowe raises her hand to his lips. "That has usually been the case."

"My point exactly. I'm unfinished business. Which is the only reason you think you want me."

"Not true. I do want you. All the time and on whatever terms you choose." Marlowe keeps her hand in his, he keeps it pressed against his lips, he can see himself reflected in her eyes. His gaze is intense and he is baffled. "Why are you so immune?" he asks wistfully.

"I got to know you too well."

"What did I do wrong?" It is never too late, he thinks. He notes that she does not pull her hand away. It is warm and soft and her hand lotion smells of something tropical, rainforest orchids perhaps.

"It's not what you did," Lilith says. "It's what you are. For a while I tried to convince myself, I actually *wanted* to convince myself, that you did have a moral compass. Never saw any trace of it, I'm afraid."

"You know," Marlowe says, furious but carefully calm, "one thing I never figured out about you and McVie. Most of us are in the game for the money and the life style, no apologies, no hypoc-risy, no remorse. And some of us have put our skills to higher use even while we indulge ourselves. I've never been quite sure what was in it for you two but I'm willing to swear it was something you got high on, something sleazy, something that gave you subversive trips with an underside as kinky as Catholic porn. Self-righteous-ness and hypocrisy make me gag and virtual virtue stinks to high heaven. I'm getting fumes off you now."

"My goodness, such passion, such a confessional spill!" Lilith pulls her hand from his then and lays it, mocking, over her own heart. "You find me completely unprepared." She raises her glass, apparently to someone behind him, but when he turns he sees them both in the mirror across the room.

"Okay," he says. "But you can't fool a fellow player. People don't play hopscotch with their names and identities unless there's some murky reason. Are you actually hoping McVie is alive?"

Her expression unreadable, Lilith meets his eyes until he finds himself studying his coaster. "I wasn't being fully honest," she says, "about why we never, you know... You understand there's always been someone else?"

Marlowe rolls his eyes. "And who can compete with the dead and perfect lover?"

Lilith says nothing.

"He *is* dead," Marlowe says. "We both know he's been dead for twenty-seven years, but denial is a powerful thing. And it's a dead end in every sense of the word." Marlowe has not intended to shout, but apparently he has. Every head in the Oyster Bar is turned in his direction. He lowers his voice. "And it's a sick and self-punishing end, witness the hysterical *Comtesse* Vanderbilt, that pathetic and desperate woman. Her inability to give up hope that her son was alive is what killed her."

Lilith seems deep in thought and far away. "I was with her

when she died," she says. "She was as close to a mother as I had."

"What? You were with her?"

"I assumed you knew."

"I saw you with her in court when the video was shown. I know you were at her side in the ambulance. But she was discharged in a matter of days and you disappeared back to Australia."

"Not immediately. I stayed with her until the end."

"You were there in her penthouse when she died?"

"I was. I was holding her hand. Celise dropped by, so I took for granted that you knew."

"My wife was there?"

"Celise, yes. Your wife. When I say Celise dropped by, I really mean she barged in. It was completely inappropriate. I find it hard to believe she didn't tell you."

Marlowe cannot conceal his agitation. Not entirely.

"I see I've internalized your surveillance," Lilith says. "I assume you're spying even when you aren't. But I did think you sent Celise to file a deathbed report."

"Okay," Marlowe says. "Okay." He broods over his whiskey. "Okay. So I've figured it out. The only way this makes sense. You and the claimant have cooked up this elaborate scam, whether for sexual reasons or financial or both, I won't presume to judge. This Queensland cattle property, if it exists, if it's not just a prop, and the claimant, if he exists, he's your farm hand. You've coached him. You've given him the family history so he has all the answers to the lawyers' trick questions."

"I would like to point out," Lilith says—she speaks patiently, as she might to some student she could be tutoring—"though it's something the media has completely and inexplicably ignored, that the claimant has never claimed anything."

"If he wins," Marlowe says, "I mean if you pull this scam off, you get your hands on a big chunk of Vanderbilt real estate and stock."

"You know something, Lucifer? You've lost your ferret capacity for inquisitorial focus. Do try to remember that the actual claimant in the legal sense of this case was the countess herself, the recently deceased mother of the heir, and the present claimant is her *estate*."

Marlowe feels winded, he feels as though all the air has been punched out of his lungs by one swing of a 400-pound weight. "Go to hell," he says, but in truth he is stunned. He is shocked by the sudden realization that he has been as blindsided as any other absorber of disinformation. The disturbing fact is—and he does know it, he does admit it to himself, on some level he must have known it—that the "claimant" has never actually been the claimant.

After Lawrence Gwynne Vanderbilt died in 1994, the Vanderbilt family took his widow to court for refusing to have her son declared dead. *La comtesse* had returned from her chateau in France to the Vanderbilt residence on Fifth Avenue in 1968, not long before her son was shipped to Vietnam. She had come for his Harvard graduation which she was, in fact, prevented from attending. She stayed on in New York because she was so shocked— as was every single relative and acquaintance of the heir—by his enlistment. She tried to dissuade him, by letters and phone calls which he did not answer. She begged. She left messages with his training officers at Fort Bragg.

She offered to buy his way out.

He went.

His platoon was ambushed. His body was never recovered.

La comtesse obstinately and persistently refused to believe that her son was dead, and this in spite of the many years that had passed since an army officer in full-dress uniform had hand-delivered official condolence and the embossed Missing-in-Action letter. On the stroke of that first dire death-knell—which had tolled in the summer of 1969—*la comtesse* had collapsed with grief and had sunk into a state of clinical depression, sometimes involving hospitalization, for seven years.

And then, almost overnight it seemed, she rallied.

She engaged in a frenzy of letter-writing to the families of soldiers who were Missing in Action or who were known to be Prisoners of War. She received many letters in reply.

After the death in 1994 of her estranged husband (who had promptly moved to his summer place on Long Island the day after his wife returned to New York in '68), she insisted ever more vehemently that her son was still alive and that she had proof, a stance which stonewalled probate proceedings.

At this point, late in 1994, she was sued by the Vanderbilt family.

Her lawyers promptly produced a photocopy of a letter, dated 1976.

Decatur, Georgia.
August 23, 1976

Dear Mrs. Vanderbilt,

I don't know how to reach you but I hope this letter will be sent on by the Atlanta Journal-Constitution. I saw an article about Vietnam MIA's that are still unaccounted for. There were photographs of the missing and one was your son, Gwynne Patrice Vanderbilt, officially declared MIA, presumed dead, in July 1969. I recognized him from the photograph. I wanted to tell you that I was in the same platoon, the same squad, as your son. We called him McVie because that's what he wanted to be called, in honor of a close friend killed in combat in '65, but our squad leader always called him

Vanderbilt. To be honest, it was confusing, because he had two sets of dog tags. We knew, because he talked about it in his sleep, that he felt he had to atone for the death of McVie. We also knew that the last thing he wanted was for anyone to think he was one of the fat cats who shipped us out to be killed. He talked a lot in his sleep. He shouted and argued. Sometimes he was Vanderbilt paying for the death of McVie. Other times he was McVie.

Your son and I arrived in Da Nang late spring '69. We were both only in country two months. Our squad was ambushed on a Search and Destroy. I actually felt your son fall against my body a few seconds before I was hit. His fall knocked me over. I was never sure if I was covered with his blood or mine. I don't remember much after that except I was taken out in a Medevac chopper (or so I was told.) I guess your son wasn't flown out because the wounded always had priority over the dead.

When I came to in the military hospital in Saigon, I was told your son did not make it. I know our squad, what was left of it, went back for the bodies two days later, but the bodies were gone. No one knew for certain if they were POW or dead, but we all assumed your son was dead.

I was in and out of Walter Reed for years (broken legs; rehab, etc.), but what I wanted to tell you is that on one of my Walter Reed stints I met this guy who'd also been in Da Nang in spring '69. He'd also been shot up on a Search and Destroy (not the same one as ours.) He was delirious for he doesn't know how long, but when he came to, he was in a fishing village being tended by South Vietnamese who were on our side. There were two others, one American, one Australian, all of them too shot up to walk. They never knew if they were kept by the village for insurance or out of the goodness of their hearts. It used to be a VC village but the VC abandoned it, and whenever the VC came through again, the whole village hid in the old VC underground tunnels and carried their wounded with them. They blocked off the entrances and the VC must have forgotten where the tunnels were or believed they'd collapsed.

My ward mate in Walter Reed said the other American called himself McVie. My ward mate said they spent so much time underground that they learned to see in the dark. For a long time, not one of the three could walk, but the villagers carried them around on bamboo stretchers. Carried lots of their own folk too. This guy said he thinks they were there for at least two years, maybe three. Hard to keep track, he said, but he remembers three rainy seasons, the tunnels flooded, mostly spending time underground, mostly delirious, mostly not expecting to live, always hungry, never anything but fish and kelp and maybe some rice to eat, but the Vietnamese kept making them drink their own potions and damned if he hadn't come to believe their medicines were better than ours. They got so they could get around on bamboo crutches although they all looked like skeletons, he said.

He said their village minders knew the end was close and they knew they weren't on any VC honor rolls, so one night the whole village, children and guests and all, took off in their own fishing boats. Thought they could get to the Philippines, no moon, no flotation devices, typhoon season. All the boats went down in the South China Sea, but anyone who managed to cling to wreckage long enough was picked up by a passing Australian ship, the **HMAS Sydney**, he thinks.

This guy in Walter Reed got flown back to L.A. from Manila, spring '73. He showed me a lock of hair from his Vietnamese woman. She drowned. His baby son drowned too. He *didn't have any pictures. He didn't know what happened to the other two vets, but he thinks he remembers seeing them on the ship. He thinks maybe they were taken from Manila to Saigon, to the embassy, or maybe they went on to Australia.*

I regret to tell you this guy died a year ago while we were both still in Walter Reed. He used to have nightmares and rave at nights, like most of us in the ward, so I can't swear how reliable he was. But there's stuff he couldn't have made up, so I wanted to let you know that your son might not have died in Vietnam, that he might have left there in a fishing boat, but after that who knows what might have happened. He may still be alive, and if he didn't return home there's a chance he's living in Australia and doesn't remember who he is. One of the doctors in Walter Reed told me that hypothermia from near drowning always causes amnesia. It can be temporary or permanent, depending on how long the survivor is in the water and how cold the water is. The survivors were pulled out of tropical waters, a hopeful sign.

Yours sincerely,
Ben Wheeler
Charlie Company, 3rd Infantry, 2nd Battalion.

The lawyers for *la comtesse* tracked down the writer of this letter and found him working as a UPS driver in Decatur, Georgia. He could give no further information than he had already given in his letter. He could remember no names except that the Vanderbilt G.I. called himself McVie and the Australian called himself Blue and the man who died in Walter Reed was Lee Jackson from Asheville, North Carolina.

Lee Jackson's family was located. They shared his stories of deprivation, his gratitude to the village, the lock of hair from his Vietnamese lover, but they could provide no further information on Blue or McVie, to both of whom, they said, their son constant-ly talked in his nightmares.

The lawyers diligently searched Australian naval records and found that the **HMAS Sydney** had no refugees or non-Australians on board on its final trip back from Vietnam. They did find a record of a cargo ship that had left Manila in May '73 and had docked in Darwin in June before proceeding on to Perth. They could find no detailed disembarkation records in Darwin. All equatorial cities are alike, the research team explained to the lawyers, who ex-plained to *la comtesse* before presenting all this evidence to the court. The bureaucracies of equatorial cities, they explained, live life on the Slow Easy and do not take for granted that efficiency is a virtue, nor can they see any compelling reason for doing today what one might just as well put off until tomorrow or next week or next year. They do not consider record-keeping a high-priority.

In Perth, the lawyers (or rather, the legal team to which the American lawyers had sub-contracted the search in Australia) did find detailed records. The team checked out every name on the list of those who had disembarked from the cargo ship that had sailed from Manila. They tracked down and interviewed every last one. Not one had been shipwrecked in the South China Sea. Not one had even been in Vietnam.

The investigative team did pick up anecdotal evidence in Dar-win that a handful of men had skipped ship in that city and had probably hitch-hiked south by cattle-transporting road-trains, possibly to Alice Springs and on to Adelaide, possibly to Cairns or to Brisbane, or so the guessing and betting went in Darwin bars. The pub tales caught the attention of the lawyers on both sides of the Vanderbilt affair. It was not until the countess was sued by her husband's family that large sums of money were wired to Darwin accounts. A list was drawn up. Generous bounties were dangled, and a small army of trackers and scouts signed on. By following every capillary creek of every tributary rumor, by working every cattle station from Katherine to Alice Springs, from Channel Country to the Darling Downs, they located a Vietnam vet on a small farm in the valley of the North Pine River in the rural district of Dayboro, north-west of Brisbane, capital city of the state of Queensland, Australia.

The possible heir—in response to what was described much later, in the court of investigative journalistic persistence, as entrapment and trickery—agreed to be interviewed on camera. This interview was the video shown in court, though whether it was proffered as evidence by the lawyers for *la comtesse* or by the lawyers for the rest of the hostile Vanderbilt family, remained an unsettled and murky question for the press.

The video begins with an aerial view of the lush coast of southern Queensland. The lens hovers above the Pacific, the white sand beaches, the rich coastal lowlands, the range of mountains which hugs the coast, the rivers that rise in those mountains. The camera pans in toward rich pasture inside an ox-bow loop of river. The slopes of the Great Dividing Range loom close, jagged and dense with rainforest. The sky is cloudless and of a blue so intense (though so normal in Queensland) that the Manhattan jury assumes a tinted lens must surely have been employed. The lens slowly zooms in toward clusters of grazing cattle and then descends like a plane coming in to a runway, closer, closer, to reveal a house with wide verandahs on all four sides. Projecting above the verandahs, and rising like a lantern from the center of the house, is a gabled loft.

The posts and decking of the screened veranda are of rainforest timbers (silky oak, black wattle, mango), polished and dark. So the documentary voiceover informs. There is a rainwater tank of corrugated and galvanized metal, which stands on a wooden platform raised on high wooden stilts, close to one side of the house. Cattle graze on lush pasture. Two Australian cattle dogs, one bluish in color, one speckled gingery gold, are in boisterous combat or play. There are two horses inside a split-rail fence. The lens zooms toward one of the horses, toward the figure of a man who now appears in close-up, a man casually leaning against his horse, the reins loose in his hands. This man is wearing frayed and faded jeans, an open-necked denim shirt, an Akubra hat. He is good-looking, tanned, fit, with a lazy genial smile. He gives the bodily impression of someone who would come off well in any-thing from a wrestling match to a cross-country run to a triathlon.

He could be an actor, he could be the Marlboro Man, except for the slightly awkward jut of one leg which might be a prosthet-ic carefully disguised by the denim jeans or might simply be a leg once broken and never properly tended to or mended. There is a large welt of a scar that rises like a knuckled line of low hills from below his open-necked shirt and covers the left side of his neck, stopping just short of his left ear.

This is the man whom the press consistently and inaccurately labels the claimant.

In the video, a voice from off-camera asks: *What is your name?*

"My name is Christy McLew," the man says with a nasal Irish-Australian drawl.

What is your occupation?

"I'm a cattleman and a butcher," Christy McLew replies. He gestures to indicate the land between the range of hills and the loop of the river. "I'm the owner of Christopher Farm, which you see around you." He laughs and one has the impression that he may be laughing at the cameraman or at his interrogator or per-haps at an audience whom he assumes to be watching somewhere out there, who knows where? He may be mocking his viewers. "But I'm not a cattleman in the usual Aussie sense."

He waits, and the off-camera voice obliges by asking: *What do you mean by the usual Australian sense?*

"I mean individual cattle stations bigger than the state of Texas. I'm not one of those. My herd is so small I'm a joke. My station runs to forty hectares."

How does that translate into acres? asks the off-camera voice (which speaks with an American accent.)

"Acres? Oh... I'd have to work that out. Let me see... um, about a hundred acres, I think. Which is a joke. When we meet in the Dayboro pub, my neighbors call me a nutter, but they tolerate me. They think I'm wacko because of the permaculture thing."

What do you mean by "the permaculture thing"?

"Natural farming. I let nature grow her own pasture. My cattle are grass-fed. I don't grow fodder crops. I don't use feed lots, which are cruel and cause kidney damage, fattening the steers up for maximum weight and profit. Not great for the health of the beef consumers either, but it will probably be a couple more decades before everyone realizes that. I'm a subsistence farmer. I have two hired hands. My slaughtering is done by a small family firm in Dayboro and I personally do my own butchering and my own cuts, from sides and quarters, all the way down to tenderloin and chops. I supply direct to a handful of restaurants and farmers' markets in Brisbane, and of course to the local butcher shop in Dayboro. I believe in small scale and I believe in humanely raised cattle. You understand?"

Interesting. Does the name Lawrence Gwynne Vanderbilt mean anything to you?

"What?!" A silence of several seconds ensues. The cattleman appears shocked, even stunned. "I thought this was for a documentary about natural farming," he protests.

Does the name Lawrence Gwynne Vanderbilt mean anything to you?

The viewer notes a slight grimace on Christy McLew's lips, perhaps not a grimace but some fleeting expression... of what?

"I would prefer not to reply," the cattleman says.

Did you know that Lawrence Gwynne Vanderbilt died over a year ago?

McLew turns away from the camera and rests his forehead against the flank of his horse. Seconds pass before he turns back. "I live off the beaten track. The only news I get is from the pub."

It seems that the death of Lawrence Gwynne Vanderbilt is of interest to you.

"It is not of interest. I was not on close terms with the deceased."

But you knew him?

"In a manner of speaking. But no, I never felt I knew him."

Did you know that the only legitimate son of Lawrence Gwynne Vanderbilt is the sole heir to his estate?

"Frankly, no. I assumed he would have disinherited his son. And believe me..."—and here there is a disarming shrug, a curious toss of the head, raised eyebrows, a particular kind of ironic smile much remarked upon by the analysts of body language—"I would imagine his only son would feel nothing but relief on that score. I'd guess that the heir would run to Timbuktu to escape the inheritance of the Vanderbilts if he could."

Did you know that the Vanderbilt family believes that the heir was killed in Vietnam?

"I did know that. And the family is correct. The heir did die there. He never left Vietnam."

How would you know that?

"Ah, well..." McLew laces and unlaces the reins around his fingers. He is increasingly nervous. "I crossed paths with him there."

You yourself were in Vietnam?

"I was. I was there when Vanderbilt died."

Does the name Isabel de la Vallière Vanderbilt mean anything to you?

Again there is a lengthy pause. The man in the Akubra turns away from the camera and fondles the neck of his horse.

"Yes," he says eventually.

In what sense does this name mean something to you?

"She was Vanderbilt's mother," the man says, or so subtitles claim, though the words are muffled and indistinct because the man has one foot in the stirrup and is swinging his other leg (the oddly disjointed one) over the horse. The horse rears, gallops away from the camera and jumps the fence. The video ends with the horseman disappearing into the distant blue-green haze of the forested slopes.

The video produced a sensation in court and in the press, especially since *la comtesse* collapsed in the gallery and had to be ferried out to an ambulance. A reporter managed to reach her as the ambulance doors were being closed. He thrust a microphone almost into the patient's mouth. "Mrs. Vanderbilt, is that man your son?" he demanded.

The eyes of the countess fluttered. "Yes," she whispered, before the paramedics roughed up the reporter and slammed the vehicle doors in his face. The breathy *yes* of the countess was amplified and much replayed—posthumously—on radio and TV. This was her last public word.

In spite of the most valiant efforts of her lawyers and their Australian retainers, Christy McLew could not be located again. He could not be reached by the press. He had gone into hiding. Local farmers and cattlemen could shed no light. When questioned, they smiled and shook their heads. Never heard of the Vanderbilt claimant, they said. We get news on the bush telegraph. It's always a few weeks old.

Of course, the Vanderbilt family's lawyers claimed, the cattle-man cannot be located because he does not exist. He's an actor or a digital concoction. He is the special-effects manifestation of his mother's desperate state of denial and grief.

On the contrary, suggested certain letters to the editor of the *New York Times*, is he a concoction of the lawyers of the Vanderbilt family? What convoluted game might they be playing?

The lawyers for *la comtesse* claimed to have received word, via several intermediary layers, that the cattleman in the video had not the slightest wish to claim any inheritance which the court might inappropriately bestow and which (should it be legally required) he would be more than happy to renounce in favor of the Vanderbilt widow.

Unfortunately, the fine print of Lawrence Gwynne Vanderbilt's will ruled out this option. Though his wife was granted permission to live in the Fifth Avenue penthouse until her demise, she was awarded no money toward its upkeep nor any income at all. Indeed, since her personal inheritance—a chateau and vineyard in France—was in disrepair and no longer producing income, the countess had been obliged to sell a number of her paintings and much of her antique furniture. Upon her death, not only her personal property in France, but the New York penthouse and all other Vanderbilt assets were bequeathed to Lawrence Gwynne's son, or to his son's issue, or—if his son were to produce no offspring—to Lawrence Gwynne's nephew William Jeremiah, known as Billy, son of Lawrence Gwynne's deceased older brother, Harold Cornelius—and his nephew's heirs.

The lawyers for the countess, therefore, had considered it essential that her son return to claim his inheritance and to establish legal title, after which he would be free either to sell the properties or to gift them to his mother, but Christy McLew remained either unreachable or immune to persuasion.

As for the countess, the medical verdict was a stroke which affected her ability to speak and paralyzed one side of her body. She was discharged and provided with round-the-clock nursing care. A few weeks later, she died in her own four-poster bed.

Legally speaking, after the death of *la comtesse,* the defendant was now her estate.

"I'm waiting for an answer," Marlowe says in the Oyster Bar. "You know that farm hick in the video, don't you? The two of you are in on this scam together."

"How is it a scam when he stated his absolute lack of interest in the Vanderbilt will?"

"Cunning, that. A well-known ploy of masters of the game. So what's your strategy?"

Lilith stares at Marlowe until he drops his eyes and studies his glass of whiskey and his coaster. "I am asked this, quite seriously," she says, "by someone who pursued and married a Vanderbilt?"

"I didn't pursue her," Marlowe says. "Quite the contrary, as a matter of fact. But here's my theory. You obviously have an intense interest in the outcome of this trial, or you wouldn't be here. If he loses the case, as he will, there'll be an appeal. When the legal surrogates track him down and interrogate him in Australia, he'll seem to know the sort of private detail that only a son (or the lover of someone intimate with the Vanderbilt family) could know. So then, if the appeal decides in his favor, you split the proceeds, right?"

"Lucifer, talking to you is like talking to someone from outer space."

"You haven't answered my question."

"There's no point. We don't speak the same language."

"I think I read you and the claimant rather well," Marlowe says.

"There you go. There's a parallel universe between your bar stool and mine," Lilith sighs. "But I'm going to make an effort to translate. At least in your public life, Lucifer—the above-ground one, and the above-ground *part* of that one—you're a wealthy man and a weirdly successful broker. Your returns are uncanny, which any sane person would consider a serious warning sign. The rich and famous flock to you. You make them feel richer and safer. So. You didn't marry Celise Vanderbilt for her money because you don't need it. So why *did* you marry her?"

Marlowe closes his eyes and tries to recall why he married Celise.

"The answer's obvious. You married her as a way to escape your Southern self which still embarrasses you. Celise was your portal to the Upper East Side where you never felt you'd really arrived."

"Lilith." Elbows on bar, Marlowe rests his head on his hands. "I never needed to *arrive* because I was always *here*. Southerners have always known, deep in their bones, that they are superior to anyone north of the Mason-Dixon line. There is no such thing as not needing money or as having enough of it. You don't even begin to understand. It's about being a Master of the Game. I compete only with myself and I never stop raising the bar. You entirely miss the point. What I'm trying to figure out is what is *your* point, and what was McVie's? No one changes their name and skips two countries for innocent reasons, so I know there's something devious going on. I want to know what it is."

"Is that why I've been subpoenaed, so to speak?"

"Who are you now? I'm not asking on behalf of the people I work for. I'm asking out of personal admiration. I truly respect counterfeit of a high and surpassing order."

"You respect counterfeit?" She laughs. "That rings true."

"I'm speaking as one master player to another," Marlowe says.

"We're not playing the same game, Lucifer. We never have been. But given that you married a Vanderbilt who's next in line once the heir is declared officially dead or dismissed as a fraud, the probable verdict should make you deliriously happy."

"That is a slander."

"Intended."

Marlowe is so visibly agitated that the bartender appears, refill in hand.

"You want another?" the bartender asks.

"Yes," Marlowe says. "Jack Daniels." He pushes his empty glass away so violently that it falls to the floor and rises as a small cloud of glittering shards.

"Jesus," the bartender says. "Not again. You don't get another one."

"Give him one. He needs it. I'll get him out of here without further damages," Lilith promises.

"McVie was a master of the game," Marlowe says. "As McVie he was good, very good, fooled me for months. Never fooled me as Boston Irish, but it did take me a while to realize he was a Vanderbilt. One thing is crystal clear though: he certainly has nothing to do with this clown of a cow hand in Australia."

"Then it's a win-win all round, isn't it? The jury is bound to agree and you'll win. So you're happy, your wife is happy, I'm happy, the ghost of McVie would be happy." She reaches in front of him, picks up his glass, raises it in a toast, and drains his newly refilled whiskey. "To your winning," she says. "And to Celise. To what you have brought upon yourselves." She reaches for her own champagne glass and drains it. "I shouldn't be drinking so much but it's been a long wait. Nice seeing you again."

"Wait," he says.

But by the time he reaches 42nd Street, she has vanished.

4.

To go back to the beginning, Lilith's version, Marlowe writes.

This, of course, will be Marlowe's version of Lilith's version, and therefore suspect, but he intends a variorum edition. He intends to be scrupulous about integrating all her redactions and flourishes, all of McVie's interpolations and refutations, all those overheard snippets of their conversation that no doubt he imperfectly recalls after so many years.

He lets his fingers rest on the computer keyboard. The lit skyline of Manhattan shimmers on the far dark side of his windows. The computer screen flickers like memory, like a trace of perfume. He closes his eyes and he can sense her beside him, here in his study, or in the Oyster Bar, or in Harvard Square, wherever and whenever, he can summon her up, she can reel him in. He can feel her hand where he pressed it against his lips mere hours ago. He can smell her hand lotion. She did not, he recalls, pull away. Not immediately. He should have found out where she is staying.

Beauty is truth, truth beauty, he writes in the dark and his fingers know where the letters are. *I was force-fed Keats in prep school, weren't we all? But as to the boundary lines between truth (i.e. received perceptions of reality) and beauty (i.e. subjective sensory ordering of the esthetic) I leave that to the moral philosophers.*

His hands lie still on the keyboard. He closes his eyes and succumbs to vertigo, falling back through a time-slide of years and hearing their voices—Lilith's voice and McVie's voice—replaying old conversations in his head, that debate to which they kept returning, though only when they believed they were not being overheard, or when they were so absorbed that they were oblivious to eavesdroppers, most of whom, in any case, were strangers in bars. As for Marlowe, he became addicted to the role of unnoticed snoop. *Debate* is not quite the right word for what obsessed them. It was more like a weirdly competitive recounting of dreams or of vague memories of dreams or of invented dreams or perhaps merely of fantasies. Conflict was at the heart of these exchanges but Marlowe had the impression that each wanted to be proved definitively right or wrong. It was as though they were both searching for keys to a forbidden room.

If Marlowe summons up the chips of evidence from these curious exchanges, they were probably around five years old when they met for the first time (though Lilith was possibly a year older than whoever McVie was at that time) and he was the strangest boy-child she had ever seen. This supposedly happened in the village of St Gilles, about two hours south-west of Paris in the wine-growing district of the valley of the Vienne, a tributary of the Loire, and the children met in the courtyard of the Chateau de Boissy whose decaying stone wall was once part of the medieval keep that surrounded the village back in the Middle Ages, thirteenth century, twelfth century, even earlier perhaps. Parts of the ancient rampart, Marlowe knows, are still standing though they are embedded as the back walls of houses in which present-day villagers live.

Marlowe has a theory—one of several, and he plays with them all, moving them this way and that as jigsaw pieces—that McVie and Lilith may have created an entire fictional childhood history for themselves, that they needed to believe their lives were mythically intertwined. McVie's sick reasons would have died with him in a rice paddy in Vietnam but what might Lilith's have been? Marlowe replays her voice, an endless loop in his brain.

"We're hush-up children," he hears her say. "Me and Petit Christophe."

"I know," McVie says. "I heard the talk. Your mothers were nuns and your father was a priest."

"So everyone believes. In St Gilles."

"Not everyone."

"Most, though. Even though they'd deny it. We had different mothers, same father."

"You can't entirely blame them," McVie says. "Happened often enough. Babies placed in good Catholic homes, no questions asked."

"But it's not true. Our father is our father and he wasn't a priest."

"Different mothers though, we do know that."

"Yes." Lilith sighs. "Some people think Petit Christophe's mother—"

McVie laughs. "I've heard that one. He's my mother's bastard. Born in the chateau."

"No. Not born in the chateau. Born in Paris. Where your mother, *la comtesse*—"

"Ridiculous."

"I know it is. Petit Christophe knew who his mother was. He *remembers* her. But Marie-Claire said *la comtesse* was away in Paris for six months before the war and before she was married. People had to ask themselves why."

"Being pregnant wasn't the why. Not even the angel Gabriel could have pried my mother's legs apart," McVie says. "She wore a cast-iron chastity belt and nobody had the key." He crosses himself reflexively. "God forgive me for being disrespectful to my mother."

"You're not fair to her. And obviously your father found the key."

"Not so obvious," McVie says.

The three of them—Marlowe, Lilith, and McVie—are in a dimly lit basement bar in Harvard Square. Marlowe leans back into shadow. The other two lean forward, toward each other, and are so close that they whisper. Marlowe has to strain to catch their words. They are below street level, looking up through basement windows at passing feet.

His mother the countess, McVie reminds Lilith, has always treated him as though he were immaculately conceived. "But I probably have half-siblings in the village. I'm sure my father kept himself busy with the maids."

Lilith is shocked. "Who?" she asks. "Who d'you think are your half-siblings?"

"I don't know. Half a dozen. Anyone same age as us."

"We're not the same age. I'm a year older than you."

"We don't know that, do we? Not for sure. There's no way to pin your birth date down."

"There might be. I was born in the convent where my mother was still in hiding. The nuns must have kept secret records. I know they would have had me baptized. There must be a record hidden somewhere."

"The nuns would have been too afraid. Hiding resisters could get you shot."

"I know I was born before the Liberation. Papa told me. And you were born after. When I was born your father had never even been to St Gilles."

"He wasn't far off," McVie says. "He was in Paris. Doing his stint in the US Army."

"But your mother wasn't in Paris. She spent the Occupation in St Gilles. In the chateau."

"She did. But at first word of the Liberation, she went to Paris. She was staying with some aunt or other, doing the round of the balls, husband hunting. All that froth was part of late '44 when they met. Dances every night, U.S. uniforms and pretty French women."

"I was already born," Lilith says.

"No you weren't. *Maman* told me. The earliest you could have been born was late February '45, maybe March. There was no sign of a baby in the gardener's cottage in February '45 when my parents were married. If you'd been born, you would have been at the wedding."

"No I wouldn't have been. I was still in the convent in Tours and the nuns were still hiding me. Marie-Claire says it was springtime, April '45, when the priest brought me to St Gilles and she's sure I was already six months old. She thinks I was born November '44. She was at your parents" wedding, in the church and in the chateau afterwards. She danced with the stable boys. She said your father was besotted with your mother. Everyone says that."

"Hard to believe, but I know it's true. He wrote to his buddies in the army and they wrote letters home and I've got copies."

"How did you get them?"

"Found them in an anthology, which is as disturbing as it gets. Total strangers reading my father's drunken thoughts." The memory makes McVie so angry that he folds a cardboard coaster into a pellet and throws it across the bar. *Soldiers' Letters home from post-Liberation Paris.* Lots of jokes about some little French beauty who's put a ring through Vanderbilt's nose and is leading him into her trap. My father sent her flowers and champagne for weeks on end."

"So obviously that did the trick. Unlocked the chastity belt."

"Apparently. More's the pity."

Now this is the sort of comment that piques insatiable curiosity. Doesn't McVie consider himself fortunate, Marlowe asks, to have proof that his parents were in love? Were madly in love? At least on their wedding night?

Of course it is stupid of him to interject. McVie and Lilith both stare as though horns are sprouting from his forehead. "Sorry," he says. "None of my business. Shouldn't have been listening and didn't mean to."

"In your experience," McVie asks in his grave intellectual way, "how long does passionate love last?"

"Five minutes." Marlowe laughs. "Actually, I've never seen it close up. It was certainly never in evidence in my family."

"In my experience," McVie says, "it turns into its flip side very fast."

"Flip side?"

"Passionate hate," he says.

His parents, he says, were married in the Catholic church (the one and only church) in St Gilles in February '45. His father had a week's leave from the U.S. army and at the end of that week, he packed his bride off to his family in New York. His father was still in Europe when McVie was born in a Vanderbilt penthouse in Manhattan.

Marlowe does not think McVie gives a second thought to these tossed-off comments. The three are drinking beer and passing a reefer around, though Marlowe suspects McVie is faking being drunk or high because there is something so guarded about him. Even so, he must be out of it, he must be elsewhere, or he would never reveal so much. It does not seem to occur to him that Marlowe keeps records.

"I arrived exactly nine months later," McVie says, "so I must have been conceived in the chateau. It must have been wedding-night duty on *maman's* part, or wedding-night rape on my father's. I'm sure they never did it again."

"But while he was bridegroom-in-residence," Lilith says, "you think your father might have dallied with the maids?"

"With more than one, I'm willing to bet. Though my mother would have jerked the reins very fast."

"You're grossly unfair to your mother. I know her better than you do."

"You know her differently."

"You don't really know her at all."

"She never let me know her." McVie closes his eyes. He could be praying.

"She turned my life around and I love her," Lilith says.

"She turned my life upside down and I don't forgive her."

"Now that she's moved back to New York," Lilith says, "I hope you won't get angry if I visit her. If I stay with her."

"Do whatever you want. Just don't expect me to go with you. And don't tell her anything about me."

"There's not much I know about you anymore."

McVie covers his face with his hands. "There's too much we don't know about too many things, that's our problem. How much did the nuns never tell your father? And Petit Christophe, how much did he know that he never had a chance to tell us or never could?"

"Ti-Christophe." Lilith lowers her head and lets her long hair fall over her face

"I take sleeping pills," McVie says.

"I just lie awake."

"They don't stop my nightmares," he says.

"I can't stop mine either. Even though I don't sleep, I still have them."

Something very strange happens then. There is something un-nervingly intense about the way they hold each other's eyes. Seconds pass and Marlowe is asking himself: *Just what the hell is going on here? What is this really about?*

"Sometimes," McVie says, "you look so like him that I'm spooked—"

"I know," Lilith says. "I see him in the mirror all the time. It's like an electric shock. Like Banquo showing up for dinner at Macbeth's."

"What happened to Petit Christophe?" Marlowe asks.

It is as though he has touched their wrists with a cattle prod. There is a beat or two of stunned silence, then McVie shakes himself and laughs in a lightly dismissive way that strikes Marlowe as totally fake. "This is just a weird kind of game we play," he says.

"Sort of like chess for people at a wake," Lilith says. "You know. The way folks do things to keep the time passing. We take turns."

"What's the point of it?" Marlowe wants to know.

"The point is to avoid checkmate."

"Not the point of chess," Marlowe says. "I mean the point of your game."

"Same thing." The way McVie smiles, Marlowe knows he is deemed to be caught out, that discussion has been cut off, that his own king has been placed in check or his own queen captured. "It's about strategies," McVie says.

Marlowe thinks: *You are three moves away from checkmate.*

"It's about memory," Lilith offers. "About rearranging the pieces on the board. We had..."—she pauses for what seems like a very long time but is probably only a minute—"we had *unconventional* childhoods, I think that might be the right word, so we..."

"We re-do them," McVie says. "Give them a makeover."

"Re-imagine them," Lilith suggests. "Try to make them turn out better."

"It doesn't mean anything," McVie adds. "But it does make the past more interesting."

"And more tolerable," Lilith says.

"We make up strategy as we go. And we change the plays each time."

"So Petit Christophe?" Marlowe asks. "What happened to him?"

McVie busies himself with writing something on his paper napkin. Marlowe cannot see what he writes. Lilith is folding her napkin, origami style, into a bird. "It depends," she says, "on the strategy. On which chess board we happen to be on."

"Do you mean," Marlowe persists, "that you invent people?"

"We do, sometimes. When it helps. Yes."

"So you invented Petit Christophe?"

"In a way, yes."

"He doesn't exist?"

Lilith points her paper swallow at the ceiling and lofts it into the room. "Right," she says. "He doesn't exist. Not anymore."

Marlowe sees them make some kind of sign, a secret sign, as though they are passing imaginary beads between their fingers. He thinks he sees that. He knows that in the years since that moment he has often seen, in dreams, with the utmost clarity, several versions of what McVie writes on his napkin.

Queen's bishop to castle, he sees. There are arrows and diagrams.

Faut pas rêver, McVie writes another time.

Once he writes in Latin, not French. *Noli me tangere.*

In the bar in Harvard Square, when he catches Marlowe looking over his shoulder, McVie scrunches the napkin into a ball and tosses it into a bin behind the bar.

"Bull's eye!" the bartender calls.

"Let's get back to the game," McVie says. "If you want to play, you can write yourself into the script."

"I had a pretty strange childhood myself," Marlowe says. "In spite of family privilege and affluence and parents who couldn't stand each other and all that stuff."

"OK," McVie says. "You're a contender. Pitch in."

"What did Petit Christophe look like?" Marlowe wants to know.

"Before or after?" McVie asks.

"Like me and my father," Lilith says. "Before, that is."

From that moment on, Marlowe has never known whether to believe a word that either one of them says. He already knows the rules of this game. He has been playing it all his life. You plan your moves. If you can get away with it, when your opponent is glancing across the room, you change the board. You slide a pawn this way or that. You deny the evidence. Even when you and your hearer both know you are making it up, you still tell elaborate lies without blinking. You cross your heart and swear you are telling the truth.

5.

No court ruling is requiring Marlowe to keep to strict chronological order and certainly nobody's memory works that way.
Memory: now there's an inexhaustibly interesting topic, he thinks,
because memory is never linear, never. It is holographic, a multi-di-
rectional detour-rich extremely faulty retrieval system. One day,
inevitably and democratically, everyone's hard drive crashes, but
until it does Marlowe's personal credo is this: follow every byway,
every meander, every swerve.

And so he falls back down the rabbit hole to Harvard Square
in the sixties.

What was he doing there?

He was a runaway from elite prep schools in Massachusetts,
from expectations that weighed like a lead jacket on his shoulders.
He often felt that rogue genes might have intruded, (and, quite
frankly, what does he know of his mother's possible erotic de-
tours?) though the official genes protected him for years. He was
first sent to Dryden Academy and ran away and then got kicked
out. Dryden Academy! Miles from nowhere in western Massachusetts. Runaways were not uncommon. Boys would hitch rides
with the local farmers down to Springfield and to the Mass Pike
and then take a Greyhound to Boston. Local farmers were sympathetic, seeing the defections as evidence of character and genuine
worth. "Sick of all those spoiled rich kids, huh? Want a little fun

with some girls?" Marlowe's time there, it must be understood, was three decades before Dryden went co-ed. He lasted almost two years, on and off.

After his expulsion, he was diplomatically transferred to other elite pastoral campuses, scraped through by parental intervention, got into Yale, flunked out through not bothering to take exams, was finagled into West Point and finagled out again in the nick of time before being expelled. His father made the requisite reparations to land him a desirable position. (He did have sky-high IQ scores on his side.) His father and grandfather and great-grandfather and great-great-whatevers before that were military officers and heroes (the Revolutionary Army, the Confederate Army, the US Army) so naturally he joined the marches against the Vietnam war. He was the perfect double agent, an insider/outsider with high analytical skills. He was already keeping an eye on subversives, but also indulging his private protest against excessive ancestral control.

Hey, hey, LBJ, he chanted as he marched. *How many kids did you kill today?*

It is one of the few things that he truly regrets, one of the things that gives him nightmares. Well, nothing gives him nightmares, but some things do cause him unease and that is one of them. He has not changed his mind about Vietnam (we did it badly, he thinks, very badly, but we had to do it) but he has changed his mind about Johnson. Johnson was a vulgar son-of-a-bitch but he knew what would work and what wouldn't and he knew how to get Congress to move. Also he was a fellow Southerner. Also there is the huge added pleasure of knowing that the Civil Rights Act—which no one but Johnson could have got through Congress—enraged most of Marlowe's male relatives and doubtless made earlier generations turn in their graves. Also (setting aside the coarse language) LBJ reminds Marlowe of his father who died before his son was able to ask forgiveness and make peace.

Marlowe knows his future readers will think he is trying to whitewash himself, to show that he has a political conscience in spite of being without any discernible morality when it comes to accountability, personal or financial. He, however, sees himself in the Robin Hood camp. God and country first; after that, to fleece a few of the mega-rich and give to the poor is fair game.

Not, he is obliged to confess, that he has ever given much to the poor (though he has certainly enjoyed fleecing the rich.)

Odd what a skittering thing memory is, the way it branches and swerves like the Mississippi splaying out across its flood plain, overtopping the levees, a natural phenomenon that made Marlowe's ancestors rich (cotton rich, slave rich), a capillary network that can leak into hollows and coves that time forgot.

There is a certain march that comes back to him, hyper-realistic in detail. Students are milling about in July 1968, hundreds of them, on Cambridge Common, where George Washington assembled his troops. "In 1775," Marlowe explains to Lilith who seems to know almost nothing of American history. "You know. Concord. The shot heard round the world, General Gage, all that."

"No," she says vaguely. "I've got a lot of gaps to fill in. Have you seen McVie?"

Of course Marlowe has seen McVie. He wants him out of the way. He has arranged it.

"I believe he's got a paper due," he says.

"We've all got papers due, but that's not the point."

"He's decided to stay and work on it in Widener."

"What? I don't believe you."

"That's what he told me."

"Fucking aristocrat."

Bodies are buffeting them, politicians-to-be are shouting through megaphones. They are all being herded along Massachusetts Avenue toward the bridge across the Charles and then on to Fenway Park. Marlowe links his arm through hers. Her hair smells of something earthy, like anise or cloves.

He takes a photograph of her. He is taking many photographs of the crowd.

"We really can change the world," she says.

"How do you know McVie?" he asks.

She frowns. "Same way as you."

"I don't think that's true. You act as though you already knew each other."

"Oh," she says. "That. No. That's just... it's a silly game that we play."

"Why did you call him an aristocrat?"

"Don't you think he gives himself airs? Are you going to vote for McCarthy?"

"Of course," he says. "Are you?"

"If I'm able to vote," she says.

"What do you mean?"

"I have complications with documents. Can't register to vote until they get sorted out."

"Aren't you American?"

"Yes. But I wasn't born here. My parents were trapped in occupied France, my mother was killed, my father survived and stayed on after the war and I grew up there."

"Until when?"

"Until I came as a student to NYU. Art History degree, which got me the internship here."

"So. Dual citizenship. That explains why your English is so good. You don't have any accent at all."

"I don't have an accent in French either. It's my first language."

"Speaking of which, don't you think there's something odd about McVie's accent?"

"Is there?" she asks. "I'm not good on American regional variations. He's Boston Irish."

"I don't think so," Marlowe says.

She says, "I wouldn't know."

"Perhaps I can help you," he offers. "With your document issues."

"How could you help me?"

"My family has considerable clout and my father can pull strings all over the place, including in Washington, whenever he wants. It's who you know that counts."

"I'll keep that in mind."

Marlowe puts his arm around her shoulders. "Let's discuss this after the demonstration."

Fenway Park is carnivalesque. While Pete Seeger is singing, Marlowe kisses her. "You want to come back to my apartment?" he asks.

"Well, I'm sort of in a relationship," she says. "A kind of relationship. At least, I think I am. I hope I am."

"Sounds as though he isn't too interested."

"You could be right, but that doesn't mean I'm disengaged."

"Next week," he says, "there's a protest planned for New York, a huge sit-in in Central Park, and I'm driving down. You want to come with me?"

"I'll think about it." Then she says: "I have family in New York. Well, almost family. My French godmother. And my other... another set of godparents, French. I haven't seen them for two months. I'd love to spend time with them. Would that be okay?"

"Sure," he says. "We could stay overnight if you like."

"Okay," she says. "Yes. Okay. That would be great."

Marlowe has this thing about McVie in his head. It is like waking from a dream that he knows is thick with meaning and of crucial significance, but it's gone. All he can see is the dusty cobweb it leaves behind.

In his apartment, he jots down notes about the demonstration. He lists names, students and faculty he recognized, conversations engaged in, other conversations overheard. He forwards this information to assorted authorities. They are paying him well.

He has his rolls of film developed and sends those on too, though he keeps the ones of Lilith for himself. This is mostly selfish, partly altruistic. He does not want her locked into J. Edgar Hoover's files, does not want to share her with all those prurient prying eyes.

And then he sits in the dark for hours with his fingers pressed against his temples until it comes to him, quite suddenly, in the way such things will rocket up from bottomless places, leaping like phosphorescent fish from black water. He pulls out desk drawers in a state of manic excitement. He riffles through book shelves and wicker baskets chockfull of yearbooks and high-school magazines.

He locates them: the magazines from the miserable year-and-a-half he spent at Dryden. He turns page after page until he finds the face he is searching for. Freshman. Latin club, Medieval History club, theater, chess club, cross-country. Third from left, front row, under-sized loner from the year behind Marlowe, identified below the photograph as Gwynne Vanderbilt who stares out with that somber brainy look that never fails to trigger in Marlowe an intense allergic reaction. They overlapped by a mere three semesters and the closest contact they ever had was from being assigned to the same dining table for two weeks before Marlowe bailed out. Dryden students were ten to a table and Marlowe never sat next to McVie (who was Vanderbilt then) but he has a certain kind of instinct for prey. Mentally he put Vanderbilt on his usable list.

Theater club? That does not surprise Marlowe. He knew from

the first moment that Vanderbilt was a mask with no one behind it. On the club pages, in the photograph spreads, there he is on stage in an Oscar Wilde play. Vanderbilt a brilliant mimic, the caption reads. Can do Scottish, Irish, French-English, Italian-English, the latter two especially hilarious. In short, he can pull any accent out of the hat.

But cross-country? How could he possibly have made that team? Even back then, in spite of jelly-fish nothingness, there must have been something stubborn and persistent—or a sense of entitlement?—about him. He is small. He looks as though a footballer could snap his frail little ribcage in two. He must surely have been the runt of the litter on the track team.

This recognition on Marlowe's part would not count as proof in a court of law. If he were to pass the magazine around in their summer-school class or at a demo and point to the photograph, probably less than twenty percent would say: Hey, that's McVie. Or: I think that's Vanderbilt. I knew him at Dryden. Or: He's my grad school tutor. His name's McVie.

Whatever they might say, Marlowe knows.

There is something about the haunted eyes and the solemnity, a boy with the weight of the world on his limp but ancestrally entitled shoulders.

Nailed you! he thinks, you fake Boston-Irish Mick. But who or what are you running from? And what un-American activities are you covering up?

Nobody goes to that sort of hassle (name change, fake accent, fake past) for nothing. Or for innocent reasons. Marlowe does what he does very thoroughly. He is diligent in research and he has access to more sources of information than most people have.

He files his report to the CIA and he also alerts the FBI.

He does not mention Lilith Jardine.

6.

The jury is closeted for one week but the verdict makes instant headline news.

JURY FINDS VANDERBILT CLAIMANT A FRAUD.

Marlowe scans the papers in the lobby of his building.

"Who's surprised?" the doorman says. "Never had a snow-flake's chance in hell."

"You think he should have? You think he's the real thing?"

The doorman shrugs and spreads his hands, palms up. "What would I know?" he asks, careful. "But we had a ten-dollar bet. You said he was the heir. I bet the jury would be against."

"I owe you ten dollars." Marlowe pulls a bill from his wal-let. "You were right about the jury. But do you agree with them? What do you really think?"

"They don't pay me enough to tell you that," the doorman says.

Smart man, Marlowe thinks. Is Lilith equally smart? What is she thinking right now? Why didn't he follow her? Why has he not tracked down the source of his Fedex-delivered invitation to the Oyster Bar? Why has he let himself get so heavily leveraged that he has been paying more attention to notes due and to the jury than to locating Lilith's hotel. He takes all the papers up to his apartment and spreads them out on his desk. He listens to the news. He channel-surfs TV.

He learns that details such as when sentencing will be pronounced, and who will be sentenced, and how, are difficult to come by. Money is being liberally dispensed to track down every existing descendant of the Vanderbilt family (of which there turn out to be hundreds), to contact and interrogate every juror, to fly journalists to France and Australia, to run up thousands of dollars in long-distance telephone calls to French villages and Outback Australian pubs.

Until the jury went into seclusion, all media attention was focused on Australia, on attempts to locate the claimant or to dig up gossip about him. Now there is a sudden swerve of media focus, a frenzy of interest in the village of St Gilles, in the crumbling chateau of the deceased countess.

Waves of Breaking News—real and surreal, probable, improbable, and absurd—crash in like surf.

Vanderbilt Claimant is really Christophe Jardinier, village butcher in France, believed murdered decades ago but found to be living in Australia.

Vanderbilt claimant may be murderer of village butcher in France.

Anonymous sources say claimant may have murdered Vanderbilt heir.

Claimant abandoned dying Vanderbilt heir in Da Nang, claims family member.

Claimant stole dog tags and identity of the heir, claims a Vietnam vet.

Claimant an Australian drifter coached by disaffected former Vanderbilt servant.

Claimant revealed to be noted con man coached by former maid of French countess…

Every news anchor's opening line is about the media trial and the tabloid trial that are following the courthouse trial and the avalanche of fresh evidence (much of it dubious, none of it well documented) that no lawyer even tried to present in court. The press constantly referred to "the claimant's lawyers" but it is now clear that, legally speaking, the Australian cattleman was never the claimant. For reasons of financial survival and to stave off eviction, the Countess de la Vallière Vanderbilt did find it necessary to retain defense counsel, but it was the Vanderbilt lawyers who first filed suit.

The question is: Why?

Given Vanderbilt wealth, who in the family could be sufficiently needy and greedy to want to turn a frail old lady out on the street? Perhaps the law firm itself? Perhaps the deceased husband of the countess was secretly as deeply in debt as his wife? Perhaps the lawyers aided in this cover-up or simply wanted to perpetuate their inherited role? A random telephone poll finds that majority opinion now considers the law firm (or a rogue member of that law firm) the fraudulent party.

Murkier details follow, and Marlowe absorbs them avidly. Documentation (in the form of family correspondence obtained from an unknown source for an undisclosed sum of money) shows that at the time of the Vanderbilt/de la Vallière marriage—a matrimonial union that never greatly warmed the hearts of the American side of the family—only modest affluence was involved as the inheritance of Lawrence Gwynne Vanderbilt who was still in uniform and still on duty with the allied forces in Europe. Though they did of course insist on a pre-nuptial contract, family lawyers advised that it hardly seemed worth the trouble to obstruct a marital alliance with a neurotic but aristocratically connected French countess. There were adequate compensatory factors: a chateau in one of the best wine-growing valleys in France and a genealogical link to Louis XIV.

No one knows who sold this cache of private correspondence to the press, but the press makes hay with it. Marlowe is instantly sure that the Vanderbilt lawyers and many members of the family, including perhaps his wife, will suspect that he is the source. What scares him is that he is not. Who is the mole? He does not know, unless it is the law firm itself. Marlowe learns, along with the public, that the war-time marriage in Paris took place because Lawrence Gwynne Vanderbilt's modest financial expectations at the time were not worth squabbling about.

Small changes in initial conditions, however, can have huge consequence, and an odd set of accidents, a series of Vanderbilts succumbing to untimely deaths like a row of dominoes falling, altered the future. Lawrence Gwynne's uncle, the heir at the time of Lawrence Gwynne's French-village marriage, succumbed to cardiac arrest during a dalliance with a prostitute, a condition that seems to have been a genetically inherited flaw. Following that: there was a drowning of that uncle's oldest son, and a few years later, the steeplechase death of the next in line, then the storm-wreckage of a younger Vanderbilt's yacht. If there is a moral to the fall of the House of Vanderbilt it would seem to be: *Beware adultery, horses, and ships.* One more equestrian death during a hunt, this time of Lawrence Gwynne's nephew (cousin of the purported claimant) has meant that several parcels of inheritance have devolved into an estate much larger than anticipated for Lawrence Gwynne, and hence for his son—long presumed dead—and hence for the next-in-line beyond that son.

Suddenly, on television and radio, bio-pics of the Comtesse Isabelle de la Vallière Vanderbilt proliferate. Everyone now knows that the countess, grief-stricken by the absence of her son, and also because of mounting debts in connection with the maintenance of the chateau, moved back to her husband's penthouse in the summer of 1968 just in time for her son's graduation. For reasons that have not been fully determined (though speculation runs rampant) neither parent actually attended the graduation ceremony in

Harvard Yard. Nevertheless, the countess remained in Manhattan and her husband promptly decamped for the Hamptons and spent most of his time thereafter either in Montauk or in Europe until his scandalous death *in flagrante delicto* and *in coitus* in Paris in 1994.

Both parents apparently did exert considerable effort to make contact and to meet with their son when—to the bemused shock of all, and against all possible prior political indications—he enlisted in the infantry in late '68. He did not respond in any way to the overtures of either of his parents and declined to meet with either before being shipped to Vietnam in '69.

But back in 1945 in France, in the pre-nuptial contract, the Vanderbilt family lawyers had specified a separation of assets. Should the Comtesse Isabelle be pre-deceased by her husband, the widow would keep her chateau and vineyard (from which, by French law and by seventeenth-century royal decree, neither she nor her heirs could be alienated) but Lawrence Gwynne's legal descendants would be sole heirs of their father's estate. Consequently, in 1995, a year after the death of her husband and twenty-six years after the official designation of her son as MIA, the lawyers for the Vanderbilt family notified *la comtesse* that they required her to declare her son dead and to vacate the Fifth Avenue penthouse.

The countess responded, through her own lawyers, that she did not believe, and had never believed, that her son was dead. She produced the letter from a Vietnam Vet, a fellow platoon member, dated 1976. *Dear Mrs. Vanderbilt...I served in the same platoon, the same squad, as your son in Vietnam...*

One week after the court finding of fraudulence, the frenzy of newly-focused and redirected media attention reveals that members of the Vanderbilt family law firm are themselves executors of the estate of the late *comtesse*. This seemingly flagrant conflict-of-interest has been made possible, following the Lady Isabelle's death, by opaque legal contracts dating back several generations. It is revealed that, sheltering under that judicial umbrella, the family has dismissed the lawyers for the estate of the countess and has appointed lawyers of their own choosing. In effect, the Vanderbilt law firm has become judge and jury. They own both the lawyers for the prosecution and for the defense.

Pandemonium breaks out.

There is a rush of commentary on ABC, NBC, CBS, CNN and on the newly minted and salaciously inclined FOX, all channels hastily dispatching reporters and camera crews to the valleys of the Loire and the Vienne.

There are villagers from a tiny hamlet south-west of Paris whose rural accents (as unintelligible to Parisians as to New Yorkers) instantly mutate into subtitles, English ones, not always white against dark background, not always readable, a flaw which irritates many viewers. The networks are deluged with calls and promptly switch to dubbing.

The one who was murdered was not Christophe le Jardinier, explains an elderly priest in the incongruously large church in St Gilles. *It was his son, Petit Christophe. Actually, we don't know for certain he was murdered. He disappeared and people assumed...*

Yes, of course we remember him, the older villagers say. *His father was the head gardener at the chateau and Petit Christophe was apprenticed to Monsieur Monsard, the village butcher. He had a younger sister but she went to America....*

Some people say that Petit Christophe is living in Australia...

Petit Christophe and his little sister and the young Vanderbilt son, they were close friends, but they all went away...

He was very well-liked, Petit Christophe, very handsome, a la-dies' man who got himself into trouble—(Here the dubbing falters, the translator—in spite of long experience in simultaneous translation—bamboozled by the thick rural accent.)

It was very mysterious, what happened. Petit Christophe, the gardener's son—

The butcher's daughter—

The gist of these fragmented reports is that the butcher's daughter was unwed and pregnant when Petit Christophe disappeared. Shortly after he vanished, she killed herself. Some people believe that Petit Christophe simply fled—fearful of the girl's father—and is living in Paris or Algeria or maybe even in Australia. Many in the village privately believe that the butcher—the pregnant girl's father—killed Petit Christophe and many privately think he was justified. *She was, you understand, a certain kind of woman, his daughter...* Others believe that the pregnant girl's older brother was the killer, but since the body of Petit Christophe was never found, no charges were ever brought.

Petit Christophe, the gardener's son.... It was 1960 when he disappeared—

We think he was murdered but no one knows. He might be living somewhere else.

Journalists ask if they might interview the gardener, the father of Petit Christophe. The villagers lower their eyes. *Christophe le père,* they say sadly, *Christophe le Jardinier, he is no longer alive but even before he died, he was somewhere else in his head after the death—after the disappearance—of his son. He had a stroke. He was never right again after that.*

He died in 1964 but he was somewhere else in his head long before that...

His daughter stayed with him until the end but then she went to New York...

American journalists thrust photographs of the Vanderbilt claimant (stills from the video) in front of the people of the village of St Gilles. Roughly fifty percent of those interviewed, speaking to global television, identify the Australian cattleman as Petit Christophe. As a butcher, he was an artist, they say. He was better than Monsieur Monsard, the butcher who trained him. Approximately thirty percent of those willing to give an opinion recognize the Australian not as the son of the chateau gardener but as the son of the Comtesse Isabelle de la Vallière Vanderbilt, a woman *un peu énervée* and very devout, who died of a broken heart because the courts had put a wall between her son and what was rightfully his and hers.

"*Elle se mettait dans tous ses états tout le temps,*" one old man says.

"She wasn't too stable," the dubber supplies, translating freely.

"It is very sad," another old man says. The old man is fishing in the village pond. "Speaking for myself, I believe it was the lawyers who killed *la comtesse*. They milked her, they squeezed out every last cent, and then she couldn't afford the repairs to the chateau. Me, I knew the heir when he was a child but I haven't seen him since. I take the Comtesse Isabelle's word. A mother knows her own son, but her husband's family, they would never let her son touch their money. Filthy English."

"Tell him," the reporter says to the translator, "that the Vanderbilts are American, not English."

"*La même chose,*" the old man spits. "*Tout à fait, la même chose.*"

The translator summarizes. "Same difference," he says.

CNN reports that twenty percent of the inhabitants of St Gilles, looking a little bemused as they face the cameras, say they have never heard of the Vanderbilt claimant, do not recognize the man in the photograph, and insist that no one—unless one counts goats and chickens—has lived in the chateau for many years. It is badly in need of major repairs, the villagers say. It is a ruin. Part of the roof has fallen in.

As for Marlowe, watching and listening to all this, he goes to the Oyster Bar every late afternoon and waits for hours, drinking whiskey and checking his phone. He curses himself for not having asked where Lilith was staying, in which hotel. He calls Sotheby's, but is told they do not give out contact information on appraisers. He calls former intelligence contacts but his calls are not being returned. He keeps one eye on the mirror and the bar but Lilith never appears. He wants to ask about Petit Christophe.

Exactly how unreal was he? Was he her brother or not? Has McVie always been Petit Christophe? Did they swap ID's?

Lilith never shows up.

What does show up is a messenger boy.

"Sir? Are you Mr. Lucifer?"

Marlowe glares. "Why?" He sees the envelope in the messenger's hand: **For Lucifer, Oyster Bar.** "Yes, that's for me," he says, reaching for a five-dollar tip. "Wait," he says. "Wait. Who gave this to you?"

"The doorman at the Grand Hyatt, sir."

"Wait," Marlowe says. "Wait until I've read this. There might be a message in return and another tip."

Marlowe finds a note, handwritten on Hyatt stationery.

Dear Lucifer:

I misjudged you. One mystery has been cleared up and I realize you were not behind the free flights or the two free weeks at this hotel. Whoever arranged that has sent a very specific threat and it has nothing to do with the trial. The timing was pure coincidence. Later today I'll either meet that person or possibly I'll simply be disappeared. Those are the rules of the game and I knew that when I signed up to play.

As for who arranged our meeting in the Oyster Bar, I haven't the slightest idea, but I don't see how it could possibly have any-

thing to do with whoever arranged my trip.

The jury's verdict should have made you very happy. Congrat-ulations to you and Celise on getting the chateau and everything else. But be careful what you wish for.

Sincerely,

Lilith.

Marlowe instantly scribbles a reply on a paper Oyster Bar napkin.

Dear Lilith:

Can we meet? Fuck the chateau and my wife. I don't give a damn about the Vanderbilts. It's you I want. I'm in the Oyster Bar and I'll stay here until you come. Tell me what you want. Any-thing, everything, I'll arrange it. My cell phone number is below. Call me now.

Marlowe.

P.S. Please call. I'll do anything you want.

He folds the napkin into the Hyatt-embossed envelope, cross-es out her hand-printed upper-case letters, and prints **For Lilith Jardine, Grand Hyatt.** He gives the messenger boy a ten-dollar tip with very specific directions: "Give this to the concierge him-self. Immediately."

He waits. He keeps watching the door. Drink after drink, he keeps checking his phone. Ambient noise is considerable, but how can he have missed an incoming call? Apparently, however, there has been one. She now has his cell phone number, so his nap-kin-note must have been received. He keeps replaying her voice-mail: *There's your problem, Lucifer. I don't want anything. I've already got what I want.*

He hits callback on his cell phone and gets the reception desk at the Hyatt. "I just missed a call from one of your guests," he explains. "Can you connect me?"

"Certainly, sir. What name?"

"Ahh… I believe she is registered as Lilith Jardine."

"I'm sorry, sir. There is no answer from her room."

He leaves a message. "I'll be in the downstairs lounge at your hotel."

Marlowe rushes out of the Oyster Bar, emerges onto East 42nd, turns left, and enters the cavernous lobby of the Grand Hyatt. He sits in the lobby lounge where he can watch anyone entering from the street. He picks up the hotel's free copy of the *New York Post,* a trashy society-gossip rag that he has often successfully trolled for investors. In fact, he knows very well that apart from people like himself, only Republican campaign managers and desperate art-museum fundraisers, sniffing for big money whatever it smells like, read the *Post*'s journalistic swill.

VANDERBILT BUTTERFLY LAYS LOW, the headline reads.

There is a photograph of Celise in a strapless gown. Startled, Marlowe reads on.

Social butterfly Celise Vanderbilt, who kept her widowed name after the death of her second husband, and after re-marrying into Old South money and Old South plantation aristocracy, says she is dumbfounded to learn she is next in line to inherit properties in the Hamptons and in France, as well as a handsome Fifth Avenue penthouse. A fellow socialite fundraiser who described herself as a friend —but who declined to be identified—said this was not surprising. *Celise eats properties the way she eats men,* this friend said.

There have been rumors that Ms. Vanderbilt and her most recent husband—her third, a legendary investment broker—were splitting up. Ms. Vanderbilt has denied this adamantly. "My husband and I are very much in love," she said.

Asked if she wished to comment on speculation that an SEC investigation into her husband's affairs was imminent and that allegations of major financial irregularities were pending, Ms. Vanderbilt said: "You'll have to speak to my husband about that. I was brought up to believe that for a lady to speak about money was quite vulgar."

The case of the Vanderbilt claimant and the jury's finding have set off a frenzy of investigative journalism in this country, in France, and in Australia. The claimant has been tentatively identified—perhaps, to be more precise, creatively and theoretically identified—as Christophe Jardinier the Younger, a village butcher from France (though this evidence is as yet unsubstantiated and was not uncovered in time to be presented at the trial.)

The jury has convicted the claimant of fraud, but it transpires that legally speaking the claimant was actually *la comtesse* herself, mother of the Vanderbilt heir, and—at the time of the verdict—the claimant was in fact *the estate* of the recently deceased *comtesse*. It is not yet clear if the courts consider that the deceased countess was deliberately guilty of fraud or of desperate grief-stricken hope. It is not yet clear if she was duped by her lawyers or if her lawyers may be charged with fiduciary misconduct.

Investigative research has uncovered that Christophe Jardinier the Younger, known in his native French village as Petit Christophe, mysteriously disappeared in 1960. He was the son of the head gardener of the chateau owned by the Vanderbilt heir's French mother, and he was apprenticed to the village butcher. It was rumored for many years that he had been murdered by Monsieur Monsard, the butcher himself, father of the young woman whom Petit Christophe had made pregnant. Evidence now suggests that, fearful of the wrath of his lover's father, it is possible that Petit Christophe fled the country. Some sources (not yet verified) claim that he fled to Australia. He may have been, for many years, the butcher in a rural town in Queensland, which is to say that the claimant as seen in the courtroom video may be Petit Christophe. Nevertheless, at this point, there is no DNA confirmation that the claimant is indeed Christophe the Younger. Nor, in spite of the jury's finding, is there DNA confirmation that the claimant is <u>not</u> Gwynne Patrice Vanderbilt.

Several sources, who have insisted on anonymity because they feel themselves to be at personal risk, suggested that there were members of the Vanderbilt family who were eager for the claimant to disappear— or to be disappeared—before further information comes to light. Unidentified sources in France, in particular members of the gendarmerie in small Loire valley towns, suggest that whoever killed Christophe the Younger acquired a taste for blood and may still be at large. He may be a serial killer and is probably still killing, they claim, though they believe he is no longer in France. It is even possible, these sources suggest, that the heir himself killed Christophe the Younger and that is why he immediately fled to the USA and why he subsequently vanished in Vietnam, supposedly vanished, and why he might not be dead at all.

Marlowe downs several whiskies and keeps his eye on the revolving doors that give onto 42nd Street until his eye is caught by a television screen anchored to one of the pillars in the lounge. He is obliged to watch his wife giving an interview on FOX News.

"It has been so embarrassing for the family," Marlowe's wife says demurely, "to have someone who is essentially a farm hand claim to be heir to my uncle's will."

"That is to say, your uncle by marriage," the interviewer says.

"My uncle by marriage, yes. The uncle of my deceased husband."

"That is, of your former *second* husband, now deceased."

"Yes. We were very close. I mean, my husband's uncle and I were very close. He was the younger brother of my father-in-law who was tragically killed in a steeplechase incident. I was quite devastated when my husband's uncle died."

"Is it true, Ms. Vanderbilt," the interviewer asks, "that if the jury's verdict stands, and is not overturned by appeal, then you yourself are next in line to inherit?"

"You know," Marlowe's wife responds sweetly, "I am married to a very wealthy man—"

"Your third husband."

"Yes. He's a brilliant financier. The inheritance, per se, is obviously not an issue that concerns us."

Okay. Enough. Leave it right there, Marlowe says to the television screen. He is, by now, quite drunk, and considers hurling his glass at the TV.

An aerial photograph of the Chateau de Boissy and the village of St Gilles fills the screen. The outer wall of the chateau is crumbling. A voice-over explains that a natural system of village conservation is in process. Once a building begins to decay, the villagers cart away the stone for re-use elsewhere. An oak tree branches up through a hole in the roof of the chateau. "Ms. Vanderbilt," the interviewer asks, "it would appear that the chateau is a ruin. If you inherit, what do you intend to do with it?"

"Well, bless your heart," Marlowe's wife replies. "I haven't given the matter any thought."

"Did you ever meet the Comtesse Isabelle de la Vallière Vanderbilt, the former owner of the chateau?"

"Oh indeed. We were very fond of each other. We met on many formal family occasions in the Fifth Avenue penthouse and in the Hamptons," Marlowe's wife says, "before the tragic death of my second husband. The countess moved back to New York in the summer of 1968 and I had married into the family not long before that. After Gwynne Patrice was killed in Vietnam, I dropped by as often as I could. I like to think I was a source of comfort to her."

"You know that she recognized the claimant as her son?"

"Yes." Marlowe's wife sighs. "Poor Isabelle. Grief does terrible things to people, and denial is only one of these things. The fear of destitution compounds the problem. To be frank, and to be as gentle as possible, I think Isabelle would have identified a chimpanzee as her son if that would have paid for repairs to the chateau and would have covered the upkeep on the penthouse and the association fee."

"The penthouse on Fifth Avenue?"

"Yes. She lived there in apparent splendor, you know, but she was a pauper. I happen to know that her black domestic did the grocery shopping and had begun to pay for the food. That was when I chipped in. It was the least I could do."

"Could you explain to our audience exactly the nature of your relationship to the actual heir, should he be found to be alive."

"I am his cousin by marriage," Marlowe's wife says. "My second husband was the heir's cousin."

"Why did you keep the Vanderbilt name after you remarried?"

"Out of respect for the Vanderbilt family. They had become very dear to me."

"The heir has never been declared legally dead, though he was officially declared MIA in Vietnam. Should he be declared officially dead, or should the verdict of fraudulence on the part of the claimant be upheld, it is our understanding that the estate of your deceased husband stands to benefit."

"That is correct. The Comtesse Isabelle, as we all know, for the saddest and most moving of reasons and irrational hopes, refused to have her son declared dead."

"She had substantive proof that he was alive, isn't that so?"

"I can't comment," Marlowe's wife says. "On the advice of my lawyers. Except to say that she alone, the Comtesse Isabelle, of the entire extended family, insisted that the claimant, who in no way resembled Gwynne Patrice, was her son. Far be it from me to say that what mattered to her was the inheritance which would have enabled her to remain in the penthouse and with which she could pay for repairs to the chateau."

"Since our inquiries in France have given us to understand that the chateau was given in perpetuity, by royal decree, to the family of the countess, can you explain to our viewers how it became part of this lawsuit?"

"After the death of the Comtesse Isabelle, her estate passed into her husband's estate, and hence on to his heirs. Which is to say, given the death in Vietnam of his only son, the estate of the countess passed from her husband to his nephew, my deceased husband."

"And since your second husband, now deceased, left his entire estate to you, you are now next in line to inherit the chateau as well as the Vanderbilt holdings in this country?"

"So my lawyers tell me," Marlowe's wife says, with a disarming shrug of her shoulders. "I might, you know, donate the chateau to the Metropolitan Museum of Art as exhibition space for their fine collection of paintings by Cezanne and Monet."

"Ms. Vanderbilt," the interviewer explains to the TV audience and to the world, "has a distinguished record of sponsorship of the Metropolitan Museum of Art, as well as of MOMA and of the Metropolitan Opera. Nevertheless," he says, "I am obligated to ask you, Ms Vanderbilt, if there is any substance to the rumors that you yourself had an affair with the heir's father before your marriage to—"

"Oh my goodness!" Celise raises her eyes heavenward. "Have we come to this? I won't dignify that question with an answer."

"As I'm sure you're aware, Ms. Vanderbilt, photographs taken in night clubs in the sixties—"

"Ah yes," Celise sighs. "Fakes. Doctored collages. What everyone expects from the tabloids. They settled out of court years ago."

Marlowe pours himself another glass of whiskey.

He checks his phone for messages but there are none.

He calls Sotheby's and asks if he can speak to one of their appraisers, the one based in Australia, the one who is currently a guest at the Grand Hyatt. He gets a standard after-hours recording and a number to call in emergency. He calls that number and speaks to an unknown live person. "You have reached our answering service," the live person says. "Sotheby's does not give out personal information on appraisers when they are traveling, but we can take a message and it will be relayed to the appraiser's hotel room. Please leave your message after the tone."

"Lilith," he says after the tone. "I'm waiting downstairs. I'm going to wait here until you come." He keeps downing whiskies but Lilith never comes.

"Sir," a steward says, waking him. "Can I escort you to your room, or should I call you a cab?"

7.

A man named Marlowe is taken home from the Grand Hyatt in a cab. Between them, the doorman and the taxi driver manage to get Marlowe across the lobby. He wakes in his own apartment with a terrible hangover. His dreams have been mangled. In one fragment, he is on Interstate 95 driving down from Boston to New York for an anti-war sit-in in Central Park. The car radio is dissecting the fallout of the assassinations (Martin Luther King and Bobby Kennedy) and is predicting violence for the upcoming Democratic convention in Chicago. Lilith is in the passenger seat. Marlowe has to swerve for an oncoming car that is going the wrong way at high speed, head-on collision imminent. The other driver must have come up the off-ramp, must be crazy or drunk or high. In mid-swerve the passenger door is flung open and Lilith is ejected like a rocket. Marlowe jams on the brakes, not a wise reflex, because cars and trucks pile up on him from the rear and crush his vehicle like a tin-foil can in a garbage compactor.

Marlowe wakes briefly with an excruciating headache, tries to claw his way out of the wreckage of his dream, and gives up. In any case, he has to go back for Lilith. He can't just take the exit ramp and leave her in the rubble of the interstate, of a nightmare, of his life. Has he lost her permanently? It is now as clear as the shard of windshield sticking out of his throbbing eye that what he wants is so much more than mere conquest. He wants her to want him. He wants her to think well of him. He wants to want to be the kind of person she would think well of. Well, almost. In lieu of becoming someone else, he wants her to think she sees the kind of man she admires.

Beneath him, shockingly, suddenly, the interstate gapes open and he falls down the sink-hole, turning and tumbling into darkness. He finds himself in a tunnel, scraped and bruised and slick with sewage, but otherwise unharmed. He crawls forward. Ahead of him a toll booth appears and in the booth, all buck teeth and smirk, the white rabbit demands to see his interstate ticket. "It's here somewhere," Marlowe says, anxiously searching his pockets. "I know I've got it. I came on in Boston at that interchange of the Mass Pike with I-95." He can feel a panic attack closing in. On the lowered boom ahead of him sits the Cheshire cat. The cat is almost nothing but grin. "If you don't have your toll receipt," the Cheshire cat says, "the boom will not let you through. It has a dual function, you know."

"I've got it, I know I've got it," Marlowe says. "As a matter of fact, you don't even have the right to ask because I have an E-Z pass. I always get through. I'm never stopped. I don't even have to pause. I have permanent right of way."

"So show me your E-Z pass."

"It's on my windshield, naturally, under that pile-up. How can I find it? Especially since I have to find Lilith first."

"Better find both of them fast," the white rabbit advises, checking his fob watch, "because the queen's on her way. Patience is not her strong suit and she's not inclined to make allowances. She doesn't cut slack for mistakes."

"I know my toll ticket's here somewhere," Marlowe says, oddly desperate and seriously offended. He is not used to being put on the defensive. He is not used to a racing heartbeat, hyperventilation, and panic. None of this is normal. He is always the one in control. "I have to save Lilith," he explains. "She was thrown clear but she'll be in critical condition. Call for an ambulance."

"Not until I see your pass or your ticket," the white rabbit says.

"What? But that makes no sense. It's not fair."

"Since when have you cared about fairness?"

"It's a matter of life and death, for God's sake. Call 911."

"Ticket first. Those are the rules."

"What the hell is the matter with you bureaucrats?"

"You must hurry," the white rabbit says, checking his watch. "The queen doesn't tolerate delays. Oh dear, oh dear, she's late as usual, she's always late, but here she is."

"Guilty!" the queen shouts. "Off with his head!" and when Marlowe turns, the face is that of his wife, Celise, whom he has not yet even met. He does not yet even know of her existence in this late summer week of 1968 though (as it turns out) she does know of his, she is waiting for him, watching for him, the black widow at the hub of her web. As it turns out—much too late for his own future fate—she already has an alarmingly thick dossier on him. She is reeling him in. In less than twenty-four hours they will meet in New York.

"I have to rescue Lilith," he explains to his future wife.

"She has never needed rescuing," the queen says icily. "And her name is Alice."

"How many names does she have?"

"You may well ask," says the queen. "But your time is up. Off with his head!"

The interstate tollbooth boom comes down with its bright angled shimmering guillotine blade. Marlowe does not even feel pain. He is eye to eye with the queen as she holds up his own head by its hair.

"I do think that was overkill," the white rabbit says.

"Don't imagine I can be shuffled off," Celise warns, dangling his head like a toy. "You're not the card sharp you think you are, and you're certainly not the sharpest card in the pack. You don't even begin to know how many aces I have up my sleeve."

All that is left of the Cheshire cat is its smile.

Marlowe, holding his head (now reattached to his body) in his hands, palms pressed against throbbing temples, stumbles out of his dream and into the kitchen to make coffee. There is a note propped against the coffee machine.

Darling:

Eggs and bacon in the fridge. Cappuccino machine loaded and ready to go. Just push the green button. Quite a turn of events in the past few days, all that mayhem in the news. And is the claim-ant a murderer?

La pauvre comtesse. *She must be turning in her grave. I've ac-tually been asked to do an interview with* VANITY FAIR *about my close familial relationship with the countess. They know I was at her side when she was dying. They've set up a photo shoot for next week in the Vanderbilt penthouse.*

I'm not sure how well you'd remember the penthouse but it's where we met the first time, though I don't think we've been back there together since then. Do you remember the magnificent mar-ble lobby with its floor-to-ceiling French baroque mirror? And do you remember that on the opposite wall there's a huge seven-teenth-century painting of the Virgin and Child. It's worth a for-tune. I thought I'd suggest to VANITY FAIR *that I sit in one of the Louis XIV chairs in front of the painting and their photographer could arrange things so that the painting and Yours Truly would also be reflected in the mirror.*

What do you think?

It won't hurt your client list, will it? to get a full-color spread in VANITY FAIR.

Don't forget the fundraiser at MOMA tonight. I've arranged a

car for you. Be all tuxed up and ready to go at 7.30.
Celise.

    P.S. A little bird told me that the gardener's daughter is back in town and at the Grand Hyatt, at least for another few days. Now why would that be? She's always tried to keep her claws in the countess. Be careful.

Marlowe swallows a handful of powerful painkillers, fills his mug with coffee and sinks into his favorite armchair looking out over Central Park. His windows face east. He can see the lake, the boathouse, tourists plying their paddles already. Though he is not someone given to the interpretation of dreams—in fact, he has always despised gullible people who see meaning in dreams—he feels an odd sense of dread.

He is not used to feeling anything at all. He thinks of feelings the way he thinks of clouds or fantasies. They drift. They do not touch him. They have no substance. There is no proof that they exist at all. Other people claim to have feelings or to observe their effect but he is a non-believer.

He is never anxious. So why does he have this tense sensation of driving a car whose brakes have failed? Even if he were indeed driving a car whose brakes had failed, he could pilot his way out of the spin. He knows this. Just as tightrope walkers are born with their own unique skills, their squirrel genes—they can walk across Niagara on a wire, they can walk from one skyscraper tower to another, hundreds of feet above traffic—so he was born with the ability to remain always and perpetually unscathed. There is no crash from which he cannot steer free. This is something he knows as surely as he knows he is alive. Why then does he feel as though the steering wheel itself is utterly unresponsive, wobbling like a plastic propeller on a fairground stick?

Beyond his windows, floating above the lake in Central

Park, is the toothy smile of the Cheshire cat. "Stop smirking," Marlowe snaps.

"Stop pretending you're the only player who has control," the Cheshire cat smirks back. "There are other players and you happen to be up against another master of the game. Get used to it."

"Do you mean Lilith or do you mean Celise?" Marlowe asks

"That is the sixty-four-thousand dollar question," the Cheshire cat says, beginning to disappear into thin air. First the tip of the long curled tail fades away, then the rest of the tail, then the body, then the ears and the head, then the whiskers, and last of all the smirk full of teeth.

The state Marlowe is in is so far from normal that it interests him. He does believe in intuition and he does trust his gut instincts, which have, after all, made him obscenely rich. They have also made him a valuable conduit of information for which he has been rewarded with greater access to further conduits of otherwise private and even classified information which have in turn brought him access to ever more massive influxes of fresh blood.

Fresh blood? Fresh blood-money.

Dear God, Mrs. Malaprop! he reprimands the chattering goblin in his head. *Let us please be circumspect and keep to the rules of decorum. We are speaking of cash flow here, a neutral entity where the sole and only moral duty is to the shareholders and the investors and where any unfortunate side effects are merely collateral damage, regrettable of course, though essential to the well-oiled working of the national economic machine.*

Is this current abnormal malaise an intuition about his investment business? No. He thinks not. Certainly that is a high-risk game, but he loves high risk. He is a master of any juggling act and will invariably finesse his way out, even though at this particular moment in time he must admit to himself that there is some worrying shakiness in his intricate house of cards. But his whole life has been one glorious gamble. He has always rolled the dice and they have always come up double six. He really could not bear life without that adrenaline rush.

The sense of impending disaster is something outside of all that, but he cannot quite put his finger on what it is. Probably simply the hangover. Perhaps the trial?

Perhaps seeing Lilith again? Perhaps her disdain? Perhaps his memory of the way she had withdrawn into herself all those years ago when McVie was first reported Missing in Action. She would not return phone calls. She would not answer the door. He had gone to the Fogg and the Boston Museum of Fine Arts and asked to see her and was told she had taken a leave of absence. For how long? he had wanted to know. An extended leave, he was told. How extended? he asked. That depends on the verdict of her doctor, he was told.

A month later when he went back to the Fogg, she was in her office but acted as though nothing had happened. "Where were you?" he asked.

"I was staying with friends in New York," she said lightly.

"That French countess?"

She said politely: "I don't think I'm required to file reports with you, Lucifer."

"Can I take you to dinner?" he asked.

"I don't think so."

"Is this still because of the anti-war demo and the Oyster Bar? Because you thought I'd stood you up?"

"It's because I don't want to go out for dinner."

"With me, you mean. Which means you've heard rumors about my supposed affair."

Lilith raised one eyebrow. "No, I haven't heard rumors. They wouldn't interest me if I had. Do you want me to ask with whom you are rumored to be having an affair?"

"With the niece of your countess," he said. "Or rather, her niece by marriage. But there's no truth to it. Billy Vanderbilt and I have become close and I spend weekends with them in the Hamptons. That's all there is to it. So let me take you to dinner to cheer you up."

"Lucifer," she said, "I'm sure that is kindly intended, but I've been on leave for a month. I have to catch up on a lot of work."

He could not stop himself from saying: "But if McVie were asking, you'd find time. Oh, and by the way, just so you know, McVie's cover is blown. We overlapped at Dryden and I recognized him. I know he's really a Vanderbilt. I know he's the son of your countess. I already knew it before I drove you to New York."

"How predictable of you, Lucifer."

"I'm right, aren't I? If McVie were asking you out to dinner, you'd find time."

She said quietly: "McVie is no longer able to ask anyone anything."

"Life goes on," Marlowe said.

"Does it? How would you know, Lucifer? What losses have you survived?"

"Oh, for God's sake. Get over it. McVie was a flea bite, not a mortal wound."

"McVie and I didn't part on good terms. I was angry with him. It's not an easy thing to live with."

"You were right to be angry. He enlisted pointlessly." Marlowe was thinking that he would love to see her angry, love to see her snarl and bite, love to take her by force. "But he's not worth grief. He was a sanctimonious prick. He stalked martyrdom."

"It's a terrible thing, a terminal quarrel… The last chance for forgiveness has gone."

"You still have to get on with your life."

"Do I? Why?"

"Because otherwise you wallow in self-pity. Come on, I'm in-sisting. Dinner."

"Thank you, but no. I'd prefer to wallow. I'm trying to find a way to forgive myself."

Was she telling the truth then?

Was she telling it now? Was there really someone unknown who had sent her pre-paid airfare and a hotel reservation? He knows he himself did not do it. Did anyone? Really, what does he know? What does anyone know? He himself has told thousands of lies, yet people instinctively trust him. Is it possible that Lilith is simply better at the game than he is?

Is she one of the truly great Masters of the Game?

Everyone trusts him, and yet Lilith does not, which is a chal-lenge he cannot let go. He did not send her a pre-paid round-trip Sydney-New York air ticket. He did not make her hotel reserva-tion. He did not send her a message re an Oyster Bar rendezvous, specific date, specific time.

Someone *did* send him—Marlowe—a message about a rendez-vous at the Oyster Bar, same specific date, same time, quite specific about the woman he would find there.

What proof does he have that Lilith did not pay for her own airfare, did not make her own reservation, did not herself send him the message about the Oyster Bar? She will deserve at least one whole chapter in his manuscript of *Masters of the Game*. What proof does he have that she is not the mastermind behind the fraudulent claimant and that she has yet to play the ace up her sleeve?

Certainly there are many people in the world of illicit art trad-ing, and many more in international intelligence circles, who could have been tracking her and luring her for reasons of their own. But if Lilith herself is not playing games with him, if she is not out-gaming him, there is only one other person who could have known where she would be staying, only one other person who could have coordinated meeting times, could have sent the Oyster Bar invitation to Marlowe by Fedex, and could have known he would take the bait. Head throbbing, Marlowe makes a few phone calls. He is still connected to multiple data nodes.

He has one simple question. Like everyone else, he now knows that the Vanderbilt law firm has displaced the lawyers for the countess. This is his question: which family member, in particular, is the executor of the estate of the Vanderbilt widow?

In the late summer of 1968, a man named Marlowe is driving south on Interstate 95 to what is planned as a peaceful demonstration in New York. He has a camera and intends to take hundreds of pictures. These will be sent to appropriate authorities and kept on file, an activity he considers a serious moral obligation. He knows that many of the demonstrators will be naive though genuine pacifists and idealists. Others will not be.

Lilith is in the passenger seat and Marlowe has reserved a room at the Grand Hyatt for their overnight stay in Manhattan. They left Boston at eight in the morning and they expect to be in Manhattan in time for lunch. Marlowe keeps giving his passenger sidelong glances. Her window is open, her hair streaming and flapping like a flag. She appears luminous, excited by something: the demonstration? the prospect of their affair? It is a hot summer day, the atmosphere steamy, everything loose and easy. Marlowe has to force himself not to take the first exit after they cross into Connecticut. He could drive deep into the state forest that hugs the Atlantic shore. There will be curtains of conifers, oaks, and maples on all sides and he could simply press the button that turns the front seats into a bed.

Better not to rush things, perhaps.

"Can I ask a favor?" she says. "Before the demo, could you

drop me off at Fifth and East 72nd? I told you I'd be visiting family. To be perfectly honest, that's why I accepted your offer."

"Why don't I come with you?" he says. "I'd like to meet your family."

"Oh... Well, they're not exactly family, strictly speaking, but we go back a long way. To childhood in fact. I'd prefer to have time alone."

Marlowe is recalling, with extreme and prurient interest, the strangely obsessive conversations he has heard and reheard, the staccato glimpses of odd personal histories, perhaps the pure inventions of Lilith and McVie, perhaps his own private embroidery of what he thinks he remembers he has heard.

"How about you simply introduce me?" he suggests. "And then I'll take off."

"But why?"

Of course, he is mightily tempted to say: *Because I've nailed McVie as a Vanderbilt and I'm curious about his family and your "almost family" in New York.* But he says, "Because you matter to me, you know, and therefore your friends matter."

"Let me think about it," she says.

Somewhere in Connecticut—his memory is on the bridge across the Housatonic River—she says: "Well, look, the two families I'll be visiting are French so they're not comfortable meeting strangers the way Americans are. They're not unfriendly, not at all, well they wouldn't seem unfriendly to anyone European, but they'd just find it odd... They would find it very impolite and intrusive of me to show up with someone they've never met."

"Okay," Marlowe says. "I understand. Look, the closest I'll be able to park for the demo is in the underground lot at the Metropolitan Museum. It's impossible even to pause on Fifth Avenue, except for stop lights, so why don't I just park under the Met and we'll leave the car there for the day."

"Okay," she says, relieved. "Okay. That's a great idea. Thanks."

"And then let's meet at the Met again," he says, "at, say, 3 p.m., in time for the demo."

"Well," Lilith says, "I'll probably have lunch with my friends, so I can't say for sure when I'll be free. How about we leave that open and just make our separate ways to Central Park?"

"In that case," he says, "in case we don't connect at the demo, let's agree to meet at the Oyster Bar in Grand Central at 6 p.m."

"Okay," she says. "Yes. Good idea. Because I'm not quite sure I'll be willing to leave my friends in time for the demo."

He raises his eyebrows. "But I can count on the Oyster Bar at 6?"

"Well, I'll certainly try..." She hesitates. "Yes, okay, that's a promise. I do owe you for the ride down. I couldn't have afforded this visit without it."

"My pleasure. My gift. And not the only one either because I've booked a room for us at the Grand Hyatt. More or less next door to the Oyster Bar."

Marlowe is startled by how startled Lilith is. "Oh," she says. "Uh... I'm sorry. But there's been a terrible misunderstanding. I'll be staying with my godmother overnight."

"Ahh. Well. Yes. A small misunderstanding. But are we still on for the Oyster Bar?"

"Sure," Lilith says. "Yes. I promise. My treat, to make up for the misunderstanding."

"If you couldn't afford the trip down, you can't pick up the tab at the Oyster Bar. And it's still my pleasure."

When the car is safely stowed, Marlowe walks her to a high-rise on Fifth Avenue. "First call," Lilith says. "I'll be here for a while. My other friends live on Madison, a few blocks away."

"You won't all get together in one place?"

"Oh no!" Lilith cannot quite suppress a laugh. "No. That

wouldn't work. My friends come from two very different worlds. In France, the boundary lines are very distinct and you can't transgress."

"Apparently *you* can."

"That's because I don't count. I'm like stealth aircraft. I don't show up on the radar."

"Isn't this where the Vanderbilts have a penthouse?" he asks.

"How do you know that?"

"The Vanderbilt holdings aren't exactly unknown," he says. "You can look them up in any guide book." He does not tell her that he has already nailed McVie as a Vanderbilt. He does not tell her that he and Vanderbilt/McVie overlapped at the same prep school in Massachusetts. "So you know the Vanderbilts?"

Lilith is visibly nervous. "Not really," she says. "But Mrs. Vanderbilt is a French countess from the village where I grew up. I've known her since I was a child. She's very formal, but I'm fond of her and she's fond of me and I have an obligation to pay my respects. She's only just come back to New York. She spent most of her life in France."

"What about Mr. Vanderbilt? Will he be here?"

"I don't think so. He has a house in the Hamptons. And, uh, I think he and Lady Isabelle prefer to live apart."

Marlowe is immensely tempted to say, for the sheer thrill of shocking her: "And the countess is McVie's mother, right?" But he says only, "I really would love to meet a French *comtesse*."

"I just don't think—"

"You could introduce me and say I've driven you down from Boston and then I'd leave."

"But why? Why would you want to meet her?"

"Put it down to crass American curiosity about genuine blue-blood aristocrats. I understand she's a descendant of Louis XIV. Wrong side of the sheets, of course."

"Yes, she is. But how do you know that?"

"I think you don't understand the role of the Vanderbilts in American history, or realize just how much everyone knows about them. We own them, you know, the way we own Jackie Kennedy. I don't think you understand that."

"Probably not," Lilith sighs. "I suppose I owe you. For the drive down, I mean. But I should warn you that the countess is not going to be amused. She will be gracious in a very formal way, but believe me, she will not be pleased to meet you. She will not like you. And she is going to consider this very bad behavior on my part. I wish you wouldn't ask this of me."

"Objection overruled."

Lilith gives him a long puzzled look.

He smiles disarmingly. "When I really want something, I get it. Always." He shrugs and extends his hands, palms turned upwards, a gesture of surrender. "Badly brought up, I guess. But it's like the law of gravity. I get what I want. That's simply the way things are."

"Really?" Lilith raises one eyebrow. "If that's what you believe, I'd say beware of what you want."

"A dare always whets my appetite. Beware yourself. If you won't introduce me, your pumpkin coach will disappear and you'll have to take a Greyhound bus back to Boston."

"I've just decided I'll do that anyway," she says.

"Oh, come on. Can't you take a joke? All I'm asking for is a sighting of a French countess and a one-minute introduction."

"Are you sure you don't mean you want a Vanderbilt connection for your financial sideline?"

"I won't pretend I'd find the connection a problem. How do you know I have a financial sideline?"

"There's talk among other summer-school students. There's talk in anti-war circles."

"Is there?" Marlowe is disconcerted but grateful for the warning. He covers quickly. "It's because I'm Southern, you know. To be Southern in Boston is like being Jewish in Germany. The ugliest prejudice floats up."

"Oh, right," Lilith says. "I've noticed the barbed wire and the concentration camps for Southerners in Harvard Square."

"Ouch," Marlowe says. "Okay. So I'm slightly overstating the case. But who's maligning me?"

"A couple of guys in our seminar told me they'd invested with you. They said they'd made money. They said you get uncanny returns. "

Marlowe smiles disarmingly. "My secret's out. I do have financial skills. It's just a hobby. Something I do for friends. You want to invest?"

"I don't have anything to invest."

"Well, when you do, I'll triple it for you. In return for an introduction to a French countess and a quick peek inside a Vanderbilt penthouse."

"If I did have anything to invest, I wouldn't trust a company that calls itself Lucifer Investments. But I'm willing to introduce you as the devil incarnate."

Marlowe laughs. "I'll consider it an endorsement. Free advertising."

"And I *will* go back by Greyhound. I don't care for imposed obligations but I do meet those I impose on myself. See you at six at the Oyster Bar."

There is a doorman on the desk in the lobby of the building on Fifth Avenue, but Lilith presses the buzzer for the penthouse.

"*C'est qui?*" a voice responds.

"*C'est moi, ma chère marraine. Je viens d'arriver de Boston.*"

"*Melusine? C'est vraiment toi?*"

"*Oui, ma marreine. C'est moi.*"

"*Monte, monte, ma petite enfant.*"

"*Madame Isabelle*, I have a guest with me. He has driven me down from Boston. He would very much like to meet you."

"*C'est mon fils?*"

"*Je suis désolée, ma marreine. Mais non.* Your son has a paper due and he is teaching a class. He could not get away. My guest is an American friend. I am obligated to him for the ride. He will only stay for one minute."

There is a pause. "*Il me faut?*"

"*Mais non, pas du tout,* of course you don't *have* to, *ma marreine*. It would be a case of *noblesse oblige.* Americans are besotted with the very idea of aristocrats."

"*Je le ferai si'l me faut,*" the countess says. "*Bien.* Let him come up."

"If she has to, then she has to," Lilith explains. "I think you may have noticed a lack of enthusiasm in the tone."

"I'm tone-deaf," Marlowe says cheerfully.

"I've noticed," Lilith responds.

"I know a bit of French," he says, "but I don't know what *marreine* means."

"It means godmother. The countess is like a mother to me." In the elevator she tells him: "I've been here before, but it was when the countess was still in France. It was before she shipped her furniture back. I know she will have changed things. I'm not sure what to expect."

The elevator doors open onto the marble lobby of the penthouse floor. Opposite, there is a gilded and ornate baroque mirror, baseboard to ceiling, twelve feet high, and Marlowe notes Lilith's sudden intake of breath, the kind of startle that indicates *déjà vu.* On the antique sideboard facing them is a potted orchid that curves in a long graceful arc to the right, its ivory flowers displaying their speckled pink throats. Reflected obliquely in the mirror is a large canvas of the Virgin and Child. Marlowe has the usual level of knowledge about art—the kind necessary for black-tie opening-night chatter at art museums—and he thinks he recalls that this portrait is famous and worth a fortune.

"I should not have brought you," Lilith says. The painting seems to overwhelm her. But a door is even now opening onto the marble entryway and the slender form of a woman once and still beautiful is emerging, a woman in softly draped silk, a woman who is accustomed to having her wishes received as law, a woman who expects to be perceived as beautiful even though she is well beyond a certain age. She wears a long double string of pearls to which is attached a jeweled crucifix that she clasps constantly with her right hand.

"Melusine!" she says. "*Quel plaisir!*"

The two women embrace, formal French style, kissing the air beside each other's cheeks, right, left, right, three times.

"*Votre fils vous embrasse aussi,*" Lilith says.

"*Tu mentes,*" the countess responds sadly.

"No, no, I'm not lying," Lilith protests. "But you know how it is. *Madame la Comtesse*, may I present the American friend?"

"*Enchantée,*" the countess says.

Marlowe takes the hands of the countess in his own and kisses them one by one. "*Madame la Comtesse,*" he says. "Such a privilege. Will you permit me to say that you bear a striking resemblance to Poussin's portrait of 'The Assumption of the Virgin'? You must surely have stepped out of the seventeenth-century French court."

Lilith rolls her eyes.

"How very charming of you," the countess says. "Though Poussin was living in Rome when he painted that series. He spent more of his life in Rome than in France."

"The nomads of history," Marlowe says smoothly. "Art and

commerce owe everything to them."

"Do you think so?"

"Those who move, move history. Like yourself, *Madame la Comtesse*. And like myself too. I'm a Southerner living in Boston, but I have been a guest at Biltmore, your Vanderbilt chateau in the south."

"Indeed?" the countess says politely. "You refer to that *nouveau riche* country house in North Carolina? I haven't been there myself. It belongs to my husband's family. It is not, you understand, a chateau in the French sense."

"I understand the spiral staircase was copied from the chateau at Blois."

"Is that so?" The countess inclines her head graciously. "Will you join us for an apéritif?"

"Oh no, he can't stay," Lilith says.

"I could stay for a little while," Marlowe offers.

"As it happens, I have another guest at the moment," the countess says. "The timing is most opportune. You are both Americans. You can amuse each other out on the terrace while Melusine and I converse in private." She raises her voice slightly to call back into the salon. "Celise, come and entertain a fellow American for me."

The woman who appears is probably about his own age, mid-twenties, or perhaps she is thirty. She seems colorless. There is something oddly diffident, bashful (*staged*, he senses) and yet overly eager about her. Marlowe sees that she wants to please. She very much wants to please. She advances on Lilith as though they are childhood friends, long parted. "Melusine," she says, with altogether more ardor than seems appropriate. "I am so happy to meet you. *La comtesse* never stops talking about you."

Over the top, Marlowe thinks, wincing, feeling ostentatiously American, and wishing he could rewind his own performance.

"I hope *ma belle-mère* will grant us a formal introduction,"

Celise murmurs.

"Forgive me," the countess says, exquisitely polite, ice crystals on the tips of her words. "This is Celise, the bride of my husband's nephew, a young man much involved with horses." She invests this statement with the most refined nuance of disdain. She waves Celise toward Marlowe. "Take this American out to the terrace and talk horses with him," she orders her niece-in-law. Marlowe is close enough to hear what she then murmurs in Lilith's ear. She speaks in French, which Marlowe understands only slightly, but he picks up the gist of her comment. *That woman does meekness well*, the countess says. *Gentille comme un scorpion.*

Ah. In retrospect, Marlowe wishes he had paid more attention to that warning.

"And to whom do I have the pleasure of speaking?" Celise asks.

"His name is Lucifer," Lilith says.

Marlowe notes a sudden quiver, like a small electric charge, pass through the body and cross the face of Celise. He is used to having this effect on women. "So," he says, offering his arm. "Horses?"

"Race horses," Celise explains. Out on the terrace, she takes Marlowe's hand between both of her own soft palms and waits for him to raise hers to his lips. When he does so, she says demurely: "A Southern gentleman. It's unmistakable, really, and such a pleasure. When were you at Biltmore?"

"Oh, years ago," Marlowe says lightly. "Weekend house parties. My family's connected."

"Then that means *we* are connected. Who are your folks?"

"Let's talk about race horses," Marlowe says. "It's a much more interesting topic. Your husband's an owner?"

"An owner, a breeder, a trainer, and a very fine horseman himself. Kentucky Derby, Preakness, Belmont, Ascot." She looks up at him from under her lashes. "We were invited to the queen's box at Ascot."

"Is that so? Racing royalty then," Marlowe feels obliged to say.

Is it possible to reconstruct his first impression? Can he recall what she looked like on the penthouse terrace? He knows he would not have looked at her twice if they were anywhere else. *Simpering*, he might have said if asked for an opinion at the time. He cannot really remember what she looked like. She did indeed do meekness well. But then, who was he to cast stones? He did what the occasion required and so did she. In that sense, they were well matched from the start.

"Yes," she agrees. "We *were* treated as royalty at Ascot. In fact, the queen was seriously interested in our breeding line. She asked if her equerry could contact ours."

"Is that so?" Marlowe murmurs again. He is trying to see where the countess and Lilith have gone.

"We do of course have our own equerry," Celise explains. "On Long Island. And he has been in contact with Buckingham Palace."

"Yes?" Marlowe says, beginning to feel desperate to escape. "I regret," he says, "that I must—"

"By the way, the countess has her own little whims but I'm hardly a bride. Billy and I have been married for nearly two years, and we would absolutely adore to have you come for a weekend to the Hamptons," she says. "Oh, you really must come. How is the weekend after this?"

"Ah... I'm afraid that won't be possible," he says. "I live in Boston."

"Boston! We have friends who've discovered the most amazing investment broker in Boston. You wouldn't by any chance be the Lucifer of Lucifer Investments, would you?"

"As a matter of fact—" In retrospect, how obtuse could he have been? How stupidly narcissistic, how slow-witted?

"Oh my God," she says. "Somehow I knew it. Our friends

swear that you have the Midas touch."

"Combination of good luck and good management."

"That's not what our friends say. We have so many more who'd be interested. They'd love to meet you."

"Actually, I'm about to sell the business and start over. Trade under a different name."

"Oh, that's such a shame. *Lucifer* is perfect. What will your new name be?"

"Can't share that," he says. "Secrecy is the point. I don't advertise. People come to me."

"How tantalizing. Do say you'll come the weekend after this."

"I'll be back in Boston, I'm afraid."

"Oh, that's hardly a problem," Celise says. "Billy could send his private jet. We have the most extraordinary weekend house parties. Not just horse people but baseball superstars, painters, musicians, even writers. One weekend we had Placido Domingo and Robert Rauschenberg at the same dinner party and all they could talk about was John Cage. The rest of us might as well not have even been there. Of course, Rasuchenberg was at college with John Cage. "

John Cage? The name sounds familiar, although symphony concerts are not Marlowe's thing. Isn't Cage that modern composer who writes music no one can listen to?

"Do you know we've had Norman Mailer and Joseph Heller as guests at the same party? As a matter of fact—" and here she leans close, confidentially—"at one of our dinners, Mailer got so drunk that he climbed across the table and fell into my lap."

"Must have been a bit of a shock," Marlowe says, though at that very instant the word *hungry* drops into his mind. Celise is hungry, he thinks, not just hungry but *voracious*, and the thought arrives with a weird visual image, the letters of *voracious* scrunched into alphabetic pulp in the talons of a great bird of prey. The bird has the face of Wallis Simpson, which should have been adequate warning. Where did that come from? he wonders. All because of Celise's predator eyes? He is puzzled by the associations his own retrieval system makes.

But the truth is, the down-swooping eagle also carries arrows and sparklers in its claws and danger has always been a turn-on. Contacts, he is thinking. Investors. It is not as though he is short of links to people with more money than sense but the nature of his business requires constant infusions of new blood, innocent blood, and he has already felt the need to sell his current corporate name while the going is good. He needs to restart: a new name, a new set of contacts. Possibilities swarm: British royalty, Ascot toffs, the Hamptons, the upper east side, massive inflows of cash to keep the delicate house of cards standing, the sky the limit.

"You really must come," Celise says. "We'll invite Mailer and Heller and anyone else you'd like to meet."

"Well," he says. "I'll think about it."

From this moment, he now realizes in retrospect, he is a marked man. He remembers reading somewhere that when multiple piranhas are placed in an aquarium, they hunt as a school and strip the flesh from all other forms of aquatic life, but when only two are in the same tank, they tear each other to shreds. No one wins.

How does one piranha perceive another one? he wonders.

Is there a quiver of recognition when fin slithers against fin in a school? Probably not.

Obviously not.

Something he does now know: it is profoundly disorienting—a shocking heart-stopping moment—for a master of the game to understand that he has been conned.

Marlowe refills his coffee mug and reads again the note propped against his cappuccino machine. It is not handwritten. Celise's printer is set always to print in turquoise ink and an imitation calligraphic font.

He has never before thought much about the premature death of Billy Vanderbilt in a hunting accident, convenient though that had been. He and Celise had been involved for two years by then. He has never even been curious about Celise's first husband but now he is. He has never even inquired as to whether she was widowed or divorced the first time round. He has never been sufficiently interested, but now he is. He has all the right contacts, all the best access to coroners' reports.

The coroner's verdict in both cases is "Premature death due to accidental causes." He is given a name for that first husband: Tom Boykin, of Asheville, North Carolina, a groundsman on the Biltmore Estate, killed in a tractor accident.

As to Billy Vanderbilt, her second husband: the bit in the horse's mouth had corroded, become suddenly acidic, driving the horse mad with pain. Billy had been dragged across three hurdles. A groom in the Vanderbilt stables was charged with negligent use of the wrong kind of brass polish and was sentenced to three years of house arrest.

Marlowe's phone calls to sundry legal offices are returned. There are two answers to his question *Who is the executor of the estate of the Vanderbilt widow?*

The first answer is another question: *Which Vanderbilt widow?*

The second answer is unequivocal. *Celise Vanderbilt is executor of the estate of the French countess.* As to how such a thing could have possibly come about: there, all answers are tentative and obscure. Marlowe is confident—well, reasonably confident— that he will have the last laugh but there are matters that require his urgent attention before the collapse of his own house of cards.

As to the imperatives of memory: he never made it to the

demonstration in Central Park. He cannot quite remember the stages by which he and Celise Vanderbilt shared the night in a suite at the Grand Hyatt, but he can remember with horrible clarity that moment at 6.20 p.m. when he heard Lilith's voice. *I'm not going to wait any longer,* she said. *I have a dinner engagement with my friends.* It was, of course, a vocal hallucination from some layer deep in his subconscious mind, but he *heard* it, he actually heard it like a voice in the room.

"What's wrong?" Celise asked with alarm, because he had bolted upright in bed and doubled over with something that felt like heartburn.

"Nothing," he assured her, gasping, staggering out of bed and pulling on clothes. "I've got a crucial business meeting that I inexplicably forgot. That's the kind of power you have. I'll be late. I'll grab a taxi. Wait here until I get back."

"I'm not going anywhere," Celise promised him, pulling the sheet up to her shoulders.

And he ran. He actually ran. He ran to the elevator, zoomed down to the street-level floor, and then he ran across the lobby. He ran along East 42nd and into the Oyster Bar. His shirt was only partially buttoned up and not fully tucked into his pants. Lilith was still there. She was just sliding down from her bar stool and was smiling at the bartender and a tip was passing from her hand to his.

"Sorry I'm late," he gasped. "The demo got a little wild. We were detained by the police."

"Really?" she said, and the word was covered with burrs. She pointed to the television set over the bar. "I've been watching. I guess they didn't show the violent part."

"Can we have a table?" he asked the waiter.

But Lilith said, "I'm sorry. I've called a taxi. My friends made a restaurant reservation for seven and I'm meeting them there.

Enjoy your weekend, Lucifer, and thanks for the ride. I'll take the Greyhound back to Boston in the morning."

"I don't think you realize," he flung after her, "how much I know. I know your real name is Capucine and you're really French."

"*Félicitations*," she said, waving backwards over her shoulder. "Good luck with that."

BOOK II
CAPUCINE

1.

There is a bench in Central Park on a rocky spine that juts into the lake from the densely wooded labyrinth of the Ramble. From this bench, close to the water, Capucine is watching a covey of ducks glide in and out of the dappled light. Some are preening and drying their wings on rock islets that stick out of the shallows like mooring posts. If she shades her eyes, she can see across the blinding shimmer of water to Bethesda Terrace where the young are already gathering on the fountain rim and strumming guitars, or emerging like meteors from out of the shadowy arches of the arcade to perform arabesques on their rollerblades. Tourists are storing all this exotic movement in video cameras.

It is early morning.

The sun is punching its blazing fist between the skyscrapers on Fifth Avenue. Cap cannot see the Loeb Boathouse on the eastern shore of the lake because more spiny and wooded outcrops of the Ramble block it from view. Nevertheless a few boats are already out, the rowers sometimes waving, more often as busy with cameras as with the oars. The important thing for the boaters is to photograph the Dakota, where John Lennon lived and in front of which he was shot down, and where Yoko Ono still lives. The Dakota rises massively on Central Park West, brown and bulky above the colossal crowns of the trees, and can only be adequately captured from a boat on the lake. Hundreds of thousands of such

110

images are mailed around the world and sometimes are sent instantly via the newfangled World Wide Web to friends, relatives, newspapers, police departments, intelligence agencies. Sometimes the boaters focus their cameras on Cap, so peaceful on her park bench with the woods in their brilliant autumnal hues behind her, the ducks and the rocks in the foreground, the water as frame. She wonders, uneasily, how many people around the world might eventually see her image in a snapshot enclosed in a family letter. One of the boats appears to have a news crew on board—she can see the CNN logo on the equipment—and the cameraman makes panoramic sweeps of skyline and shore. Is this for a travel documentary on the city? Is it for the national or international news?

Will there be friends in Harvard Square who might pause, startled, and ask themselves: *Was that Lilith Jardine?*

How many viewers across the planet might see this?

In Australia? In France? In the village of St Gilles?

Will there be puzzled people who ask themselves and each other *Hey, isn't that...?*

Capucine has lived in all these places and possibly hundreds of people would recognize her, though she doubts that she will be beamed back to St Gilles, and if she is she knows few people in the village will be watching world news on TV. But if her image should reach the Middle East? Or the Balkans? Or Hong Kong? Or certain African nations?

That could be a different kettle of fish. She is acquainted with only a handful of people in such places, and only a handful know her, but her image is in multiple files. She has two sets of contacts which are as different as day is from night, and each set keeps files on the other. When she travels, she is hosted by the wealthy and powerful as an appraiser of works of art that have been newly (though often secretly and often illicitly) put on the market or just acquired. Unofficially and covertly she meets with families in hiding, families whose relatives have been arrested or are missing or dead. She gathers evidence. She passes this information on.

Possibly, at this very instant, the keepers of sundry files are recognizing her, tracking her, logging information about her, passing it on. She feels anxiety, but that anxiety goes with the turf. It is part of her life, at every airport, every border crossing, every port of entry or exit. She never knows when she might be detained. Given the occupations and history of both of her parents, she probably has a genetic disposition toward this particular kind of risk. Still. She knows the plot. These narratives rarely end well. Anxiety is constant. You get used to living with this but you never completely relax. The cool and courteous mask of the unflappable persona behind which you hide is always in place, but your fight-or-flight reflex never ceases to be on red alert.

Does the unsigned typed note slipped under her hotel door that morning just before she checked out have any bearing on her anxiety?

Negotiations necessary. You are being watched and monitored, the note says. *Be at the Loeb Boathouse in Central Park, in the outdoor bar, at 1 p.m.*

The note was in a sealed envelope bearing the Grand Hyatt logo.

It is the kind of note that Lucifer might send, except that Lucifer has never bothered to be melodramatic or indirect. If it were not for the fact that someone has brought her to New York and paid for her to stay in the Grand Hyatt during the final week of the trial, Cap would not even entertain the idea that the note could have any bearing on the Vanderbilt affair. Perhaps the timing is purely coincidental. But then again, who else besides Lucifer might have or could have set up the meeting in the Oyster Bar?

Actually, there are a number of people in New York who no doubt tap multiple sources of information on her whereabouts and her contacts. In particular, there are two collectors who do seem more likely sources of surveillance than Lucifer and more likely writers of the note pushed under the door. The encounters with these art collectors had been subtly menacing. One involved an African dictator's mistress infamous for her lavish lifestyle. That meeting had taken place in London a little over a year ago when Cap's advice had been sought for the furnishing of a sumptuous palace under construction in Zimbabwe. An article had appeared in the Guardian the day after Cap's meeting with the dictator's mistress suggesting that both the art-buying spree and the palace were financed by blood diamonds. There was another article in the *Independent* on the corrupt misuse of government funds for luxury living in a nation where starvation was rampant.

Cap was actually reading the articles in her hotel room in London when reception called to say a distinguished African diplomat wished to meet her in the lobby lounge. Who is it? she asked. He does not wish to identify himself, the reception clerk replied, but he says you will recognize him.

When Cap emerged from the elevator doors in the lobby, the distinguished diplomat raised his eyebrows and his Scotch and beckoned for Cap to join him. He had described himself, a day earlier, as Personal Assistant to the Art Collector, who was not only the dictator's mistress but the mother of the dictator's son. The diplomat cum Personal Assistant to the mother of the dictator-in-waiting had the look of a bodyguard.

"I suppose you'd like white wine," he said.

"Scotch is fine."

The diplomat raised his eyebrows again, smirked, and snapped his fingers for a steward. "The little lady would like a Scotch with soda and ice."

"Straight up," Cap said. "No ice."

"Well, well," the bodyguard said. He raised his glass. "To a cordial establishment of ground rules."

"The ground rules for art appraisal are rigorous," Cap said, clinking her glass against his. "We are subject to international standards."

"I believe that client confidentiality is one of the bedrock rules," the bodyguard said.

"It is indeed."

"Then why did you speak to the press?"

"I did not speak to the press," Cap said. "I never speak to the press about my clients or my appraisal advice."

"I see. Obviously someone did. We will find out who that was. Whoever that loose-lip was will suffer consequences. Am I understood?"

"This is not an issue that concerns me."

"Let us hope that is true." The Personal Assistant sipped his Scotch and rolled the viscous fire in his mouth. He smiled. Cap had a list of smiles that sometimes showed up in nightmares and this smile would be added to the list. "If the source of the leak turns out to concern you," the bodyguard said, "not only will your invitation to supervise the palace placement of paintings and antiques be revoked, but you will look back to these cocktails as the last safe moment in your life." The bodyguard chuckled. "Or possibly after all we will send your visa and air tickets for the palace's interior decoration, but you will mysteriously disappear. Am I understood?"

Cap raised her glass. "You are always free to make do with second-rate appraisal and art-placement advice. It's nothing to me."

The bodyguard's smile grew broader. "I think I will enjoy taking you on." He laughed again and raised his glass. "I think we will make your flight reservations."

So far, to Cap's disappointment (and also to her relief), nothing has come of the invitation, a devastating blow to those survivors-in-hiding who are awaiting and praying for her visit. They have photographs and eye-witness accounts to loft into the outside world like paper planes.

Cap shies away from sending back word that the world already knows and does not care.

Nevertheless, she does want to retrieve those photographs and those recorded accounts. She wants to preserve them. Decades from now, they will matter. Decades from now, they may give comfort and crucial historical data to the descendants of those who have been tortured, if any descendants survive.

Last week, just before the Vanderbilt jury verdict, she read in the *New York Times* that a Zimbabwean art collector—her own Zimbabwean art collector—was currently in Manhattan on a shopping spree involving designer clothing and shoes. The *New York Post* carried a front-page photograph of the dictator's mistress in Prada, with Manolo Blahnik shoes. EXOTIC BEAUTY, the headline read. Also visible at the edge of the photograph was a body guard. Cap recognized him. He had bought her Scotch in a London hotel.

The other meeting (the other suspect for the surveillance and for the note slipped under her hotel door) had taken place in Shanghai with a Chinese official who was shipping his art collection to the U.S. Cap's appraisal estimate had been required by insurance companies. The Chinese official had been cited for corruption in Beijing and word was that he was not only under imminent threat of expulsion from the party but also of imminent confiscation of his passport. He too is currently in New York.

It is certain that the dictator's mistress and the Chinese official would have their own agents and lobbyists in Washington and New York, lobbyists whose task it would be to keep an eye on Cap and on anyone else in possession of evidence damaging to their image. One or other of these two clients, she is sure —or one of their emissaries—is planning to meet her for lunch.

Cap thinks of leaving the bench, of retreating into the impenetrable woodland cover of the Ramble, of moving out of the lines of sight of the boaters and their cameras, but then again, what difference would it make? The die has been cast. She wants to sit and watch the ducks and watch the light on the water.

She thinks it would be a desirable afterimage on the retina's final *Lights Out.*

She discovered the Ramble when she was an undergraduate at NYU, newly arrived from rural France and homesick for the Forest of Chinon and for the quicksilver movement of deer and for ponds with snapping turtles and for the vineyards in the valley of the Vienne.

Dislocated, Cap used to walk for hours every day in Central Park. The Ramble was paradise, a miraculous illusion, a place from within whose wooded trails she could neither see nor hear the roar of the metropolis. For an hour at a time she could pretend she was back in the woods surrounding St Gilles.

She is mesmerized by the random circling of ducks and boats, a geometry of chaos, as bewildering as the map of her life. Is it possible that she has traveled from a gardener's cottage in rural France to this point of repose in Central Park while a sensational trial has just concluded in Manhattan and while two fabulously wealthy and fabulously corrupt clients are staying in nearby hotels?

This does not seem credible. Most of Cap's life does not seem credible to her.

Occasionally other devotees of the Ramble, other meditative loiterers, leave one of the woodland trails and encroach on the little promontory where Cap sits. But there is an instinctive mutual respect among those who love the Ramble. They pause, they exchange brief polite greetings, or perhaps they merely nod and smile and say nothing, and then they withdraw.

Cap notes the first red and gold leaves of the fall eddying on the surface of the lake. Do they make patterns? Perhaps. She could impose form: a ragged spiral; a cluster disrupted by ducks; a single leaf caught between reeds. She could impose symbolic meaning. She believes this may be life's primary requirement: to impose a tolerable meaning on randomness. A gold leaf is washed up at her feet. That is the way her own life drifts through her memory, one bright fragment at a time, the sequence unpredictable and not under any conscious control because recollection never keeps chronological rules.

Here is a maple leaf, bright crimson, caught in a funnel between two rocks, turning but going nowhere, lovely as the red quilt in the loft of the gardener's cottage in the grounds of the Chateau de Boissy on the banks of the Vienne, a half-mile outside the village of St Gilles, which is thirty minutes by car from the railway station in Tours, which is just one hour south-west of Paris by TGV, *Train à Grande Vitesse,* the high-speed rail cars that travel at 200 mph though they certainly did not exist when Cap was a child. Nevertheless, she can hear the mice in the eaves of the gardener's cottage, feel the shifting lumpiness of the straw mattress, smell the remnants of the cassoulet, see the smoke that seems to settle and reside permanently in the attic from the cast-iron stove below, hear the heavy breathing and soft snores of her father from his couch in front of the stove. She can smell her brother on the pallet at the other side of the loft. He smells of the vegetable garden, of compost, of the vineyard, of fish fresh-caught in the Vienne.

Above all three of them—above her father, her brother, her small self; above the gardener's cottage; above the village of St Gilles—looms the great hulking shadow of the empty chateau. It is almost as large as the twelfth-century church of St Gilles. The two buildings, pocked and turreted rock monoliths, hover like guardian angels over the handful of people who live between.

Capucine's father is the manager of the estate of the chateau—also its gardener and its *viticulteur*—but he concerns himself only with the earth on which the chateau stands, all twenty hectares or fifty acres of it, and with the tilling and the blossoming and the caretaking of those hectares. He alone has the keys to the wrought-iron gates of the walled courtyard and to the great oak doors of the chateau itself, but he never goes inside the mansion. Once a month, he lets Marie-Claire into the chateau to dust and sweep the cobwebs away and check that the aged pipes have not burst. Three dogs, guardians, prowl the courtyard to guard against intrusion. Cap's father cares for these dogs and the dogs adore him. He feeds them daily. In the evenings, he lets them loose for a couple of hours in the Forest of Chinon. When he whistles, they come obediently—each usually has a rabbit or a rodent in its mouth and drops its trophy at her father's feet—after which her father locks them back in the courtyard.

Cap also adores the dogs. They are as lean as wolves and full of wolf-like energy, and Cap is jealous of the rabbits so delicately held between their teeth. She rolls with the dogs in the woods and on the sandy grit of the chateau courtyard.

She has never been inside the chateau. "Can we, Papa?" she sometimes asks.

"There's nothing to see," her father says.

"Can I see the nothing?" It is such a huge nothing. It fills her with awe.

"I used to go there every day," her father says, "when *la comtesse* was young, when her mother was still alive, when we were both children. But I haven't set foot in the building since the Nazis were quartered there. I'd rather step through the gates of Hell. If you want to see inside, you'll have to get Marie-Claire to take you."

Marie-Claire lives in the village and has her own family but she also cooks for the gardener and keeps the empty chateau under wraps. When Cap begs to accompany her, *just to see inside,* Marie-Claire is brusque. "It's a castle of ghosts," she says. "It's damned. It's the devil's outhouse. It's full of lost souls. Every piece of furniture is covered in white canvas. You want to see inside a grave? You want to go down where the shrouds and the cobwebs are?"

Caps shudders. "No," she says. "Yes," she says. "Maybe."

"I won't take you. Believe me, you don't want to see inside the chateau. Bad things happened there."

"What bad things?"

"Never mind. It's no place for a child. I don't like going there myself and I'll never go there after dark. I can hear the walls scream."

"So why do you go?"

"Because I'm paid to do so," Marie-Claire says. "Just like your father is paid to look after the vines and the grounds."

"Papa?" Cap asks at the dinner table in the gardener's cottage, "Who pays you to look after the chateau?"

"*La comtesse* pays me. Who told you I'm paid?"

"Marie-Claire did. Where is *la comtesse*?"

"In New York. She went there after the war. No one lives in the chateau now."

"Why not?" Cap wants to know.

"Because the war wore itself out. Because *la comtesse* married an American and went to live over there."

"Will she come back?"

"Who knows?" her father says.

"She'll never come back," Petit Christophe says, brushing a cloud of imaginary mosquitoes from his face, "because she knows

119

she'd be eaten alive by Cap's questions." Cap mock-punches her brother, who is eight years her senior, and he responds by picking her up, grappling with her, tickling her, wrestling her, both of them thrashing about playfully on the floor.

"Marie-Claire says bad things happened in the chateau," Cap gasps between shoulder-locks. "What happened?"

"The war happened," her father says. "And we are not going to talk about the war."

This is the way it goes. Depending on the season and on the budget provided by *la comtesse*—Cap visualizes this absent mythical person as the Virgin Mary, queen of heaven, powerful but invisible, enthroned in stained glass above the altar in the village church—the gardener hires laborers from the village for the vines and the orchard and the *potager*. He hires Marie-Claire as housekeeper for the empty chateau and also, part-time, for his own cottage. She cooks and cleans and does laundry.

From the time she can crawl, Cap has a sense of herself as part of the earth. On hands and knees, she makes her way between the tomato towers and bean trellises. Her wrists smell of lavender, her ankles of sage. She fancies she began as a seedling, like lettuce, like radishes, and that she reached for the sun and grew taller, smelling of compost and rosemary and thyme. She is tolerated by her father, her brother, and the laborers, much as an earthworm is tolerated: a slight thing to be placed gently to one side of spade or hoe. As soon as she can walk, she joins her brother and the laborers to pick beans and tomatoes or to hunt for mushrooms in the woods, or she helps her father on the stony terraces where the vines spread their wide woody arms along wires.

"Everyone thinks making wine is about the grapes," Christophe le Jardinier explains solemnly to his five-year-old daughter. "It is only partly about the grapes. Much more important is the drainage. Vines do best on the slopes, but only if the channels are kept clear."

Her father works with a shovel, Capucine follows with her trowel. They expose the channels, row upon row of clay tiles. They pull out, with bare hands, clotted hairballs of roots and of silt. The soil is poor and stony and sandy.

"The soil doesn't matter," Capucine's father tells her. "Rich soil is not the issue. The vines must be made to suffer to make the best wine. The deep-rooted vines, the ones that have to reach down and down and down to touch the wet, they survive when no rain comes and when the sun burns."

When rain does not come, which is often, Capucine and her father lug buckets of well-water up the slopes and anoint the root of each plant. Capucine learns the art of digging and footing the posts, of threading the wires so that the vines grow like a green fence, arms crucified, stretched and strained sideways like Christ on the cross. Guiding the new tendrils along the wires, fixing the thickening vines to the posts, Capucine begins to feel unable to drive a nail through the woody wrist of a runner.

"I can't do it, Papa."

"The vines that suffer," her father says, "make the best wine."

"Just the same, Papa, I can't do it."

"I'll do it then," he says. "You do the planting and the watering."

Capucine learns to plant. She learns that it takes three years before a vine can yield grapes, four years before the fruit is legal for making wine. She learns that a vine can live for a century, but that its best years come after it turns fifteen and before it turns forty years old.

"Same for women," her father tells her. "Best child-bearing years. Your *maman* was only twenty when you were born."

Capucine holds her breath. She counts to twenty, thirty, sixty. "Yes?" she prompts.

"When you are eighteen or twenty, you'll find a husband and we'll have a wedding and the whole village will come."

"I want a husband like you, Papa."

"I'm not a good example, Capucine. I never had me a legal wife." He turns away and looks down the terraces toward his cottage.

"Papa?"

"I'm a lucky man, Capucine," Christophe le Jardinier says. "I'm a lucky man."

"My *maman*?" Capucine prompts.

"I have loved two women, beautiful women, brave as she lions. And they gave me Petit Christophe and you."

"Papa?" Cap lays down her shovel and nuzzles up against her father.

"Ours are old vines," her father says. "Thirty years old. Which is why our wines are so fine, and why the *Appellation Controlée du Chateau de Boissy de St Gilles* was so appealing to that fat cat from America. People say he was bewitched by *la comtesse*. I say he was bewitched by our wine."

2.

The ducks converge, like a summoned flotilla, toward Capucine's bench in the Ramble, but what she sees are the old men reeling in their lines at the village pond in St Gilles and the little funnels made in the water by the silvery fish fighting for their lives. No fish survives the hook. Not one lives long enough to pass on the warning—*Beware the dangling worm!*—to the next generation. All that the infant fishlings see is the parent ascending into heaven like lightning.

Capucine takes the white envelope from the pocket of her jacket and looks at it again. It was slipped under her door along with the bill for the room which was marked: PAID. COMPLIMENTS OF THE GRAND HYATT. The white envelope is addressed to Lilith Jardine and inside is a note typed in a hand-script font. She reads it again.

Negotiations necessary. You are being watched and monitored. Be at the Loeb Boathouse in Central Park, in the outdoor bar, at 1 p.m.

The note is unsigned.

Capucine now feels certain that the airfares, the hotel reservation, and the note did not come from Lucifer, though she knows well enough that watching and monitoring the lives of others is his business. She has never been afraid of him. She *has* been afraid of certain professional watchers, border guards, foreign military personnel, to whom Lucifer may or may not have passed on information, but she also believes she is under the protective umbrella of the powerful rulers and bureaucrats who buy and sell art. They need her appraisals. They value her knowledge of the artifacts of the seventeenth and eighteenth centuries and of the global art market in paintings and antiques. She is the seal of approval on their million-dollar tastes and cultural standing. What she offers is proof of the perks of power. Thus an unspoken deal is being made, admittedly without the knowledge of the art collectors.

Cap often feels anxious, but if things go wrong (and she knows they frequently do and always could) she is placing herself on the line for something that matters. She is lighting candles for her mother, for Petit Christophe's mother, for her father, for Marie-Claire's husband. Some risks are worth the cost though the costs can be terrifyingly high.

You are being watched and monitored.

So what's new?

A night spent in a cell on the Slovak side of the Czech border suddenly comes back to her with acute sensory detail: the cement floor, the stink from the latrine in the corner, the vomit in the sink, the hunched form of the only other person in the cell, the leering guard on the other side of the bars, patting his crotch and licking her confiscated passport.

"I'd advise you not to try," Cap says in English, looking him in the eye. The guard laughs, staring back at her, making slurping sounds with his tongue. Cap meets his eyes intensely until he drops his gaze and turns away. He makes a parting gesture, an obscene one, over his shoulder. "Try anything rough," Cap says in a strong steady voice, "and there'll be reprisals you are going to regret."

"Lucky for you he doesn't understand a word." The cellmate is young, perhaps eighteen. Her English is thickly Slavic. "What are you?" she demands derisively. "One of the Holy Innocents or a stupid American?"

"I'm French."

"Don't believe you." The guard has moved on and can be heard guffawing with fellow armed border officers from an adjacent room. The cellmate gestures with her thumb toward the sound. "Get it? Either you're retarded or you're not from Europe. No way you are French."

"I was born and grew up in France, but I've lived in the States a long time."

"That explains it." Cap's cellmate thumps the cement wall with her fist. "You people. You're so naive, you're like rat poison for the rest of us."

Cap is shocked and distressed. "But we can't let that thug think he's omnipotent."

"Right now, he is. There's only one way out of here and that's bribery, cash or sex, same difference to them."

"There's not only one way out," Cap insists. "There's never only one way out."

"Well, I forgot to mention death," her cell-mate says. "Sorry."

"You can't be serious," Cap says. "They wouldn't dare. They want to join NATO and the bad PR would destroy their chances."

"And I bet you believe in elves."

"I believe in resistance."

"Piss off that guard, and you've got both of us a one-way ticket to gang-rape and a beating that I promise will have you begging to trade your resistance for your life. It will make both us want to die. I've been there. Just my fucking bad luck to be put in a cell with you."

"I have embassy contacts. They'll notice if I'm missing or de-layed. There'll be diplomatic intervention."

The girl smacked her forehead with the palms of her hands. "Mother of God! Do you have any idea how easy it is for them to put you out of diplomatic reach? They can do it in five minutes. They'll find heroin in your backpack, and then what embassy will touch you?"

"Where are you from?"

"Russia."

"Why are you here?"

"No visa. Third try to get to France where my sister is. Got caught and sent back."

"What happened?"

"Detention center. Broke out last week. I won't forgive you if you fuck up my third try. For God's sake, make nice."

"I won't be intimidated," Cap says.

"Oh yeah? Want to bet on that? " The girl pulls up her top. The skin above her ribs is purple and black. She lets her jeans fall to her knees. Her inner thighs are the color of carbon. "You'll find offering sex is simpler," she says. "And less painful."

"What's your name?"

"Natasha."

Cap and Natasha, between them, pay a fine and sign a document in which they admit to being wrongfully in Slovakia. Cap pays in American dollars. She does not ask how Natasha pays. Their passports are stamped *Persona non grata,* or at least that is the gist of the translation which Natasha provides. No subsequent entry into Slovakia permitted. Ever. "Is that a promise?" Cap asks in English.

"Mother of God!" Natasha says. "Can't you keep your mouth shut? Lucky for us they don't understand."

The women are escorted to the railway station and put on a train to Prague. Cap pays for both tickets. At the train station in Prague, they part company. "Can I buy your ticket to Paris?" Cap asks. "In return for the survival advice?"

"No thanks. I have my own ways and means."

"Good luck," Cap says.

"Fuck luck. What counts is what's decided in here." Natasha taps her forehead. "Nothing will stop me."

The blur of Czech woods as seen from the window of the train smudges into the Ramble. Cap shuts her eyes tight and opens them again. The signals have changed, someone has flipped a switch, the train brakes, a child's voice shrieks piercingly, "He ate it, Mama. The duck ate my bagel!"

Cap, shocked, presses a hand to her heart and lurches forward.

"I'm so sorry," a woman says. "Didn't mean to frighten you. He's only three."

"Uh... no problem. I was miles away."

"That's a Mallard, Richie," the woman says. "See the green on its back?" To Cap she says, "I wonder if you'd mind?" She proffers a camera. "Of me and Richie and the ducks."

"With pleasure," Cap says. She focuses. She clicks the shutter. "There," she says. "You and Richie and the ducks. You all look wonderful."

"Thank you so much," the woman says. "You live here?"

"No. I used to. Now I'm just visiting."

"So are we," the woman says. "We're from Texas. We're staying at the Grand Hyatt."

"I was staying there too," Cap says. "I've just checked out."

She has checked out of the Grand Hyatt. She has left her one small suitcase with the concierge but has put everything essential—passport, air tickets, change of underwear—into her very large shoulder bag. Should this become necessary, she can abandon the suitcase. She has not quite made up her mind as to whether or not she will show up at the Loeb Boathouse bar. She is not sure why, but she feels like a fish watching the slick slithering temptation

127

of a worm. Somewhere there must be a hidden hook. Why was the date of her return ticket left open? Who is expecting to detain her—and for how long—after her checkout date? What kind of detour might she be taken on before she gets a flight back to Australia?

Will the mistress of an African dictator arrange her visit to Zimbabwe? Under certain conditions, of course. Is a Chinese defector—corrupt, it goes without saying—seeking to buy silence or to get the highest price for his paintings? Curiosity may have killed the cat but it has led Capucine through at least nine interesting lives.

The hunted is curious about the hunter.

Capucine has genetic ties to the hunted: to her mother, her father, the mother of Petit Christophe, to Marie-Claire, to Marie-Claire's husband.

The walls of the gardener's cottage at the Chateau de Boissy in St Gilles are of stone so thick that the width of the door frame is as long as a man's arm from shoulder to wrist. Even in mid-summer the place feels chilled. In all seasons, the kitchen is the best place to be. Marie-Claire arrives at sunrise. She has been doing this every morning since the miraculous arrival of Capucine. Back then, Marie-Claire made coffee, cooked breakfast for Christophe le Père and Petit Christophe, fed the baby. With one hand she waved father and son out the door.

She sang as she tended the baby and the house. Her song was without words but expressive, a narrative chant, full of mourning. The lamentations of Marie-Claire were set always in the minor key of the Renaissance mass and that music is imprinted in Cap's brain. She thinks of Marie-Claire whenever she hears Palestrina or Tallis or Couperin.

Marie-Claire sang of sorrow, of loss, of fear, of her husband living like a wild animal in the woods, of her insistent belief that somehow there was meaning behind the chaos. Her husband visited by night when he could. The Resistance was their beacon in the dark, their only hope, it was an article of faith. Her husband left before the first light of dawn. There were fifty acres of woods on the chateau grounds and within them was an underground room, a sealed-off wing of the wine cellars, forgotten, that served as safe house. It was a stone's throw from the German officers bivouacked in the chateau.

"I'll stay in the safe house till dark," her husband told her the last time he kissed her goodbye. "Someone's going to meet me with a cart at the edge of the woods. We'll take back roads to Orléans. We're going to blow up the railway line to Paris."

But the next evening it was Christophe le Jardinier who knocked on her door. "I have bad news, Marie-Claire. They have taken him. Someone informed."

"Who informed?"

"We don't know."

"Same person who informed on you last year." This was not a question. "So they know about the safe house."

"They know we have one. They don't know where it is."

"Christophe, when will this end?"

"Soon," the chateau gardener promised. "They won't kill your husband because they need information. They know the tide's turning. They know the end's near."

"We've been saying that for four years."

"This is different. The Americans have landed in Normandy."

"How do you know?"

"Short-wave radio."

"Normandy's a long way from Paris."

"But they'll get there. And we have to hang on until then. It won't be long."

"Yes it will. Until then nowhere is safe. He'll be tortured." Christophe le Père held Marie-Claire. There was no other comfort he could offer. "And you were tortured for nothing," she said.

"It wasn't for nothing. They didn't find the safe house. Your husband was taken on the road to Orléans, not in our woods. But they're watching. We'll have to stop using the old cellar."

"Do you think *la comtesse*...?"

"No. Not that she wouldn't perhaps, if it came to arrest, but she hasn't the faintest idea."

"Are you sure?"

"I'm sure. She's never even set foot in the cellars. When I offered to show her the pre-war vintages, she wouldn't go. It's like stepping into a grave, she said. So she doesn't even know that one tunnel got blocked off from her side."

"I wouldn't count on that," Marie-Claire said. "I've done her laundry, remember, and the laundry of the SS in the chateau. She's not as naive as she seems. She gets along very well with the Boche."

"It's an act."

"I think the naïveté is an act."

"Maybe. But she's good at being naive. Her naïveté saved my life."

"How?"

"She intervened. She went to the commandant and convinced the Boche to let me go."

"You didn't tell me that when I was putting you back together and patching you up."

"No. Well. The less we all say, the safer, right? Better you knew nothing about that."

"Why did she go to the commandant?"

"I don't know. Courage? French patriotism?"

"How did she even know you were taken?"

"Servants whispering. Village rumor. Or maybe the vines. Maybe she was worried about neglect. She speaks German. She told them one of her mother's lovers was German."

"I should have guessed. Is that supposed to make me trust her? She speaks German."

"She did what worked."

"She sucked up to them. She gave them a whole wing of the chateau."

"She didn't have much choice. Look, she's a religious neurotic, she's crazy, she's a very sad and lonely woman, but she's no informer."

"Not sure I agree. But if it's not *la comtesse,* then who?"

"Who knows? The butcher? The baker? The candlestick maker?"

"The butcher."

"We have no proof. Say nothing to anyone, Marie-Claire. Not even to the priest."

"You think *the priest...*?" Marie-Claire crossed herself.

"Not yes and not no. I don't know. That blocked-off cave dates from the Revolution. A tunnel ran all the way from the church to the chateau. It saved priests from the guillotine. Doesn't mean that every priest since then has known, but it means they *might* know. Don't trust anyone. Don't take chances."

Marie-Claire did not know if her husband was dead or alive, but in the weeks that followed she took the baby in her belly as both comfort and sign. The Americans were in Normandy. They were coming.

The Americans arrived in Paris.

The Liberation arrived with a pealing of all the bells in the village church.

The baby of Marie-Claire tried to arrive but never had time to draw breath.

All night Marie-Claire was in labor with the midwife promising, promising, promising.

But then the midwife sent for the priest.

The moment of seeing the priest, Marie-Claire told Capucine, she sang the memory to the infant Capucine—this musical movement was slow and profoundly sorrowful, *adagio lacrimoso*—that moment lasts forever and ever, world without end. The priest is standing forever at her bedside waiting to baptize the bluish-purple baby who will never cry out. The midwife slapped the coiled monkey-shape gently on the shoulders, then sharply, then pummeled the tiny lungs, but no sound came.

"A boy," the midwife told Marie-Claire.

Time stood still. Marie-Claire grew one hundred years old in one minute.

Time passed. Time must have passed.

The priest came to her door early one morning, weeks later. "God takes, God gives," he said. "A life is lost, a life can be saved. There is something that must be done." The priest led her through the woods to the gardener's cottage. It was still dark. There were branches piled against the secret back entrance to the chateau cellar where her husband had hidden in the pre-dawn hours before he was caught. The priest did not even glance in that direction.

Who informed?

Who informed on Christophe le Jardinier?

There was a star above the hidden entrance to the cellars.

"You see?" the priest said to Marie-Claire. "A sign from God. Who of us can understand his ways?"

"Do you think God will forgive collaborators?" Marie-Claire asked.

"His mercy is infinite," the priest said.

Christophe le Jardinier was standing at the door of his stone cottage with a baby, a girl child, in his arms. "This is the duty God has assigned to you," the priest explained. "I will leave you to your task, Marie-Claire. And you, Monsieur le Jardinier, to your penance."

"Christophe?"

"I am her father," the gardener said, after the priest had left. "Her mother was Lilith."

"They caught Lilith too?"

"No. The nuns at the convent in Tours have been hiding her. She died in childbirth. The baby is three weeks old."

"Christophe," Marie-Claire said gently, taking the child. "This baby is at least six months old, maybe more."

"No," the gardener protested. "No! That's not possible. Lilith died in the convent. Three weeks ago."

"The war is over, Christophe. If she died three weeks ago, why wouldn't the nuns summon you?"

"Because there are soldiers everywhere. Americans, British, Canadians, Australians. The convent is dealing with chaos."

"Why wouldn't they inform you of her death? Think about it, Christophe. Why wouldn't they summon you to the funeral?"

The gardener leaned back against the door frame of his cottage, his face contorted. He closed his eyes. He took the baby back from Marie-Claire and held her against his chest, the tiny heart beating with his. "The nuns were overwhelmed," he said. "They told me Lilith was at peace when she died. Her last words were *Tell her father that all is well.*"

"May it be so," Marie-Claire said, crossing herself. "Pray God, may it be so. You have her child. *Your* child. The nuns must have hidden the baby after Lilith was taken. That would have put them at great risk."

"Lilith died in childbirth," the gardener insisted. "My daughter is three weeks old."

When Cap was four (or five?) years old, the husband of Ma-

133

rie-Claire was dropped off in the village square from a military jeep driven by American soldiers. Dental records, the Americans explained. We think this is where he belongs, but he doesn't remember too much. The Gestapo had him and then he was in an Allied hospital. He doesn't remember his name.

When Marie-Claire saw her husband, she first screamed and then she fainted.

When Cap was about five (or six?), two events dominated village talk.

La comtesse is returning with a young American son, the village said. The news was everywhere, bouncing off garden walls. It filled the church like the sonorous din of the organ.

Marie-Claire is enceinte again, the antiphon chanted. *Her husband, who still does not remember his name, her husband who nevertheless smiles when his wife comes into the room, her husband is the father.*

Gloria in excelsis Deo sang the angels in the organ loft.

This baby—the product of the reunion of Marie-Claire and the husband who does not know his name—this baby lives and Marie-Claire brings her baby to the gardener's cottage every day for a month or so. She prepares the evening meal then she leaves the family to fend for itself. She has a running joke. "Manna from heaven," she says, leaving a platter of food on the kitchen table. She hoists her own baby on her shoulder. "Capucine found the platter on the doorstep. The angels don't know if she is five years old, or six, but they know she can look after this house."

"Angels brought you," her father tells Capucine.

"But you don't look like one," her brother says. "You look like a monkey."

Capucine punches him on the arm.

When Marie-Claire explains that she cannot come anymore, she needs to stay home, she needs to care for her own baby and her damaged husband, Petit Christophe says: "You will have to hire a housekeeper, Papa. As well as the extra farm hands."

"What he means," Cap's father explains, "is that the butcher has offered Petit Christophe an apprenticeship, and Petit Christophe wants to accept."

Cap looks from her father to her brother, sensing some shadow in the air. "Is that good?" she asks.

"I'll be able to bring home off-cuts of meat," Petit Christophe says. "The parts no one wants to buy. Free food. You can make sausages and *rillettes*. Marie-Claire can teach you how."

"I already know how. She already taught me."

"So. More food. No cost."

"Nothing is without cost," the gardener says.

"The countess is coming back," Petit Christophe tells Capucine. "She's bringing her American son."

"You said she'd never come back."

"I was wrong. She's crazy though, and so is her son."

"Her son's the same age as you," Cap's father says, but Petit Christophe contradicts.

"He's younger, and he's a mama's boy and very strange." Cap's brother taps his forehead to suggest defective clockwork inside the boy's skull. "But the countess is loaded. She'll spread money around. Papa will earn more, the butcher will earn more, I will earn more, and I won't have to live and die a farm hand."

This is the way it goes. The countess is willing to hire extra laborers from the village for the vines and the orchard and the *potager*. She also trains domestic servants for the chateau. The gardener himself hires a housekeeper, part-time, for cleaning and laundry and cooking the evening meal. Father, son, and Capucine rise at dawn and fix their own breakfast. Then Petit Christophe rides his bicycle into the village and enters the cobbled courtyard of Monsieur Monsard, *Boucherie.*

Cap climbs her favorite apple tree and drops over the high stone wall into the chateau courtyard. A boy in a blue dress stands watching.

"You are not allowed in here," he says. "You have to stay outside the gate."

"Papa told me you were back. Why are you wearing a dress?"

"Go," he says, pointing.

"I won't go. Does your *maman* make you wear dresses? My brother says your mother is crazy."

"*Maman* prays a lot," the boy concedes. "I'm an answer to prayer. I'm a gift from the Virgin Mary. That's why I wear blue."

"Are you going to wear blue dresses all your life?"

"Not after my first communion."

"Is your *Maman* really crazy?"

"My mother," he says stiffly, "and my father too, are both listed in the *Dictionanaire de la Noblesse de France* and in *Burke's Peerage.*"

"What's that?"

"You are very ignorant. You wouldn't understand."

"Yes I do," she says. "You are a fat cat, *un gros Richard.* We don't think much of fat cats in St Gilles."

"My mother's great-great-great grandmother," the boy says, reciting family catechism, was the daughter of a mistress of the king of France. This house was a gift from the king to his mistress and to her descendants for ever and ever and one day it will be mine."

"No it won't," the girl says. "It's ours. We've always lived here and we do all the work. If we didn't do it, the chateau would be a ruin."

"Your father is my mother's servant. You are the gardener's daughter and you don't even have a mother," the boy says.

136

"I do so."

"Where is she then?"

The girl picks up a pebble from the courtyard and tosses it over the wall. She says with dignity: "I don't have to tell you where she is."

"You talk like a peasant. You don't wash your hair and you don't bathe. *Maman* says I am not to talk to you because you are dirty and wild."

The girl puts a hand over her mouth to hold back a rush of anger. The boy smooths down his silken shift but his hand is trembling and the girl's rage instantly turns into pity.

"You want to climb the tree and escape?" she asks gently. "That's how I get in."

"You are not allowed inside the gate."

"I never come through the gate. You want to see the secret entrance to the cellar that no one remembers?"

"Where is it?"

"In the woods. Nobody knows where except my father and my brother and Marie-Claire and me. Can't show you," she says, "this side of the wall."

"What's in the secret cellar?"

"Nothing's in it. People used to hide there."

From the window of the chateau a voice calls.

"It's *maman*," the boy says, alarmed. "I have to go."

When Petit Christophe cycles home from the village, he and Cap work together in the *potager* throughout the long twilit evenings of the summer, though this practice is becoming intermittent. Petit Christophe does not always come home anymore, but when he does he is a patient teacher. "You can't get the best tomatoes or beans, year after year," he explains, "unless you take precautions in between."

He teaches her to mix lime and bone meal in the right proportions and how to work this mixture into the soil. He teaches her the cover-crop routine—how to grow winter wheat, winter rye, and clovers—and then how to plough them in. "The soil gets exhausted, just like we do. You've got to find a way to let it sleep, to give it fresh juice. This is the best way. It's like falling in love."

"You mean like you and Chantal?"

"What do you know about me and Chantal?"

"I saw you kissing in the slaughter yard."

Petit Christophe pushes his garden fork into the soil with a furious boot. "Did you tell papa?"

"No. I'm not a snitch."

"Good. Look, Cap..." Her brother leans on his pitchfork. "The butcher and papa, during the Occupation, they were on different sides. Not on different sides, exactly, because everyone hated the Boche. But they had different opinions about how to survive."

"Papa was on our side."

"What has he told you?"

"Nothing. He didn't tell me anything. You did. You said papa worked for the Resistance, like our mothers. And like Marie-Claire's husband. It was terrible, what the Boche did to her husband."

"Yes, it was terrible."

"Did the Gestapo do that to our mothers?"

Petit Christophe crosses himself. "Don't think about it," he says. "It doesn't bear thinking about. Nobody knows. The butcher was afraid they would do that to everyone."

"So he joined the German side?"

"It wasn't so simple, Cap. No one was *for* the Germans but everyone was afraid. No one will talk about it, ever. So, see, me working for Monsieur Monsard, papa doesn't like it."

"I don't like it either," Cap says.

"Why not?"

"Because you don't come home as much."

"Sometimes I'm just too tired at the end of the day and Monsieur Monsard gives me a room. Less food expense for you and papa. I'll come home when I can."

"Was the butcher a collaborator?"

"Who told you about collaborators?"

"Marie-Claire did. She says even kids did it for money."

"Did she say which kids?"

"Yes. She thinks Michel Monsard was doing it. He always had extra money, she says. She blames him for what happened to her husband. She thinks he saw something and told his father, and his father informed."

Petit Christophe lays his pitchfork, carefully, tines down, at the edge of the bean patch. He sits down beside it. He begins picking beans, one by one. "That was such a bad time, Cap. I don't like to think about it at all. Can you bring me the basket?"

"Are you sure the beans are ready?" Cap asks.

Petit Christophe goes on picking, making a small mound of beans in the basket. "Marie-Claire shouldn't talk about that time. Especially not to you."

"She doesn't exactly talk to me. She talks out loud to herself. Is it true about the butcher and Michel?"

"Everyone was afraid, Cap. Everyone needed money and food." Petit Christophe snaps a bean between his teeth and eats it raw. "These are good," he says. "We weren't allowed to eat our own beans, back then. The Boche took everything for their army. Eat, Cap. Eat while you can."

Cap takes a bean from the basket and snaps it with her fingers and eats. "Michel just wanted to eat?"

"Yes. Doesn't mean I forgive him, but I don't forgive myself even more. I did something stupid."

"What?"

"I told him there was a safe-house in the woods where papa hid people. I didn't show him where it was, thank God. It's that stupid sort of thing you do when you're a kid. You just can't keep a secret and you want to show off."

"What did he do?"

"Told his father what I told him, I suppose. So what happened is all my fault."

"Does Marie-Claire think that?"

"I don't know. I don't know what she knows. I don't know what anyone knows. And I don't know anything either, Cap. No one does, no one talks, but we all have suspicions. Probably we all have bad dreams. I know I do."

"Marie-Claire told me that papa never let the Boche into our cellars and he never let them take any of our wine."

"The Boche did go into our cellars and they did take the wine. La comtesse told them: *Take what you want.* What they never found was the cave blocked off from the chateau. It's blocked off inside. You can't tell. Did Marie-Claire tell you what the Gestapo did to papa?"

Cap shakes her head.

"Then I don't want to tell you either."

"Tell me," Cap begs. "Otherwise I will have nightmares."

"You'll have nightmares anyway. I have nightmares. They hung papa up like a steer and beat him till he was wet with his own blood and turned purple."

Cap squeezes her eyes shut and claps a hand over her mouth. She cannot speak.

"I shouldn't have told you," Ti-Christophe says. "I had no right. And no right not to."

"How do you know what they did?"

"Because I watched them. Michel Monsard and I were hiding

in his bedroom. The curtains were closed, but there was a crack between them, and we both saw. Papa doesn't know this and I don't want him to know, but I know he told the Boche nothing. You need to understand, Cap. I think that's why the butcher is hiring me. To make amends. I'm sure Michel told him I saw. I just want you to understand why it's not so easy for me to come home now that I'm working for Monsieur Monsard, and it's not easy for papa either. You must never mention any of this to anyone ever. "

Cap feels her heart beating so fast that she is afraid it will fly out of her ribcage like a bird. "I told the boy in the chateau," she confessses. "About the safe house. I couldn't keep a secret either. But I didn't show him."

"You must tell him you made the story up."

Cap crosses her heart. "I promise," she says. "But Monsieur Monsard and Michel...? Does everyone know?"

"Everyone suspects. I think I'm the only one who knows, and they know I know, and they're afraid of me. They would like to make me disappear but I am watchful and I am biding my time. I will make Michel pay and I will make the butcher pay."

"What people did papa hide in the cellars?"

"What people do you think?" Petit Christophe asks.

"I don't know."

"People who had to get out of France."

In the lake in Central Park, a mini-whirlpool forms between two rocks. Perhaps the wake of a boat causes this, perhaps the webbed feet of the ducks. The liquid funnel yawns wider and wider and the morning sun fills it with flame. Cap is mesmerized. She is staring into the cast-iron stove in the kitchen of the gardener's cottage of the Chateau de Boissy, just outside the village of St Gilles.

She is wrapping a rag around the hooked hotplate-lever and fitting it into the slot on the iron circle that rests on the black surface of the stove. In spite of the multiple folds of cloth, the heat is fierce against the palm of her hand. She lifts the plate with her right hand and with her left pushes wood chips through the hole into the furnace. Flames leap out and lick at the rag around her hand. She leans as far back as she can but her cheeks feel scorched. With her left hand, she reaches for more kindling and feeds the fire. The wood spits and crackles and snaps.

She lets the iron plate settle back into its circular groove and wipes her hands on the rag. Her face is flushed.

She lifts a pot of water from the stone floor and sets it over the stove-plate. The pot is so heavy that she almost trips forward and sears herself. This has happened. She breathes heavily. She moves slowly and carefully, having scalded herself on arms and legs more than once. She wishes Petit Christophe came home more often to lift the pots.

She returns to peeling potatoes. She and her father are never short of food though the menu is limited. Potatoes, carrots, beans, eggs, the birds her father shoots, the fish he catches in the Vienne, the flesh of chickens that are no longer laying, whatever throwaways Petit Christophe can scavenge from the carcass-cutting room at Monsieur Monsard's: tripe, tongue, pig's trotters, *tête de veau*, pork intestines and the fattiest parts of hog shoulder from which Cap makes *rillettes*. To a hungry stomach, *rillettes* on toast taste like the sacrament. But it is more often Cap who has to go to the butcher's to collect.

Petit Christophe is a man now and seems to avoid coming home. Cap misses him. She misses his help chopping wood and lifting pots. She misses his company, his stories, his laughter, his easy joy. He used to tell stories that made their father laugh. Sometimes Cap can make her father laugh when she mimics the village priest and the women who go to mass, but her father does not laugh so often now.

Papa wants to believe what the nuns told him, but Cap knows what everyone else believes. People disappeared without trace back then. No one wanted to know how they died.

And now Petit Christophe has gone too.

Peeling potatoes then dropping them into the boiling water, she rubs her eyes with the back of her hand. Tomorrow, she will visit the butcher's. She will reproach her brother: *You haven't brought us any meat for a week.*

She knows why.

Chantal, the butcher's daughter, is a year younger than Petit Christophe. Capucine has seen them kissing over the block where her brother slices tenderloin from rib. Her brother and the butcher's daughter had just come in from the killing yard and were both smeared with blood. She watched as Chantal ran a finger through a red splat on her wrist then drew a crimson X on her brother's lips. Cap could tell that her brother was hot and bothered.

His bone-saw hung by a rope from his belt. His boning knife was sheathed at his waist. He grasped it by the handle and laid the flat of the blade, soft, against Chantal's forehead, then against her chin, then against one cheek, then the other. The fierce point of his boning knife nicked one cheek. Chantal crossed herself and kissed Petit Christophe on the lips.

Capucine also crossed herself.

3.

"P'tit Christophe," Cap whispers. "Are you awake?"

"Mmm," he mumbles.

"I saw the American boy in the chateau courtyard today. He looks like a girl."

"I know. His *maman* is crazy. They are both of them, the boy and his *maman*, quite crazy, and they are both fat cats, *gros richards*."

"You said they'd never come back."

"I was wrong."

"Where do they come from?"

"They come from here. *La comtesse* married an American soldier. She married him here in St Gilles. I went to the church with papa. The whole village was there in the church and then the whole village danced in the chateau courtyard. After the wedding, they went to America and now they've come back."

"The American soldier too?"

"No. He stayed over there. People say he packed them off and shipped them out. He didn't want a son in a dress and a crazy wife."

"P'tit Christophe," Cap ventures. "Were our mothers crazy?"

"No. Well, a little, maybe. Crazy brave maybe."

"Do you remember your *maman*?"

A long silence ensues. Cap can hear the heavy breathing of

her brother.

"Ti-Christophe?"

"Hnnn."

"Are you awake?"

"No."

"Do you remember your *maman*?"

Petit Christophe sighs heavily and lifts himself to lean on one elbow. "Cap, don't ask these questions. It's like picking a scab. You start bleeding all over again."

Cap curls herself up very tight and small on her palette. "I'm sorry," she says. "I won't ask."

Cap is certainly not asleep but she has floated to somewhere else when her brother says into the darkness, "I think I remember her. I'm not sure. I was only three when she joined the Resistance. Papa joined too, but he stayed here and ran the safe house. My mother and your mother were on the move all the time. They were escorts. People came and went in the dark."

"Were you scared?"

"All the time. The Germans were right there in the chateau. I had bad dreams every night."

"I'm afraid to ask papa about my *maman*."

"Papa's afraid to remember."

"I think about her all the time."

"Same for me." Petit Christophe punches his pillow into a ball and buries his face in it. Just when Cap fears he may be suffocating himself, he rolls over and stares at the underside of the joists and the roof tiles above. "This is what I think I remember," he says. "*Maman* on one side, papa on the other, sleeping in front of the fire. I think I can smell my *maman*. I think this was every night until I was three, and I think something happened then, but it might be a dream I keep having."

"What happened?"

"I remember they lit three candles and let them burn in the windowsill all night long. I remember they said *Bon anniversaire, Ti-Christophe.* I think she left the next day. She went to London with De Gaulle just before the Germans took Paris."

"Why didn't she take you with her?"

"That's a question I never stop asking."

"Do you ask Papa?"

"Never. I ask *myself.* The schoolmaster told me most of what I know, which isn't much. *Maman* was parachuted back behind enemy lines when I was four, so she came sometimes at nights."

"What was her name?"

"Papa says her name was Fleur, but that was her code name. No one ever used real names, not even with each other. It wasn't safe."

"What happened to her?"

"She was escorting four people to Chinon and Papa was supposed to meet them there and then bring them here. That's what the escorts did. They met people at one safe house and took them to the next one. The escape route was from Paris to Tours. There was a safe house in a convent in Tours. After that, fishermen took people in rowboats down the Loire by night to the fishing village of La Croix. There was a safe house there. Then escorts took them after dark through the forest to Chinon. After that, sometimes they came by night in rowboats up the Vienne to St Gilles and sometimes they came on farmers' carts through the Forest of Chinon. They stayed in our safe house. Then they crossed the Vienne by night and went on south to Loudun. From there, they went from safe house to safe house until they got into Spain and then Portugal. From Portugal they took whatever ships they could pay for, to Shanghai, to New York, to wherever. The Gestapo got my mother in Chinon and we don't know what happened after that."

"Did you meet my *maman?*"

146

Petit Christophe does not answer for some time. Cap keeps her eyes tightly closed until, when she opens them again, she can see in the dark. She can see the heavy oak beams and the slate tiles in the thick black over her head. She counts the tiles.

"I think so," Petit Christophe says at last.

"What was she like?"

"I was only five years old, Cap, maybe six. I'm not sure what I remember. It's like the way you remember dreams. Papa used to say, I'm going to Chinon to collect a package. I remember he took me with him one time. We went by rowboat down the Vienne and we brought three people back. We took two of them to the safe house. I think the other one was your *maman* and she stayed here for the night."

"Here? In our cottage?"

"Yes. Up here in the loft."

"My *maman* slept up here?"

"In your bed. They laughed a lot."

"Papa laughed?"

"When he made you, he was laughing. I had to sleep by the stove downstairs and I listened until I fell asleep."

"Was she pretty?"

"Your *maman*? Yes. Very beautiful. Papa was afraid the German officers would see her and if they saw her, they'd take her. We could hear them singing and drinking in the chateau like the noisy barbarians they were. That's how close we came every day to being gutted."

"Did she look like an angel, my *maman*?"

"Yes. She did."

"Did she have wings?"

"She didn't have wings, but she acted as though she did. She wasn't afraid of anything, papa says. But she was not as beautiful as you, Cap."

"Am I beautiful?"

"Yes." Petit Christophe sighs. "It's not such a good thing, Cap. It's dangerous. If any boy touches you, you have to tell me."

"No one's going to touch me," Cap protests. "I don't even like boys, except for you. But where is my *maman* now?"

"We don't know. Nobody knows."

"What is her name?"

"Her code name was Lilith. Papa never knew her real name and she didn't know his. Her base was the convent in Tours. The last time papa went to meet her she didn't show up. She was supposed to have six people with her. We don't know what happened to them and papa never got another message from her."

"Did he ever find out what happened?"

"No. He tried. Lilith had two covers. She was a laundry maid at the convent in Tours and she was a farm hand who sold vegetables in the markets in Chinon. Whenever we could, papa and I would take the horse and cart or the old truck to the markets but she wasn't there. No one knew where she was. No one would talk. Back then, no one would say anything to anyone. No one ever saw anything. Everyone was afraid. Finally Papa couldn't stand it and he drove the truck all the way into the cathedral in Tours and he took me with him. He asked the priest if he knew Lilith but of course he didn't use her code name. He described her. The priest said the woman was a laundry maid in the convent but that she was in a state of sin."

"What did he mean?"

"He meant she had a big belly. That turned out to be you."

"Did you see her?"

"Not that time. Papa wanted to but the priest said it would be too dangerous for the nuns. He told papa that the wages of sin were punishment. He asked papa if he wanted to make confession, and papa said yes. He asked me if I wanted to make confession, and I said no. I don't know why but I didn't trust him. Papa made his confession and we drove home. I asked papa if Lilith would come back and papa said he hoped so and she would bring us a present when she came. The priest said the present would be papa's act of contrition."

"What's an act of contrition?"

"That was you. The priest brought you in a basket. I remember that day. I was eight maybe nine years old, and it was just after the Liberation. Papa took you from the basket the way he candles eggs in the hen house."

Cap buries her face in the pillow. She sees her father's willow basket lined with old quilting, the gentle way he lifts the eggs from warm straw, his thick gnarled fingers, the way he holds the eggs close to the candle flame to watch for the dark spot of blood, the fertile spot, the way he places eggs that are germinating side by side in the cushiony cloth.

"If the priest brought me, why didn't he bring my *maman*?"

"He told papa that your *maman* died in childbirth and that's what papa believes. That's what he wants to believe. But Marie-Claire told me the Gestapo took her. The nuns hid you until they couldn't hide you anymore."

"My *maman* is dead?"

"Cap. Cap! Don't cry." Petit Christophe crosses the loft and takes his little sister in his arms. He strokes her hair. "Listen," he says. "I know they got my *maman* but she is with me all the time inside my head. She's here in the loft. And so is yours." He tightens his arms around her. "Can't you feel her?" he asks.

Cap weeps silently into his shoulder. "I wish I could," she says. "I don't even know what she looked like. Does papa have a photograph?"

"No," Petit Christophe says. "No one in the Resistance carried photographs. Too dangerous. They could be used by the Gestapo to destroy the will. But papa says every time he looks at you, he sees your *maman*."

4.

Drifting across Central Park and the lake from midtown, Cap can hear the bells of the Church of St Thomas on Fifth Avenue at West 53rd, and from two blocks further south, the bells of St Patrick's on the east side of Fifth Avenue at 51st. Both churches have a bearing on the trial of the Vanderbilt claimant. In the Episcopal church of St Thomas, on November 6, 1895, Consuelo Vanderbilt, great-granddaughter of the Commodore, became the most unwilling and desperately unhappy bride of the Duke of Marlborough, dragooned into the match by her mother. Fifty years later, the Lady Isabelle de la Vallière, equally desolate French bride of Lawrence Gwynne Vanderbilt, sought comfort by attending daily mass at St Patrick's Catholic cathedral.

Cap knows she is not actually hearing those church bells, which is not possible from the Ramble. What she is hearing are the bells of the village church in St Gilles where she sits between her father and her brother. The village church is cavernous. Built in the twelfth century, it can hold a thousand people but fewer than thirty attend mass on Sunday mornings. Father Boniface presides and two boys from the village serve at the altar. In the past, Petit Christophe has been an altar boy, but Petit Christophe no longer goes to confession and he walks out of the nave after the act of consecration but before the sacrament is offered to the faithful. He has not explained why. His father has not asked. When the priest visits the gardener's cottage and asks for Petit Christophe, Cap's father explains: "My son doesn't live here anymore. He has a room at the butcher's establishment."

The priest says: "I visited Monsieur Monsard. The butcher claims he does not live there, he lives here."

"The butcher is mistaken."

"But Petit Christophe sits with you on Sunday mornings at mass. He comes every week."

"Yes. We are a close family."

"And yet he does not take the sacrament. And he has not made confession for more than a year. What is the reason? And why does he still attend the mass?"

"You will have to ask my son," Cap's father says.

"Do you know what sin is lying heavy on his heart?" the priest wants to know.

"I believe that is between my son and God. It is not my business."

"It is mine," the priest says.

"Then you must speak to him."

"Father Boniface is looking for you," Cap whispers to her brother in church.

"I know."

"Why are you hiding from him? And why don't you sleep at home anymore?"

"It's too complicated," her brother whispers back, "to explain."

"Look!" Cap murmurs, excited. "Look! It's the boy from the chateau and his mother. We never see them at Mass."

"They have a private chapel in the chateau. The priest goes there."

"Why are they here today?"

"Because it's the Feast of the Annunciation."

From her catechism and her preparation for First Communion,

Cap knows the meaning of the feast. It marks the anniversary of the Angel Gabriel's appearance before the Blessed Virgin to tell her that a child has been miraculously conceived in her womb. Cap closes her eyes and imagines the rush and swish of gigantic luminous wings. How alarmed the Virgin Mary must have been. Was this how Gwynne Something Something's birth had been announced? *I'm a gift from the Virgin Mary. That's why I wear blue.*

Capucine and Petit Christophe watch as the countess and the strange boy in his sky-blue shift walk down the center aisle, genuflect, cross themselves, and move into the front pew. The countess never lets go of her son's hand. Father Boniface bows toward them which causes Petit Christophe to mutter something angry under his breath. Cap casts a quizzical eye at her father, who shrugs. "The priest does what he has to do," her father murmurs. "He has to answer to the bishop. We only have to answer to God."

Cap keeps her eye on the lamp suspended above the altar. A foggy red-gold shimmer comes off it. God is in that shimmer and the thought fills her with awe, especially since God is happy to snap his fingers at the difference between a countess and her gardener, between the gardener's daughter and the son of the chateau. She mumbles the Latin in the wake of the congregation and the priest. Though she does not know many of the words or the meaning of them, she knows their music and the music thrills her.

Kyrie eleison...

Gloria Patri et Filio et Spiritui Sancto...in secula seculorum, amen.

Two pews in front of Cap sit Monsieur Monsard and Madame Monsard and their daughter Chantal and Chantal's older brother Michel. Cap studies Chantal's dark curls and the blue ribbon in her hair. She studies Monsieur Monsard. There are black hairs beginning to turn gray which are matted like wires, or perhaps like stiffened cat's fur, that run from the butcher's collar to the top of his neck where the dark nest of his head-hair sits. His neck hairs are coiled like very fine charcoal-gray springs and Cap can see the skin of his neck between the spirals. His skin reminds her of a chicken that has been plucked.

The priest is lifting the chalice high above his head. The altar boy is ringing the bell. The priest drinks the wine that has now been turned into blood. He drinks all of it, every last drop, though Cap sees a tiny crimson thread trickle down his chin. The priest catches the trickle with his hand and licks his fingers. If he does not do this, the mass will not be valid. This Capucine knows.

One by one, the members of the congregation are to file out from the pews to kneel in front of the priest. *La comtesse* and her son go forward first and everyone else waits, as though to receive the host at the same time as the chatelaine and the heir to the chateau would be improper. The countess is dressed in black and wears a black veil edged in lace that covers her head and her face. Her cheeks are pale, like twin moons floating behind a gossamer rain cloud. A long double string of pearls chinks very softly against the buttons on her bodice as she walks. She looks very distinguished and very graceful. She glides like a black swan across the dark surface of a tarn. The boy in the blue shift keeps his eyes on his feet. His mother holds his hand tightly and they kneel side by side before the priest.

Cap can see only a quarter-profile but she imagines the boy's mother with her tongue stuck far out for the host. Cap's mind wanders to the idea of the tongue, such a strange part of the body. She experiments with moving her own behind and in front of her teeth, with poking it into the fleshy pockets on each side of the soft pink cavern where her tongue is leashed. She nudges Petit Christophe so that he can see the odd protrusion in the middle of her left cheek. From his perspective, she thinks, it would look like a cork popping out of a champagne bottle. He grins, then gives her an admonitory frown, and presses the popped cork with his thumb. Her tongue, this strange thing which she shares with animals, birds, even whales, settles back into its bed between her teeth. Petit Christophe has told her that the tongue of a whale weighs more than an elephant.

What kind of elephant? she asked.

How many kinds do you know? Petit Christophe asked back.

Petit Christophe often answers questions with other questions and the answer is always crimped inside his question like a walnut within its hard shell. It is always difficult to pry that answer out, but his questions frequently make her laugh.

Cap tries to imagine the tongue of a whale without success.

She switches to calf's tongue, which is easier, which she has often seen. She thinks of how it resembles a gigantic slug or perhaps a monstrous snail without its shell, slimy and slick, but with a leathery blister-crowded skin. That is what she thought when Petit Christophe first brought one home. Cap did not even want to touch it, but Marie-Claire told her: "Calf's tongue is a delicacy. A supreme delight." Marie-Claire taught her what was required.

Cap thinks of how the tongue must be soaked for such a long time, six hours, and how the water has to be changed several times, and then how the pink slug has to be boiled and simmered for an hour at least, with an onion and some garlic cloves in the pot, and how she has to keep skimming the grey foam from off the top. She wonders why the tongue is not green on its upper side, given how often the leathery muscle has turned grass into weedy swamp-soup. She has asked Petit Christophe about this. "Why doesn't a calf's tongue turn green?"

"Why doesn't yours?" he responded, tickling her. "You eat spinach; you eat green beans. Why doesn't your tongue turn green?"

She giggled. "You are so silly," she said. "But where does the foam come from when I'm boiling it? And why is it grey?"

"When you watch cows chewing grass, what do you see?"

"There's foamy stuff coming out of the sides of their mouths."

"Exactly. That drool gets stored in their tongues with all the grey dust from the field. That's what you are boiling out."

Cap decides she does not want to eat calf's tongue anymore.

If Petit Christophe brings another one home, she will still have to prepare it for her father. After the tongue-slug has been boiled forever and forever and cooled, she has to peel it. The skin of a calf's tongue makes her think of Monsieur Monsard's neck. Both are covered with tiny pimples and blisters. Both make her want to throw up.

Both make her think about what happened to the husband of Marie-Claire and what happened to her own mother and to the mother of Petit Christophe. She wants to know and she doesn't want to know what things were done to her father.

She thinks about peeling the butcher's neck from his hairline to the top of his collar. How can the butcher and her father sit in the same church and receive the sacrament at the same time? Then she remembers: Monsieur Monsard does not go forward for the sacrament.

"Why doesn't he?" she asks her brother.

"Why do you think?" her brother says. "He has a guilty conscience, that's why."

"Is that why you won't make confession or take the sacrament anymore?"

"Yes. But I can't tell the priest because I don't trust him. Remember that papa doesn't know what I know. No one knows anything. Nobody talks. And everyone has to go on living in this village."

"Michel knows that you know. And everyone knows what happened to the husband of Marie-Claire," Capucine objects. "And if you saw the Boche with papa in the slaughter yard, then papa *must* know it was the butcher—"

"People know," Petit Christophe acknowledges. "But nobody wants to know and they want to forget. The priest knows. Monsieur Monsard knows. Michel knows. Papa knows. But they keep on trying not to know."

Cap would like to peel Monsieur Monsard all the way down to his heels. She imagines the butcher's tongue on their kitchen table, how she would slice it, extra thin, and then sautée it, and then feed it to the dogs.

"P'tit Christophe," she whispers in church, "did *la comtesse* know?"

"Shh," her brother warns.

The countess is accepting the host on her outstretched tongue. The priest puts his hand on the blue boy's head and blesses him. Like Cap, the blue boy has not yet made his first communion. He is too young.

As *la comtesse* and her son are returning to their pew, Cap and her father move forward. Petit Christophe leaves the church. His footsteps, on the long stone walk to the west door, sound loud. Cap wonders what Father Boniface is thinking. She is level with the countess and her son. For a moment, the boy raises his head and his eyes meet those of Capucine. Two seconds pass. They can see themselves in each other's eyes and Cap can hear the boy's voice replaying itself in her head. *You're the gardener's daughter, you don't have a mother, you don't bathe and you don't wash your hair, you are dirty and wild.* The insult feels as rank and sharp as a freshly dropped cow-pat. She pulls her eyes slanty with her fingers and pokes out her tongue. She notes the nervous way the boy looks swiftly at his mother. She notes his relief (the way his shoulders go slack) when he realizes that his mother did not see.

At the altar rail, Cap finds herself kneeling between her father and Chantal Monsard. Monsieur Monsard does not leave the church but he does not come forward for the sacrament either.

Nor does his son Michel. (At least, Cap's brother tells her later, at least they acknowledge they are in a state of mortal sin. They know what they have done.) On the other side of Chantal is her mother. Chantal has been confirmed; Cap receives only the hand of the priest on her head, but she has a close-up view of all the tongues stretched out, waiting for the wafer as for manna from heaven.

The tongue is not an attractive part of the body, Cap thinks. She decides she will never eat calf's tongue again. She will not soak it or boil it or peel it. In particular, she will never slice it again. She watches all the tongues of St Gilles tasting the body of Christ. They are swallowing His flesh and blood.

In the slaughtering yard, Petit Christophe sees so much blood every day. He sees stone channels flowing with blood. Perhaps that is why he can no longer bear to watch it being drunk, let alone drink it himself. Perhaps his reaction is no different from how Capucine feels about calf's tongue. Perhaps he is remembering what he saw in the killing yard when the Boche did things to their father. Why did this happen in the slaughtering yard? Her father never goes there, had no reason to go there, so the trap must have been carefully planned.

Did the butcher invite her father for *pastis* and then suddenly...?

Afterwards, outside the church, the gardener and the butcher nod to each other but do not speak. Petit Christophe and Chantal stand talking under an oak. Cap can see that the two fathers do not like this and nor does Michel, Chantal's brother, who no longer lives in St Gilles but comes home for Sunday dinner. He is a big surly young man who works at the motorcycle plant in Tours and whose own moto leans against the oak.

There is a roar and a belching of black exhaust and another moto blasts through the quiet. This is Olivier, friend and fellow worker of Michel Monsard. They are both employed on the assembly line in the same factory and live in the same boarding house in Tours. Olivier guns his moto so close to Chantal that she and Petit Christophe are forced to scramble aside. Olivier doffs his cloth cap and offers his pillion seat to Chantal.

She hesitates.

It is known that Olivier has been courting Chantal and that her father and her brother approve. Chantal looks from Petit Christophe to Olivier and back again. She lowers her head, afraid to decide. Olivier guns his moto and roars off in the direction of Tours. Michel Monsard jumps onto his own moto and follows.

Cap is only partly watching her brother and Chantal. She is waiting for the countess and the boy in blue to come out of the church. Now she can see them below the great rose window, the cobalt and crimson circle that is scattering color and light on the priest. Father Boniface stands in the arched entry of the western facade, below the sculpted apostles, one eye on Petit Christophe and Chantal and on the motos heading back toward Tours. The priest startles when the countess touches his arm. He bows slightly. The countess never lets go of her son's hand.

Cap does not remember making a decision or moving from her father's side but here she is, close enough to the boy to touch his blue dress, close enough to touch his mother and the priest.

"You should apologize," she says to the boy. "You said I was dirty and wild. And you should also apologize, *Madame la Comtesse*, for telling him that."

Neither Father Boniface nor *Madame la Comtesse* seems able to speak. They look as stunned as though one of the stray churchyard cats has made a statement in impeccable French. Cap and the boy in the blue shift lock eyes but Cap cannot read what the boy's eyes say.

"Capucine!" her father calls. "*Madame la Comtesse*," he says, nodding politely. "I ask your pardon. She is an impetuous child

159

without a mother."

"It is nothing, *Monsieur le Jardinier*," the countess says, leading her son away.

"Bravo!" Petit Christophe whispers in her ear, tousling her hair. "Come to the butcher's tomorrow. Bring a basket and I'll fill it with off-cuts and bones. Rib bones, leg bones, perfect for soup."

"But no calf's tongue," Caps warns. "I don't want any more tongue."

"Your own tongue will get you into quite enough trouble, *ma petite soeur*," her brother says.

5.

On her park bench, Cap is still staring at the white envelope which someone slid under her hotel door that morning, the envelope which contains an unsigned note. She does not need to read the note again. For some reason, doubtless to do with superstition or vague atavistic anxiety, she does not wish to re-open the envelope, but she makes her way around the northern shore of the lake to the boat house restaurant. She settles at a table in the outdoor bar and orders a small dish of olives and a glass of wine. "Someone will be joining me," she explains. "I won't order lunch until then."

"No problem," the waiter assures her. "Chef's special is Garlic Shrimp."

Because of the autumn chill, and because the terrace is in shadow, Cap huddles in her jacket and watches the slow gliding of the rowers and boats. The air is fragrant with garlic and herbs and grilled fish and steamed vegetables and she is back in St Gilles, back in the gardener's cottage, back in the kitchen where the potatoes are gently bumping against each other in boiling water. When they are cooked Cap spears them one by one with a long-handled fork and places them in a blue ceramic dish. They are new potatoes, quite small, freshly harvested, and look like delicate eggs in a nest. A tiny fog of steam comes off them. Cap tosses a slice of butter into the cobalt bowl and watches it melt. With a wooden spoon, she stirs the potatoes until each looks like a golden egg.

She chops parsley and rosemary and lavender and sprinkles the clippings over her buttered jewels. They are really too beautiful to eat, but papa will love them.

Her hands wrapped with toweling, Cap opens the oven door and slides out the roasting pan. Three rabbits huddle against each other in the way of children spooning their little bodies in a cot. The vessel is so hot that the rabbits twitch and flinch from contact with the searing sides of the pan. Cap moves slowly and carefully toward the oak slab of the kitchen table where the cooling rack stands. Any minute now her father will appear in the doorway, smeared with dirt, weary, and ravenous for supper.

There it is: the sound of boots being scraped at the door.

She sets the heavy pan on the table, but when she turns it is not her father she sees. It is the boy in the blue dress. He is clasping and unclasping his hands. He blinks rapidly. "I came," he says.

For several whole seconds, Cap is too astonished to speak. Then she asks: "Came for what?"

"To apologize."

"Oh. That's... " Cap is not prepared for this. What she has really wanted, she suddenly knows, is not to get an apology, but to make the mother and the boy feel buffeted, to shock them, to wind them. She wants them to sense that they are not immune to being treated with disdain, not immune to being *scraped*, not immune to contempt. She wants them to know what that feels like.

"And to see the secret entrance to the cellars," the boy adds.

"Ah..." Cap grasps the edge of the kitchen table to steady herself. "That. I made that up. I was joking. There's no secret entrance."

"Oh." The boy seems crestfallen. "*Maman* thought there might be."

"No. There isn't. You told your mother what I said?"

"No," the boy says with nervous urgency. "No. I didn't. Maman says there have always been stories. There was supposed to be a

162

tunnel from the church to the chateau since before the Revolution. It was supposed to end in our cellars, but if it did it got destroyed in the First World War. *Maman* never believed the stories anyway, but when you said... I thought perhaps they were true."

"No," Cap says. "No. They're just stories. Everyone in the village tells those stories." She feels a handful of the boy's dress. "Is it silk?" she asks.

"Yes."

"I've never felt silk before." She lets it slip between her fingers. "It's so soft. But aren't you ashamed to wear a dress?"

"Yes."

"So why do you do it?"

"My mother is too sad if I don't. She made a vow." He takes a deep trembling breath. He speaks nervously, too softly, into the heavy fragrant silence of roasted rabbit. "I *believed* you," he accuses, in some anguish, as though a terrible betrayal has occurred. "You said there was a secret cellar. You promised you'd show me if I came outside the wall."

"I'm sorry." Cap does feel compunction. She feels complicit. She feels the way she feels about the soft dead rabbits before she skins them and puts them in the oven. "I lied to you. You were so... I wanted to trick you outside the courtyard. But you ran away."

"Because *maman* called me. She could see me from the house and I'm not allowed to talk to you."

"What would she do to you?"

"She wouldn't do anything. But she would be sad and I don't... Her sadness is heavy, it is very heavy, it is like a... like something I can't carry. So I can't talk to you."

"You're talking to me now."

"I know. But it's dark and no one can see us." The boy in the blue dress bites his lip. "I climbed out my window," he explains, part plaintive, part boasting, part resentful. Just look at the trou-

Go to page 166

163

"*Maman* says your father is a poacher. He is trapping our rabbits."

"Nobody owns rabbits," Cap says.

"*Maman* says she should report him to the *gendarmerie* but she will turn a blind eye..."

"How dare you! The *gendarmerie* don't have enough food for their children. They need the rabbits my father gives. He is a fine *braconneur*, my papa. Go!" She points to the door. "Let your *maman* snitch on my papa. The gendarmes, like the dogs, are our friends, *tu con!*"

"Who's going to snitch on me?" The great bulk of Christophe le Jardinier darkens the doorway. "And who's a stupid asshole here?"

"He is!" Capucine says.

The boy is visibly trembling. "I came to apologize," he pleads.

Cap's father laughs, an amused, gentle, friendly Gargantuan kind of laugh. "What's all this then?" He lifts the frail slip of the girly-boy with his hands—he might have been picking up a kitten—and holds him at eye-level. "Well. If it isn't the Vanderbilt cub," he says. "You poor little sod." He sets the child down. "Your *maman* and I were children together. What's your name?"

"His name is Gwynne Something Something Something," Capucine says.

"My name is Gwynne Patrice de la Vallière Vanderbilt," the boy says.

"*Sacré bleu,* what a mouthful!" Christophe le Jardinier laughs. "I'll call you Petit Loup, the little wolf cub, because you're the Vanderbilt whelp. Got Petit Christophe's old coveralls I can give you if you want to make yourself look decent for supper."

A small amber puddle appears between the boy's feet, under the hem of the blue dress. Gwynne Something Something Vanderbilt is mortified. Christophe le Jardinier tousles his hair. "*Tiens!*" he says. "There, there, little man. You can wear whatever you want,

164

c'est pas grand chose. Capucine, set an extra plate and a fork for P'tit Loup."

"He won't eat our rabbits. He says you're a poacher and his *maman* is going to snitch."

"Is she now?"

"No, she isn't," the boy quickly insists. "She said she won't because—"

"Exactly," Cap's father says. "We have an understanding, your mother and I, and it goes back many years. Many many years, from before you or Capucine were born. Your mother and I were children who played together. Ever eaten rabbit, P'tit Loup?"

"No, Monsieur le Jardinier."

"A rabbit caught in a poacher's trap tastes much better than a rabbit shot by a hunter because our traps don't hurt them. The rabbits just lie there quiet with the shakes, same as you. When I check the traps, I break their necks quick as a wink. I don't let God's creatures suffer. That's why a poacher's rabbit tastes like heaven. Here. Open your mouth and stick out your tongue."

The little wolf cub obediently accepts a forkful and chews. He closes his eyes and breathes in. His eyelids flutter. He holds his breath. He breathes out. "It tastes like heaven," he concurs.

"P'tit Loup," Cap's father says, "no boy can be comfortable in a wet dress. Come with me."

When the man and the boy return from the loft, P'tit Loup is wearing the torn and cast-off coveralls of Cap's brother. He seems to have become someone else, someone else altogether.

"You look bigger, P'tit Loup," Cap says. "It's strange how much bigger you look."

"I *am* bigger," Gwynne Something Something Vanderbilt says.

"Capucine, hang this blue thing in front of the stove to dry out. Now you listen to me, P'tit Loup. I have been gardener and *viticulteur* for your *maman*'s family for a very long time, for many years

go to page 167

165

ble I've taken. And all to please you. He is trying very hard not to cry. Cap cannot quite decide whether she is full of exasperation or full of guilt for lying to him twice. She thinks that maybe she liked him better when he was giving orders and being a shit.

"You'll have to climb back in through your window," she says.

It is immediately clear that such a consequence has not occurred to the boy in advance. He puts his hands to his cheeks. He looks stricken.

Cap studies him, puzzled. "Are you afraid of your mother?"

The boy's eyebrows buckle upwards, deeply startled. "No, no," he says emphatically. "No!" He stamps his foot. For a moment, the imperious son of the chateau is back on stage. "My *maman* is in the *Dictionnaire de la Noblesse*—"

"Yes," Cap says. "You told me. So you had better climb back in through your window."

"I don't know if I can reach."

Something about his intense anxiety touches Cap. "I can help you. You can climb on my back."

"*Maman* might see us."

"In the dark? Anyway, what if she does? I'm not scared of her."

"I don't like to make her sad," the boy confesses. "She is always sad, my *maman*. "

"Why is she sad?"

"I don't know, but I think it is my fault."

Cap frowns, trying to unpuzzle the boy. She asks suddenly: "You want to stay and have supper with us? With me and papa?"

The boy's face changes. It is animated by a hungry look that has nothing to do with food. His eyes glitter.

"It's potatoes and roast rabbit," Cap offers.

Something about this statement makes the boy instantly uneasy. He turns away. "I've eaten supper already," he says.

"Don't you like rabbit?"

go to p. 164

166

before you were born. Your mother knows she cannot do without me. So you will stay here tonight and I will speak to your mother tomorrow and you need have no fear. "

"My *maman*—" the boy begins nervously.

"Do not worry about your mother. I will set her mind at ease."

That night, Gwynne Patrice de la Vallière Vanderbilt lies on the mattress in the loft alongside Capucine. He has never been happier.

"Do you see your father every day?" he asks Capucine in amazement.

"Of course I do. What do you mean?"

"You have supper every evening with your papa?"

"Of course I do."

"In New York," he says, "when we lived with my father, I only saw him to say goodnight. Just before bed."

"You didn't have supper with your father?"

"No. Never. My parents had a dinner party every night. With guests. And with the servants. I had my supper in the nursery with Shannay. She was my nanny."

"But you see your *maman* every day."

"Yes," the boy sighs.

Cap tells him, "I wish I could see my *maman*."

fact that since 1950 he has not needed the daily delivery of blocks of ice, but now has mechanical refrigeration installed. The fourth side, facing the back of the shop, is also refrigerated in a year-long chill and is the cutting room where sides of beef and pork and lamb hang from hooks on a steel ceiling-track and jostle each other, pale as corpses in a morgue.

This fourth wing also permits direct entry to the courtyard from the laneway behind the *boucherie*. It is through these huge double oak gates—directly opposite the entrance from the street—that the live animals arrive, terrified, via wooden ramps, shunted from farmers' carts into the narrow chute that is their corridor to death. There, hugged by the sides of the movable stall, the beasts feel the cold press of the stun-gun against their foreheads, their final sensory puzzle. Though their hearts are still beating and pumping blood, they do not feel the shackles attached to their legs, nor the winch that drags them into the cobbled square, nor the steel blade that slashes the trachea, nor the grappling iron that clenches one rear ankle and hauls them up and suspends them so that their slack tongues do not quite lick the stones.

The courtyard is the kill floor.

With its scaffolds for skinning, gutting, draining blood, with its block and tackle devices, with its great ghastly hooks and leg irons that make possible the sawing of a carcass in half, the yard resembles a torturer's chamber.

Gwynne Patrice *etcetera etcetera* tugs his hand free from Capucine and vomits into one of the drains.

"Monsieur Monsard will give you hell," Cap warns. "I'll have to get P'tit Christophe to sluice that away before he sees."

Outside the chateau grounds, Gwynne Patrice is such a timid child. Cap finds it difficult to understand. Inside the chateau walls, he is a pompous little king of the world and ridiculous. Outside, he is like a mouse quivering between the paws of a cat. He is afraid of everything, even though he is still wearing P'tit Christophe's old work clothes. He exasperates Cap. "You eat sausage, you eat roast beef," she says scornfully. "Where do you think it comes from?"

Gwynne Patrice etcetera wipes his sleeve across his mouth and turns away from the blood and vomit in the stone canal. "It comes from the butcher's," he says meekly. "Can we go home now?"

" *This* is the butcher's," Cap explains, "and no, we are not going home. We just got here. My brother lives here."

"*Maman* will be worried about me. She will be frightened." The boy has not been home since he climbed out of his window the night before. "I don't want to make her sad."

"Papa will look after that. Your *maman* trusts him."

"He can't make her un-sad. I have to go."

Cap grabs hold of his wrist. "Monsieur Monsard cuts the meat for the chateau. He'll give us lamb cutlets and lamb shank and you can give them to your *maman* and she'll be happy."

The boy frowns, slightly horrified. "Our cook brings our meat. *Maman* will be very upset if I— "

"What's the matter with you?"

"It's not proper to touch raw flesh. Or touch blood. Only servants do that."

"I touch raw flesh," Cap tells him, hands on her hips. "I touch liver, calf's tongue, pigs' intestines. I make sausages and *rillettes*. You better stay away from me, Gwynne Patrice Whatever Whatever."

"I don't mean you," the boy says miserably.

"Monsieur Monsard gives us scraps for sausage meat and Ti-Christophe gives him fruit from the orchard and some wine."

"That is our fruit and our wine," Gwynne Vanderbilt says, pulling free, trying to reassert himself. "Petit Christophe does not have the right."

"Oh, shut up! Okay. These are your cattle, your pigs, your sheep, even your rabbits. They all come from the chateau. They all

go to p. 171

169

6.

Cap takes Petit Loup's hand and almost pulls him across the courtyard of the butcher's compound. The courtyard is cobbled and square and slopes slightly from all four sides toward the middle which is marked by the great iron grid of a drain, three feet square, a trapdoor to nothingness, all black. Four stone trenches, six inches wide and six inches deep, run from the corners of the courtyard to spill themselves into this gaping grated hole. Sometimes rain sluices down these small canals with such ferocity that a waterspout skyrockets up at the point of collision. Chantal, the butcher's daughter, calls it the Witches' Fountain.

More often, however—as now—the gutters run blood.

The courtyard is surrounded on all four sides by one-story wings of stone. The front side, facing the street, is the shop where the villagers buy their meat. The entrance to the courtyard is through a stone arch at one side of the shop. The arch faces the street and frames huge oak doors bolted shut from inside. At right angles to the shop, on the left if one stands inside the courtyard with one's back to the store, are the living quarters of the butcher and his family. Within this wing, one small room at the far end, with direct access to the courtyard, is set aside for an apprentice. (This room—at present and intermittently—is occupied by Petit Christophe.) The opposite wing, parallel to the living quarters, is for cold storage. Monsieur Monsard is inordinately proud of the

go to p. 168

end up on your table, as well as on ours, as well as on every other table in the village. You should know how they get there. Don't you understand anything at all?"

"No." The boy says this so softly that Cap can barely hear. He crosses the cobbles, stepping delicately to avoid moist lumps of fat and gristle, wet clouts of blood. He leans his forehead against one of the stone walls. He is whispering something, possibly praying.

"What? I can't hear you," Cap says.

"I think I don't understand anything at all."

"But don't you want to? Don't you want to watch Ti-Christophe cut up a steer?"

"I think I don't want to," the boy says.

"Fine," Cap says, exasperated. "Go and recite the rosary with your mother. Me, I'm going into the cutting room. You'll have to go home by yourself."

"Wait! Wait!" the boy pleads, running after her. "I don't want to go home on my own. I want to watch P'tit Christophe. I do."

Cap turns, her hands on her hips. "If you embarrass me," she warns, "if you cry or throw up, I'll make you walk back through the village by yourself. And I'll get papa to tell your *maman* that you snitched on her." The boy's eyes widen with such shock and he looks so appalled that Cap promptly relents. "I won't tell Papa," she promises.

"I didn't snitch on *maman*. How did I snitch on her?"

"You said she's always sad."

The boy looks miserable. "I shouldn't have told you."

"I won't tell Papa," Cap repeats. "But you do have to help me carry the guts and brains and the other stuff that Ti-Christophe will give us."

The boy takes a deep trembling breath, but he nods.

"There'll be chunks of bone and cartilage and liver and intestines, and we have to scoop it all up with our hands," she warns.

171

She feels the buzz of a slightly sadistic frisson.

The boy nods.

"All right, then," she says. "Follow me."

The great wooden doors to the cutting room are kept closed, but light pours down through a skylight in the roof. Cap pulls the boy inside and closes the doors again. She pushes her way through hanging sides of beef, through dangling forequarters and hindquarters, as though pushing aside clothes in a closet. The oak floor is pale gold and bleached clean. "No blood," she points out. "That's all drained out in the courtyard before the sides are brought in. No slaughtering in here. I don't like to watch it either. Here, it's just boning and cutting. "

The boy almost smiles.

"Ti-Christophe," Cap calls out. "I brought the boy from the chateau. Papa gave him your old coveralls last night and he slept on your mattress."

Petit Christophe's left arm is extended high above his head. His left hand holds a clawed boning hook which is plunged deep into a fatty shoulder of steer. The hook steadies the forequarter while Petit Christophe traces a deep slow curve with the boning knife which he holds in his right hand. His concentration is intense. He may or may not be aware of his visitors. The long slim blade follows the curve of the breast bone and feels for the joint of the foreshank. There the blade pauses. Petit Christophe is so close to the carcass he might be caressing it with his cheek. He seems to be listening, to be thinking, to be sensing his way toward the soft spaces between the bones. He finds the seam, plunges deep with the blade, and suddenly the foreshank is hanging loose and he is cutting a path through the brisket toward the ribs. He pauses, sets down his knife, tugs on the boning hook and pulls the foreshank free. He holds it up like a trophy, admiring.

He is startled by the watching children.

"I didn't hear you come in," he says. "What do you think of this?" he asks Cap. "Great stewing meat. Great *osso bucco*."

"This is the boy from the chateau," Cap says. "His name is Gwynne Something Something Vanderbilt."

"My name is Petit Loup," the boy says emphatically. He is mesmerized. "How did you cut through the bone?"

"I never cut through the bone," Petit Christophe says. "My knife feels for the spaces between the bones. Here." Petit Christophe hoists the boy onto his shoulders. "Now I'm going to separate the chuck from the rib. Do you see this seam of fat?" Petit Christophe runs his forefinger along a line of suet. "Do you see that? Feel it. Press it."

"It's soft," the boy says. "Like a pillow."

"It's a laneway between the bones. I'm going to mark it with my boning knife, like this, see? Now I'm going to cut, following the line of the bone, and you are going to pull on my boning hook. Okay?"

"Okay."

"You see how the chuck is coming away? It's just falling away."

"It's like a peach," the boy says, amazed, excited. "When you bite and it comes away from the pit."

"Exactly," Petit Christophe says. "That's exactly what it's like."

"I want to be a butcher," the boy says fervently, "when I grow up."

In the outdoor bar at the boathouse restaurant, the waiters have stopped serving lunch. Cap is drinking her second glass of wine and has eaten a chicken salad. People have come and gone or moved inside. In spite of the afternoon sun, the temperature is dropping. Cap huddles into her jacket and pulls the white envelope from her pocket again and reads the note.

You are being watched and monitored. Be at the Loeb Boathouse in Central Park, in the outdoor bar, at 1 p.m.

It is now 2.30 p.m.

Cap signals her waiter. "I guess I've been stood up," she says ruefully. "Can you bring my check?"

A messenger boy on a bicycle swoops into the patio and brakes at Cap's table. "Are you Lilith Jardine?"

"Yes."

"Delivery for you." He hands her a brown manila envelope. It is addressed to Lilith Jardine, Loeb Boathouse Outdoor Bar. "You have to sign for it."

"I'm not going to sign for this," Cap says calmly. "You can take it back."

The messenger boy is flummoxed. "Keep it anyway," he says. "I don't give a damn." He swings one leg over his bicycle.

"I think I'll have another glass of wine," Cap tells the waiter when he brings her check.

"Bad news?" the waiter asks, nodding at the envelope.

"Don't know yet," she says. "But I guess I'm about to find out."

7.

Over breakfast in the gardener's cottage, Christophe le Jardinier tells his daughter: "*La comtesse* wants to see you."

"Is it because I took Ti-Loup to the butcher's?"

"I don't think so. How would she know?"

"From the servants. From gossip. And because Ti-Loup was missing for one night."

"Turns out she wasn't aware. She has breakfast brought to her room and doesn't see her son before lunch. She and I had a little chat when I delivered the vegetables this morning."

"She doesn't know he spent the night here?"

"I don't think so."

"So why does she want to see me?"

"Maybe she isn't used to being confronted on the church porch. In public."

"Have I made trouble for you, Papa?"

"Right from the start." The gardener laughs. "Trouble is what makes life interesting. And you are the kind of trouble I wouldn't want to live without."

"Papa, during the Occupation— "

"Ah. Shh." Cap's father places his fingers against her lips. She notes that he winces, that his body instinctively curves and slightly folds inwards, cradling itself against what memory? "Don't speak of it," he says. "Different kind of trouble. The kind we can do without."

Cap closes her own fingers around her father's wrist. "Please, Papa, tell me what happened. Otherwise I will have bad dreams. I do have bad dreams, but they will be worse—"

"There's nothing to tell. The Boche came, they made threats, I didn't give them what they wanted, they let me go. That's all."

"What did they want?"

"Betrayals. Names. I wouldn't give them any names."

"Did some people betray—?"

"Yes. Some people did. We shouldn't blame them. The Gestapo had very persuasive methods."

"What happened when there were betrayals?"

"You know what happened. You saw the husband of Marie-Claire. Someone betrayed him."

"The butcher?"

"Maybe. Possibly. But we really don't know. We have no proof."

"And someone betrayed you."

"Apparently."

"What happened to you, Papa?"

Her father spreads his arms, palms up. "I was lucky. As you can see. In fact it was *la comtesse* who saved me, although she doesn't understand that she did. She never knew enough to betray. She's smart enough not to know a lot of things."

"But what happened?"

"What happened is what happened. I survived. We don't need to speak of this, Capucine, because it's done with. It was before you were born. You must treat *la comtesse* with respect."

"Ti-Loup said she called me a wild thing."

"You *are* a wild thing, like your *maman*."

Cap can scarcely breathe. "I am like my *maman*?"

"You are very much like your *maman*. And I wouldn't want either of you different. You look like her too."

Cap waits. The silence stretches on and on. She knows her father will say nothing more on this subject but it is enough. It is like a jeweled relic that she will keep in a secret coffer in her mind. To break the silence, she says, "*La comtesse* told Ti-Loup that I don't wash my hair and I stink. She should apologize."

"You know, Cap, that is like asking a fish to apologize for swimming. *La comtesse* lives in a different world from the rest of us. But Ti-Loup came to apologize and that is a remarkable thing. Be gentle with that sad little boy. And don't forget that I owe my life to his mother. Treat her with respect. Treat everyone with respect."

"But she doesn't treat me with respect. And you told me I should never kowtow."

"To treat her with respect does not mean you have to kowtow."

Cap bathes and washes her hair. She wears shoes and her church dress. At the oak gates in the stone wall of the outer courtyard of the chateau she pauses, hesitates, and decides to climb the tree and drop over the wall instead, her habitual method of entry. She has done it this way since she was three years old, even though her father has a key to the great gates. Nested in the crook between the trunk and the branch that hangs over the wall, she can see the world. On one side of the wall is the chateau, the crushed-stone court, the wing of the grange above the underground cellars, the manicured chateau garden within its boxwood knots. On the other side is the gardener's cottage, the *potager*, the herb garden, the orchard, the woods with their secret cellar, the vineyards stretching away toward the river on one side and the church spire on the other, the gray cluster of stone houses surrounding the church, the terracotta roof tiles of the village of St Gilles within which is the establishment of Monsieur Monsard, the butcher. Cap can see everything. She could be God. She feels comfortable in trees, as though she were perhaps part bird, which maybe she is, given that her mother had flown from the nest the minute that Capucine was hatched.

In trees, there are so many footholds and handholds that walking a limb is as easy as walking down a lane. Easier. Cap steps lightly along her branch, sees below her the thick line of the stone wall, passes it, then eases down into saddle position, one leg on each side. She bends forward, flattens her body along the apple-wood limb, her arms forward and fully outstretched. There surely cannot be anything more beautiful than the smell of living wood and crushed leaves, the view of the grass below. She bracelets the narrowing end of the branch with her hands and swings herself out to dangle her body above the six-foot-drop. As her shoulders arc, her dress billows and catches on something. She feels the thud of the landing a split second after she hears the rip. She pitches forward and brakes her momentum with her hands.

There is a sharp jarring pain in her wrists. She has made this crossing so many times, more times than anyone could count, but always in farm-work coveralls, never in her best Sunday dress. Apparently this has made a difference. Her hands are blackened with earth and she wipes them carefully on the grass before she wipes them on her dress. She notes the tear, from hemline to waist. Fortunately, it is at the back of her skirt and she can mend it before next Sunday. It will be important, of course, always to face *la comtesse* on this visit, never to let her backside be seen.

She is late for her rendezvous now.

She runs across the gravel court, her feet crunching the stones with a soft percussive sound. She pulls on the bell-rope at the great carved doors of the chateau.

A pageboy dressed in red velvet pantaloons greets her. Cap knows the boy, who is a couple of years older than she. The boy's father raises goats and Cap has been to the farm with her father to buy goat's milk and cheese. "Hi, Pierre," she says.

"What shall I say is your business?" Pierre asks.

Capucine grins. She puts a hand over her mouth but cannot keep her laughter stoppered in. "Pierre," she says. "It's me."

"What shall I say is your business?"

"Why are you talking funny?"

"Because I'm not still a peasant like you. Why are you here?"

"*La comtesse* wants to see me," she says. "She sent for me. Remember, Pierre, I've seen your dick. I've watched you showing it to the goats."

"Follow me," Pierre says with icy dignity. "Wait here," he says, leaving her just inside the doors. "And by the way, you have mud all over the front of your dress. *La comtesse* will not be impressed." He walks away from her down a hallway which seems to stretch to the end of the world.

Capucine leans back against the doors. She is in a small room with a stone floor that apparently exists solely to separate the lofty entry space from the hallway, down which a crimson river of carpet flows into the interior horizon of the chateau. Cap wonders if she should take off her shoes and leave them on the stone floor before she steps onto—or into?—such rich softness. A stone arch separates the entry room from the hall. There is a vaulted ceiling far above her head, though otherwise the dimensions of the entry room are small. Against one wall, the one on Cap's left, is a narrow sideboard and above it a window. The flowered arc of a white potted orchid on the sideboard catches the light. When Cap looks to her right, she confronts herself in the most astonishing mirror she has ever seen. It stretches from floor to ceiling and is framed with elaborate gilt molding. The top of the mirror is a golden forest of vines twisted around a fleur-de-lys. She is so awed by the mirror itself that at first she is barely conscious of the reflected vision of her unkempt self, of the mud on her dress, of the leaves and twigs caught in her hair, or of the reflection of the sideboard and the orchid behind her. Then she is charmed and confused by the reflection of the window above the sideboard and the seemingly infinite view down the boxwood hedges in the courtyard.

She approaches the mirror as though she might walk into it, through it, directly into the paths between the hedges. She thinks of pressing her mouth against her own lips.

She does not hear Pierre behind her.

"*Mon Dieu!*" he says. "Your dress is torn."

Cap whirls, clutching her skirt, holding its tattered hind-wings together.

"I saw your underthings and your derrière," Pierre smirks.

"That must be a shock," Cap says, "given how well acquainted you are with the backsides of goats."

"*La comtesse* is coming," Pierre says coldly. "Follow me. You are to wait in the salon."

Cap enters a space so vast and so grand that it seems to her she may have crossed that river which separates this world from the next. In the hallway, there is a staircase. The banister is a coiled whorl of mahogany that Capucine wishes to stroke. There are intricately carved spindles that mount with the stairs. There are huge woven tapestries hung from high on the wall above.

"The salon is in there." Pierre points through the doorway to the right, at the foot of the stairs. In the salon, there is another carpet, darkly crimson and intricate in design, which glows against the stone floor like the red lamp above the altar in the church. There is a great carved wooden candlestick, taller than Cap. She caresses it, sliding her hand up and down its double-spiral whorl. She strokes the surface of a heavy sideboard with her fingertips. The dark wood feels like satin. She touches a porcelain vase, a marble bust. For a reason she does not understand, she feels as though she may begin to weep.

"So you like beautiful things?" *La comtesse*, in pale blue silk, stands on the staircase, her hand on the banister. "That is a Louis XIV," *la comtesse* says. "Walnut. Do you like it?"

Cap nods. She does not feel able to speak. Slowly the countess descends the stairs. "Well," she says, "is it possible, after all, to make a silk purse from a sow's ear?" She studies Cap carefully. "You really are a wild thing, aren't you? Completely wild." She is now on the third lowest stair but still far above Cap. "How old are you, child?"

"I think I am nearly seven. But my father says I am not quite six."

"Indeed? And how does it come about that you and your father disagree about your age?"

"Because we don't have a birth certificate. The priest from St Gatien in Tours brought me. Papa says I was three weeks old, but Marie-Claire says I was older. She says I was born in the last weeks of the Occupation," Cap explains.

"I see. I was here during the Occupation and you were not. I was married here in February 1945. You were not born then."

"I think I was, Madame la Comtesse, but the nuns were still hiding me in Tours. The priest didn't bring me here until later."

"I see." For a long time, the countess touches the crucifix that hangs from a gold chain around her neck. She touches it to her lips. She closes her eyes in prayer. Cap notes that her hands are trembling. After what seems to Cap an eternity, the countess says calmly, "Let us assume you are not quite seven. The same as my son. So you will make your first communion together next year. My son is a gift from the Blessed Virgin."

"Yes," Cap says. "I know. He told me."

"When I was not quite seven...," the countess says, but she trails into silence.

"Did you live here?" Cap asks. "With all these beautiful things?"

The countess raises her eyebrows. "Yes," she says, "I did. I spent my childhood here. Between here and Paris."

"Oh!" Cap is enchanted. "The chateau and Paris! You must have been so happy!" Such a childhood seems to her as seductively mythical as the rose courtyards of troubadours and their fair ladies. When he is working in the vineyards, her father sings songs about that golden time. He sings in some strange kind of French— *Old French,* he says—that Cap does not understand. He has told her the tales of Tristan and Iseult, of Lancelot and Guinevere, of lovers who will die of their love and for their love. *That time is not past,* he has told her.

Do you mean you and maman? she asked.

All the great love stories end in loss, he said. *They are all as much about sorrow as they are about love.*

"Why do you think my childhood was happy?" the countess asks.

"Because of all these beautiful things. Because you love them. But Papa says love is always about sorrow and loss, and Petit Loup says you are always sad. Why are you sad?"

La comtesse is too stunned to speak. Her hand tightens on the banister. She leans against it, then slowly, very slowly, subsides until she is sitting on one of the stairs, her silk skirt sighing around her and settling like a slowly deflating balloon.

"Ti-Loup thinks it is his fault," Cap explains.

La comtesse stares at her blankly. "Who?"

"Ti-Loup. Your son. He thinks it is his fault that you are sad."

"My son is my sole source of happiness," *la comtesse* contradicts sharply. Then she corrects herself: "My son and my devotion to God. These are the sources of contentment. My son is a gift from the Virgin Mary. You may refer to him as Monsieur le Vicomte Gwynne Patrice de la Vallière Vanderbilt."

"*Madame la Comtesse,*" Cap says politely, "if Ti-Loup is your happiness, why do you want to make him so unhappy? You should

182

not make him wear a dress."

La comtesse, astonished, affronted, energized, stands and slaps Cap on the face. She is abruptly appalled by her own act. "*Je m'excuse,*" she says. "I do not strike servants."

Cap presses one hand to the sting on her cheek.

La comtesse is trembling. "I have never struck a servant before," she says, slowly subsiding again to sit on a stair.

"I am not your servant, *Madame la Comtesse.*"

During several long seconds of silence, the countess and the child do not break eye contact.

La comtesse draws several deep slow breaths. "I am not someone who strikes servants," she says. She fiddles with the silk ribbons on her cuffs and her fingers begin to braid them absently. "It is also beneath me to answer the questions of servants."

"I apologize, *Madame la Comtesse.* My father says I must treat you with respect. We just wish, my papa and me, we wish he wasn't such a sad little boy."

The eyes of the countess widen with shock. "I would give my life for him," she says passionately. She takes short gasping breaths. She appears to be having trouble speaking. "I protect him from all possible harm. His father is trying to take him away from me. He is afraid of his father. I would die if anything—"

"Madame!" Cap says in alarm. "Madame, I will bring my papa."

"No," the countess says. "Wait." She breathes slowly. "I have taken a vow," she explains. "My son is dressed to give thanks to the Virgin until his First Communion. Like Louis XIV. Do you understand? Do you know history?"

"Not very much history, *Madame la Comtesse.*"

"The queen, the mother of Louis XIV, had four stillborn children before her son Louis was born. For sixteen years after her marriage to Louis XIII, she was childless and mocked by the court.

When Louis XIV was born, he was called *Louis le Dieu-donné*, the God-given child, not only by his mother but by all the princes and courtiers of the realm, and he was promised to God. He wore a dress until his first communion. And then he became the Sun King. My son, *le vicomte,* will also have a great destiny if I fulfill my vow."

"Now I understand why you are so sad, *Madame la Comtesse.* Did you also have stillborn children?"

"No, I did not." Again *la comtesse* seems shocked and angry. "You are extremely impertinent, child. You have no idea of your station."

"I am sorry, *Madame la Comtesse.* I don't know what my station is."

"Indeed you do not. I will have to speak to your father."

"My father says he owes you his life."

"*Il a dit quoi?!*" demands the countess, astonished.

Impulsively, Cap hugs the countess. "Thank you, thank you, Madame."

The countess stiffens and turns away. She scrunches her eyes tightly shut, and when she opens them she stares fixedly beyond the window, down the boxwood lanes, into the orchard. "Your father is a good man," she says at last. "We were children together. He danced at my wedding. I remember that. He was present with your little brother."

"*Madame la Comtesse*, my brother is much older than I am."

"At my wedding, he was a little boy. I waited a long time to marry. I was considered... *une vieille fille*, an old maid, you understand?" The countess pauses, dazed, her eyes fixed on air as though her words are floating there and she is reading them back, unable to believe she has spoken them. "These questions... You have no understanding of your station, child. Absolutely none." *La comtesse* rubs her hands together as though scrubbing off mud.

"I am sorry, *Madame la Comtesse*. I did not mean to upset you." Impulsively, instinctively, Cap leans forward and kisses the countess on the cheek, three times, left, right, left, in the formal French manner. "My father says we should question everything."

La comtesse turns her head aside, much preoccupied with the lace cuff and the ribbons on her sleeve. After some time, she says, "Your father, yes. He is an unusual man, your father. Sit here." She pats the space beside her on the stair.

"*Le vicomte* is my only child. I made a vow on my wedding night and a vow must be fulfilled. And now," *la comtesse* presses one hand over her heart, "you have so disturbed me that I must meditate and pray. You will join me."

Her wrist taken in a vice-like grip, Cap is led to one corner of the great salon. Two *prie-dieux*, twins, in lustrous oiled walnut, intricately carved, stand side by side. There are red velvet cushions on the kneelers. On each desktop rests an illuminated Book of Hours and a rosary. *La comtesse* kneels at the prie-dieu on the left and passes the rosary through her fingers, murmuring softly, her lips forming almost silent words. Her eyes are closed. She is in an intense and private state. *Elle est ailleurs*, Cap marvels. *La comtesse* is not here, she is somewhere else. Cap is amazed, fascinated, aware that if she were to touch the countess at this moment, lightning might strike.

Rosaries have never been part of life in the gardener's cottage. Cap has never been quite sure of the rules. Pass the beads through one's fingers, yes, that is obvious, but then what? Count them? Recite a psalm for each bead? Say a Hail Mary or a Paternoster for each bead? The rosary on the *prie-dieu* where she herself kneels is made of cobalt blue beads strung on a silver chain. Cap moves the beads through her fingers, delighted by the rich color, the smooth texture. Every eleventh bead is a small silver ball. She notes that the rosary of the countess seems to be made of pearls with a cloudy and pale green bead between the decades. She notes that the countess pauses at each bead and murmurs a prayer. Cap summons an image for each of her own intensely blue beads as they pass between her fingers.

First bead: for her father. She imagines his face candling eggs, gazing at the baby brought by the priest, watering the new vines, winding the new runners along the wires.

Second bead: for Petit Christophe. She sees him training the runner beans, mulching tomatoes, plowing-in cover crops with a hoe, moving his boning knife through the channels between the bones, wiping blood off his hands, kissing Chantal.

Third bead: for her mother. Where is she? What happened to her? Did she look like the Virgin Mary? Did she hold her baby, kiss her, make promises, before surrendering her to the nuns? Yes. Suddenly Cap is certain of this. The blue beads pass through her fingers like a string of days, all of them sunlit, all of them smelling of the fragrant skin of her mother. She feels a most wondrous calm, a benediction, settling on her like perfume, like ashes of roses, like peace. She can feel tears coursing down her cheeks.

"That is the power of praying the rosary," *la comtesse* says. "I consider this a sign from the Virgin. She has placed the mark of her blessing on your forehead."

"The rosaries are very beautiful," Cap says.

"Your beads are of lapis lazuli. Mine are pearls with jade for the Our Fathers."

Cap nods solemnly.

"So, child, I understand you want an apology from me?"

Cap thinks of saying: I wanted you to know what it feels like to be insulted. But instead she lowers her eyes and says: "No, Madame la Comtesse. I'm the one who was disrespectful. I ask for your pardon."

La comtesse rests a hand on Cap's shoulder. "I will speak to your father," she says. "Your father and I have always been frank with each other. I would be willing to take you into service. You are intelligent, you have good taste, you could be trained."

Cap says nothing.

"This idea does not please you?" *la comtesse* demands.

"I like to be with my father," Cap says. "I like to work with him."

"You would see and touch beautiful things every day," *la comtesse* entices. "You would be my personal maid."

Seconds pass.

"I always wanted a daughter," the countess sighs. "It was a daughter I prayed for because fathers take sons for themselves. My own father ignored me. I did not exist for him. I only saw him three times because my mother was his mistress, not his wife. I am descended from a long line of mistresses, and so I made a vow. If I could just be a wife and not a mistress, if I could have a child instead of a chateau...

"And so I must keep my vow, although it was a daughter I prayed for, a girl who would not be illegitimate like me. But one must accept what God gives. His ways are beyond understanding. One accepts what He gives, even when his ways seem most... seem least... seem intended to mock us."

8.

The day following their First Communion, the day le Petit Loup is released from his blue dress, is the day Cap becomes someone else and pulls a different dress entirely over her own head and shoulders. Tricked out in black silk and white lace, she can feel the fabric like dragonfly wings against her skin. There are many small round black buttons, hard as seed-pods, to be fastened one by one between neckline and waist. The lace cuffs must be attended to, the lace collar adjusted, the apron tied.

La comtesse stands behind Cap, her hands on the girl's shoulders. Both woman and child are reflected in the baroque mirror, one of many in the chateau, all the mirrors at least seven feet tall, some of them ten feet, some of them twelve, all of them stretching like pools of light toward a domed or a vaulted ceiling, all of them framed in convoluted moldings of gold. The mirrors telegraph spaces to one another, they commune in a semaphore of arcades, they beckon into rooms that are not there.

There is only one small mirror in the gardener's cottage and Cap has to stand on tiptoe to see into it, not that she has ever felt a need to look at herself. People who live with vast mirrors, she realizes, know there are invisible worlds. They understand that they don't know themselves.

La comtesse lifts the mass of Cap's nut-brown hair from her shoulders and twists it into a knot which she ties with a black velvet ribbon. "What do you think?" she asks.

"I don't know," Cap says. "I don't know who that girl is." An entire corridor of her new selves stretches toward infinity, curving slightly toward the right then bouncing back from the mirror on the opposite wall of the boudoir. Cap feels dizzy. "May I sit down?"

"Here," *la comtesse* says. "At my dressing table." Capucine sinks into a velvet-upholstered chair with gilded arms and legs. "Cabriole chair," *la comtesse* instructs, checking off an article in a new catechism. "You must learn these things. The chair legs, do you see how they curve out at the knee? The slim ankles? The dainty feet of a lion cub? There are many new rules you must master."

Cap is seated in front of a two-tiered ornate table with multiple drawers. Attached to the table is a hinged mirror which *la comtesse* tilts toward her personal maid. "My dressing table is Louis XV. You see the difference from the Louis XIV pieces in the salon? Those are baroque. This is rococo. This piece was done by an *ebeniste* whom one of my ancestors knew personally. He was, I believe, her lover. It was the fashionable thing in the eighteenth century, to have fine furniture and a lover."

Cap thinks of asking: *Have you ever had a lover, Madame la Comtesse?* and as though she has heard Cap's thoughts, la comtesse says: "I have never wanted a lover, but I have always wanted fine furniture and fine fabrics and art. And I wanted to be married and have my own child who would be the legitimate heir of his father's property as well as mine."

Capucine runs her fingertips across the satiny and visually intricate surface of the dressing table, a jungle of acanthus leaves and vines, light and dark, some of them lustrous, some of them as unreflecting as midnight. "That is marquetry work," *la comtesse* explains. "Tortoiseshell, ivory, beech, exotic timbers, all inlaid in layers to give us so many colors, so many sensations of one thing turning into another by pure enchantment. The *ebenistes* were magicians."

Now, via the tilted dresser mirror, Capucine can see two branching corridors of herself, of her new unrecognizable self—or of the unknown girl in the mirrors—one fork curling toward the gardener's cottage, the other coiling into a padded silk-covered apricot wall-panel which self-multiplies infinitely and spirals back into one of the dressing-table drawers. *La comtesse* also seems transfixed by this split image. "We must call you Melusine," she says, animated. "Yes. It is perfect. That will be your name."

"Melusine." Cap says it aloud to the multiplicity of images she faces. Why not? She does not know the girls in the mirrors. She does not know their names. Melusine, the ravishingly beautiful woman of French folktales who was secretly a mermaid one night a week, why not? Everyone knows that story. Cap can feel the black silk of her dress whispering against her thighs as lightly as fish passing each other underwater. She fingers her lace collar and cuffs. She touches the tasseled handle of a small drawer in the dressing table, the drawer which appears to be the vanishing point of the serpentine coil of the Melusines.

"Ahh," la comtesse says. "I think I realized from the moment you dared to confront me in the porch of the church that you had unusual powers, *ma petite* Melusine. That is one of the secret drawers that you are touching, and here is the secret key." La comtesse trails her fingers below the neckline of her own gown and pulls up a fine gold chain, very long, at the end of which is a small golden key. She inserts the key into the lock on the drawer. "What do you see?" she asks.

The drawer is very small, only four inches wide, and when Cap opens it, only five inches deep. "I see a very small drawer. It is empty."

"But there is a drawer behind the drawer," la comtesse says. "Pull the drawer out entirely and set it on my dressing table. Now, make your hand small and reach in and press against the back of that space. Tell me what you find."

"The back has popped open like a trapdoor."

"Feel behind it. Whatever you find, pull it out."

"It is a silk sac of gold thread," Cap says, displaying it.

"It contains a lock of *le petit vicomte's* hair. His first haircut, when he was one year old. I did not wish his hair to be cut at all, but his father insisted. Did you know that during the years of the plague, the first-cut lock of a boy-child's hair could stave off death in that family? It could cure the sickness of the boy-child's mother."

"Are there other secret drawers?" Cap asks.

"Many. There are many secret drawers and hidden panels in my boudoir and throughout the chateau. There are underground tunnels whose maps and exits have been lost. Places to keep secrets are essential. In my family history, secrecy was the essence of survival. I will show you." La comtesse removes a painting from one of the padded and silk-paneled segments of the wall. She props the painting against one of the sofas. The silk panel is embroidered with ravishing mermaids who have spangled tails of cobalt sequins and gold thread and seed pearls. *La comtesse* presses the navel of the central sea-nymph, the Melusine, and one side of the panel moves soundlessly away from its frame. "A lover could be hidden here," *la comtesse* explains. "Or the king could be hidden when an inconvenient visitor arrived. A reputation or a life could be saved." Cap thinks of asking: Why are you showing me these secrets? "There is even, it is said, a mysterious room in the cellars with a tunnel to an exit in the forest. I don't know where it is. Perhaps it's nothing more than a rumor, but I've always believed it could be true. I've heard it said that your father

191

knows something."

"My father knows everything there is to know," Cap says, "about grapes and vintages and wine. He says there's no secret to making good wine. The vines must suffer."

"Hmm," la comtesse says. "And he has a daughter as cleverly discreet as her father. He has superintended some very fine vintages for me. And now there are many things you must learn about your new duties. First, my jewelry. You will be responsible for the care and cleaning and for making ready the pieces that I choose to wear for any particular occasion. Sometimes, perhaps, if I am buying jewelry or art or antique furniture, I may require you to come to Paris with me. Ah, I see the thought of Paris excites you."

"Yes, *Madame la Comtesse*. It does."

"Good. That pleases me. And now my gowns. Can you tell the difference between silk and cashmere and fine linen?"

"I'm not sure, Madame. I think I know silk."

"I will teach you. And then the furniture. You must learn to distinguish baroque from régence from rococo. You must know which must be oiled and which must never be oiled."

"Yes, Madame."

"You must recognize Empire, you must distinguish between Restoration and Louis Philippe. I do not own very much from these periods. I prefer the seventeenth and eighteenth centuries. Those were more civilized times."

"Before the Occupation, Madame?"

"*Mon Dieu!*" the countess says, dumbfounded. "Melusine, *mon Dieu!* What else don't you know?"

"Papa says that the Occupation proved we are only one hair's breadth removed from barbarians."

"Indeed," the countess says. She takes fast shallow breaths as she paces the room. She seems highly agitated. "Indeed. Is that so? Is that what your father believes?"

192

"Yes, *Madame la Comtesse*. But since you saved his life he knows you are not numbered among the barbarians."

The countess is too stunned to speak. She regards her maid as though something truly strange, far stranger than a mermaid, is in her boudoir.

"Your father is a believer, yes? He goes to Mass? He takes the sacrament."

"Yes, *Madame la Comtesse*. You know that. You have seen him at Mass."

"We must pray," *la comtesse* says, agitated. "We must beseech the Virgin for peace." She places one hand over her heart. Cap notes the tremor in the countess's hand. She is aware that the countess is having considerable difficulty with her breathing.

"*Madame la Comtesse*," she says, alarmed. "Should I call the doctor?"

"No. Doctors cannot help us in these situations. We must pray," *la comtesse* says. "We must beseech the Virgin for inner calm."

At the *prie-dieux* in the salon, Cap and *la comtesse* kneel side by side. Cap lets the smooth cobalt beads of the rosary slide between her fingers.

"You must meditate on the face of the Virgin," la comtesse says. "Meditate on her face." She points to a painting. "That is by Philippe de Champaigne, late seventeenth century, *La vierge Marie donnant la couronne et le sceptre à Louis XIV.* You can see why I acquired it. The Virgin is giving the crown and the sceptre to the boy king, and there is his younger brother, the Duc d'Orléans, at his side."

"The Duc d'Orléans looks like Ti-Loup. I mean Ti-Loup before his First Communion."

"The Duc d'Orléans was as yet unbreeched at the time of the painting. It was done in 1643."

"He is wearing a blue dress."

"Look upon the virgin's face, Melusine. Direct your attention there. Meditate upon it. It is the face of all mothers who feel anxiety for their sons."

Cap studies the painting. The Virgin, whose chubby and energetic child seems barely contained on his mother's slippery silk robe, looks placid, half smiling, not too interesting. In fact, the child Jesus is clearly focused on grabbing the coronet that his mother is offering the five-year-old king. Within a minute, two at most, Jesus will slide from his mother's lap, clutch at the crown, and catapult himself into the Sun King who will in turn be knocked like a domino into the frail and angelic body of his three-year-old brother, the Duc d'Orléans, who looks so much like Ti-Loup, sweet and bewildered and sad.

The boy king reminds Cap of Pierre, the chateau footman, in his ridiculous velvet pantaloons. Both are bad actors, dressed up, on stage, and unconvincing.

What rivets Cap is the woman in black silk, white lace collar, white cuffs, who stands between the two children. Surely this is the queen, their mother, the woman who has endured four stillbirths and sixteen years of public humiliation at court before the birth of Louis XIV. Now *there* is an interesting face, sad and beautiful. In the painting, she has no status, this woman. She could have been the nursery maid. She could have been a housemaid in the clearly sumptuous chateau of the Virgin.

Cap meditates upon this face.

One day she will ask her father if the nuns told him anything, anything at all. She will ask if her father made inquiries. She will ask if they can visit the convent and talk to the nuns.

The face of the woman in the painting is the face of a woman who knows she will be required to surrender her children to forces beyond her control. In the painting, everyone is watching the wriggling Child Jesus, not the Virgin, but then quite suddenly it is apparent to Cap that the woman in black, the mother queen, has turned slightly and that the woman's sorrowful eyes are meeting Cap's. Capucine—or Melusine? or the child who must have been given by her own mother a name unknown?—feels a high-voltage infusion of energy, as though the sun itself has touched her and filled her with light.

"Did you meditate on the face in the painting, Melusine?"

"Yes, *Madame la Comtesse.*"

"Do you feel at peace now?"

"Yes, madame."

"That is the Virgin's gift," *la comtesse* says. "That is ever her gift. And now we must continue with your duties."

She begins to take inlaid boxes from drawers and armoires. She begins to spread necklaces on the satin bedspread, a spill of diamonds, pearls, rubies, emeralds. "We all had to protect our treasures as best we could," she says. "Hiding places are the secret of survival. But Melusine, Melusine, you must be educated. We must see to it. When was the Sun King's reign?"

"I don't know, Madame la Comtesse."

"Seventeenth century. You must remember that. And the eighteenth century belongs to Louis XV and to the unfortunate Louis XVI, but I do not collect anything from after the Revolution. Now. When was the reign of Louis XIV?"

"Seventeenth century, Madame."

La comtesse sighs with relief. "So we have a starting point. We have a base. But there must be history lessons. Furniture, jewelry, fabrics. And then the paintings and sculptures. If a visitor from Paris should ask: *Is that an Antoine Watteau or a Francois Boucher? Is this Poussin?* you should be able to answer correctly, you understand? But also demurely. One does not want a personal maid to be a Georges Sand, but one does not want her to be ignorant either. I will attend to your education on these matters."

9.

In the outdoor bar at the boathouse restaurant in Central Park, Cap tucks the requisite number of twenty dollar bills into the folder the waiter has brought, but she finds herself doodling on an envelope—manila-sized, delivered by a messenger boy on a bicycle, not yet opened—with the monogrammed ballpoint pen. She finds she has drawn a mermaid. She draws a line, the surface of the ocean, and the mermaid is below this line. She draws a shoreline of sheer rock which rises steeply and abruptly from the water, hostile as a granite cliff or the wall of a fortress. Beneath the waterline, the rock wall opens into a cave which is lit by some kind of oceanic phosphorescence and seems to beckon, seems to imply interior depth, seems to indicate a pathway to a safe interior cocoon.

"Hey, wow, that's not bad," the waiter says, returning for the check. "How do you get that effect in black and white? Are you an artist?"

"Just a doodler. Okay if I sit here until I finish this glass of wine?"

"You want to keep shivering? Feel free." He taps the manila envelope. "Bad news or not?"

"I still don't know," Cap says. "Hence the wine."

"Procrastinating, huh? That means you're expecting bad news. Should I bring a martini?"

"No. No. God, no. I've definitely had enough."

"Well, good luck."

In fact, Cap is not really expecting bad news, at least not out of the normal range of the kind of bad news she must deal with all the time, collecting and relaying evidence of the darkest side of human behavior. For this kind of news she has had to develop a kind of working detachment, not always easy to maintain. However, she is not expecting *personal* bad news, and so she is unable to account for the fog of anxiety that now seems to have settled on her table. She cannot really understand her extreme reluctance to open the envelope. She tries to analyze her reaction.

The packet, like the threatening summons under her hotel door, is either from one of the two art-buying clients who are currently in New York, or from persons unknown, the usual persons unknown, generic thugs from the worldwide Ministry of Intimidation. This is hardly a new experience, though the method of delivery is new, and intimidation on American soil is without precedent. Is this why Cap feels so apprehensive?

Perhaps the package itself is leaking malevolence.

This would mean that it contains photographs of the horrendous aftermath of beatings and torture. Such photographs are always profoundly disturbing, but they are also valuable evidence, each image being one small goal scored, one cog in the wheel that turns global attention to a dark corner, one inch toward generating action. Each photograph smuggled across a border is a moment of triumph. Perhaps this entire trip was planned by a mole in the entourage of the African dictator or the Chinese defector and this was his carefully planned method of getting the evidence to Cap. If so, she has been spared both further travel and danger.

And yet the note under her hotel door and the method of delivery of the envelope suggest menace and the crux of her anxiety is suddenly apparent to her. She is terrified that the desecrated faces and bodies will be those of people she knows, other field workers who gather what evidence they can from the killing fields. The point will be threat and intimidation and one of the primary survival rules of field workers is to shield themselves from paralyzing fear.

Then again, the packet may merely contain something that will restrict Cap's ability to cross borders or will discredit the evidence she collects. That is another common tactic. Cap cannot think of anything that could be used for blackmail but that means nothing. She knows of other field workers whose usefulness has been snuffed out that way.

A fog of dread envelops her table like a comic-book cloud, but she does open the envelope and extracts a sheaf of stiff papers, all standard letter size, all heavy stock of the kind used to photocopy old snapshots. The top sheet induces a shock of violation so intense that Cap folds herself forward over the image until her forehead comes to rest on the table. She forces herself to count to ten, to inhale slowly, to exhale, before she looks at the image again. It is a photocopy of a portrait taken long ago by an old box-camera, in sepia tones, but certain details on the original photograph have been hand-tinted. The image is of a child, an androgynous child with long pale curls, wearing a shift that has been painted pale blue. The vertical punctuation point of the blue shift is the only splash of color in a field of beige and dark shadow. The original photograph was taken in a studio in front of a sepia-painted backdrop of the Chateau de Boissy. Cap stares at the small sad frightened face of Ti-Loup and instinctively strokes his cheek with her index finger.

"Are you okay?" the waiter asks.

"What?"

"Should I bring that martini?"

Cap frowns slightly, trying to translate.

"Is that you?" the waiter asks. "You as a child?"

"Oh... no. It's, uh, he was a childhood friend."

"That's a boy?"

"A boy, yes. He was shipped to Vietnam in '69 and never came back."

"Oh shit. I'm sorry. Didn't mean to pry. Just checking that you are okay."

"Kind of you. Thanks. I'm fine."

Cap moves the image of the little boy in the blue dress to the back of the sheaf and uncovers a photocopy of another black-and-white photograph. She is stunned. The photograph shows the forequarter of a steer punctured by a huge steel hook that is suspended from a ceiling track. Light from a high window falls on the hook, making it flash like a sun. There are two figures in the photograph, in profile and mostly in shadow, but the flash of light from the steel hook illuminates their faces. One face is that of Petit Christophe, the other the face of Ti-Loup who holds a boning knife in his right hand. Petit Christophe is demonstrating with his index finger the line that the boning knife should follow.

Cap is stunned. Who could possibly have taken this photograph? Who had preserved it? Who had photocopied it? And how could it possibly have reached Cap in a manila envelope in Central Park? She feels dizzy. She feels caught in a wind tunnel of time and grasps the bistro table with both hands to keep herself anchored to the present. The last thing she feels is the imprint of the aluminum mesh of the table against her cheek.

There are voices.

"We should call 911."

"No," another voice says. "She's just drunk. Throw some iced water on her face."

"That would ruin the photographs."

"I don't think photographs are top priority at the moment."

199

"This has something to do with the photographs. I could tell she was expecting bad news."

Cap pushes herself upright in her chair. "I'm fine," she says groggily. "Too much to drink and bad news. Sorry about this." She stuffs the photographs back into the envelope. She stands and sways. "I'm fine," she says. "Truly. Terribly sorry to have caused a fuss."

"You're not in great shape," the waiter says. "Can I call you a cab?"

"No. Thanks. A walk in the cold air is what I need."

She manages, though she seems to have boots of lead on her feet. People are watching and this makes it possible to concentrate on lifting one heavy foot after the other and placing it on the ground without falling. She waves lightly and dismissively. Manila envelope clutched to her chest, she leaves the outdoor bar and heads back into the Ramble. In the late fall afternoon, the light is fading. She knows it is not wise to stay long, but there is something about the bench at the lakeshore, something about the rocks and the ducks, something that promises sanctuary.

There will always be safe houses. There will always be tiny islands of repose.

They will never be permanently safe.

On the bench in the Ramble, she reaches into the envelope again and looks at the third sheet. It is also a photocopy of a black-and-white snapshot and shows two children in white smocks in front of an altar. A crucifix rises behind and between them like a sword with a jeweled hilt. It is a photograph of a First Communion. The children, a boy and a girl, Ti-Loup and Cap, are holding hands. Cap brushes her eyes and cheeks with the sleeve of her jacket. She herself has a wallet-size version of this very photograph in her purse but she is certain that the only other place in America where a copy might possibly exist would be in a secret drawer in an antique desk in the private possession of the deceased Countess of the Chateau de Boissy. That desk had been shipped to Fifth Avenue in 1968 when the countess moved back to New York. It had probably been sold off as the countess became more desperate for money. Someone must have found the secret drawers.

Of course, Ti-Loup once kept a wallet-size copy with him at all times, but who knew where that copy might be now?

Cap is not equal to seeing anything more at the moment. She leaves the Ramble, crosses the East Drive and follows a trail to Conservatory Water where she sits on a bench to watch the miniature sailboats buzzing across the surface, responding to radio remotes in the hands of grandfathers and children. One of the miniature sailboats is a replica of the *Santa Maria*. It zips toward Cap and then pauses, facing her, vibrating like a humming bird, before swooping away in a graceful arc. Could Columbus possibly have imagined such a future for the ship in which he reached the New World?

10.

Father John Gabriel is a young English Jesuit, delicate as a Da Vinci drawing, who is fluent in French. He arrives at the chateau in 1953 and is given his own suite of three rooms by the countess. She summons him to the great salon for orientation.

"This is my son, *le vicomte*," she explains.

"What a beautiful child!" The fervent gaze of Father John Gabriel disconcerts the countess and silences her for several seconds. Her son's hand is held firmly in her own. She pauses in the act of extending the boy's hand toward that of the priest so that the locked hands of mother and son hover uncertainly like mating doves, fluttering slightly, neither moving forward nor back. Then the hands lower themselves, curving back into the silken nesting place of the countess's voluminous skirt.

"You will be his private tutor for six hours every day," the countess instructs. "One of your rooms is intended to be the classroom, which I have had well supplied with books and maps. I have also arranged that any book you desire to add to the collection, any book which will be of profit to my son's education, will be swiftly supplied. My son must learn Greek and Latin, English Language and Literature—because his father is English-speaking—French History, in particular the accounts of how French support made the American Revolution possible—because his father, you see, is American, but I find that Americans are shockingly ill-informed on their debt to France. Also French Literature, French Art and Architecture. And of course Aquinas and Catholic theology. You come well recommended."

"If I might inquire, *Madame la Comtesse*," Father John Gabriel says, "will there be boys from other great estates in the Loire valley in the classroom?"

"Definitely not," the countess responds. "My son will be your sole responsibility and preoccupation."

"If I may be so bold," Father John Gabriel says, "it is my experience that my students learn so much more and so much more quickly if there is at least one other student—and preferably more than one—in the class. I would not describe this as simple or crude competitiveness. Rather I've become aware that a dynamic force operates in the give and take of different opinions and calls forth the best in each student. If you wish your son to excel—and clearly that is your intention, *Madame la Comtesse*—if you wish to sharpen his mind to the highest degree, then may I recommend that you add at least one more student to my class?"

"Indeed?" the countess says icily. "I will consider your recommendation. You may retire to your rooms."

"Father John Gabriel," the countess says, "I have given your suggestion considerable thought and I acknowledge the strength of your argument. You will have two students."

"That is most welcome news, *Madame la Comtesse*."

"Your second student will be the daughter of my gardener. Her name is Melusine and I consider myself responsible for her education. She is the same age as my son."

"A girl, Madame?" Father John Gabriel seems taken aback, even stunned. "I am not sure, *Madame la Comtesse*... I have no experience with teaching female students."

"Melusine!" the countess calls. "*Mon fils, le vicomte*! You may come to the salon now."

"I am not sure, *Madame la Comtesse*," Father John Gabriel says, "that a female student will have the desired effect of which I spoke. Indeed, it is possible that, ah, an undesirable, an unforeseen element—"

"It is my personal intuition," the countess explains as the children enter the salon, "that Melusine is as intelligent as my son and has a more—how shall I put it?—a more animated, a more audacious personality. I think she has a beneficial effect on my son who is inclined to timidity. They are both eight years old."

"*Madame la Comtesse*," Cap says, "I think I am nine."

The countess frowns momentarily, then smiles, then rests her fingers gently on Capucine's lips. "As you see, Father John Gabriel, Melusine has an independent mind. She will be a challenge to which I am sure you will be equal. And the children, as you see, are inseparable. I expect you to prepare both for *le bac* and for eventual admission to the Sorbonne."

Father John Gabriel bows. "I hope I will not disappoint you, *Madame la Comtesse*."

Capucine and le Petit Loup roll their eyes at each other.

"What is the Sorbonne?" Cap wants to know.

Father John Gabriel raises his eyebrows. "We have a long way to go, *Madame la Comtesse*," he says.

"We should begin, I think," Father John Gabriel says in the classroom, "with a pivotal moment in the history of French-English relations, that is with the meeting of the English and French kings—Henry VIII and François I—at the Field of the Cloth of Gold in June 1520."

Ti-Loup says: "*Maman* has a woodcut of the Field of the Cloth of Gold."

"Many copies exist. In due course," Father John Gabriel says,

"I hope we will visit the site of that historic 1520 encounter and the even more hallowed site of a much earlier engagement, the Battle of Agincourt in 1415, a glorious victory."

"Whose glorious victory?" Ti-Loup asks.

"Ah." There is a careful and diplomatic pause. "A glorious victory for Shakespeare," the Jesuit says. "No battle in history has a more lasting or triumphant monument than the king's speech in *Henry V*. I hope *la comtesse* will allow field trips to these iconic spaces."

Cap and Ti-Loup exchange a quick look, shining-eyed.

"Now let us study this famous painting of *The Field of the Cloth of Gold*." Father John Gabriel displays a book with a wing span that covers his desk. There are colored plates that stretch across the ravine between the two pages. "This reproduction, I regret to say, is not a photographic reprint of the original, but is merely a copy of a copy. Art historians have not been able to determine who painted the original, but it has been ascribed to Hans Holbein. He was not present at the meeting of the two kings in 1520 but he had access to detailed eye-witness accounts. The painting is part of the Royal Collection at Hampton Court Palace in London. Study this print closely and tell me what you can see."

"A lake," Cap says, pointing to the upper left corner of the painting.

"Ocean?" suggests Petit Loup.

"Correct," Father John Gabriel says. "*Monsieur le Vicomte*, you should not be so tentative. Rest assured, your intelligence is superior." Out of sight of Father John Gabriel's eyes, Cap pokes out her tongue, sticks her thumbs into her ears and waggles her fingers. She mouths the words *Monsieur le Supérieur, ooh la la!* Petit Loup folds his hands together in mock prayer and rolls his eyes heavenward. "That's the English Channel, in fact," explains Father John Gabriel. "The encounter took place on French soil near Calais. Can you see Henry VIII?" The children pore over the image. "I will give you a hint. He is not wearing a crown. He is riding a white horse and his cloak is richly embroidered in gold. The horse's bridle and saddle cloth are also gold."

"Here he is!" Suddenly excited, both children identify the royal figure.

"He's fat," Cap says.

"I note that your mode of perception veers toward the literal and material, mademoiselle, rather than the metaphorical or the metaphysical. But yes, Henry VIII was already, shall we say, substantial in figure in 1520 and he became considerably more substantial. Late in life, no horse could be found to support the king and his armor. There was a winch to lift his majesty, in full battle dress, onto his mount, but no winch could prevent that mount from collapsing. You understand that at the time of the Field of the Cloth of Gold the king was still the Defender of the Faith and not the traitor to the Pope and to Holy Mother Church that he later became."

"When did he become a traitor to Holy Mother Church?" Petit Loup asks.

"In 1535."

"Why?" Cap wants to know.

"Because of his lust for the witch Anne Boleyn," the priest replies. "And because of his lust for the riches of Holy Mother Church. His empty treasury was the most direct cause of the Sack of the Monasteries in England. The king had already defied the pope by his marriage to Boleyn in 1533, but the formal schism with Rome did not take place until two years later. Curiously enough, by the way, both the mother and the sister of Anne Boleyn were present at the Field of the Cloth of Gold, but the future queen herself was not there. At the time, both her mother and her sister were mistresses of the king."

Capucine's eyes widen with fascination and with the frisson of what seems like deliciously forbidden information. "Should you be telling us this?" she asks.

"I beg your pardon, Mademoiselle Melusine?"

"Does my mother know?" asks Petit Loup.

"Does she know about the debaucheries of Henry VIII? "

The children regard him with silent awe, uncertain of how to respond.

"Of course she knows. Everyone knows about his six wives and his countless mistresses and every Catholic knows what harm he did to the church. *Madame la Comtesse* has entrusted me with giving you a thorough education and I take that task very seriously. This is French history. It is also English history. It is also the history of the church and of faith itself. So, what else do you notice in the painting. Can you see the royal tents and pavilions made of gold?"

Yes. These are easily identified. Here, and here, and here.

"They were woven of silk and pure gold thread," the Jesuit explains. "Fabulous sums of money were spent. The nobles were taxed, the church was taxed, the poor were taxed to pay for the extravaganza. You might even say that the seeds of the beheading of Charles I of England as well as of the French Revolution were sown here by these two profligate kings.

"And look, do you see this fountain near the center of the painting? See the large stone basin in which it stands? That was one of Henry VIII's contributions, a fountain of wine. Free silver goblets were provided for anyone who wanted to dip and drink. Note the crowd of drunks stumbling around the rim, some of them vomiting. Study them with this magnifying glass.

"And why was this sumptuous extravaganza staged?

"I'll tell you. It was the age-old game of jockeying for power. The main rivals of both kings were Charles V, the Holy Roman

Emperor, on the one hand; and the Protestant princes of the Netherlands and Germany on the other. The French and the English kings hoped they might outwit these threats by forging their own alliance. The more things change, the more they remain the same: *The enemy of my enemy is my friend.*

"You understand that this was no different from today, not one whit different. Today England and France are friends with Germany who was our deadly enemy a decade ago. Why? Because Germany is an enemy of Russia.

"In 1520, it was Cardinal Wolsey who planned the whole extravagant circus, planned it as a pure act of seduction. He was courting France for the hand of England, he was pimping for England, tricking her out like a whore in silk and gold. But at the same time he was secretly meeting with the Holy Roman Emperor Charles V. A mutual non-aggression pact between England and France was signed on the Field of the Cloth of Gold, but it lasted less than a year. Within months, Wolsey, who was as duplicitous as any modern politician, signed a different deal with Charles V and that was the end of French-English trust for a long long time. In fact, even now, in spite of being allies during the war, the English and the French don't trust each other."

"But my mother trusts you," Petit Loup points out. "And you are English."

"I am Catholic," the Jesuit says. "There are loyalties that transcend the boundaries of nation states."

"I am half-American," Petit Loup says. "And half-Protestant."

"I think you are very French and very Catholic," the priest replies. "Also your mother trusts me because two world wars *have* made a difference."

"My father says America won the war," Petit Loup says. "Without America, Hitler would have won."

"Papa says it was the Resistance," Cap protests, "who saved us from Hitler. Not France, and not America. Papa says that France was stabbed by collaborators from inside."

"Ahh," the priest says. "That is a very painful and complicated question and... ah... we will eventually explore it."

"Was Wolsey a collaborator?" Cap wants to know.

"That is... that was not even an intelligible question in 1520," Father John Gabriel says. "We will discuss it, in due course, but not until we have covered a few earlier centuries, all of which have a bearing on these twentieth-century wars. To return to the meeting on the Field of the Cloth of Gold, that encounter was as much about royal strutting as about diplomacy. Both kings were aggrandizing themselves with conspicuous consumption and sumptuous architecture. Chateau Chambord was being built, with its double-spiral staircase designed by Da Vinci. And Hampton Court Palace was also being built, by and for Cardinal Wolsey, in point of fact, but let anyone who tries to outdo a king beware. Less than a decade later, the king had banished Wolsey and confiscated Hampton Court Palace for himself.

"But back to 1520. Each king brought six thousand attendants to the meeting. They pitched thousands of tents. There were feasts and music and dancing and jousts and tournaments. Both kings took part in the jousts and both distinguished themselves. On impulse, a one-on-one wrestling match between the kings was proposed. Henry was 29 years old and had already been king of England for eleven years, and, as you have observed, Mademoiselle Melusine, he was already a man of considerable weight in all senses. He expected to win. François was younger, 26 years old, had only been king for five years, and was as frisky and arrogant as an unbroken colt. To the shock of all observers, he wrestled Henry to the ground, and from the point of view of the French historians, Henry never forgave the humiliation. The alliance with France was doomed before anyone even left the Field of the Cloth of Gold. That is the end of your first history lesson.

"Your assignment is to spend the rest of the morning studying the painting with a magnifying glass. Discuss with each other the details you find. Look for the symbol of the Tudor rose on the white silk tent. Study the platters and the food on the tables. Study the dragon flying over the channel and tell me what you think it might mean.

"The second part of your first assignment is to ponder this question: Would the history of France and England and the Holy Roman Empire, and indeed of Europe, have been dramatically different if Henry VIII had won the wrestling match? Or if the match had never taken place?

"I expect you to be able to argue your case, and to support it, and that is how we will spend the whole afternoon.

"Tomorrow, we will discuss the wives and mistresses of these kings, and we will discuss whether women have any influence on the course of history."

"Of course women influence the course of history," Cap says.

"Indeed, Mademoiselle Melusine? Do you think so? And what are your reasons?"

"Queen Anne, the mother of Louis XIV, was regent of France for eight years. *La comtesse* told me."

"It is true," Father John Gabriel acknowledges, "that the queen held that *title* for eight years, as the mother of the infant king. But the real ruler during the Regency was Cardinal Mazarin."

"The Regency was full of secrets," Cap says. "*La comtesse* told me. Secrecy was essential to survival, *la comtesse* says. Your desk, Father, is a Regency desk, like the one in the salon. It has secret drawers."

"One of Queen Anne's secrets," Father John Gabriel responds, "with respect to Cardinal Mazarin, was that people believed he was her lover. But perhaps it is better that I not tell you what court gossip claimed. Tomorrow, we will discuss the issue of women and power, or of women and the illusion of power, or of women and the particular kind of power they held."

11.

In Central Park, collisions are rare on Conservatory Water but they do happen. The miniature *Santa Maria* is privately owned and its remote-control gizmo is held by its owner, a boy who is perhaps twelve years old. He is dressed in expensive casual clothing from The Gap. The rented boats and their pilots clearly resent him and his tiny custom-built vessel. Some sort of collective decision seems to have been made in the same mysterious way in which Canada geese suddenly take off in V formation to fly thousands of miles behind a leader.

The rented boats converge on the target like iron filings moving toward a magnet. There is turbulence. There is buffeting.

The *Santa Maria* lists and goes suddenly under.

Cap has an instant sensation of nausea. She has never traveled by sea, never been on a ship, but she has a shipwreck phobia. It did not begin until she was in her thirties (until the countess received a letter about the flotilla of boats that went down in the South China Sea) but now, in recurrent nightmares, she is underwater, desperately kicking for the surface, thrashing about with her long fishtail and straining to catch the hand of someone who is drowning, someone she can never quite reach. She has watched too many documentaries of Vietnamese boat people, of vessels insanely overloaded. She no longer watches such reports. She avoids them.

Life is a matter of random collisions and catastrophes, she thinks, watching the shocked eyes of the owner of the *Santa Maria*. Perhaps his ship was a birthday present. He has been letting it zoom around the pond with such manifest pride and pleasure. It has not even occurred to him that resentment might swamp him and capsize his boat and wreck his unalloyed joy. Cap wonders if the boy has a sense of historical doom, or if he will have one from this moment on. He has the look of a private-school student from the Upper East Side and so probably knows that the original *Santa Maria* was wrecked on Christmas Day in 1492. Even the faces of the boys who have ganged up on the three-master now look subdued rather than triumphant. In fact, one of the pirates takes off his shoes, rolls up his jeans, and wades into the pond to retrieve the sunken vessel. Two of its masts are broken and the sails droop like torn sodden wings. The buccaneer offers the wreck to its owner. "Sorry," he says. "Didn't mean to break her."

The master of the *Santa Maria* will not meet her salvager's eyes. He nods, cradles his shattered sailboat in his arms, turns away, and then runs toward Fifth Avenue. Cap suspects that he does not want to be seen crying.

Cap ponders the idea of randomness and pattern. Random catastrophes, random rescues, weird repetitions.

Every week, in the church of St Gilles, her father lit a candle for her mother. He gave thanks to the Virgin that Cap's mother had died in a convent, surrounded by prayers and nuns. But whenever there was a loud banging on the door at night, he woke with a start and expected dire news. Sometimes he would talk in his sleep and when he did so he argued—with the nuns? with Marie-Claire? with himself? He would insist that if Cap's mother had not died in childbirth, then she had moved from safe house to safe house until she reached the Pyrenees and Spain and the coast of Portugal and a ship called the *Santa Maria*. If it had not been for a storm in the

213

Atlantic, or for a German torpedo, her ship would have reached New York instead of the afterlife. Sometimes he dreamed that she did indeed reach American shores. Sometimes he believed this on waking. It was known, it was a matter of record, that from time to time survivors of torpedoed wrecks were picked up by Allied crews.

"Who's that?" Christophe le Jardinier asks, waking with a start.

"It's Ti-Loup's signal," Cap says, sleepy. "I'll let him in."

"No. I'll go. Never open the door at night."

"Papa, if it's not Ti-Loup, it's Ti-Christophe getting home late."

"Someone saw your *maman* in Hendaye," her father says. "On the Spanish border."

"What? Who saw her? When?"

"Just before Normandy."

Nineteen-forty-four, Cap thinks. And where was I? If she asks, he will say: *She left you with the nuns,* but later, fully awake, he will remember the articles of his personal catechism: *She died in childbirth.* "Papa, I think you are still inside your dream. I'm going to open the door. Ti-Loup?" she calls.

Ti-Loup emerges from the shadows. "I climbed out my window. Can I stay?"

"Come in."

"Is your father all right?"

"You woke him up from a dream. When he has bad dreams, he talks in his sleep."

"I was not asleep," her father says.

"I don't want you to ask me why," Ti-Loup says. "And if you do, I won't tell you. But I won't sleep at the chateau any more. Can I stay?"

"Of course you can stay," Cap's father says. "This is your safe house."

It becomes established illicit practice. At night, after his mother has bid him goodnight, Petit Loup climbs out his window and makes his way to the gardener's cottage where he has supper for the second time. He spends the night on a palliasse in the loft—on the straw mattress where Petit Christophe used to sleep—and climbs back into his own bedroom at the chateau before dawn so the servants won't see. Cap has to go with him. She has to crouch like a tortoise in front of his window, elbows pressed against knees. Petit Loup stands on her back, reaches for the sill, and hoists himself over. Then he leans out. He kisses his fingertips, Cap kisses hers, and they reach and touch hands.

"You are putting on weight," Cap warns him one evening as her father urges second helpings on the boy. "Your *maman* will want to know why."

"She knows why."

"You told her you are having two dinners?"

"No. She says happiness makes the body bloom and she knows I'm happy. It's because the Virgin Mary has answered her prayers, she says."

Cap makes her eyes go slanty with the tips of her thumbs. "And because of me," she reminds.

Ti-Loup pulls his mouth into a gargoyle slit with his index fingers. "You're here because the Virgin Mary sent you."

"I'm here because I do what I want. No one makes me do anything. Not even the Virgin Mary."

"If you don't watch out," Ti-Loup warns, "the Virgin Mary will strike you dead."

"If you don't watch out," Cap responds, "I won't help you climb back through your window. And I won't sneak you into

Petit Christophe's back window at Monsieur Monsard's and you won't be able to get into the cutting room without being seen."

"If you ever do that," Ti-Loup says, "I would ask the Virgin Mary to strike you dead."

In fact, when Petit Loup turns twelve and Cap is perhaps thirteen, a curious act of trans-substantiation comes to pass. The countess summons her gardener and explains that she has provided a room in the chateau for Melusine. The room has a solid Louis XIV bed and two baroque mirrors and a charming Louis XV *escritoire.*

"She is a young woman now," the countess explains. "It is not proper that she does not have her own bedroom and a chaperone."

It comes to pass that Capucine spends the night in a four-poster bed in the chateau and Ti-Loup, unknown to his mother, sleeps in the loft in the gardener's cottage. Ti-Loup no longer needs help to climb in or out of his window. Cap has no need whatsoever of entry by window. The countess brushes her hair every night.

The arrangement keeps both children happy.

However, Father John Gabriel is less than happy.

"Night after night," he tells his primary charge, "I come by your room to help with your assignments. But you are never there. I begin to think you are a werewolf."

"I change shape at night," Petit Loup acknowledges gravely. "I am someone else after dark. But I will tell *maman* that you come to my room every night. She can meet us there."

"There is no need to speak of this to your mother," Father John Gabriel says. "It is not of any consequence as long as your home-work is done."

There are subsidiary benefits to secret knowledge.

Father John Gabriel is a strong believer in the educational val-ue of field trips. On Saturdays there are excursions of historical benefit: Chinon, Tours, the chateaux at Chenonceau, Amboise,

Saumur, the royal abbey of Fontevraud, all so close by. These trips are made in Father John Gabriel's car. There are vague plans to go as far as Calais and Agincourt but the countess has not yet given permission. When the children are older, she says.

It transpires that Father John Gabriel has a close friend in Tours, a Dominican friar who also serves the Cathedral of St Gatien as a curate. The Jesuit and the Dominican are close friends who like to spend time in scholarly research and discussion. The Jesuit tutor is amenable to an arrangement proposed by his students: that three Saturdays of every four, *le vicomte* Gwynne Patrice will spend the day with a friend at some unspecified place in the village of St Gilles; that Melusine, personal maid and ward of the countess, will spend the day wandering dreamily through the Musée des Beaux Arts in Tours, studying the seventeenth and eighteenth century paintings, visually memorizing them. Sometimes she will sit in front of a single painting for an hour at a time. She is particularly fascinated by a seventeenth-century canvas by Claude Vignon. The painting is called "Croesus demanding tribute from a peasant." The portrait of the peasant captivates her. It could be her father: gnarled hands, fingers twisted from hard work, a gentle face weary and luminous with a kind of sublime resignation but a form of resignation that also suggests irony. The worst will go on happening, the face says, and behold what it does to the tyrant.

Bored, comfortable, ruthless, impervious, indifferent, the obscenely rich Croesus lounges in his sumptuous chair, counting the spill of coins from the old peasant's small leather purse. Croesus has the face of a Gestapo officer who expects betrayal as a matter of course.

Goodness will outlast him, the face of the peasant says.

Three Saturdays in every four, a ritual pattern is well established. Father John Gabriel in his Citroen picks up Cap and Ti-Loup at the entrance to the chateau. All three wave to the countess as they leave. Father John Gabriel stops in the village square in St Gilles for a pitcher of wine and a *croque-monsieur* at the Lion d'Or. While he is there, Cap visits her brother and takes Ti-Loup with her. They do not enter the butcher's establishment from the street. They do not cross the courtyard. Rather, they follow the drainage ditch and narrow footpath from the back of the Lion d'Or to the back of *la boucherie*. Cap knocks on her brother's window and he lets them climb into his private quarters. No one can see them from courtyard or street. Petit Christophe offers them lime tea and madeleines and they exchange a week's worth of news. Then Cap climbs back out of the window and makes her way to the Lion d'Or and on to Tours, chaperoned by her tutor.

Petit Christophe has his own key and his own private door that leads directly from his small apartment to the cutting room. Under his tutelage, Ti-Loup studies the art of the boning hook and knife. He is acquiring a sixth sense, an instinct for the passageways between muscle and joint. He is learning to navigate inter-bone alleyways with his knife. He knows how to separate tenderloin from flank and tenderloin from rump without ever scraping a bone.

"Sometimes," Petit Christophe tells him, "there's no avoiding the boning saw. After the animals are killed and hung in the slaughter yard, there's no other way to get halves and quarters. You have to saw through the spine. Monsieur Monsard does that; I won't do it. Just the same, when the carcasses are brought inside, I have to use the saw to separate the neck from the spine." He demonstrates this, but he uses the saw very rarely. "It's a matter of finding the canals," he says. "A matter of knowing the sluicegate codes. The knife floats through them."

"Did Monsieur Monsard teach you this?"

"In the beginning, yes. But then the carcasses taught me. I'm a better butcher than he is and the customers know it. So now he leaves the butchering to me."

"I want to be as good as you," Ti-Loup says.

"Then you must pay close attention to the carcasses. You must listen to them. You must let them teach you."

"It's so exciting," Ti-Loup tells Capucine. "It's like solving a riddle in Greek."

"You're not just listening to the carcasses," Cap says. "You've been listening to Ti-Christophe and papa so much that you sound exactly like them when you're with us. You sound like a peasant. Next thing I know you'll be able to talk to dead steers."

"And you," Ti-Loup accuses, "when you're in the chateau, you sound exactly like my *maman*."

"I do not."

"You do. It just happens. We don't even notice. I can do Father JG."

"Do Father JG."

"Ask yourself," Ti-Loup says in a tight and slightly prissy British accent, "if the history of Europe might be altogether different if François I had not beaten Henry VIII in a wrestling match in 1520."

Both children collapse with laughter.

Ti-Loup and Cap are stranded together in St Gilles in the apprentice's room (that is, in Ti-Christophe's room) at Monsieur Monsard's place. Father John Gabriel is taking Ti-Christophe with him to Tours. Cap's brother has insisted that his sister should not come along.

"But why?" Cap demands.

"Because," her brother says. "There's something private I have to attend to."

"Is this something to do with Olivier and Chantal?"

"That is none of your business."

"It might be," Cap says. "Will you be safe? Pierre and others, servants I mean, say Olivier works the black market. They say he's killed people."

"I can look after myself," her brother says.

Cap has a book and is curled up on her brother's bed, reading. Ti-Loup is carving up a lamb in the cutting room next door. This is the first time he has been unsupervised, but Petit Christophe says he is learning well, he is attentive to the scaffolding and rigging and river systems of the animal body. Lamb is carved on the butcher-block table, not while suspended from a hook. The gutted body of the lamb seems so small, the ribs so fragile, that Ti-Loup has the uneasy sense of cutting up a child. He has noted the particular tenderness, the reverence, with which Petit Christophe dissects lamb. Always, in fact, before cutting, Petit Christophe crosses himself. Ti-Loup does the same.

First he removes the shanks, then the neck. Then he reaches into the carcass and counts the ribs down from the neck. He makes a mark between the fifth and sixth ribs on both sides (inside and out) and cuts. He is preparing a Frenched rack of lamb.

"What are you doing here?"

The interruption startles Ti-Loup and causes his knife to scrape against a rib. A young woman pushes through the insulated door from the courtyard and faces him across the butcher block. "You've spoiled my cut," he accuses.

"How did you get into this room?"

"Petit Christophe let me in."

"How come I didn't see you in the courtyard?"

"I must have come when you weren't looking," Ti-Loup says.

"Where's Petit Christophe?"

"He has gone into Tours."

"Tours?" The young woman looks disturbed. "Why Tours?"

"I don't know why."

"He didn't tell me he was going to Tours." The voice of the young woman rises a notch. Cap opens the door from her brother's room a crack and watches and listens. "Why didn't he tell me?" The young woman crosses her arms and hugs herself. She is shivering. The room is always kept cold and Ti-Loup wears two sweaters and a warm undershirt. "I know you," she says. "You are le vicomte from the chateau. Petit Christophe talks about you all the time, but I never see you. What are you doing here?"

"Petit Christophe is teaching me. I only come when the butcher shop is closed. Are you Chantal?"

"Yes. Does he talk about me?"

"Not to me," Ti-Loup admits. "But he talks to his sister and she talks to me."

"What does she say?"

Ti-Loup flicks his eyes toward the door that leads to Ti-Christophe's quarters and is aware of Cap's presence. "Sometimes she talks to me," he says carefully. "But she never tells much. She says your father and brother don't like Petit Christophe. They don't approve of him."

"I don't care what they think."

"She says that Ti-Christophe knows you spend time with Olivier and it makes him angry."

"That's a lie! I don't spend time with Olivier! I hide from him whenever he comes! Why doesn't Ti-Christophe know that?"

"Your brother told him you are going to marry Olivier."

"I'm not. I will never marry Olivier. I'm frightened of him." They can both hear footsteps in the courtyard. Chantal looks terrified. "It's my father," she says. "Or my brother. Where can I hide?"

"Uh—" Before Ti-Loup can think of any response, she leaps at the U-curve of the steel hook from which one of the carcasses is suspended and presses herself inside the steer's husk of flesh and bone. The hook screeches on its track and the carcass swings like

221

a pendulum possessed, spinning and twisting, but coming to rest with its severed gut facing the wall. Chantal is curled inside like a chrysalis inside its cocoon, her hands just visible on the steel loop above the severed neck of the steer.

The door from the courtyard bangs open. "What the hell are you doing here?" Michel Monsard demands. "And how the hell did you get in?"

"Petit Christophe let me in. I'm his assistant."

"What? My father never hires extras. Where is he?"

"Your father?"

"I know where my father is. Where is Petit Christophe? He can't hire anyone."

"He hasn't hired me. I don't get paid. I just help. Petit Christophe is teaching me."

"Not on our carcasses, he isn't. Not if I have any say. I recognize you. You're the son of *la comtesse*. Where is Petit Christophe?"

"He's in Tours."

"In Tours! Why?"

"I don't know why."

"He's looking for me or Olivier, that's why." Michel Monsard is pacing around the cutting room, opening refrigerated lockers. "I saw my sister come in here. Where is she?"

"Your sister?" Ti-Loup looks convincingly astonished. "No one ever comes in here except Petit Christophe." Ti-Loup gestures at the scrubbed and bleached floorboards, the freezer cubicles lining the walls. "You can check the lockers. There's no one here except me."

"And you've got no business here," Michel Monsard says. He snatches the cutting knife from Ti-Loup's hand and grabs the boy by the scruff of the neck. He presses the tip of the blade to Ti-Loup's throat and draws blood. One crimson bead appears on the pale skin, then two, then three. "You're the *fifi* American boy who wears dresses. We don't let homos touch our meat because the meat turns rotten if homos touch it. Get the hell out and don't come back. Stay inside the chateau where you belong, *fifi* boy."

Ti-Loup does not flinch. "You are right," he says calmly, seeming to be calm, though Cap can hear the kettledrum beat of his heart on the far side of the door. "The chateau should not deal with Monsieur Monsard. We should take our business to the butcher in Chinon."

Michel Monsard is arrested in the act of toying with the knife-blade and Ti-Loup's throat. He lets go of the boy and hurls the knife like a dart at the butcher block. It lodges in the flank of the lamb. He punches savagely at the row of carcasses and they screech and career across the ceiling tracks. Ti-Loup and Cap watch the clasped hands of Chantal speed across the room and get lost in the crowded huddle of the chilled and ghostly overcoats of former cattle.

"I will speak to my mother, *la comtesse,*" Petit Loup says. "I will tell her that Monsieur Monsard no longer wants her business. We should deal with the butcher in Chinon."

Michel spits on the floor. "We'll see about that," he says. "If your mother speaks to my father, you'll have to answer to me. *You*! To *me*! Understand?" He pushes Ti-Loup ahead of him into the courtyard and bangs the door shut behind them.

"You can come out now," Cap tells Chantal. "They've gone."

"I'm frozen," Chantal says. "I can't move my arms. I think I might have dislocated my shoulders."

"Here." Cap reaches up and wraps herself around Chantal's hips. "Just let go your hands and I'll hold you." The sensation of a center of gravity changing is slow and then sudden. Cap falls and feels pain in her buttocks and arms. Chantal is on top of her. Neither can move.

223

"I don't think I can walk," Chantal says.

"I don't know if I can either."

"Why did Petit Christophe go to Tours?"

"I don't know," Cap says. "I'm afraid he's looking for a fight with Olivier."

"Olivier will kill him."

"No he won't. My brother can look after himself. Ugh! My back hurts, but I think I can move." She stands, assessing the pain. "I'll probably have a bruise the size of France on my backside, but I think I'm okay. You need to get warm." She hooks Chantal by her underarms and drags her into Ti-Christophe's room.

"I won't be able to leave here," Chantal says. "My brother will see me and he'll kill me."

"First you have to get warmed up, and then I'll get you out so no one sees you."

"How?"

"The way Ti-Loup and I get in." She hoists Chantal into Petit Christophe's bed. "Get warm first," she orders, piling a quilt on the bed.

"Is he in love with me?" Chantal asks. "Or does he just enjoy annoying my brother and my father?"

"I think he's in love with you but he doesn't want to be. He knows your father will never permit it."

"We could leave," Chantal says. "We could live somewhere else. Maybe that's why he went to Tours. If he finds work in a butcher shop there, we could run away and get married."

"You could get married in St Gatien. My father says that's where I was born."

"In the church?"

"In the convent. The nuns had a hiding place. The crypt, perhaps."

"The crypt! With skeletons and coffins all around you?"

"I suppose."

"What a terrible omen."

"Yes. It was. My mother died. I never knew her."

Chantal crosses herself. "Petit Christophe and I will have to get married secretly but I won't get married in a crypt. Surrounded by skeletons? It would be a terrible omen."

Cap refrains from indicating the clothes-racks of carcasses in the frigid room next door. She stops herself from saying: *You are a butcher's daughter. You are surrounded by blood and slaughter every day.*

Instead she says: "The crypt is a sanctuary where babies were born during the war. It kept them safe. It can only be a good omen."

12.

In the wake of the sinking of the *Santa Maria*, Cap is too agitated to remain on the park bench at Conservatory Water. She is also too agitated to re-open the manila envelope. She is afraid of what else she will find. She is deeply moved to discover which photographs the countess must have treasured and retained, which ones she had brought with her when she reluctantly returned to New York. But the photograph of Ti-Loup and Petit Christophe in the cutting room is so disturbing that Cap finds it necessary to take brief refuge in a cubicle in the public bathrooms. She is not able, not entirely, to hold back the need to weep. She blots her cheeks with toilet paper. When she washes her hands, she notes that they are trembling. She hates to feel exposed in this way. She nods and smiles to other women in the restroom. Outside, she pats dogs and exchanges small talk, functioning on automatic pilot, but the storm weather inside her head persists.

That photograph, the existence of which is a shock, could only have been taken by Michel Monsard or his father. But when and how? And they must have sent it (or shown it) to the countess as an act of revenge. This would at last—nearly forty years later—explain what had happened next. Since it must have caused the countess extreme distress, why had she preserved it? What other archival material—pictorial, textual, tactile (a lock of Ti-Loup's hair, for example?)—might be quietly lying in hidden drawers or in cavities behind quilted silk panels in the crumbling walls of the chateau? Will anyone ever know?

Perhaps the countess left sealed directives with her lawyers, open-sesame instructions for recessed spaces not visible to the eye. Who is now in possession of these codes? How much of the chateau furniture was shipped to New York when the countess moved back in '68? Certainly some of it was. There were pieces Cap saw in the penthouse. They had the air of refugees bemused by the Fifth Avenue din. But there were so many, so many beautiful things she had never seen since she herself left the chateau. Were they in New York? If so, those items had not been on display when Cap visited. Had they been held in storage? Or were they sold off in France? Were those extraordinary Louis XIV and Louis XV pieces currently showing up around the world in exclusive— and quite possibly illicit and private—auction rooms? For years, Cap has been watching for them in Sotheby's catalogues, in Christie's, in Bonhams, but has never seen an item she knows. And she does know them intimately. The mere memory of stroking those consoles and armoires, the mere fact of having once been in the same room as them, of having fallen in love with them, still casts an extraordinary aura of happiness and awe. Are they now owned by Saudi princes? By rock stars with indiscriminate acquisitive instincts? By internet billionaires who know more about the stock market than art?

Or are they in dusty flea-market displays at the Porte de Clignancourt in the eighteenth arrondissement of Paris? Where are they?

And where is the talismanic blond curl from Ti-Loup's very first haircut?

In any case, Cap is as touched by the fact that the countess has kept the First Communion photograph as she is distressed that persons unknown must now have one of the originals in their

hands. Who could have managed access to the private possessions and secret drawers of the Vanderbilt penthouse? The family
lawyers perhaps? Celise, perhaps, who kept a key? The bankers?
The foreclosure team? The eviction movers subcontracted by the
bank? Any or all of them might have sold off boxes of memora-
bilia for peanuts at a second-hand store. Any or all of them might
have sold items for much larger sums of money to traffickers in
intelligence or scandal. It seems to Cap that the image of the First
Communion has been smudged and tainted and desecrated by the
photocopier's finger pads.

Cap herself keeps one of the originals, untainted, wallet-size,
in her purse or under her pillow at all times. She is not superstitious, but nevertheless keeping that photograph within reach was
a source of comfort after Ti-Loup was lost in Vietnam. Perhaps
the countess had kept the golden lock of his infant hair under
her pillow.

Perhaps she had believed it would keep Ti-Loup alive. Perhaps
it had.

Naturally Cap does not believe in this sort of primitive sympathetic magic. Nevertheless, furtively, she rummages in her purse
and takes the photo from her wallet. She brushes it with her lips,
slides it into the pocket of her jeans, keeps her hand in contact.
Obviously whoever sent the packet of photographs understands
the psychology of violation.

The question is, who would find this necessary and why? Cap
can think of no logical reason, no possible advantage to be had
from the flaunting of access to archival footage of her life. Precisely for this reason the escalating activity feels ominous. She has a
sense of waiting for a hurricane to make landfall, a sense that it
will be a Category 5 with spin-off tornadoes, hail, a storm surge
that will wash across Battery Park and rampage up Broadway,
split into tidal gangs, smash the Village and Chelsea, vandalize

228

Midtown, pickle Central Park in brine, clump overturned lives into matchstick heaps of sand-swamped debris.

This is ridiculous.

Nevertheless, she does trust her instincts. Her intuition and her premonitions have saved her life more than once and she finds that she is bracing for the funnel of wind that will suck her back to the moment when the Gestapo held her mother's head under water. Or shot her. Or did whatever they did.

How many hours or days after Cap's birth had they done this?

Certain moments in any war, certain intersections of anxiety and threat, certain ways of thinking engendered by cultural or economic fear: all these hone the capacity for desecration. At such times, brutality acquires finesse. It becomes sophisticated. It becomes a monstrous form of art. It can even mask itself as virtue. It sees itself, in its own mirror, as patriotic duty.

Lucifer is well trained in the psychology of violation but Cap does not believe he would ever assault her in this way. He would never be so crude and indirect. On the other hand, he has colleagues—who knows how many?—who would certainly be less scrupulous. And of course there are agents of shady and dysfunctional governments—who knows how many?—who have been burned in the court of international opinion, who wish to curtail Cap's ability to travel, have her passport impounded, undermine the credibility of any evidence she might amass. But how would these photographs help them? And how could the photographs have come into their hands?

Could Celise have sensed blackmail potential and sold to the highest bidder? Cap has never found Celise even marginally interesting or intelligent but nor has she ever had any illusions about the woman once married to Ti-Loup's cousin and then to Lucifer. She has never considered Celise worth attention, but perhaps she has been naive.

In the final weeks of the life of *la comtesse,* Cap sat at her god-mother's bedside every day. Daily the concierge would call up to say that Mrs. Celise Vanderbilt was in the lobby and wished to pay her respects. By then, in the aftermath of her stroke, the countess could speak but not in a manner easily understood. She could make half-words and grunting sounds but Cap could translate. Tell him to keep that vulture away from me, the countess said.

Nevertheless, flowers would be sent up daily. *From your loving niece, Celise.*

"Niece Celise, call the police," the countess whispered fiercely one day, with startling clarity, pulling aside her oxygen tubes. The effort exhausted her.

"Shh, don't tire yourself." Cap replaced the tubes. "What a wicked mouth you have," she said affectionately. "And you are the one who claimed *I* was a wild thing."

The countess spluttered with laughter but the laughter turned into a harrowing coughing fit. In alarm, Cap pressed Medic Alert and within minutes the emergency nurse was there.

"You should buffer her from any source of agitation," the nurse reproved.

"I'll speak to the doorman," Cap promised.

But two days later Celise was suddenly there at the bedroom door. There must have been minutes when the doorman was otherwise engaged...

"Oh my poor dear Isabelle," Celise said unctuously. She leaned over the bed and stroked the cheek of the dying woman with one hand. The voice and the touch had the effect of a violent adrenaline surge. The Lady Isabelle de la Vallière Vanderbilt, bedridden for weeks, too frail to walk, fed by a drip from a plastic bag, kept breathing by an oxygen tank, suddenly tried to sit upright in bed. "*Out!*" she ordered, ripping away her nasal tubes, smacking away her niece's hand with surprising force.

"Poor dear Isabelle," Celise murmured, unperturbed. "I just wanted to see how you were." Her digital camera clicked and flashed.

The countess subsided, exhausted, onto her pillows.

"I'm calling the doorman," Cap said and buzzed the intercom.

"Oh, don't worry," Celise said smoothly, leaving the room.

Between the sailboat pond and the edge of the park, Cap leans against a tree until the image of Celise by the deathbed fades. She emerges from the park at Fifth Avenue and East 72nd. Crossing Fifth, she is almost hit by a bus and knows that she remains in an unsafe state. She anchors her body to the light pole on the corner until her heartbeat returns to something approximating normal. One person stops to ask if she needs help. Most pass without a second glance or assume she is drunk or stoned and turn away.

Cap takes deep slow breaths and steadies herself and walks down Fifth to the Frick, then along East 70th to Madison. She is heading for the first sanctuary she knew after she left the chateau and the gardener's cottage. The Goldbergs are no longer there. They moved to the Beth Shalom retirement community in Florida months ago. But their old pre-war apartment building and its interior court and garden still cast an aura of calm. Cap only has to think of the Goldbergs and their apartment (crammed with books and art, floor to ceiling, two paintings on each side of every door, Soutine in the bathroom, Cocteau above the toilet, Modigliani in the bedroom), she has only to visualize the enclosed garden of their building to feel safe, something which, she realizes now, is profoundly ironic.

How could two people so utterly subject to Category 5 dangers through so many years of their lives have made her feel so secure?

The doorman to what was once the Goldbergs' apartment building is young and new and Cap does not know him.

"I used to live here," she tells him. "A long time ago, apartment 6A, early sixties."

"People come back all the time," the doorman says. "Famous people. Sign the Former Residents Book, over there. We've got artists, writers, CEOs, ambassadors, secretaries of state, and gangsters. What are you famous for?"

"Oh nothing at all. Except maybe for having lived in this building."

"Well, sign the book and press the 6A buzzer," the doorman says. "You can talk on the intercom."

"No, no. I don't know the people who live there now. I don't want to bother them. I don't know anyone in the building anymore. I was just wondering if you'd let me sit in the courtyard garden for a while."

"I'm not allowed to let anyone in unless they're vouched for by a resident."

"I know," Cap says. "Good rule. I know the rules. This is... well, it's a nostalgia thing. You lived in Manhattan all your life?"

"Never lived in Manhattan. Can't afford it. I go home to Newark every night."

"Grow up in New Jersey?"

"No. Grew up in Minnesota and escaped to NYU six years ago. Theater. Working here part-time between auditions and bit parts on stage."

"Ever go back to Minnesota?"

"Thanksgiving. Christmas."

"To the house you grew up in?"

"Yeah."

"Think of it twenty, thirty, forty years from now. Strangers living there. You think you might want to knock on the door and tell whoever opens it: *I grew up in this house. I wonder if I could just sit under the apple tree my mother planted in the back yard?*"

The doorman smiles. "Point made," he says. "Wow. Convincing

232

case. You a theater major too?"

"Art History. I was an undergrad at NYU when I lived here."

"Okay," the doorman says. "But don't leave the courtyard garden. You still have to sign in, and make sure you sign out before the end of my shift."

From a bench in the courtyard garden, Cap studies the hostas and ferns, the lacy birch trees, the massed white caladiums, the bronze Lipchitz sculpture rising like an elongated supplicant from the waving green lily-turf lawn. There is a plaque, Cap knows, on its pedestal. *Gift of Aaron and Myriam Goldberg,* it says. *In tribute to Lilith and Grand Loup.*

In the sixth year of the tutelage of Father John Gabriel who is dedicated to the preparation of his pupils for *le bac* and for eventual distinguished acceptance at La Sorbonne, in the year when Petit Loup is thirteen years old and Cap is whatever age she is, during Latin translation and under their schoolmaster's stern policing eye, Ti-Loup slips a note across the table to Cap under his text of Cicero's *De Re Publica.*

Something to tell you at mid-morning break. Meet you under the apple tree.

Under the very apple tree where they first met, Ti-Loup tells Capucine, "Two strangers, Americans who speak good French, are walking around the village every day. Have you heard?"

"No."

"Marie-Claire told me. She was at your father's cottage last night. Marie-Claire says everyone's talking about them, but she hasn't seen them herself. Their names are Monsieur and Madame Goldberg."

These strangers are not staying in the village—which has no place for visitors to stay—but they have a hotel room in Chinon. They come every day in a car which they park in the village square.

They talk to everyone. They eat lunch at Le Lion d'Or. They are very charming but everyone is wary. The visitors say they spent a few days in St Gilles when they were young, and they wanted to come back after all these years. They speak very good French, but no one remembers them. Sometimes they ask if Monsieur Grand Loup is still alive. No one knows who they mean. They say they will know Monsieur Grand Loup, if he is still alive, when they see him.

"What did papa say?"

"He said, 'Marie-Claire, everyone promised they would return, but no one did.' And Marie-Claire said, 'We don't know how many ever got that chance.' She said, 'They speak Parisian French, not country French.'"

Ti-Loup runs agitated fingers through his hair. "Cap, do you think...? Grand Loup, Petit Loup...? What do you think?"

"Did you ask Papa?"

"I asked him if he knew who the strangers were. He said he would know the answer to that when he saw them. I asked him if he knew who Monsieur Grand Loup was, and he said yes, but this was not a subject about which he wanted to talk."

Father John Gabriel's afternoon class is interrupted by Pierre of the velvet pantaloons. "*Madame la Comtesse* wishes her son and Melusine to come to the salon immediately. She says distinguished visitors from America are here."

In the salon, the countess is elegant in pale grey silk. Almost forty now, her body looks younger but her face looks older, still striking with its high cheek bones and large eyes, but with something dark in the hollows beneath the eye sockets and something disturbing in the lustrous intensity of her gaze.

"Madame and Monsieur Goldberg," she says, "may I present my son, *le vicomte* Gwynne Patrice—"

"*Mon Dieu!*" Madame Goldberg says, with an intake of breath. "Lilith!" She presses a hand over her heart before taking Cap's hand between her own. "*Lilith, c'est toi!*"

"And also," the countess says, with a courteous though starched intimation that impropriety has occurred, "I present Melusine, my gardener's daughter. *Mes enfants*," she says, "the Goldbergs used to live in Paris before the war. They are art collectors from New York and my personal collection has come to their attention."

"*C'est toi,*" Madame Goldberg says again, in a whisper. She is still holding Cap's hand. And then, collecting herself, she says, "*Enchantée.*"

Cap senses the electricity of possibility, of some barely imaginable state of being that is far beyond the village, far beyond the valleys of the Vienne and the Cher and the Loire, far beyond Paris, far beyond France, back to the mists of a prior incarnation. For a second she has a fogged image of a Romanesque crypt, of nuns, of bloodied sheets, but the image dissolves and she is studying the face of Madame Goldberg as intensely as Madame Goldberg is studying hers.

If the countess reminds her of the austerely beautiful and sorrowing face of the mother of Louis XIV in Philippe de Champaigne's painting, then Madame Goldberg reminds her of a portrait de Champaigne did of his own wife, Charlotte Duchesne, daughter of his patron at court. It is a delicate face with dark hair and warm eyes, a hint of a smile on the lips. The eyes are cordial but intense. They suggest a churn of inquiry, of equivocation, of rebuttal and parrying in the mind behind the eyes. Cap is extremely familiar with this face. In the Musée des Beaux Arts in Tours, she has spent hours in contemplation of de Champaigne's preliminary sketch for the painting of his wife, black chalk on parchment, highlights in white chalk, some red chalk accents. She is transfixed by the face of Myriam Goldberg, quite unaware that Madame and

Monsieur Goldberg, in return, are equally transfixed by her own.

"Lilith!" Madame Goldberg murmurs. "*Mon Dieu!*" She leans forward to kiss Cap's cheek three times in the formal French manner. "You have come back to us." This is a whisper that only Capucine can hear.

"You remind us of someone," Monsieur Goldberg explains, to cover an awkward stretch of silence. "Someone we knew in St Gilles."

"You had relatives in our village?" the countess inquires.

"Not relatives," Monsieur Goldberg responds. "Not exactly. But people close to us, yes."

"And you, Madame Goldberg?" the countess inquires with a hint of steel in her voice. "Melusine reminds you of this person?"

Madame Goldberg seems not to hear. She has touched Cap's cheek with her hand, but her eye has been arrested by a watercolor-tinted charcoal sketch on the wall beyond Cap's head. The sketch—of a man and a woman—consists of strong dark minimalist strokes —black clothing, stark white collars and cuffs—but is luminous with a wash of rose-gold flesh. The work is quite small, about twenty inches high and ten wide.

"Ah yes," the countess says, following the sightline of her guest. "Rather out of keeping with the rest of my collection. It's modern, not my taste at all, but my dealer applied an unusual amount of pressure. Very odd, when I think back. I bought it in '41 or '42, I think. My dealer was selling it cheaply, dirt cheap, to be honest, I don't even know what happened to him, he just disappeared. The sketch isn't signed, but my current appraiser says it could be an early Modigliani and quite valuable. Could be a preliminary sketch of a portrait of Jacques and Berthe Lipchitz, he thinks, but there's no signature. He left drawings and paintings, you know, all over Paris. Modigliani, I mean. He kept being evicted and leaving canvases behind, or using them to pay overdue bills. His life was a mess. My dealer says his early work shows up in flea markets from time to time. The dealer said this sketch was called *Man and Wife*."

"It is definitely an early Modigliani," Monsieur Goldberg says. "As a knowledgeable collector of Modigliani, I can confirm that."

"So it is valuable?" the countess asks.

"Extremely. And rare. And uncatalogued. How did your dealer acquire it?"

"At the time, you know," the countess explains, "it was prudent not to ask questions about the provenance.... You are collectors yourselves."

"Yes. We have a considerable collection. We have bequeathed it to the Metropolitan Museum of Art."

"Ah," the countess says fondly. "I used to spend so many hours there. I lived in New York for five years when I was first married. When Gwynne Patrice was an infant. But then I came back here to France."

"Were you here in 1944?" Madame Goldberg asks.

"Oh, indeed, yes," the countess says. "That was before I was married. Before I left France. That is not a year I will ever forget though it is not a year I like to remember. My mother died the winter before, I think from the shock of having German officers move into our rooms. The rains came at the wrong time, the vintage was disappointing, and in other respects, we never knew how many mouths we would have to feed or how many hands we would have at harvest. We made what accommodations were necessary, you understand, but we never made them willingly. The Germans informed us that they would be billeting officers in the chateau. We had to feed them. They had to have the best wines, the best lamb, the best steaks, the best of everything. My mother had a heart attack and a German officer moved into her bedroom one week after she was buried. That's the way it was all through

go to p. 240

Myriam cannot take her eyes off Capucine. "She was so beautiful and so quick-thinking."

"Reckless," Marie-Claire says.

"Young." Christophe le Jardinier busies himself with stoking the fire. "I made the false floor in the laundry van."

"I still smell fresh linen above, gasoline below," Myriam says. "I have suffocation nightmares. Still."

"We were squashed under that false floor in Chinon," her husband explains. "Lilith took the river road, ten miles to St Gilles, but it felt like a hundred. A daylight trip because Lilith thought that would be less suspicious."

"But we were stopped." Myriam closes her eyes, sees and hears it all again: the German soldiers, Lilith explaining she is taking linens back to military officers, Lilith flirting, asking the soldiers if she can give them a lift into St Gilles. On the sub-floor, the Goldbergs are lying flat on their backs with ten inches of space between their faces and the sheets stacked above. They cannot see what i s happening but they can hear. Yes, the soldiers are saying, they would like a lift, and Lilith says, "Get in. But be careful y o u d o n ' t p u t a s i n g l e mark on those starched sheets because the SS are fanatics when it comes to their laundry." And the soldiers change their minds and wave her on.

Christophe le Jardinier smiles. "She had a dangerous sense of humor."

"By then, I'd stopped breathing," Myriam says.

The Goldbergs lay under the van floor till nightfall. They had cramps in their legs. They were afraid they would moan from the pain. The baskets of laundry were unloaded in the chateau courtyard with the SS watching.

The gardener smiles at a memory. "Lilith and I did it together. We should have been terrified but it gave us a bit of a thrill."

"I remember that," Ti-Christophe says.

"No. You couldn't. You weren't at the chateau. What you remember happened later."

"What happened later?" Cap asks.

"We drove the van to our cottage and we got the Goldbergs out after dark."

"That's what I remember," Ti-Christophe says. "Walking through the woods without a candle. That's how I learned where the safe house was."

"We were there for two days," Myriam recalls. "Grand Loup brought food and candles. Then he took us across the Vienne in a row boat on a night with no moon."

"In fact there was a young moon," the gardener says, "but we waited for a night with thick cloud."

"Papa?" Cap prompts. "And then?"

"One of our people met us," her father says, "and then I rowed back."

"For years we have wanted to return and find Grand Loup and Lilith to thank them," Myriam says. "And... I'm afraid to ask. Where is Lilith?"

"She died in the convent in Tours," Christophe le Jardinier reports. "In childbirth." He strokes his daughter's hair. "She left me this gift."

Christophe the Younger and Capucine lock eyes. Her brother places his index finger against his lips.

"We lost a child," Myriam Goldberg says. "It was not a time when anyone wanted to be pregnant, or should have been..."

They had gone the long way around. Their ship went via Lisbon, then Morocco—a month in Morocco —the Canary Islands, the Bahamas, Florida, and finally New York. Myriam's uncle was supposed to meet them there. He checked the port manifestos every day for months on end but the information was always days behind. Myriam went into premature labor in Arrivals, the Man-

go to p. 241

'42 and '43 and '44, right up until the Liberation. They were terrible years."

"Yes," Monsieur Goldberg agrees. "Terrible years."

"And that dreadful winter of '44. What a strange year. From the darkest of darks before June, and then suddenly a sunrise of hope. And then, end of August, the Free French and De Gaulle on the Champs Elysées! Well, we went giddy with champagne and dances. I met my husband in Paris then. But before that, we had to take risks," the countess says. "Sometimes we had to put our own lives on the line. I personally— Well, never mind. The war ended and we survived."

Six people are gathered in front of the cast-iron stove in the gardener's cottage: the Goldbergs; Christophe le Jardinier and his two children, now aged twenty-two and fourteen; also Marie-Claire, though many years have passed since she was the gardener's housekeeper.

"It's quite unnerving, Lilith, to see you again," Madame Goldberg says. "Unchanged."

"I'm Capucine."

"Yes. Yes, of course. But you look so like your mother." Madame Goldberg presses the back of one wrist against her lips. "I'm Myriam. Call me Myriam. Being here, seeing you, it brings back all the anxiety, all the dangerous excitement of hope."

Myriam bows her head, fingertips pressed to her brow. "Lilith was extraordinary, the most extraordinary woman—"

"She was just a slip of a girl," Monsieur Goldberg says.

"She was twenty," the gardener says gruffly.

"Such courage. Such ingenuity."

"She was an escort," the gardener says. "She was doing her job. There were many young women and young men who did the same thing. Some survived, but more didn't."

go to p. 238

hattan Pier, Immigration and Customs. It was chaos.

"A girl," Aaron Goldberg says. "It is possible she was conceived in your safe house. We called her Lilith but she died."

Marie-Claire moves from her chair near the fireplace to sit beside Myriam Goldberg. She places one hand on Myriam's arm. "We all lost..." she begins to say, but is unable to finish her sentence.

"We never had other children," Myriam says.

Christophe le Jardinier busies himself with heating a pot of tea. "We all lost someone," he says. "But here we are."

"You know that sketch?" Myriam Goldberg is suddenly struck by a memory, energized by it, pulling herself out of sorrow. "That Modigliani in the chateau? We used to own it. It's a drawing of my own grandparents because Modigliani was, you know, a family friend. He probably did use that sketch as a template for his *Jacques and Berthe Lipchiz*. We had to sell it, of course, to buy hiding time and to fund our escape."

"Lipchiz got out earlier than we did," Aaron Goldberg explains, "but he got out the same way. Safe house to safe house. Over the Pyrenees. And then a ship out of Portugal. He got there years ahead of us, but we met up again in New York. Good friends."

"Lilith," Myriam Goldberg says—

"I'm Capucine."

"Yes. Forgive me. We owe you and Grand Loup everything... We hope to repay you."

13.

Afternoons are for Latin. Father John Gabriel is discoursing on Dionysius, tyrant of Syracuse, and on his courtier Damocles, and on the sword suspended by a hair above the head of Damocles, and on the idiomatic meaning of the phrase *de pilo pendet*.

"Translate," Father JG orders Ti-Loup. "Literally."

"It hangs by a hair," Ti-Loup responds.

"Good. And colloquially?"

"What happens next is in the lap of the gods," Ti-Loup says.

"A rather free translation, but well put. The question inevitably arises: are we merely the playthings of the gods, or can we influence fate? As Brutus expressed it, *There is a tide in the affairs of men, which, taken at the flood...* Melusine, continue this quotation and tell us what was on the mind of Brutus when Shakespeare had him speak these words."

"*Which, taken at the flood,*" Cap recites, "*leads on to fortune. Omitted, all the voyage of their life / Is bound in shallows and in miseries...* He was considering whether or not to take part in the assassination of Julius Caesar."

"Good. And do you have a sense, *mon jeune vicomte*, that the decision of Brutus was hanging by a hair? That it could have gone either way?"

"Do you mean Shakespeare's Brutus or Plutarch's Brutus or the actual historical Brutus?" Ti-Loup asks.

Father JG raises his eyebrows. "And what sources other than Plutarch can you cite, Monsieur le Vicomte, for the 'actual historical Brutus' as you put it?"

"Well, Cicero," Ti-Loup says.

"Yes. Go on."

"Plutarch was born one hundred years after the death of Julius Caesar, but Cicero and Caesar knew each other. Cicero's letters to Atticus were Plutarch's source, and Plutarch was Shakespeare's source, and Brutus is different each time."

"True. In what way?"

"Cicero was hostile toward both Caesar and Mark Antony, and Plutarch was ambivalent about both. Plutarch raises the possibility that Brutus was actually the illegitimate son of Caesar, and that both Caesar and Brutus were aware of this, and if that was true, then yes, I think the decision of Brutus must have been agonizing and could have gone either way."

"It is true," Father JG acknowledges. "Plutarch raises the specter of the Oedipal struggle, which Shakespeare surely picked up with his *Et tu, Brute.* But, as you point out, there is no hint of this in Cicero, who was Caesar's contemporary, and who hosted Caesar in his own home. So we can probably dismiss the theory as Plutarch's invention. On the other hand, it may have seemed to Cicero a matter too risky and too delicate to mention."

"Cicero was like Pétain," Cap interjects. "He wanted to have his cake and eat it too. He wanted to stay on good terms with both sides. He sucked up to Caesar, then he sucked up to Brutus even more, but he never had the courage to face the music. The consequences were someone else's affair. He hightailed it out of Rome and fled to Greece."

Father JG frowns. He is playing with a pencil, turning it in circles with the fingers of his right hand. "That is an intemperate and ill-informed and unorthodox view, Mademoiselle Melusine."

go to p. 246

"It may take me a while to find him."

"He is not in the vinyeard or the *potager*," the countess says. "I have already sent Pierre and others. No one can find him. I fear this means he is ill. I cannot permit or order my servants into your father's home without his permission and so I am requesting you to go and find out what is wrong. I need his advice."

Cap is puzzled. If her father had shown signs of illness the night before, Ti-Loup would have told her. She pushes open the door of the gardener's cottage. If her father were ill, he would be lying on the couch in front of the cast-iron stove. The room is empty, but Cap hears sounds from the loft above. Her father's knees give him trouble now and he does not climb the ladder to the loft any more. That is Ti-Loup's space, his private lair.

Cap listens.

There is thumping and laughter. She hears the voices of Petit Christophe and Chantal.

But where is her father?

If, as the countess insisted, he is not working in the vineyard or the vegetable garden, she can think of only one possible place where he might be. She herself has never actually been inside the safe house, the lost cellar, but she knows where it is. She follows the trail into the woods to the ruined stone foundations of a seventeenth-century farmhouse. From the entrance, she measures 200 paces toward the chateau. Here there is a creek, a trickle that runs into the Vienne which runs into the Loire. A small curved stone bridge, centuries old and crumbling, and only eight feet long, crosses the creek. Nobody uses the bridge. Indeed it has been so long—more than a century—since the bridge was used that any footpath which must once have led to it has been obliterated by moss, ivy, and fungal outcrops. The bridge itself is almost invisible, matted with creepers and hidden behind clumps of holly and overhanging trees. Under the bridge, set into the supporting stone pillar on the chateau side, is a small metal door as green with oxidation and mildew and moss as the vegetation that screens it. In the center of the green door is a great iron ring.

Cap's feet sink into creek mud as she crouches under the bridge. The ring is rusty, but it must have been recently oiled. It turns easily in Cap's hands and she swings back the hinged cover to the upside-down world of roots and worms. In the middle of a dark wood and under a bridge, she feels vertigo. She can see only nothing and blackness, but she knows there are steep stone steps going down. "Papa?" she calls, and listens to her voice travel and reverberate and bounce back at her.

"Cap! What are you doing here?" The voice floats up and echoes as strangely as if her father had six voices, each ghost-like, damp, ricocheting moistly all the way from the sealed-up wall of the chateau cellars.

"The countess wants to see you," Cap calls. This is like listening to the mass in the village church, the priest's voice being chanted up and back, up and back, chorus and antiphony, from stone floor to vaulted stone ceiling. She has to pause and let her voice settle. "She said it was urgent." Cap waits for the reverberations to subside. "I don't have a flashlight. Can you come up?"

A glow of light precedes her father. His footsteps multiply themselves like muffled drum beats against the stone. When he emerges, blinking against the light, Cap blurts: "Do you know that Petit Christophe and Chantal are in our loft?"

"Yes."

"How did you know?"

"I saw them from the vineyard. Saw them go into the cottage."

"Then why come here? *Here!*"

"I don't know. I needed somewhere dark and private to be afraid. I've lost the knack of being afraid. In the war, I was afraid

245

go to p. 247

His right hand clenches in disapproval. The pencil snaps into two parts. "Cicero is the father of civilized discourse," Father JG says. "He was admired by Locke and Hume, but also by Jefferson. He was a father of the very idea of liberty. And he most certainly did face consequences. He was assassinated by the henchmen of Mark Antony just a year after Caesar's death, and he died defending the rights of citizens against dictators."

"He had some dictatorial tendencies himself," Cap argues. "When he was consul, he executed five Roman citizens without trial."

Father JG is palpably angry now. "To save the republic. He was up against the Catiline conspiracy."

"Pétain made the same argument," Cap says. "He did it to save France. So he claimed."

"The situations are not remotely comparable." Father JG is red in the face. "Your interpretation of historical evidence is perverse, Mademoiselle. Uhh... Madame la Comtesse, I beg your pardon... I hope you will excuse this heated discussion."

"Evidence of excellent teaching," the countess says from the doorway. "Father John Gabriel, I wish to have a word with Melusine."

Cap and Ti-Loup discreetly roll their eyes at each other. *Now you're in trouble,* Ti-Loup telegraphs.

But the countess simply takes Cap's hand and leads her toward the *prie-dieux* in the great salon. "When I am distressed," she says, "I pray to the Virgin for peace. Pray with me."

Cap fingers her rosary while the countess prays.

Eventually the countess says: "There have been a number of recent events, Melusine, that are very disturbing to me. I need to speak to your father. Will you bring him to the chateau?"

"Now, *Madame la Comtesse*?"

"Now."

"He will be in the vineyard or the *potager*," Cap says, puzzled.

go to p. 244

From p245

all the time and I used to come here."

"Shouldn't you have stopped them? Ti-Christophe and Chantal?"

"Should I have stopped them?" Cap's father repeats this slowly. It is a serious question, but one that he is asking himself.

"This is a bad thing, isn't it?"

"I think so," the gardener says. "I think it's a bad thing. I don't like it."

"So why didn't you stop them?"

"Why didn't I stop them?" Cristophe le Jardinier feels in the dark for his own answer. "I think what's happening is unwise and I don't think any good can come of it. But that's where your mother and I made you. In that loft. On that straw mattress. It wasn't wise then and it was extremely dangerous, but look what came of it! " He ruffles her hair and smiles. "My son has the right to choose his own dangers. Everyone has that right."

go to p. 249 – Chapter 14

say things that you'd never forgive me for saying, *Maman*."

Cap stares at him with astonishment.

A silence descends on the dinner table.

The countess says, with exquisite politeness, "I do not permit any further mention of Pétain. *Mes enfants,* we will pray together in the salon after the meal."

After dinner, Gwynne Patrice and Cap share one prie-dieu, the countess kneels alone at the other. While the countess murmurs her way through the rosary, Ti-Loup and Cap avoid each other's eyes.

"Amen," the countess murmurs.

"Amen," Ti-Loup and Cap murmur with relief.

"And now," the countess says, "we have grave matters to discuss. I have spoken with your father, Melusine. We are deeply disturbed. Monsieur Monsard has paid me a visit. The butcher tells me, Gwynne Patrice, that you have been seen at *la boucherie,* working as though you were a peasant. Is this true?"

"No, *Maman,*" Ti-Loup says evenly, meeting his mother's eyes. "How would it even be possible, with my ancestry, that I could work like a peasant?"

"Melusine has taught you many things," the countess says drily, not without the hint of a smile, "including how to answer a question with a question, like a lawyer, and how to be courteously caustic."

Ti-Loup meets his mother's eyes steadily, but says nothing.

"When do you visit *la boucherie?*" his mother demands.

Ti-Loup is silent.

"Unfortunately, Monsieur Monsard has shown me incontrovertible proof of your facility with a butcher's knife in the room where the carcasses are prepared. I expect you to explain why and how this has come about. Monsieur Monsard says that nobody

go to p. 250

14.

Dinner at the chateau is a formal though not a solemn affair. The countess sits at the head of the table, Father JG at the foot. Ti-Loup and Capucine face each other across the silver candelabra which branches between them like a tree. The butler and a housemaid wait on them. Conversation is usually lively.

"Father Jean Gabriel," the countess says, "you were having a very intense discussion about Cicero today before I interrupted the class."

"Ah, yes, *Madame la Comtesse*," Father JG says carefully.

"You were in verbal combat with Melusine, I think."

Father JG clears his throat and takes a sip of wine. "Mademoiselle Melusine has rather unorthodox views, *Madame la Comtesse*, and I felt it incumbent upon me to... to..."

"To spar with her."

"To counter her unorthodox views, *Madame la Comtesse*."

"Not a simple task, Father. Believe me, I know. She is a formidable opponent, is she not? And she has many unorthodox opinions."

"I'm not unorthodox about Cicero as a rhetorician," Cap protests. "But I don't think much of him politically. Too much like Pétain, a moral coward playing it safe and hedging his bets."

"We will not be discussing Pétain," the countess says politely but firmly.

Ti-Loup announces with unexpected vehemence: "You let Cap

 go to p248

has seen you enter and he does not know how often you are there or how you get in. I expect an explanation from you."

Ti-Loup says quietly: "I have no explanation to give you, *Maman*."

"Do Father Jean Gabriel's educational trips have anything to do with this?"

"Father Jean Gabriel knows nothing about my visits to *la boucherie, Maman*, and he is in no way responsible for them."

"*Visits!*" the countess says. "Plural. I see. How many visits? How often?"

Ti-Loup says nothing.

The countess holds herself very still for several minutes, then she kneels at her *prie-dieu*. Time passes. The only sound is the murmur of her prayers and the soft click of rosary beads. She rises and smooths down the crushed silk of her dress. "Very well," she says. "All educational trips will be cancelled. You are not to leave the chateau, Gwynne Patrice, at any time. And now Melusine, I am reluctant to ask you this question, but I know you will be truthful. Did you know that Gwynne Patrice was visiting your brother and engaging in unseemly behavior for someone of his station in life?"

Cap thinks of kneeling at her *prie-dieu*. She thinks of fingering the rosary instead of speaking. She presses her lips together.

"Melusine?"

"*Madame la Comtesse*, I do not think the work my brother does is unseemly for anyone."

"I do not mean any disrespect for your brother, Melusine. Civilized society cannot maintain itself without excellent butchers. But you have not answered my question. Did you know that Gwynne Patrice has, on at least two occasions and I don't know how many more, been engaged in butchering livestock at the establishment of Monsieur Monsard?"

"I prefer not to answer the question, *Madame la Comtesse*."

"But I am requiring you to answer the question."

"Madame, you know I would never lie to you. But you cannot make me answer a question."

"Your father and I, Melusine, have a history of mutual respect that stretches back many years. We were children together. When I was born, your grandfather was the manager and the *viticulteur* of the chateau. Neither of us was ever permitted to leave the estate. We had only each other as companions."

Ti-Loup flicks astonished eyes at Cap. "Did you know that?"

"No," she says. "Yes. I suppose I did. I don't know if I did."

"We were childhood playmates who understood our respective stations in life," the countess says.

"But since the war..." Cap says.

"Exactly," the countess admits. "The war changed things. But it did not change everything. Your father, Melusine, is deeply uneasy about your brother's relationship with the butcher's daughter. Has your father told you that Monsieur Monsard will terminate Petit Christophe's services if he has any further contact with Mademoiselle Chantal?"

Cap's sudden intake of breath is audible. "No, Madame. Papa did not tell me that."

"That just shows," Ti-Loup says hotly, "how stupid Monsieur Monsard is. If he fires Petit Christophe his business will suffer. The best butchers in Chinon and Tours will compete to hire Petit Christophe. He may even be snatched up by Paris."

"You seem to be very knowledgeable about his skills," the countess says.

"Ti-Loup is reporting what I've told him," Cap offers.

"I see. There appears to be some history that I, however, do not know, Melusine, because for five years after the war, I was in New York. Why is there enmity between your family and the family Monsard? Your father would not speak of it."

"I do not wish to speak of it either, Madame."

"Nevertheless, Melusine, I am requesting that you *do* speak of the matter and that you speak on your word of honor. Since both your father and the butcher are dependent on my patronage, I believe I have a right to know. And if there *is* enmity between the manager of my estate and the butcher, why would Monsieur Monsard offer an apprenticeship to your brother?"

"Because he is afraid of what Petit Christophe might tell about his past, Madame. About the butcher's past, I mean."

"The butcher's past? Everyone knows the butcher's past. He was born here. He has lived all his life in St Gilles. His father was the butcher before him. What do you mean, his past?"

"During the Occupation, Madame."

"Ahh..." Agitated, the countess strokes the carved arm of her chair. "Melusine, you have no sense, no awareness at all, of acceptable boundaries... You have absolutely no sense of what may be said and what may not be said... We must be calm. We must pray, *mes enfants*." The countess rises and kneels at her prie-dieu. "Let us pray, *mes enfants*."

Cap rises and kneels at her assigned *prie-dieu*.

"Gwynne Patrice!" the countess commands.

"I do not wish to pray, *Maman*. I have no need."

The countess is visibly trembling. She bows her head so low that it touches the lectern on which her missal rests, but after only two decades of the rosary she turns to Cap and says: "You are implying something very grave, Melusine. Terrible things, terrible things were done in the wake of the war to anyone who was accused... In Paris, after the Liberation, I saw things that no one should ever see. You should not even *suggest...*"

"Everyone knows there were informers and collaborators in St Gilles, Madame, but nobody knows for certain—"

"Enough, Melusine! Enough! You are not to speak of these

matters. Do you know that your father, if not for me—?"

"Yes, Madame, I do know. My father is profoundly grateful and so am I. But what of the lives of my mother, and of my brother's mother, and of the husband of Marie-Claire? It is difficult for me... it is, to be honest, *impossible* for me to understand how you could have fed German officers and offered them the chateau wines."

Madame la Comtesse clutches a hand to her chest and winces with pain. "Do you think I had any choice?" she gasps. She fingers her rosary.

Ti-Loup and Cap observe her in nervous silence.

15.

A mutinous silence presides over morning literature and Father John Gabriel is visibly apprehensive. Between two acts in Racine's *Bérénice*, he abruptly demands: "Why is *Madame la Comtesse* so displeased with me? What have you said to her?"

"She is not displeased with you," Ti-Loup tells him, "but with me."

"And with me," Cap says.

"Not with you," Ti-Loup says bitterly.

"What have you said about me?" Father JG demands.

"I said nothing about you," Ti-Loup says. "This has nothing to do with you."

"Then why have I been told that all field trips are now forbidden?"

"Not for you," Cap says. "You can go wherever you want on weekends. You can't take us with you, that's all."

"We are prisoners of the chateau," Ti-Loup says glumly.

"I am hired at the pleasure of *la comtesse*." Father JG paces the classroom. "I have been instructed that we will now hold regular classes on Saturdays. And on Sunday afternoons, we will have readings and discussions on the history of Holy Mother Church."

"So you've had your wings clipped too, Father," Cap says. "I'm sorry."

"I'm particularly sorry," Ti-Loup says.

"We're both sorry," Cap assures Father JG. "It's really our fault."

"I am to monitor your movements," the Jesuit says. "I hope there will be nothing negative to report."

"What's next?" Ti-Loup demands morosely.

Across the breakfast table in the chateau, a meal for which neither the countess nor Father JG is ever up and about, Cap raises her eyebrows at Ti-Loup. "What happened last night?" she asks, when the housemaid returns to the kitchen. "Did you manage to climb out and back in?"

"Yes."

"So no problems?"

"Petit Christophe slept in the loft with me. He has been fired."

"*Merde!*" Cap thinks about this. "But he loves the vineyard and the *potager*. He'll work with papa again."

"No, he won't. He knew this was coming. That's why he went into Tours, and he is going into Chinon today to visit the butchers. All of them want him." Ti-Loup rests his elbows on the table and thumps his temples with the palms of his hands. "It's not fair. You can go back to your father's whenever you want, but I've got nowhere to go. I'm caged."

"No you're not. You climbed out of your window last night."

"You don't understand," Ti-Loup says.

"I do."

"No, you don't. You've always been free as a bird."

"You've always been rich and spoiled, *tu con!* Just how much does it take to make you happy?"

"I can't ever remember being happy until the night I climbed out my window and slept in your loft. But I'm happiest when I'm with Ti-Christophe and when I've got a boning knife in my hands. And my mother has taken that away."

"Only if you let her."

"I can't stop her."

"Yes you can. You plan your safe house. You plan your escape route. If your escape route is blocked, you plan a new route."

"My safe house is the loft in your cottage."

"So stay there. And plan a new route for after Ti-Christophe is hired in Chinon or Tours."

"How could I go there?" Ti-Loup asks, "when I'm not allowed to leave the chateau?"

"Before you moved back from New York, I'd never been inside the chateau. You told me I wasn't even allowed in the grounds, but I came in anyway. We both need a new way to get to Tours and we'll find it."

"My father is coming to get me," Ti-Loup announces.

"What? Why?"

"I'm to go to boarding school in Massachusetts, the same one my father went to. Turns out my mother suggested it. It's so stupid and so ironic. *Maman's* always been paranoid that my father would kidnap me and send me there.

"When is he coming?"

"Soon. Read this. It's the letter my mother wrote to my father. He sent me a copy."

My esteemed husband:

I know we have always had different views about our son's education. You wanted him to attend your own boarding school (for what I consider a barely competent American education) and I felt strongly that the least I owed him was the excellence of a Jesuit and French education with the Sorbonne as goal. However, I regret to report that unanticipated connections with the village have arisen and I now think it advisable to put a moat between our son and current influences which we would both find undesirable.

"So I'm an undesirable influence," Cap says. "That hurts."

"Not you. Your brother. We descendants of the De la Vallières

256

and the Vanderbilts are not supposed to dirty our hands."

"Your kind already have blood on their hands."

"*My* kind? What do you mean, *my kind*? Whose side are you on?"

"I don't know. Whose side are *you* on?"

"Ti-Christophe's side. Your father's side. The side of the gardener's cottage. But you. You've crossed over. You'd rather live in the chateau."

"I do love the chateau and I love spending time with your mother. I love what she's taught me. And I love papa's cottage and I love working in the *potager* and with the vines. No one's making me choose between them. I would die for papa and Ti-Christophe. I would die for you too. I don't want you to leave."

"Then speak to *maman*. Stop her."

"You can stop her. You can refuse to go."

"Didn't you read her letter? The only person who ever made her change her mind is you. If you won't speak to her—"

"I'll speak to her." Impulsively Cap puts her arms around Ti-Loup and kisses him on the lips. For two seconds, Ti-Loup leans into the embrace then pulls sharply away.

"Father JG will see us," he says nervously. "He'll tell *maman*."

"I don't care," Cap says.

16.

"I'm sorry," Cap whispers. "I tried. I couldn't make her change her mind. She says I don't understand but she claims that my father does and that he agrees with her."

"Mademoiselle Melusine," Father JG says sternly. "Do you have something you wish to tell us in Latin?"

"No, Father."

"Then attend to Cicero, please. Your translation, *Monsieur le Vicomte*. Next paragraph please."

"I'm sorry, Father. I haven't prepared it."

"*Monsieur le Vicomte?*" Father JG is shocked silent. "This is unprecedented."

"I'm, you know, I'm not sleeping well. My father's coming for me in two weeks and I don't want to leave."

"Focus on Cicero, *Monsieur le Vicomte*. You will find that linguistic and rhetorical perfection induces calm."

"I have to take an entrance exam for my father's school. I need study time, not Cicero."

"I believe Cicero can survive that distorted perception of his value. You must keep up with your regular assignments."

"My mother says the entrance exam has priority."

"Your mother has said nothing to me."

"She will. I have to sit for the exam two days after I arrive in New York."

258

"I do not for one second doubt," Father JG says, "that you will outperform any American student who takes the exam."

"I wish my parents were as confident, Father. No one believes that the school won't let a Vanderbilt in, but just the same, my parents, both of them, will blame you if I don't pass with distinction. There's no Latin test. But I have to know all the American presidents and the order they came in. You haven't taught us that, Father."

"I have taught you far more history than the average American schoolchild knows, not to mention more tools for critical evaluation of the American system of government. Nevertheless, I defer to the wishes of *Madame la Comtesse*. And you do seem extraordinarily agitated, *mon petit vicomte*. Mademoiselle Melusine, let us leave *le vicomte* to his presidents and their chronology."

"No, no, Father." Ti-Loup's objection is quick and vehement. "I need her to stay and study with me."

"Am I to understand that Mademoiselle Melusine will also be taking the entrance exam?"

"No, she won't. It's a boys' school. But we study better together. My mother always says so and you've said it yourself."

"You may study together," Father JG says stiffly. "I don't doubt that you will pass with distinction."

Ti-Loup rolls his eyes at the closing door. "I thought I'd never get rid of him."

"You shouldn't worry about that silly exam."

"It's not the exam I'm worried about. Something terrible happened last night."

"What? Where?"

"In your father's cottage. All hell broke loose. Someone was banging on door, banging and banging and wouldn't stop. Gave all of us a dreadful fright, especially your father."

"A knock at night gives him bad dreams."

259

"Wasn't a knock. It was a battering."

"What time?"

"I don't know what time. After midnight. We were asleep, in deep sleep, so we were slow to wake up, but the banging went on and on. "

"Who was it?"

"Chantal."

"Chantal!?"

"She had a black eye. She was hysterical. Bruises on her face and her arms and all over. She said she was pregnant."

Cap crosses herself.

Ti-Loup asks irritably: "For God's sake, what good do you think that will do?"

"None. It's a reflex. Makes me feel less anxious, that's all. Is my brother the father?"

"He thinks so. He hopes so. He asked who beat her up but she couldn't answer, she couldn't speak. She kept sobbing and Ti-Christophe kept saying 'It's okay. It's okay. We'll get married.' She couldn't catch her breath and she started turning blue around the lips. Your father gave her whisky and she passed out."

"Yes?" Cap prods, to nudge Ti-Loup from a lengthy pause.

"I can't help wondering if that's what my father was like. Is like."

"Like Ti-Christophe?"

"Not remotely like Ti-Christophe. Like Olivier. Like Michel Monsard. I mean someone who treats women badly. This morning, Chantal told us her brother and Olivier came into her room last night. Her father must have known, she said. He must have heard. There's no way he wouldn't have heard. She said her brother watched while Olivier raped her. They both beat her. Her brother told her she was a whore."

"Where is she now? Where's Ti-Christophe?"

"Both at your place. In the cottage. Chantal said her father and brother found out she was pregnant. She went to the village doctor and the doctor told the priest and the butcher. They knew before Ti-Christophe knew. Chantal said her brother and Olivier are planning to kill Ti-Christophe."

"Ti-Christophe's not here," Grand Loup tells his daughter and Ti-Loup. "A village boy came with a message. He has gone to meet Michel Monsard in the woods."

"Papa! Papa! How could you let him go when you know what you know?"

"A man's honor is his own business," her father says. "I trust my son's instincts. Besides, Michel Monsard needs a good thrashing. Olivier, on the other hand, we will report to the police."

"But Olivier will be there too. They'll gang up on Petit Christophe," Ti-Loup protests. "It won't be a fair fight."

"They ganged up on me," Cap's father says. "It wasn't a fair fight. But here I am. Ti-Christophe's strong as an ox. He'll win. I'll bet on that, if it comes to an unfair fight."

"It's going to come to an unfair fight," Ti-Loup says.

"Where is Chantal?" Cap wants to know.

"Upstairs. In the loft. She's sleeping. I'll keep her safe here."

"Where's Ti-Christophe meeting them?"

"Meeting *him*, meeting Michel, that's what the boy said. Near the safe house, which means Michel has a sixth sense about that place and he's trying to smoke out the location."

"Is that what he said? *Near the safe house?*"

"Of course not. He said *By the old stone bridge.* You are not to go there, Capucine. Ti-Christophe can look after himself. Trust me. Trust your brother."

"I trust you and I trust my brother," Cap says. "I don't trust Michel Monsard or his father and I don't trust Olivier."

"No more do I," her father says. "But Ti-Christophe can look after himself and he won't thank you if you meddle with his honor. Chantal's not what I would have wanted for him, but probably his mother and your mother were not what my own father would have wanted. We'll have a quiet church wedding for my son and the butcher's daughter in Chinon and we'll throw a party when my grandchild arrives."

Cap and Ti-Loup huddle under the bridge.

"There's Ti-Christophe," Cap whispers.

"Is the entrance to the safe house somewhere here?"

"Yes. Shh."

"This iron ring?"

"Yes."

"You told me you made that up."

"I lied to you. Ti-Christophe told me to say I made it up."

"Ti-Christophe doesn't trust me?"

"Back then he didn't. Now he does."

"Why didn't he trust me back then?"

Cap stares at him. "Why do you think? Nazis used to sleep in your bedroom. Your mother used to dine with them every night. At the same table where we have dinner."

"Why haven't you told me that?"

"I thought you knew. Anyway Papa says your mother saved him. Shh. Look."

"Michel and Olivier, two against one. We *knew* that would happen."

Cap and Ti-Loup are fifty feet from the confrontation. Voices are raised, there is buffeting, knives are flashed. Olivier and Michel, blades drawn, rush Ti-Christophe who steps back and braces himself against a tree. He pulls his boning blade from his belt and parries the double onslaught. Olivier falls. Michel slashes.

Ti-Christophe is caught off-balance and falls. Michel stabs and stabs again, more times than the children will remember, though they will try for the rest of their lives to replay these minutes. Ti-Christophe's fingers are still clenched on his boning knife and he slashes wildly, blinded by blood. He misses Michel by a mile. He stumbles on the prone body of Olivier and sinks his blade in Olivier's heart. Then his own body convulses and pushes him back. He flails, like somebody drowning, before he lies still.

Michel Monsard runs, crashing through the woods, leaving two bodies on the ground.

Neither Ti-Loup nor Cap can move. They hold each other. Cap clamps one hand over her mouth to mute the strange sounds that rise from her throat. Ti-Loup vomits.

"We should have stopped them," he says, wiping his mouth on his sleeve.

"We couldn't—" Cap says. "We couldn't have—"

"We could have." Ti-Loup has trouble catching his breath. "We should have rushed between... I should have."

"Then *you* would have been killed."

"I wouldn't care. Ti-Christophe would still be alive."

There is so much blood on Ti-Christophe's body, so much on the ground around him, that Cap slips and falls when she tries to touch her brother's body. Ti-Loup kneels in a puddle of red. Ti-Christophe and Olivier are arranged in a weirdly graceful Gothic arc, arms extended, fingertips to fingertips, touching. The handle of Ti-Christophe's boning knife, vertical, stands like a flagpole planted in Olivier's heart.

Cap places her fingers first on one wrist, then on the other.

"Yes," she sighs. "We should have stopped them."

"What will we do?"

"We have to tell Papa."

"We can't tell him. It will break his heart."

"His heart has been broken before."

"Not this way," Ti-Loup says. "Ti-Christophe will be charged with murder. Michel Monsard will tell."

"He won't dare. We saw him kill Ti-Christophe."

"But Michel doesn't know that," Ti-Loup points out. "He doesn't know that we saw."

"Won't matter. There'll be too much evidence against him. Which body was stabbed more often? Which stab wounds match Michel's knife?"

"Whose knife is in Olivier's heart?"

Ti-Loup creeps into the bloodied space between the bodies. He nestles up against Ti-Christophe's chest. He lifts Ti-Christophe's lifeless arm and drapes it around his own shoulders. "I'm not going to leave him," he says.

Cap pulls him out of the bloody circle. They cling to each other and thrash about in the undergrowth in a passion of need and horror and fear. Afterwards they will not remember how much time has passed. They will only remember lying near the bridge, exhausted, looking up through the treetops at the sky.

"We have to tell Papa," Cap says.

"We can't. We can't let him see Ti-Christophe's knife in Olivier's heart. Once the police see that, they will charge Ti-Christophe with murder. Two killers, is what they will say. Who killed each other. Michel will plead self-defense. What we saw won't count because we're children in the eyes of the courts and because you are Ti-Christophe's sister. Father Boniface will forbid Christian burial because Ti-Christophe killed and that will break your father's heart. If we say nothing, nothing will happen until the bodies are found, and then it will be a great mystery. Michel won't dare say anything. He'll claim he knows nothing, saw nothing, and by now his knife's at the bottom of the Vienne."

"We have to tell Papa that Ti-Christophe is dead."

"But we don't have to tell *everything*," Ti-Loup says.

17.

"Papa, we have something to tell you."

"I hope you didn't interfere between Ti-Christophe and Michel Monsard."

"Ti-Christophe was killed, Papa."

Christophe le Jardinier crosses himself and leans his forehead against the wall of his cottage. "God disposes," he says, his voice breaking, "as He sees fit. It is no dishonor to die in an honorable fight."

"It wasn't an honorable fight, Papa. It was two against one."

"Olivier was there too?"

"You knew that would happen, Papa. They ganged up on him."

The gardener shakes his head. He pulls a chair back from the table and slumps into it. "How do people with no shame manage their lives? Cowards! Two against one, and my son is dead, but they live, and Olivier who abused Chantal is still alive."

"No, Papa. Michel Monsard is alive. Ti-Christophe tried to defend himself and killed Olivier but then Michel stabbed Ti-Christophe. Many more times than he needed. And then he ran away. He doesn't know that we saw."

"Cap, come to me." The gardener holds his daughter fiercely close. "We are all that we have left," he says.

"Papa, we have Ti-Loup also."

"Yes," her father says. "We have Ti-Loup also. Of course we

do." He pulls the boy into the triad of comfort and they hold each other. They simply stand and hold each other.

After some time the gardener says: "So then. Take me to my son's body."

"It was here, Papa. Both bodies were here. Someone has moved them. You can see where they have been dragged."

"They've covered up the blood," Ti-Loup says. He pushes away leaves with his foot. The soil beneath is unstained. "They used shovels. Look: scrape marks. But no trace of blood."

Christophe le Jardinier leans against a tree to steady himself. He covers his eyes with the back of his right forearm.

"Papa?" Cap rests her body against his and holds his left hand.

"I never saw the bodies or the burial places of his mother or of your mother, Cap. I didn't think it could happen again." He shakes his head and butts his forehead against the tree. "I didn't think that was possible."

"It must have been Michel Monsard and his father," Cap says. "They've taken the bodies."

"But where would they take Ti-Christophe?" Ti-Loup is wide-eyed and disbelieving. "And why?"

"We know *why*," Cap says.

"Yes, we know why," her father says. "Collaborators have ghosts at their heels. But I cannot bear it. I cannot bear it that I don't have my son's body."

"We have evidence, Papa. We know what we saw. We can tell the police."

Ti-Loup meets her eyes and holds them. "What can we tell the police?" he asks. His eyes say more. *There could be no requiem mass,* his eyes say.

"We tell them nothing," the gardener says. "We have no body. We have no proof of death. We have no way of knowing what

267

deals the police made with the butcher back then. We have no way of knowing what deals they are making now. They can tell the police that my son murdered Olivier and fled. We tell them nothing. We wait for them to tell us or for them to ask and then all we can say is that Petit Christophe is missing. Of Olivier we say and know nothing." He closes his eyes. "Three times. Three times. *Why?*"

Cap whispers to Ti-Loup: "What are we going to tell Chantal?"

18.

"My mother gave me this," Ti-Loup says. "Pearls and jade. What sort of gift is that for a boy? It's like having to wear a blue dress."

"It's her own rosary. She's giving you everything that makes her feel safe."

"I hate it the way I hated my blue dress. I'm supposed to keep it under my pillow, which I won't."

"I know this is a stupid thing to say," Cap admits, "but I believe it will keep you safe."

"What?! Even Father JG would be annoyed if he heard you. Superstition's for peasants."

"I'm a peasant, remember? And the rosary makes me feel calmer. Your mother, though... this means she is very afraid for you."

"I know she is. I'm supposed to come back each Christmas, but she's afraid my father won't let me."

"I'm afraid of that too."

"How can she be less afraid of losing me to my father than of having me work as a butcher? Right here in St Gilles where she could see me every day? It makes no sense."

"It makes sense to her," Cap's father says quietly. "Be gentle with your mother, Ti-Loup. Behind her back, the village makes fun of her. A son who's a butcher proves their point. She'd be a laughing stock."

"Is that what you think? That she'd be a laughing stock?"

"In St Gilles, she will be. She is. You're not the only person who hurts or feels lonely, Ti-Loup, and nor am I."

"If I ever pray my mother's rosary," Ti-Loup tells Cap, "but I won't... But if I did, at every bead I would think of you and Grand Loup and Ti-Christophe."

"I'll move back to the loft. I can't leave Papa alone. But I shouldn't leave your *maman* alone either. I don't know what to do."

"*Maman* has *chosen* to be alone. She's arranged it. She's *ordered* it. Don't waste your sympathy. And your father won't be alone. Chantal is there now."

"Can anyone keep Chantal safe?"

"Grand Loup will keep her safe. He wants to keep his grandchild safe."

"Yes. Yes, he does. But you are a son to him too. He's lost Ti-Christophe. I'm not sure he'll be able to bear it when you go."

"I'm going to write every day. To him and to you."

"And I'll write back."

It is the talk of the butcher shop, the baker shop, the markets, and the village square, but Cap and Ti-Loup have to hear it from Pierre of the velvet pantaloons and from the countess herself.

"Everyone knows your mother's sending you away," Pierre tells Ti-Loup, "because you smell like a butcher shop. And everyone knows your own father doesn't want you. He's going to pack you off to a concentration camp the minute you get there."

"I'll be going to the school my father went to."

"It's run like a concentration camp. Everyone knows that."

"Everyone knows what you do with goats," Cap tells him.

"Everyone knows that your brother knocked up the butcher's daughter," Pierre snaps back. "And everyone knows he ran away because he was scared shitless of her father and Michel."

"My brother did not run away."

"Where is he then? Why'd he disappear?"

Cap says with dignity and composure, "Ti-Christophe and my father are taking care of Chantal until the baby is born."

Pierre laughs. "Everyone knows Monsieur Monsard sent for the gendarmerie in Tours to arrest your brother. Everyone knows he's on the run. The butcher told the police he's armed and dangerous."

"Armed with what?"

"He stole all the butcher's knives and cleavers. That's why the police are taking Chantal back to her father's."

"They can't do that."

"They can. They've done it. Her father has the right and it's for her own safety

"I don't believe you," Ti-Loup says.

"You don't have a clue," Pierre taunts, "about how much you don't know. How much everyone knows except you."

"We know Ti-Christophe did not run away," Cap says quietly. "And we know Chantal is with my father."

"Not anymore. The gendarmes took her."

Ti-Loup is disbelieving. "When?"

"This morning. After you left. After you climbed back through the chateau window. You think we don't know?" Pierre laughs. "You think we don't see? You think we didn't tell your mother? Everyone knows."

"Pierre," the countess says from the doorway. "You may go now."

"*Madame la Comtesse*," Pierre says, bowing. He backs out of the room, step by careful backward step. "I thought they should know, Madame. I thought you would want them to know that you know."

"I will speak to your father," the countess says, "about your returning to the farm."

From behind the back of the countess, as he exits the room, Pierre makes an obscene gesture with one finger toward Ti-Loup and Cap.

"*Madame la Comtesse,*" Cap says with a very sweet smile, "I believe Pierre has something further to say to you," though Pierre has vanished when the countess turns.

"*Mes enfants,*" she says. "I have very distressing news. It is true that the gendarmes took the butcher's daughter back to her father, but then...." The countess passes the beads of an invisible rosary through her fingers. Her eyes are closed. "It seems the young woman swallowed poison and has killed both herself and the child."

"Sometimes," Cap's father says, "people come back long after you have given up hope."

"I will come back," Ti-Loup promises.

"I will wait for you," Cap's father says. Absent-mindedly he tousles Ti-Loup's hair and strokes the boy's face almost as though he has gone blind and is reading Braille and committing a likeness to memory. "But they don't come back from the dead," he says sadly.

"Papa?"

"They don't go away either. They are always with you. Especially when there is no body and no funeral and no proof." With the iron lever, he lifts one of the cast-iron circles from the top of the stove and studies the flame intently. "They are all here," he says. "They all sleep in the loft now."

"He is somewhere else," Ti-Loup whispers to Cap.

"Everyone is leaving me," Cap murmurs. "Don't go."

"I don't want to."

"You could refuse. You could stay with us."

"And you'd stay in the chateau."

"I told your *maman* that I'd be staying with Papa tonight. If you go away, I won't leave him alone."

"If I leave, I promise I'll come back."

"I won't forgive you if you don't."

"This is the last supper," Cap's father says suddenly, as though they have all just arrived. "Roasted rabbits and roasted potatoes. I prepared them myself. That was the first supper you had with us, Ti-Loup. You remember?"

Ti-Loup nods. He cannot speak.

"That was the first supper, and this is the last one," the gardener says.

"Except I roasted those rabbits," Cap reminds him. "For the first supper."

"Years ago," the gardener says. "Years and years and years ago."

He looks back down the tunnel of those years and gets lost there, the serving ladle sliding from his hands. The spoon rests on the crisped browned body of a rabbit.

Ti-Loup whispers again: "He is somewhere else."

Gently, Cap takes the ladle from her father and serves.

The fiery glow from the cast-iron stove throws a warm red-gold light on three faces. We are like Cezanne's *Card Players,* Cap thinks. Three of us leaning in over the table, the ghost of Ti-Christophe watching us with his back against the wall.

She says, "There's a painting in one of Father JG's books. It reminds me of us, right now, in front of the fire."

"Ah!" Cap's father says, startled, as though awareness has suddenly pricked him like a dart and he has returned from wherever he was to the table in front of the stove. "Speaking of paintings. A package came in the mail from Myriam Goldberg. Two things. A letter for me and a small padded envelope for you, Cap. Wait. I'll get it."

Cap studies the padded envelope with wonder. "American stamps!" she says, fascinated. "What's in it?"

"I haven't opened it. It's addressed to you."

Cap tugs on the red thread that says *Pull to open* and extracts something that is hidden between two stiff pieces of cardboard. It is a small painting, about the size of a postcard, done in watercolors on thick white stock.

"It's Cap!" Ti-Loup says. "It's a portrait of Cap."

"No, it's of her mother Lilith," Grand Loup says. "Myriam Goldberg wrote that she painted it from memory not long after they first arrived in New York."

19.

In the tranquil inner courtyard of what was once the address of the Goldbergs on Madison Avenue, and indeed was once her own address during four years at NYU, Cap finally feels sufficiently calm to open the manila envelope that had been delivered to the Loeb Boathouse in Central Park. She can, she hopes, manage to subject herself to a view of the final photographs in the pack.

There are two that she has been holding at bay.

The fourth one is ghastly.

It is a close-up of the corpse of Olivier, full body length, face in three-quarter profile, Ti-Christophe's boning knife protruding like a stake from his heart. The photograph is black-and-white, the body a ghostly pale gray. It lies on its right side, the left arm falling limply across the torso, the right arm, on which the head rests, extended in a graceful arc like the curve of Adam's arm in Michelangelo's Sistine Chapel, but it touches no finger of God, no reaching finger at all. The potent space where Petit Christophe's hand would have brushed Olivier's index finger is empty and white. It is the stark blank margin of the photocopier paper. Not until after Petit Christophe had been sheared out of context by scissors had the copy been made.

No one but Michel Monsard or his father could have taken the original photograph.

And what had they done after that? What had they done with

the other half of the image? What had they done with the body?

Cap wills herself to stay calm. The next photograph, she knows, will be of the body of her brother and she needs to prepare herself. She focuses on the Lipchitz bronze, gift of the Goldbergs, rising from a foam of white caladiums, green-veined, and a wider inland sea of hostas. The sculpture itself is as full of space as it is of mass and seems to loft itself into flight from the dense groundcover like an eddying upward wisp of prayer.

Cap recalls that long-ago moment in the gardener's cottage when Myriam Goldberg first seemed to mistake her for Lilith, the mother she never knew. Petit Christophe was there. *I remember that,* her brother said. He meant the unloading of linens from the laundry van with the SS watching. But her father said *No. What you remember was later.*

Safe houses, Cap thinks. The courtyard of the building on Madison Avenue is one of her safe houses. She can look at the final photograph now.

It is not the photograph she was expecting.

The image is of Ti-Loup, aged fourteen, passing beneath massive alphabetic caryatids whose ominous forms glower above sliding glass doors.

AÉROPORT DE PARIS.
DÉPARTS—VOLS INTERNATIONAUX—PASSAGERS SEULEMENT
CONTRÔLE DE SÛRETÉ

The sliding doors are of textured glass and are opaque. They are closing and Ti-Loup is turning back to wave. His eyes are huge and haunted, his face stricken, the mournful falling gesture of his hand spelling out a line from the third canto of Dante's <u>Inferno</u>. *Abandon hope, all ye who enter here.*

That moment is as deeply imprinted in Cap's memory as the smell of roasting rabbits and the moment when Ti-Loup first appeared in the gardener's kitchen. She does know who took this photograph. The countess took it. The flashlight startled Cap and startled Ti-Loup.

"I don't know if I focused properly," the countess said at the time. "All these glaring fluorescent tubes, it's horrible. I'm not even sure what I took." She was scrunching up her eyes and rubbing them with her silk handkerchief.

"I didn't know you owned a camera, Madame la Comtesse."

"I sent to Paris for it. I bought it this week to preserve this wrenching moment, Melusine."

"Madame la Comtesse...?" Cap hesitates. The countess turns towards her and Cap makes direct eye contact and does not drop her gaze. "Who made this moment wrenching? And why was it necessary?"

The countess turns away and stares at the doors that have closed behind Ti-Loup. "You think I am cruel but it is life that is cruel."

"I know life is cruel," Cap says. Every night the bloodied arms of her brother reach for her. Every night, his face floats above her bed. *Help me*, he says. *Find me.* "That is why we should not do cruel things. We should not make life more painful than it is."

"I know you think I'm not aware of the grief of others but I'm all too aware. For the time being, trust me, this is the only wise thing to do, the only *safe* thing. I don't only mean for social reasons although I know that's what you think and what my son thinks. But the butcher and his son... I have come to see that you and your father are right. They are barbarians. I have proof you don't even know about. My son won't be safe if he stays here and you won't be safe either. I'm making arrangements for your safety. Don't cry, my child."

"I'm not crying. I never cry."

"I know you don't, and nor do I. This won't be a long separation. It will be like the blink of an eye before Gwynne Patrice is back and you'll both be attending the Sorbonne. And then we can all look at this photograph—if I managed to capture what I meant to capture, that is—and we can all smile at each other and say *It seemed such a wrenching parting back then, but it was absolutely necessary and it was nothing in the grand scheme of things.*"

20.

In the grand scheme of things, Cap is not sure whether she has been blackmailed or warned. She is not sure whether she is yet to be approached by the Zimbabwean body guard or by the Chinese defector or by someone she has not yet met. The pre-paid round-trip airfare sent to Sydney left the return flights open for her to choose date and time. Why was that? She does not want to walk into a trap. She does not want to advertise when she will leave. She does not want to be publicly detained at the airport.

She decides to walk all the way down Madison and then Broadway to Union Square. The four miles take her more than an hour and the crisp air makes her feel calmer. She walks on south another eight blocks to Washington Square Park, where she is surrounded by the old haven of NYU and Greenwich Village. She finds a small undistinguished slightly rundown hotel and checks in for five days and pays cash.

Much as she is tempted, she will not make a phone call to Australia. She has often had the phones in her hotel rooms tapped. Why make it easy for surveillance to trace the person making or answering the call?

She walks miles every day. She walks to Wall Street, to Battery Park, she takes the ferry to Staten Island. She walks across the Brooklyn Bridge and back. Every night, in her hotel room, she watches the news on TV. The trial of the Vanderbilt claimant and the finding of the jury are still being analyzed. Interviews are being filed from a village in France. Bemused, Cap sees old fishermen in St Gilles.

*The gardener's son...*they say. *The butcher's daughter...*
Petit Christophe, they say.
Cap buries her face in the pillow and weeps silently.

She sleeps with the envelope of photographs clutched close under her quilt and they do nothing good for her dreams. She carries them around in her shoulder bag all day. She does not want anyone to steal them, see them, copy them.

No one makes contact. There are never any messages. At the reception desk no one asks about a woman from Sotheby's. After five days, she calls the airline, quotes the ticket reservation number, and books her flights and her seats.

She is waiting at her gate at Kennedy Airport for the first leg of her long flight back: New York to Los Angeles, LAX to Sydney. The envelope containing the photographs is in her carry-on bag and she is afraid the security scan will detect something black and malevolent. An alarm will sound. Whoever bought or stole the photographs and delivered them to her surely intends to detain her, immobilize her, neutralize whatever evidence she has or might yet gather. From wherever. The sender was signaling threat. Cap will be taken aside and patted down. Her passport will be confiscated; she will not be permitted to board.

But nothing happens. She shows her boarding pass and passport, the security guard smiles, her flight is called. She finds her window seat, stows her cabin bag, snaps her seatbelt in place. The woman who takes the aisle seat beside her is flustered. She has two bags, a bottle of water, a magazine, and one of the tabloids. She cannot quite figure out how to manage things in the cramped space. "I wonder if you'd mind?" she says to Cap, tentative. "Could you hold these for me, just for two minutes until I get myself organized?" She hands the magazine and the tabloid to Cap.

"No problem," Cap smiles, and then she sees the front page of the *Post*. There is a gruesome photograph of a body with a knife blade sticking out of its heart. The caption reads:

COLD CASE HEATS UP
Fraudulent Vanderbilt claimant may be killer in unsolved 1960 murder.
Village butcher reveals evidence, makes statement to French police.
Female accomplice involved.

Unidentified sources who gave evidence on condition of anonymity say that female accomplice has history of subversive activity ...

As the airplane moves slowly away from the gate, Cap stares back through the wall of plate glass to the boarding side of security. She sees a young child, a boy, bewildered, stumbling forward as though trying to reach her plane before it leaves. Perhaps he is traveling alone. Perhaps his parents are on the aircraft or perhaps they are back in the departure lounge. He is clearly disoriented and frightened. He turns back and stands waving at the gates that have closed behind him.

BOOK III
THE COLLECTED LIVES OF PETIT LOUP

1.

August 5, 1960
Air France, Seat 34A

   Dear Cap:
   This is a window seat but all I can see through the glass pane are motorized carts piled with luggage and a man in a uniform waving orange sticks. I suppose he is giving signals to the pilot. We are still on the ground. I cannot see you or maman but I can feel you watching me, still watching, still waving. If I close my eyes I can still see you crying in that last second when I turned back. I know that you will vehemently deny that you were crying. I also saw a flash of light and realized with a shock that my mother must have taken a photograph. I did not even know she had a camera. She must have bought it for this occasion. I don't know what I feel about this. Why did she do it?
   Then the security doors closed and an officer said, "Your passport, please." He raised his eyebrows when I showed him. "American? You don't look American." I'm really French, I told him, but I was born in New York. "Say goodbye to France, young man," he said.
   Say goodbye to my life, I thought. Say goodbye to my <u>second</u> life.
   I can barely remember the first one, my five infant years in New York.

I do remember a big loud man in a uniform who frightened me. One day he was just there. "Say hello to your father, Gwynne Patrice," maman said. Apparently I was two years old when he came back from deployment in Europe.

"What the hell is he doing dressed like that?" my father roared. I don't actually remember his words. I just remember he was angry and I was frightened of him.

I think maybe I remember a birthday party, perhaps my third. There was a cake in the shape of a boat with three candles for funnels. My mother lit them and I blew them out and there were some black servants who clapped and sang Happy Birthday. I can't remember anything else.

Wait. Wait...

Yes, I do remember a black woman, a big soft cushiony woman who hugged me and stroked my hair. Of course maman always did that too, but it was different. Maman never wanted me to love anyone else (except perhaps you; I think she didn't mind that, but I'm not absolutely sure.) This black woman loved me and I loved her, but she loved everyone and she took for granted that everyone would love everyone else. Just thinking of her again feels like being back in the loft or being in the cutting room with Ti-Christophe.

The cushiony woman used to bathe me and feed me and put me to bed and sing gospel songs till I fell asleep. Swing low, sweet chariot.... I think she made the cake with three candles. I think sometimes she sang a song to tease me, though not in a mean way. She was never mean. She was lathering me up in the bathtub when she sang it and she was laughing and I sang along with her and we splashed each other.

I looked over Jordan and what did I see, coming for to carry me home?

A boy in a blue dress waiting there for me, begging me to carry him home.

I wonder if I made that up later? Or made up some of the words? I think I might have because I never left the house back then. House? No, it wasn't a house, it was a penthouse, but I didn't know that until maman used to talk about it after we came back to France. I didn't know anything. I didn't even know that other boys didn't wear dresses. We didn't need to leave the penthouse. We had a terrace and a nursery room. I remember that my father didn't want anyone to see me. Even then, I knew that I embarrassed him and that he was furious with my mother but she was never going to give in.

I can't remember if there was a cake when I turned four, but I do remember the cake for my fifth birthday. It was shaped like the figure 5 and instead of candles it had five sparklers and I was allowed to light them.

That first life must have ended soon after the fizzing cake. The only other thing I can remember is the smell of the penthouse which smelled of sadness and anger, my mother's sadness, my father's anger.

In the airport I tried to look back one last time as the doors closed on my second life. All I could think of was Dante passing through the gates of Hell. I could see the text on the green glass above the portal: Abandon hope, all ye who enter here. Obviously that was hallucination but the letters looked real.

What were you thinking when I walked through those sliding doors?

I knew what maman was thinking. Her face was like a thunderstorm closing in. She was unforgiving. "Betrayal," she was thinking. "How could my son do this to me? A butcher! How could he humiliate me like that? I will record this instance of betrayal for history. Here is the face of the traitor." And of course she was still furious that not only had my father never shown up to "collect" me in St Gilles, as he'd promised, but had not shown up in Paris either. I was glad that he never came to St Gilles because if he had you would not have been invited to come with us on the train to Paris. And if my father had been in Paris as he promised, you would not have been here at the airport.

But what are you thinking? What are you thinking right now?

What were you thinking when I walked through those security doors?

You looked like Grand Loup at our last supper. You were somewhere else. But just like Grand Loup you were determined not to cry and you almost didn't.

I'd promised myself I would not cry and I didn't. But I'll confess to what I did instead. That last morning in Grand Loup's loft I took off the pillowslip and kept it. I stuffed it into my duffel bag and I'm cuddling it now like a teddy bear, though I'm pretending it's because I'm cold. I'm holding it as unobtrusively as possible. It smells of Ti-Christophe. It smells of Grand Loup and of the loft and of you.

Here's an admission I never thought I would make. I now understand the potency of relics, which I've always mocked, which Father JG taught us to mock.

We are moving now, very slowly. I can't see the man with the orange sticks. We are turning. We are gliding down the runway like a flat-bottomed boat on the Vienne, except faster and faster. We are going to take off. I'm not scared. Well, not of flying, I'm not scared of that, not at all, in fact I wouldn't mind a quick sudden death as we leave. But I suspect I'm going to have to live long and miserably and lonely. I know I'm flying into a dark tunnel with no light at the end of it and I am scared of that. I've been there before. I'm abandoning hope. When I said that to you two weeks ago, you got angry with me, but when I looked back and *saw your face as the doors were closing, I thought you were doing it too. I thought you were abandoning hope.*

    Love,
    Ti-Loup

August 5, 1960
Air France, Seat 34 A
After take-off

    Dear Cap:
    Now all I can see are clouds. First there was blue sky with towering pillows of whipped cream but now it is all cloud, whitish-grey. There is an American woman next to me in 34B. When we took off, she grabbed my arm and held on as if the pilot had announced a crash-landing. I could feel her fingernails like a row of spikes. Remember Father JG's class on the Spanish Tickler, those iron claws the Inquisition used to scrape heretics down to the bone? That's what it felt like. I would never have believed I'd feel nostalgic for Father JG, but I'd give anything to be back in his classroom right now.
    When the plane stopped climbing and leveled out, the American woman let go of my arm and apologized. I'm sorry, she said. I didn't realize what I was doing. That's okay, I said. She said, My husband wanted to go to Paris when he retired, but I refused because I'm terrified of flying. He died one year ago and I felt as though I had to do it for him on the anniversary of his death. I should have done it with him. I'm so sorry.
    She began to cry. I offered her my pillowslip from the loft and she wiped her eyes with it. I said, I'm sorry your husband died.
    I am too, she said. How old are you?
    I'll be fifteen in November, I told her.
    Why are you flying alone? she wanted to know, and I said, My

father's meeting me in New York.

Do you want to talk about it? she asked, and I said no.

It was very kind of you—she patted my arm—to lend me your security blanket.

It's a pillowslip, I said.

And then the Air France stewardess stopped in our aisle and wanted to know if I was young Mister Vanderbilt.

Yes, I said.

Your mother asked us to check on you and make sure that everything is okay, the stewardess said. Everything is okay, I assured her. We have a very special meal prepared for you, the stewardess said. It's not on the menu. It's coq au vin, *especially requested by your mother, Mister Vanderbilt. Enjoy.*

Well, the woman in 34B said, a VIP with a security blanket, that's one for the records. Then she said, Vanderbilt? You're a Vanderbilt?

I pulled my boarding pass out of my Cicero (it was my bookmark) and flashed it.

But not one of those *Vanderbilts, surely? she said.*

And I said, No, not one of those Vanderbilts. It's actually a very common name in Europe, Dutch, you know, in Dutch it's as common as Smith, and very common in America too. New Amsterdam, New York. There are hundreds of us.

Go back a few generations, she said, and you're probably all related. But if you were part of those *Vanderbilts, you wouldn't be sardined back here. You'd be sitting up front in First Class.*

It hadn't really registered with me that I was in Second Class but I have a vague memory that when I was five and maman and I flew to Paris, we flew First Class. There was more room and it was nicer and the stewardess served maman champagne and served me orange juice in a champagne flute. That time, we had linen cloths and linen napkins. In 34A, the napkins are paper and there is no cloth, no salt and pepper shakers, just plastic and little paper packets for sugar and salt. Last week maman gave me a letter in a sealed envelope and told me to open it and read it after my flight left Paris. I am reading it now. This is what it says.

I have to warn you that your father made the arrangements for this flight. Unfortunately, by American law, I don't have access to my own money. Your father does. All I have is the chateau. As for my family stocks and bonds and cash assets, your father got those. *Toujours la même chose.* He is as parsimonious as he is rich.

I am sorry that your flight will be cheap and nasty but at least it will give you a taste of what being a butcher would be like. Believe me, that life would be even cheaper and nastier. There would be nothing remotely romantic about it, particularly since recent events have made me understand, belatedly, that your life itself would be at risk from those butchers at Boucherie Monsard. This flight to rescue you from a future of danger and unrelenting despair—the kind of despair you cannot even begin to imagine—is not the kind of flight I would have wanted for you, but that has always been your father's way.

And there is this to admit about your father's school. You won't get as good an education as you would in France, certainly not as intellectual and certainly culturally deficient in art and music, but you will be well prepared for the cut-throat world of American business. You will make all the right contacts and will learn how to be as vulgarly and stupidly rich as your father. But just the same, I'm sorry I let your father arrange this flight. I should have had my banker in Paris sell another painting and I should have sent you to New York in style.

It really doesn't matter, is what I think. First Class would have been nicer, I suppose, but I do know that I wouldn't be any less lonely and miserable sitting up there instead of back here in 34A. I feel strapped into a very small cage, but if I shut my eyes and pretend I'm sleeping in the loft, then I feel free. But then I think of Ti-Christophe and I try not to think of anything at all.

Love, Ti-Loup

August 5, 1960
New York

Dear Cap:
Well, not only did my father not show up to "collect" me in St Gilles or in Paris (as you well know) but he did not show up at the airport in New York to meet me either. He sent a driver from a limousine company. When I came out of Customs, there was a row of men in uniforms holding signs with names on them. I didn't pay any attention because I was looking for my father, but then suddenly—out of the corner of my eye—I noticed one name, black lettering on white card, that said Gwynne Vanderbilt. I was startled, but you know what is really strange? It didn't occur to me that this was me. What I thought was that one of my cousins or second cousins or third cousins or some relation or other must be arriving in New York at the same time. So I just sort of wandered around vaguely, looking for my father, wondering if I would recognize him and if he would recognize me.

I stopped at an airport bookstore because the window was eye-catching and dramatic. Multiple copies of one single title were cunningly stacked in a pyramid, a delicate castle of books. At the top of the pyramid were three flags: the American Stars and Stripes and the Confederate flag (remember Father JG's classes on the Civil War?), and in the middle, higher than either of those two, a white flag with a black symbol I don't recognize, a circle with a kind of arrowhead inside it. There was a placard that said: **The just-published instant bestseller that will break your heart no matter which flag flies on your front porch.** There was a woman standing beside me, looking at the book display, so I asked her "Excuse me, what does that flag mean?" and she said, "That's the peace symbol."

The book was called **To Kill a Mocking Bird** and the author was Harper Lee. I wanted to buy a copy but I don't know how to buy things. Servants do that. Besides, I don't have any money. I don't have French francs and I don't have American dollars. When I asked maman, she said: "You don't need money. Your father will take care of all that."

Then she said: "I never have money either. Thank God, the chateau runs on its own income and my lawyer and banker handle the bills."

"I didn't know we had a lawyer and a banker," I said.

"Their offices are in Paris. When I need things, I charge to the chateau's account. But if it were not for Melusine's father, the chateau would barely be supporting itself."

"Can my father take the chateau income too?"

"He would if he could. But by royal decree and by French inheritance laws, he can't. The chateau will always belong to me until it belongs to you."

I was still looking through the bookstore window when I heard an announcement like the voice of God. It was loud and reverberating and everywhere. From out of the hubbub of sound, I gradually distinguished these words: Would Gwynne Vanderbilt, who has just arrived from Paris on Air France 3, please report to the information desk. So I did. And there was the chauffeur in the uniform with his sign and he said, "Your father has sent me to pick you up." And so I went. And so here I am in the apartment where I spent my first five years and my father is not here either.

Does my father really exist, or did my mother invent him? That is what I am asking myself. Is he just a lawyer's office in New York? Did she have her lawyer mail back to me a copy of her own letter? Is all this just to keep me away from a butcher-block and a boning knife?

Love, Ti-Loup

August 8, 1960
New York

Dear Cap:

He exists. Apparently my father exists, although I still haven't seen him. I think I must have slept for two days. When I woke I smelled something I recognized, the smell of sadness, the smell of hopelessness, the smell of not wanting to get up and get dressed, the smell of a blue dress, the smell of a big angry man, the smell of fear. The smell was dark and damp and it made me want to put my head under the pillow and never wake up again.

Someone pulled the pillow off my head and it was a black woman in a black dress with a white apron with white lace frills and she said "Master Gwynne! Don't you remember me? I'm Shannay." And she gave me a huge hug and pulled my face into her chest and her breasts were like pillows. And I did remember. I remembered her smell. I remembered the boat cake she made and the three candles. I remembered the sparkler cake. I remembered that I used to love her and I couldn't help it, I started to cry.

"There, there, there," she said, "Oh my, how you have grown up. But ain't you jus' the same sad little boy you always been?"

"No, I ain't," I said. " I ain't that same sad little boy." I can't believe I said that, but I did. I know I did. And I know I said it in a way that sounded exactly like Shannay. I can't seem to help doing this.

Shannay threw back her head and laughed. "Maybe you ain't that sad little boy anymore," she said, "but you ain't much changed either. You still your same strange self, Master Gwynne. You always talked Upper East Side to your father, French to your mama, and black folks' talk to me. You could be on Broadway, you could."

"Where's my father?" I asked.

And she said: "Lord knows. He sure is the same son of a bitch he always was".

And then we both started laughing and we laughed and laughed and she grabbed my hands and we danced a jig and I thought maybe it will be different this time.

Love, Ti-Loup

August 9, 1960
New York

Dear Cap:

I have seen him. I have seen my father. At 5 p.m. Shannay came to my room and told me that my father expected me to join him for dinner at nine. Nine o'clock!

"That's four hours away, Shannay," I said. "I'm hungry. I didn't eat lunch. I slept through it."

"Jetlag," Shannay said. "I'll make you a snack to keep your motor running till nine, but mind you don't snitch on me." She brought me a big fat roast-beef sandwich with mustard and mayonnaise and lettuce and tomato and it was good.

I remembered the dining room though I'd hardly ever seen it before and I'd never eaten there, not even once. My parents always dined in there with the servants waiting on them and the guests, sometimes six, sometimes twelve, sometimes twenty, sometimes actors, sometimes bankers, sometimes football players, congressmen, movie stars, English royalty, White Russian princes, sheiks. Of course I didn't know who they were back then, but Shannay has shown me photographs that have signatures all over the back. I realize now that my parents were terrified of being alone with each other.

Back then, I used to eat upstairs with Shannay and the au pair. (Shannay and I spoke English; the au pair and I spoke French; my father and I spoke English; maman and I spoke French.) The servants lived up in the attic, under the gables, and my room was up there too (and still is.) The penthouse has two levels. The main level is the lobby, the living room, the dining room, the library, the ballroom, my parents' suite, and a wide outdoor terrace overlooking Central Park. The dining room is not much different from the one in the chateau. It's just as large. Even the table and chairs are Louis XIV so I don't know if maman bought them when she first got married or if my Vanderbilt relations always bought the same stuff.

My father was sitting at the head of the table when Shannay gave me a little push. I didn't feel ready so I resisted, I pushed back, but Shannay whispered in my ear: "Soonest begun, soonest done," and then I let myself be shot in like a cork from a champagne bottle and my father raised his eyebrows and laughed. He stood up. "Let's have a look at you then," he said. We shook hands.

"Not like that," he said. "Put some energy into it. That's more like it."

I think my knuckles were crushed but I was not going to let him see me wince. (Today my fingers have blue and purple bruise marks.)

He stood back and looked me up and down as though I were a horse he was buying. (He does buy horses.) "Your mother has turned you into a pampered neurotic weakling," he said, "but to her credit she recognizes what she has done and is making amends. I just hope it isn't too late." He sounded full of disgust. He dropped my hand and sort of flicked it away from him, as though he were batting a cockroach off. "Let's hope Dryden can make a man out of you," he said, "though they'll have their work cut out. Well, what do you have to say for yourself?"

I tried to think of what you would have said to him. I know you would have thrown a verbal grenade that would have stopped him in his tracks and stunned him and he would have been dumbfounded and he would have had to parry and he would have liked it. It would have challenged him. It would have excited him. Coming from you, it would have turned him on.

But I couldn't think of anything to say.

"Can you ride a horse?" he asked. "Can you hunt? Can you do steeplechase, hurdles?"

"I don't know, sir," I said. "I've never tried. I'm sure I could learn."

"I doubt it," he said.

He doesn't want me here. He despises me. This makes me as murderously angry as it makes me feel like a bug that should be squashed. We ate dinner in absolute silence, with the butler and the maid (equally nervous, I observed) coming and going and never speaking, and then my father simply got up and left. I did say something then. I said "Goodnight, Sir." But I didn't say it until he had closed the door behind him.

Love,

Ti-Loup

P.S. I put my first 3 letters in the mail to you yesterday (the two I wrote on the flight and the one I wrote on my first night here.)

I asked Shannay how to mail a letter and she said she'd take care of it. She said she'd buy the stamps. When I asked how much that would cost, she said, "Don't you go fretting yourself. I know your father too damn well. He never give your mama a tin nickel of her own to spend, and I know he don't give you nothing." I don't know how long it will take for my letters to get to St Gilles. Have you got them yet?

August 10, 1960
New York

Dear Cap:

This morning I took the Dryden entrance exam. I thought I would have to go to a courthouse or to la mairie *or somewhere like that but the examiner came to our penthouse. I sat at a table in the library—it's not as elegant as the chateau library—and the Dryden man said: "You have two hours. I will be invigilating. You may begin."*

I needn't have worried. I can imagine Father JG saying: "They call that an entrance exam?"

In the afternoon Shannay told me that my father expected me for dinner. In the dining room he said: "Well, at least you're good for something. Apparently, as far as academics go, you're in the top percentile, whatever that means. I know it doesn't mean any head for business, that's for sure. Dumbest people I ever met teach at Columbia or Harvard or Yale."

Then he clasped my upper arms in his hands and bored in with his thumbs as though he planned to push holes right through my flesh and bones until he touched his own fingers. "Good God," he said. "You're jello. You're pastry dough before it goes in the oven. Okay, so you've got a brain in your head but until you can do as well with a hunting rifle and a football, you'll bring me nothing but shame at my own school. Jenkins will serve you dinner. You may eat here. I'm going out." And that was that.

Love, Ti-Loup

August 12, 1960
New York

Dear Cap:
Every day I ask Shannay if there are any letters for me and every day she says no.
You promised you'd write. Why haven't you answered my letters?
How is Grand Loup? I had a dream last night. In the dream we were under the bridge and we saw Ti-Christophe and Michel Monsard and Olivier but this time I rushed out and ran in between. Michel Monsard and Olivier were so shocked that they stabbed each other over and over. Ti-Christophe crossed himself and said Let the dead bury the dead, then he hoisted me onto his shoulders and we walked back to the cottage. Grand Loup said Well done, well done, well done. Justice takes her time, he said, because she has to stumble in her own blind way but in the long run she always shows up.
I woke from this dream very happy.
And then Shannay came in with my breakfast and I remembered that Ti-Christophe was dead. I couldn't eat anything. Why haven't you written?
Love,
Ti-Loup.

August 14, 1960
New York

Dear Cap:

I have had a letter from maman. She says you have moved back into your father's cottage. She does not think this is a good idea.

I quote: "I fear that Melusine may slip backwards, socially speaking. There is a risk that she will revert to the habits of the wild creature she used to be. This is not a criticism of her father, for whom I have the greatest respect, but he is, after all, a peasant. I'm not sure if he owns any books and there is no moderating feminine influence in that cottage. I can only countenance this as a temporary measure. After all, my gardener is not the only one who has lost a son or who feels lonely."

She says she has arranged for you to attend one of the small convent schools in Tours in the Fall because seven years of Jesuit education should not be wasted. (Father JG, by the way, has already returned to England, as you would probably have known before I did.) She intends that you will go to the Sorbonne and be trained in art history and art appraisal. She intends that you will be a boarder at the convent during the week but will come back to St Gilles on weekends. She intends, she intends...

She does not say how you respond to her intentions. I try to imagine. You and my mother can both spit ice. In a fight to the death, I wouldn't know how to place my bet. She does say that you have reluctantly agreed to spend the week with the nuns but that you continue to insist that you will stay in your father's cottage on weekends. She says she has agreed to this provided you have Sunday dinner in the chateau.

Why haven't I heard all this from you? She says you will begin at the convent in September. Will you write before then or are you enjoying much too much being the only daughter on both sides

of the chateau wall, having the loft all to yourself, being chate-
laine-in-residence, chatelaine-in-waiting? If I've received a letter
from my mother, why haven't I received one from you?

She says your father is getting forgetful and strange since
Ti-Christophe disappeared and since Chantal killed herself and
the baby. She says the servants tell her that gossip in St Gilles is
equally divided as to whether the butcher killed Ti-Christophe (for
which most of the villagers believe he would be justified since his
daughter was carrying your brother's child) or whether Ti-Chris-
tophe fled to Paris because he was afraid that the butcher would
kill him.

So at least we have kept the lid tightly shut on what actually
happened, not that Grand Loup knows what happened. Not all
that happened. Only four people know for certain that Ti-Chris-
tophe is dead. Your father will say nothing and Michel Monsard
won't dare talk. And we two will never speak of that day. It is
always possible that your father sometimes does not believe what
we told him. It is possible that he chooses to believe Ti-Christophe
is alive, just as he sometimes seems to hope that your mother is
still alive. If that eases his grief, can we blame him? When there is
no body to bury, I think hope dies hard.

What I want to know is what is being said in Tours about the
disappearance of Olivier? Has anyone noticed? I'm not surprised
no one would notice his absence in St Gilles, but surely the news-
papers in Tours might have mentioned his disappearance? And
surely rumor would reach St Gilles? People would ask questions
in the butcher shop and stories would spawn and spread.

Maman says your father seems to have aged overnight. She
says his hands shake and he can't remember what happened yes-
terday. She says you had to water the vines by yourself last week.
Also you had to harvest the vegetables because your father forgot

to do it. She will not permit this state of affairs to continue. She may have to hire a new manager, she says.

She wants to know how I am. She says my father always wanted to own me and turn me into a proper Vanderbilt and a proper American so she's sure he's happy and she hopes I am too. She hopes I understand the sacrifice she has made. I'm not going to answer her letter. Why don't you write?

Love, Ti-Loup

August 18, 1960
New York

Dear Cap:

Today is Grand Loup's 46th birthday. Are you celebrating with roasted rabbits and roasted potatoes? I would give my father's racehorses to be there with you. Did you cook the birthday feast yourself? Did Marie-Claire come? Does her husband still not remember who he is? Was my mother invited to the birthday dinner?

Why wasn't I invited? Even though you know I wouldn't be able to come, the gesture would have mattered to me.

Why don't you write? Give Grand Loup a birthday hug from me. Tell him I love him more than anyone else in the world after Ti-Christophe and you.

Love, Ti-Loup

August 20, 1960
New York

Dear Cap:

Something very strange happened today. Shannay brought me an envelope. She said, "I was aksed (yes, arkst, that's what she *said; I see these dialects, you know. I see the words in phonetic script in my head, one of Father JG's gifts) I was aksed to give you this, Master Gwynne, but not to let anyone see. A messenger boy come to the door with it."*

Inside there was a handwritten letter and two small paintings, postcard size, both watercolors on thick white art paper, one of you (but, I know, really of your mother; the same as the one your father showed us at the last supper), and the other of him. The paintings are signed MG in the lower right corner. This is what the letter says.

Dear Petit Loup: Grand Loup gave us your father's address and wrote that you were living with him now. We thought you would like these little gifts and we send them as mementoes of two people who changed our lives as much as we believe they did yours. Do you remember us? We visited the chateau last year. We suspect that your father, Mr. Lawrence Vanderbilt, would probably not want you to have contact with us, so we are being discreet, but we would love to have you visit if you can. We are just walking distance away. Sincerely, Myriam & Aaron Goldberg.

Remember those people? My mother was impressed because they identified one of her paintings (one she didn't like very much) as an early Modigliani. They said it was worth a small fortune, which excited her. Remember? How come they have heard from Grand Loup and I haven't? How come I haven't heard from you? I will visit them if Shannay will help me escape from the building and show me the way. I will keep the paintings of you and Grand Loup under my mattress, safe between cardboard, but at night I will take them out and lean them against the dressing-table mirror. They will be the first thing I see when I wake in the morning.

Love, Ti-Loup

August 23, 1960
New York

Dear Cap:

Shannay took me for a walk in Central Park today. She had to ask my father's permission. She told him I was getting pale and pasty-looking from never going outside and he said, "Good God, get him walking! Toughen him up a bit and bronze him up before he gets to Dryden or they'll kill him. They'll tear him apart."

Central Park is just the other side of the street, but crossing Fifth Avenue is like walking in the Forest of Chinon in hunting season. You take your life in your hands. It's the first time I've been allowed out of the house. Shannay said: "We'll walk around the park for a bit, then we'll take a zigzag route to the Goldbergs, just in case someone is spying for your father."

Entering Central Park (after escaping live from Fifth Avenue) was like climbing out of my window all those years ago and walking into your kitchen. You were roasting rabbits. I understood in that moment that I had traveled from one galaxy to another.

Central Park is like that, a Midsummer Night's Dream kind of place. It's not Manhattan, it's not New York, it is somewhere else.

We walked up the Mall to the lake. There is a great fountain and a terrace and there were people in boats on the lake. There is a very beautiful bridge with woods on the other side like the woods around the chateau. I want to walk in the woods, I told Shannay, but she said "That's the Ramble and you can get lost in there. We don't have time."

So we walked back down to 59th Street and then to Madison and then north for two blocks. "This is the place," Shannay said. "We'll have to speak to the doorman first."

"Six-A," she said to the doorman, and he pressed a button and talked to someone on the phone. "Take the elevator, young man,

sixth floor," he said to me. He told Shannay she'd have to wait in the lobby.

When the elevator doors opened on the sixth floor, those people who visited us at the chateau were waiting. "Petit Loup!" they said, and they hugged me as though I were the son of Lilith (your mother Lilith) and Grand Loup. "Come in, come in," they said.

I told them Shannay had brought me and I didn't like to leave her down in the lobby, so they called the doorman on the phone and told him to send her up. They served us a cheese platter and afternoon tea and Dubonnet. Afterwards Shannay said to me, "The Goldbergs are a lot nicer than your folks, Master Gwynne."

"Grand Loup wrote to us," the Goldbergs said. "He told us about Petit Christophe."

I waited. I thought about it. And then I asked very carefully, "What did he tell you?"

They said: He told us Petit Christophe had been killed in an honorable fight with a man who had raped his fiancée. He said his son's body had not been found and he believed the killer had dragged it away and buried it, or possibly had tied weights to it and dumped it in the Vienne or the Loire. He knew the killer was the butcher's son, but he didn't know if the son or the butcher himself had disposed of the body. He said that Petit Christophe's fiancée had killed herself, either from grief or shame, and that she had killed his grandchild within her. He told us he felt that the weight of his own sorrow was crushing him.

Shannay said, "Jesus have mercy!"

"Did you know about this?" they asked me.

"Yes," I said. "I mean, I know Petit Christophe and Chantal and her baby are all dead." I asked them if they had any news about you.

Yes, they said. Grand Loup told them you are the one ray of sunlight in his life, that you are living at home with him again and *working with him in the potager and the vineyard.*

Are you happy back in the cottage and in the fields? You used to love it. You used to miss it. But then I think you crossed over. You speak French like my mother, you speak English like Father JG. I can't imagine you now with mud under your fingernails or your dress torn from climbing the apple tree and dropping over the wall.

The Goldbergs said that you will enter the convent school in Tours in September.

"Your mother," they told me, "your mother, la comtesse, has no idea, but it is the very same convent which served as a safe house during the Occupation. We spent two nights in hiding there. It is where we first met Lilith."

It is where you were born, Cap. This must mean something, don't you think? But I don't know what. I bet even Father JG would believe it means something (if he were to know the facts) but he wouldn't know what it meant either.

Even the Goldbergs said that the coincidence was so strange and so fitting that they were tempted to see it as a good omen, except that they do not believe in signs or magic or any such supernatural intervention in human life. We make our own fates, they said. We ourselves are responsible for how we play whatever hands we are dealt.

Grand Loup does *believe in signs and wonders, the Goldbergs said. He believes that the convent in Tours will be your safe house and that your mother is watching over your life. He is not sure anymore where his own safe house is, or whether he has one.*

Then Madame Goldberg took one of my hands in both of hers and looked me in the eye. "Grand Loup's daughter is depressed," she said, "because you never answer her letters."

"She never answers **my** *letters!" I said. "I write to her almost every day."*

"Ahh," they said. "Well then. Perhaps when Lilith is living in Tours, she should mail her letters from there and send them to us and we can pass them along to you. Perhaps you should bring your letters to us and we will mail them to Tours."

Shannay looked upset. "I take Master Gwynne's letters direct to the mailbox," she said.

"How do you address them?" Madame Goldberg asked me. "To the chateau," I said. "And what about mail arriving at the Vanderbilt residence?" Madame Goldberg asked.

"It doesn't arrive at the residence," Shannay said. "It arrives at Mister Vanderbilt's post office box and his personal secretary collects it."

So that explains everything and Shannay will take this letter to the Goldbergs tomorrow, but I suppose it won't reach you until you are in the convent in Tours. Anything mailed to Grand Loup would have to be addressed to the gardener's cottage, in care of the chateau, and we know what would happen to that.

Love, Ti-Loup

September 2, 1960
New York

Dear Cap:

Today a telegram arrived from my mother. Shannay answered the doorbell and it was the Western Union man. It's for you, Shannay said. This is what it said:

Christophe the gardener had heart attack. Taken to hospital in Tours. Doctors say risk of subsequent stroke is high. Will have to find new manager. He is now back in gardener's cottage and I have arranged nursing care. Melusine being difficult about convent in Tours. Refusing to leave her father. Not acceptable but diplomacy will be required. Will have to make nursing-home arrangements for gardener. *Maman.*

How is Grand Loup? How are you? I wish I could be there with both of you. I feel as though I am on the dark side of the moon.

Love, Ti-Loup.

September 5, 1960
New York

Dear Cap:

Of course I am worried sick about Grand Loup. How is he? I have had no further reports from Maman so I have to hope that means no stroke, no further decline. Today is a public holiday. It's called Labor Day here, which is strange, since everywhere else in the world Labor Day is on May 1st. Tomorrow my father will take me to Massachusetts to register me at his old boarding school. Classes begin next week and my third life will also begin. One more new world where I won't belong. My father is at his seaside house in the Hamptons for the holiday weekend. I wasn't invited. I've never been there. Anyway, I'd rather stay here with Shannay.

Tomorrow my father's chauffeur will drive us (my father and me) to the school for Fall registration. It is a four-hour drive. I cannot imagine a more unpleasant way to spend the last day of my second life: all that time in the back seat with my father.

What will we talk about?

I know the answer to that. We won't talk at all. But I am rehearsing over and over what I am going to say to him just before we get to the school. I am going to say: "Could I have my letters now please?"

I also like to imagine what you would say to him and that makes me smile.

Shannay and I walked in Central Park this morning and then we walked to the Goldbergs for lunch. How is Grand Loup? they asked. They were shocked to learn of his heart attack.

Do you ever see Michel Monsard? Has anything been said about Olivier? Surely the newspapers in Tours...? How has his disappearance been explained? Surely at least the moto factory made some police inquiry when he didn't show up for work? But of course, since the war, nobody trusts the police.

I have been practicing my questions for my father, watching myself in the mirror. "Why are you censoring my mail?" I practice saying this in a neutral way. Sometimes I practice with a drop of acid added. "What exactly are you and my mother afraid of?" I ask. I watch my face in the mirror. I practice looking calm. I practice looking confident of the right to an answer. My face in the mirror is not convincing. I try anger, which is easier to manage. "Did you know that Napoleon and Hitler and Stalin were all obsessed with reading other people's mail?" I demand. "And what happened to all those regimes? Did it save the censors from what they most feared?"

I imagine you asking any of those questions which I hope to ask, but of course I probably won't. If I do say anything it will be polite, if not downright pleading.

"Could I please have my letters from Cap?"

Love,

Ti-Loup

2.

Shannay appeared in the doorway of his room with a large flat box. It was the 6th of September 1960. "School uniform," she said. "Came from Saks on your father's account. You're supposed to put it on now."

"Oh my my my," she said, when he reappeared in wool slacks, white shirt, blazer and tie. "Ain't you the gentleman, Mister Gwynne?"

He did think he looked rather smart.

"You gonna break a lotta girls' hearts," Shannay said.

"There aren't any girls at Dryden."

"Never stopped your father, from what I hear," Shannay said. "There's girls' schools a bike ride away and plenty rich preppies that do a major in hanky-pank. Not just the boys, the girls too. I hear the jokes when the Old Dryden stags come around for cigars and drinks. I got to clean up after. Who cleans up the girls' lives, I can't say. Chauffeur waiting in the lobby, by the way."

"Is my father here?"

Shannay frowned and lifted her hands, palms up. "You think he ever checks in with me? You think he keeps me informed? Waiting in the limo, maybe?"

"I have to spend the next four hours with him in that car."

"I know, baby, I know." Shannay opened her arms wide and he walked into that warm space and was embarrassed by how much he did not want to leave. "I already sent your luggage down,"

Shannay said. "I'll be naming you in my prayers every day, you keep that in mind, Mister Gwynne. Lord bless you and keep you."

"I will miss you, Shannay."

"I will miss you too, honey chile."

His father was not in the limo. The car was a black Mercedes-Benz with a gold Vanderbilt crest on its sleek backside. The chauffeur tipped his cap—it was embroidered with the same baroque leaf-and-scroll-encircled V in gold thread—and held the back door open. "I'm Castano, Mr. Vanderbilt," the chauffeur said. "Your father's personal driver. He regrets that he is detained in the Hamptons today. He asked that I convey you to your school. I'll take care of your luggage."

"Thank you, Castano." Ti-Loup's most immediate reaction was one of massive relief. He'd been given a Get-Out-of-Jail-Free card. A bodily memory, intense, returned to him: he had just dropped, for the first time, from the window of his room in the chateau. He had paused in the shrubbery in sheer amazement at what he had done and the thrill of it. It was one of his safe houses, that memory.

His second reaction, as he sank into the cushioned glove-soft leather of the back seat, was of sensual pleasure. This wasn't just First Class, it was transcendent. He imagined his mother's gloss: *I'm surprised he didn't send a yellow cab for you. He would have, but he knew there'd be people watching: other parents, other members of the Board of Trustees, gossip columnists for the* New York Post.

"We'll be taking Interstate 95 to New Haven," Castano explained. "And then Interstate 91 to Hartford. After we cross the Mass Pike, we'll take Route 10 into Dryden. Depending on traffic, we should be there in under four hours. Make yourself comfortable, Mr. Vanderbilt. Juice and soft drinks in the fridge, fruit and cookies and candy in the cupboard. You can make your music selection from the arm rest on your right."

Ti-Loup chose Classical and passed through Connecticut enfolded in Bach.

He felt the cashmere caress of entitlement. Perhaps I will enjoy my third life, he thought. No one at Dryden knew about the blue dress. No one knew that his mother required him to say the rosary at her side every day and every night. He felt as though he were free to put on any costume he wished. He decided he would start by being as scholarly and reserved as Father JG, that his French accent would be high-class French and his English accent would be British. He would be as devoid of detectable emotion as his parents were. He would be inscrutable.

"Ivy League and Prep School Row," Castano said. "That's what all the chauffeurs call Route 10 once we get north of Springfield. You saw the turn-offs to Smith and Holyoke. Your father says that the Smith girls can be wild. Village of Dryden just ahead. We're in the Connecticut River valley and those hills are the Pocumtuck Ridge. Students climb up there to the Rock for a spectacular view of the campus, all 280 acres of it. Haven't done it myself but your father does it every time I bring him for the annual Board of Trustees. He says you should do it the first or second day. It's a ritual."

The view from the drive was breathtaking, as beautiful as the Chateau de Boissy and the valleys of the Vienne and the Loire. Ti-Loup began to feel happy.

"This is where I leave you," Castano said. "Administration building. They'll tell you what to do next. I'll get one of the staff to put your bags in your dorm."

There were other limousines scattered about the great drive like starlings crowding a ripening vineyard. There were more modestly-sized family cars too, Jaguars, Porsches, BMWs, Audis, Lin-

311

colns. Parents and new students milled about in a chaos of boxes and duffel bags. Ti-Loup had rarely ever, in his fifteen years, been in the company of more than three people at any one time, and those few occasions had been at airports and at Mass in the church of St Gilles on the occasions of special liturgical festival days. He felt dizzy. He felt slightly agoraphobic. He watched the Vanderbilt limousine receding down the long school drive and he thought it looked like one of Van Gogh's crows, a black smudge coasting on a current of air toward the horizon and the edge of the painting, flying south on Route 10. That black speck seemed to him a final punctuation point, the end of his second life.

A tall blond boy whose hair flopped over one eyebrow approached him. "Vanderbilt?" he said. He extended his right hand and Ti-Loup shook it, firmly, as his father required. "Saw you get out of the Vanderbilt limo. Honor to meet you. Welcome to Dryden. I'm Cabot." Cabot tossed his head slightly, in the manner of a cantering horse, so that the mane of blond hair lifted and then fell back again. "I'm the senior proctor on your corridor. Always confusing on your first day, but you'll get the hang of it. I'll show you to your dorm. There'll be eight freshmen in your corridor but you'll each have a room to yourself. Not everyone does, you know, but most of us do."

Ti-Loup absorbed this information as inscrutably as possible. It had not even occurred to him that he might not have a room to himself. "That will be congenial," he said in Father JG's voice.

"You sound British," Cabot said. "I thought you'd been living in France."

"France, yes. New York. Wherever." Ti-Loup shrugged in the manner of Father JG being dismissive. "My father travels a lot."

"Oh, mine too," Cabot said. "We spend summers in Italy. Florence mainly. Here's our dorm. The staff has got your bags here already. I'll leave you to yourself to get settled." He leaned against the doorframe to watch Ti-Loup getting settled. He had a habit of tossing back his forelock and then letting it fall across his eyebrows again.

"I can't tell you how delighted we are to have a Vanderbilt in our hall," he said.

Ti-Loup absorbed the astonishing information that Cabot was anxious to please him. He smiled and said nothing. He inclined his head slightly as though to the manner born.

3.

Dinner in the massive dining hall, with more than six hundred stu
dents, was both unruly and cozy, each student assigned to a table
for ten, each table presided over by a proctor or faculty member.
Cabot was not at Ti-Loup's table. The person on Ti-Loup's right
announced, "Hi, everyone. Welcome to Dryden. I'm John Semple.
I teach Math and I'm a college advisor. This will be your family
dinner table for the next three weeks and then you'll be assigned
a new table and a new dining family. Why don't we start by intro-
ducing ourselves while the first course is being served. Vanderbilt?
Can we start with you and then proceed in clockwise direction?
You should each give your name, your home town, and why you
came to Dryden."

"My name is Ti—" Ti-Loup had a moment of absolute panic.
He touched his blazer and expected to feel blue silk. He braced
for ridicule. What he touched was pure cashmere of the finest and
softest sort. He felt disoriented. Mentally, he tossed the blue dress
into an incinerator and threw in a match. He watched what happened. He *saw* it in his mind's eye: a roar of flames, highly colored,
sky-rocketing up and showering down again like birds with their
wings on fire. Bye-bye Bluebird, he said to the ashes.

"My name is Gwynne Patrice de la Vallière Vanderbilt," he said
levelly. "I was born in New York but I have spent the last ten years
in France in my mother's chateau in the Loire Valley." He spoke

in Father JG's voice, with measured authority but off-handedly, as though this were throw-away information. "My mother is a countess related to the royal house of the Bourbon kings. I came to Dryden because it is my father's old school."

John Semple, math teacher and college advisor, informed the table. "Vanderbilt's father is on the Board of Trustees and is a benefactor of our school."

Ti-Loup observed that he was regarded with deference and a certain amount of awe. The sensation was as heady as it was unprecedented. For a moment, he believed he could fly. He could not only visualize the possibility, he could feel the loft and updraft in his body.

The boy on his left said: "My name is Fouad Abdullah. My home town is Jeddah. I also came to Dryden because it is my father's old school."

John Semple provided a gloss. "Fouad's father is part of the royal family of Saud," he explained. "We owe one of our science labs to him."

And so it went, around the table. Not everyone's father had been to Dryden, but most had. Two boys explained that they were at Dryden because they had won full scholarships. The home town of one was Shreveport, Louisiana, the home town of the other was Paducah, Kentucky. John Semple greeted these introductions with great warmth. "One of the triumphs of Dryden," he said, "is that the school seeks out the highest achievers of the next generation and provides unprecedented opportunity to those from underprivileged backgrounds."

The boys from underprivileged backgrounds kept their eyes on the table while Semple led their co-diners in applause.

Between the main course and dessert, Fouad draped an arm around Ti-Loup's shoulder. "Great to meet you, Vanderbilt," he said. "My father and your father get together at Ascot every year, as you no doubt know. I hope you'll consider spending mid-term break with us in Jeddah."

"Thank you," Ti-Loup said politely. "I will certainly keep your invitation in mind."

Classes were small, never more than twelve students in any one class. Ti-Loup found his teachers quite splendid. There was never a question they could not answer in detail, they were demanding but patient and kind. He loved his courses and was pleasantly surprised to find them equally as rigorous as seminars with Father JG, though much more exciting. The Jesuit had been absolutely right about class dynamics. The greater the number of razor-sharp minds competitively chopping at a subject, the more irresistibly spiced the intellectual *cassoulet*. He felt that his brain matter, his thoughts, his ideas were being tuned to the highest pitch. His in-class and after-class discussions were like debates with Cap in spades, like having two Father JG's and eleven other Capucines in the room.

Cap! He had not thought of her in three weeks. This startled him and briefly disturbed him, but she belonged to a different life and the window between that life and his present one had closed. His life before Dryden seemed to him a dream that he could not quite remember.

He received no communication of any sort from his father but the mail brought a letter from his mother every week. He did not answer these letters. He did not read them. He did not open them. He placed them, neatly and chronologically, in a shoebox which he kept in his dresser, in the bottom drawer, the same shoebox in which he kept the rosary his mother had given him, that delicate chain of pearls and jade. He felt that if he so much as touched it, a trapdoor could open beneath him and the rosary would be his noose and he would find himself dangling from an old stone bridge, condemned to swing back and forth over two bloody corpses, back and forth, back and forth, slowly and forever, and he would never be able to breathe again but nor would he ever die, nor would his eyes ever close.

As for the miniature portraits of Lilith and Grand Loup: at first he kept them propped up on the desk in his room, his waking view and his last view at night, but they began to seem to him more like postcards from an art museum. After Cabot asked him: "Are they your French relatives?" he realized he did not want to explain. He wrapped the portraits in a silk scarf and added them to the box where he kept his mother's rosary and her letters.

In October, after more than one month at Dryden, he received a letter mailed from New York which bore the return address of Myriam Goldberg. A terrible disturbance moved through him, like the tremor that precedes an earthquake or a volcanic eruption. He held the envelope for a long time, sitting at his desk and staring out his window at the mountains. He could not control the tremor in his hands.

When the storm subsided, he slit the envelope open with his paper knife. Inside was another envelope, as well as a handwritten note from Myriam Goldberg. The enclosed envelope bore French stamps and a postmark of Tours. Myriam Goldberg's note said:

Dear Petit Loup: At last the channels of communication are safely open and no doubt Lilith will update you in her letter (which is enclosed) on her own changing circumstances and those of the chateau. (Forgive me. Of course by Lilith I mean Capucine, but she looks so like her mother at that age that it's difficult for me to remember.) We are so alarmed by the news that Grand Loup had a stroke shortly after his heart attack and so disturbed by his rapidly deteriorating condition that we plan to fly to France next week. If it is necessary, and if we can arrange it, we will bring

317

Grand Loup back to New York for medical treatment, and we will try to bring Capucine too.

In any case, we will spend time with her in Tours and in St Gilles and will give you a full report on our return. We are assuming you will spend Thanksgiving with your father in New York. We will certainly be back home by then and we hope you will visit. Of course you will observe the festival dinner with your father, but perhaps you can visit us the next day? You are welcome to drop in at any time. Fondly, Myriam Goldberg.

Ti-Loup held the envelope with the French stamps and the Tours postmark for quite some time. He ran the tip of his index finger over Cap's handwriting, slowly, tracing each letter as though deciphering code. There was a knock at his door which barely registered. There was a pause and a second knock. There was something he was supposed to do but he could not remember what it was and then the door opened and Cabot leaned in. "Hi," he said. "Are you okay?"

Ti-Loup looked at him blankly.

"Listen," Cabot said. "Everyone goes through a stage in the first few weeks. Don't let it get to you. It's normal. Can I make a suggestion as your proctor? You're not in great physical shape, I mean by Dryden standards, and there's a mind-body loop, you know. I'm on the cross-country team and I'd like to invite you to join us. We have a great coach. You don't have to be an Olympic prospect when you start but you will certainly be a few quantum leaps closer by the end of term. Practice is before breakfast, at 6 a.m. Can I count on you tomorrow morning?"

"Uh... Let me think about it."

"I'd advise against that. You'll lose your nerve. You should just jump in. Can we make a deal? If you hate it, you can quit in two weeks, but I hope I can count on you for a two-week try. Can I?"

"Sure," Ti-Loup said. "Sure. Okay. Thanks for the invitation."

"Hey. Good publicity. A Vanderbilt and a Cabot on the cross-country team? That'll give Choate and Phillips-Exeter something to chew on. I'll knock on your door in the morning. See you at dawn." Cabot flicked back his hair as he closed the door.

Ti-Loup opened the bottom drawer of his dresser and added the envelope with French stamps, unopened, to the shoebox of unread correspondence.

He had a terrible night. He could not get to sleep and when he finally did, long past midnight, he was dangling from his windowsill in the chateau. The height of the drop had increased alarmingly and he found he was twenty feet above the ground. He dropped and felt his ankle and leg bones shatter, but he knew his business was urgent, a matter of life and death. He crawled into the woods, propelling himself on his arms, dragging his broken legs behind him. He had to reach the stone bridge in time. He knew where it was, or he thought he did, but all the footpaths and trails were blocked by undergrowth that was vicious with thorns. He was punctured all over. He could see beads of blood on his arms, feel the blood trickling down his cheeks. But he would get there. He would get there. He would get to the old stone bridge and he would get there in time.

He got there just as he woke, but it was too late.

4.

At sunrise, the autumn air in rural Massachusetts was decidedly crisp. Ti-Loup, running, concentrated on gulping in enough oxygen to survive, though this felt like inhaling dry ice. His feet were killing him. Every muscle in his legs was on fire. Ten boys were running in concert, their athletic shoes pounding the earth. Cabot was slightly ahead of him and to his left. He did not know anyone else. There was no way he was going to quit before the coach, running close on his right, gave permission, but he thought the chances were high that he would drop dead before then.

He became an automaton, conscious of nothing but propulsion and pain, and then not even conscious of those.

"Listen, Vanderbilt," coach said. "I'm not going to pretend that you look like someone who could make the cross-country team, but you've got something I can work with. You're not a quitter. You serious about giving this a try? You committed?"

"I'm committed, coach."

"Cabot seems to want you on this team. But do you want it?"

"I think so, sir."

"You *think* so? Not the right answer. Do you want it or not, yes or no?"

"Yes, sir, I want it."

"But do you want it enough?"

"Yes, sir, I want it enough to do whatever you tell me to do."

"Good. Okay then. Here's what we have to do. You meet me in the gym at 5.30 a.m. every morning, before the team run. And you meet me again between study time and dinner. You lift weights. You bench-press. You do sit-ups and push-ups. We transform you from softie to Superman."

"Yes, sir."

There was another boy who thudded beside him on the morning run, footfall for footfall. This boy never spoke, at least not within Vanderbilt's hearing. This boy did not live on his hallway or in his dorm. He had not sat at the same table in dining hall. Not yet. He did not even know this boy's name although they often stood side by side in the showers after the run. At first it did not bother Vanderbilt that they did not speak, and then it did.

"Hey," he said one day as they were toweling off after the shower. "I'm Vanderbilt."

"Yeah, I know," the boy said. "I'm McVie."

"Where are you from?"

"Boston. Full scholarship." McVie announced this as though declaring a herpes infection upfront. His accent was the English equivalent of French peasant. He looked Vanderbilt directly in the eyes and held his gaze. "Boston Irish. My father's a butcher. That a problem for you?"

"No problem at all. My best friend in France was a butcher," Ti-Loup said, but without even thinking about it or making any conscious decision, without even being aware of what he was doing, he spoke as though he'd grown up on the same block as McVie.

McVie's eyes widened with shock and anger. "Fuck you," he said, "you arrogant patronizing prick."

Cabot leaned against his doorway. "Can I come in?"

"Of course."

"I have to say, you got the ancestral Vanderbilt genes in spades when it comes to competitiveness and conquest, even if you didn't get the athletic genes of your father or his racehorse body."

"Coach pushes hard," Vanderbilt said.

"*You* push hard. You push harder. No matter what pace we set, you keep up. Amazing stuff for a rookie who was skinny and... well... who wasn't exactly—"

"Who looked like a milksop," Vanderbilt supplied.

"Not what I was going to say. Hell, you're a Vanderbilt. You can look however you want to look. But you sure didn't look like a track star. And now... I begin to think I might regret inviting you to try out."

"Don't be ridiculous."

"You've got the right stuff for Dryden, that's for sure. What are your college plans?"

"My college plans?"

"Where are you applying? Where are you planning to go?"

"I haven't decided," Vanderbilt said cautiously, briefly panicked, and having no clue as to what *college plans* meant.

"I'm going to MIT," Cabot announced.

"Oh! You mean which *university*? Well, uh, the Sorbonne, I think."

"Wow. Paris. That's cool. What majors do they offer? Mine'll be Physics. What's yours?"

Vanderbilt concentrated on decoding this question. "Uh... I'm still thinking about it. Philosophy maybe."

"Good heavens!" Cabot said affectionately. "My father will wish he'd switched us at birth. Dad teaches Philosophy at Harvard. Well, actually, Political Philosophy. He's been an advisor to the State Department, a consummation devoutly *not* to be wished for in my opinion. He just can't get his head around why I would want to do Physics."

"Why do you?"

"Oh. Well. I went with Dad to a lecture by this guy named Mandelbrot who's a kind of Polish-Jewish-French refugee with IBM. No one, including Mandelbrot himself, seems to know whether he's a mathematician or a physicist or an economist and Dad thinks the Mandelbrot Man lives in sci-fi fantasyland, but I was transfixed. He said something I can't get out of my mind. He said that what appears to be chaos is really order with some missing information and I decided on the spot that I wanted to go in search of what was missing."

"Wow!" Vanderbilt said, torched by Cabot's adrenaline rush. "And your father? What sort of thing does he—?"

"Well, come to think of it, I suppose he's not so different from Mandelbrot. He studies why governments do what they do… Why did Nazi Germany do what it did? Why did Franco? Why did Stalin? Why did whole populations go along with these psychopaths? Dad's searching for the missing information so we can stop the next war before it happens."

"Wow!" Vanderbilt said again. That is what I want to do, he instantly decided. I will major in Political Philosophy at Harvard and I will study with Cabot's father.

"Listen," Cabot said, "I imagine you're going home for Thanksgiving, but just in case you're not… I mean, in case your father is in Europe or otherwise engaged or something, you're welcome to spend the weekend with us in Boston. We have a big extended family thing if you think you could stand a lot of Cabots."

"Thank you," Vanderbilt said. "I'm not sure of my plans at the moment."

Coach extended the length of practice time and the distances for the cross-country team. It became a private compulsion with Vanderbilt to run at the head of the pack regardless of the pace or the distance. Clearly the same compulsion drove McVie.

Neck and neck, thud for thud, they stayed in the lead. They never spoke.

In the showers, their teammates lobbed mock insults through the steam: *Listen, you rookies. Cross-country's not about egos, it's about the team. You newbies are going to burn yourselves out, which is not the point. The point is for the team to beat Choate.*

But coach said: "I can use people who are driven."

"Even if they sound like a thug from the Somerville crime mob?" someone murmured in a voice that he intended to be almost heard.

"You want to repeat that to my face?" McVie grabbed the boy by the shoulders and spun him around so that their eyes were inches apart. They butted foreheads.

"Enough!" Coach stepped between. "One more incident like that and you'll both be off the team. You, Benson, should know better. You've had two older brothers graduate but you've broken a cardinal Dryden rule. We expect civility and courtesy from students. Say something like that again and I'll sign you up for remedial lessons in manners. Is that understood?"

"Yes, sir." Nevertheless, everyone saw Benson give the finger to McVie behind coach's back.

5.

John Semple, college advisor, asked Vanderbilt if he knew how to play chess.

"Yes," Vanderbilt said, surprised. "I do. I love chess. I miss it. In France, I had a Jesuit tutor who taught me and sometimes I even beat him."

"Great," John Semple said. "Ideal. We have a school club. Not a large one, but those who play go for the kill. They're intense. We call it the Bobby Fischer Club and I'm the convener. We meet on Sunday afternoons in the assembly hall, six games, tournament style, and we rotate until we get an outright winner. We pick up where we left off the weekend before. Can I expect you this Sunday, 3 p.m.? We play until dinner time, and then again after, until lights out."

"I'll be there."

"McVie's also a member, by the way."

"Is Benson?"

"Benson's not the chess-playing type. The game requires patience."

Vanderbilt's first opponent was McVie.

He thought of asking John Semple: Was this arranged? And if so, why? Is this some sort of Dryden experiment? Throw two outsiders into the chess pen, pit them against each other and watch what happens?

They played for three hours and did not speak a word until McVie said, "Checkmate."

They held each other's gaze steadily, without blinking, for so long that Vanderbilt's eyes began to prickle. He wanted to say: *Well played. Congratulations.* But he was not sure which voice would come out and was afraid that whichever came out would give offense. He also wanted to ask, if he could have thought of any delicate way to put it: *Who could have taught a butcher's son to play chess like that?*

McVie seemed to sense this question. "I was sent to a Marist Brothers school in Lawrence, Mass. and we were all taught to play. My parish priest at St Ann's in Somerville went to that same school a century ago and he and I played every week. I never won."

"I was taught by my Jesuit tutor in France," Vanderbilt said. He thought he said this in his Father JG voice, but was not certain. "He almost always won, but I did beat him twice."

"You're Catholic?" McVie was astonished. "In a WASP school like this?"

"I was baptized Catholic."

"But your father's on the Board of Trustees."

"My mother's Catholic. She's French."

"So you're only half Catholic."

"I'm one-hundred percent Catholic. Baptized in St Patrick's Cathedral in New York. First communion in the parish church of St Gilles in France when I was seven."

"We're probably the only two Catholics in this school," McVie said.

Vanderbilt had never even thought about this. Was it worse than being a boy who had worn a blue dress?

"But now suddenly," McVie said, "in two weeks, there's a good chance we'll have a Catholic president in the White House. It'll be interesting to see how that's going to go over round here."

"Actually, to be perfectly honest," Vanderbilt said, "I'm *bona fide* one-hundred percent Catholic as far as baptism and confirmation goes, but I'm lapsed. Not just lapsed, but angry lapsed. I'm one hundred percent *ex*-Catholic. I don't go to confession or Mass."

"Not much opportunity at Dryden," McVie said. "But you should understand a thing or two. I had a poster of JFK for President taped to my bedroom door. Last week, it was ripped off and torn to confetti. D'you get it? This is not a time to be quitting the team."

"I'm not quitting in that sense. I'll be happy to tape a JFK poster on my door. I'll do it today. I hadn't given any of that a thought because American politics is still like outer space to me. I know the presidents and what order they came in from George Washington onwards, and I know American History up to World War II, but American politics since then... that's unknown territory. It's the New World. My Catholic problem is my mother..." Vanderbilt sighed. "I got an overdose of daily confession and daily Mass and daily praying the rosary in my childhood. I get an allergic reaction."

"Well, yeah," McVie said. "Who doesn't?" He held out his right hand as evidence. The knuckles were gnarled and swollen, the fingers crooked. "Marist Brother discipline," he said. "But that's not everything, is it? Brother Damian taught me chess."

On November 8, as election returns were bouncing back and forth, up and down, hour by hour on broadcast news, there was so much jostling around TV sets in dormitory common rooms that the whole school was invited to watch the large screen in assembly hall. Minute by minute the numbers changed, the electoral college votes swooped this way and that, the popular vote was neck-and-neck, the evening dragged on toward midnight but no one, neither masters nor students, was willing to leave the room.

Just before midnight, the *New York Times* called the election and the TV channels quoted the Times: KENNEDY DEFEATS NIXON BY NARROW MARGIN.

Some of the Dryden audience cheered, some booed, others were stunned and silent, but McVie whispered to Vanderbilt as they left: "Want to join me for a victory lap at five tomorrow morning?"

"Wouldn't miss it," Vanderbilt whispered back.

Pre-dawn on November 9 McVie and Vanderbilt met outside the gym and raised their hands high and slapped palms. "To us," McVie said. "From the potato famine to the White House. Took more than a century, but we did it. Team loyalty, Vanderbilt. I can still hardly believe it, but our team has finally won."

Vanderbilt wondered if he would ever know to which team he belonged or if any team would ever acknowledge him as a member.

In the last week of November 1960, family cars and limousines choked the Dryden drive. Limos took boys to Bradley International Airport outside Hartford, fifty-five miles south on Interstate 91, other side of the Connecticut border. From Bradley they flew to cities across the country and sometimes to assorted American embassies around the world. The international students, however, the genuine non-citizens, the mega-wealthy foreigners, were invariably invited to Thanksgiving dinners at the homes of American boys.

The family limousine arrived for Vanderbilt. "Your father is putting on quite a show for you," Castano informed him on the long drive back. "He usually spends Thanksgiving out in the Hamptons but he's arranged a caterer for Fifth Avenue this year. He's invited your Uncle Harry and your cousin Billy and I don't know who else."

"What about you, Castano?" Vanderbilt asked.

"What do you mean, Mr. Gwynne?"

"I mean, when and where will you join your own family for Thanksgiving dinner?"

"I will remain available to your father and his guests until late evening," Castano said. Then he added, in a carefully uninflected voice, "I am not required to answer personal questions, Mr. Gwynne."

Vanderbilt was startled. "Oh no, of course not," he said, embarrassed. "It's none of my business. I just wanted to wish you and your family a Happy Thanksgiving."

"Thank you, Mister Gwynne." For the next ten miles, Castano said nothing at all. "I have worked ten years as your father's chauffeur," he said at last, "but your father does not know where I live or even if I have a family. He has never asked me."

"It was quite improper of me, Castano, and quite rude. I apologize."

"We live in Newark, New Jersey, my family. Big family, very big, uncles, aunts, cousins, little ones underfoot. I have eight grandchildren."

"Wow. Congratulations. You don't look old enough—"

"Thank you, Mr. Gwynne. I am like Abraham, father of many. We have two Thanksgiving dinners, an early one for the grandchildren, nieces, nephews, all the little ones. A late one for the rest of us who have to work. My brother's a chauffeur too, and one of my sons. My father, who has passed on, was a doorman at the Carlyle."

Vanderbilt wanted to ask *How late is the late dinner?* He wanted to ask: *Do you drive the Vanderbilt limo to New Jersey? Where do you park it? Do you worry about vandalism in Newark? What time do you drive it back the next morning?* But he understood he was already far overdrawn on his decorum account.

Quite suddenly, Castano became loquacious. "We all go to my mother's house. She was born in Sicily, my mother, but she was a baby when she arrived on Ellis Island. She's eighty-eight but no one else better dare offer to stuff or roast the Thanksgiving turkey. We don't eat till midnight because by the time I get the limo parked in the underground lot and take the subway to Penn Station and then the commuter train... well, usually I miss the sweet-potato soup. But from then on, it's eating and drinking and arguing and singing and dancing until the morning hangover wakes us up."

Vanderbilt noted, with avid interest, that Castano switched accents quite radically when he spoke as patriarch of a large extended family rather than as a Fifth Avenue chauffeur. Mentally, Vanderbilt rolled the sounds around his own tongue and inside his own head, listening carefully to each one, trying them out, decoding them into phonetic symbols on the backs of his eyelids. He began to have trouble remembering his own Vanderbilt voice (his Dryden-Vanderbilt voice, which was that of Father JG) and when the limo pulled up outside his father's building on Fifth Avenue, he had still not consciously decided which voice he was going to use but his greeting came out in pure New Jersey-Sicilian. "Castano, I hope you have such a great Thanksgiving that you don't sober up until one hour before you have to pick me up next week."

Castano turned on his seat in astonishment and slid the glass divider open. He said something rapid and passionate and warmly affectionate in Sicilian.

"I'm sorry, Castano," Vanderbilt said. "I know English and French, but no Italian. I'm just good at mimicking accents, that's all, and I don't really know how or why. I don't even do it consciously. It just happens."

"You are very unusual, Mister Gwynne," Castano said in his chauffeur voice. There was a long pause. "I wish you a very happy Thanksgiving. And—uh—perhaps I should warn you...."

"Yes?"

"On second thought, perhaps I should not."

"Warn me of what, Castano?"

330

"Of nothing," Castano said. "A chauffeur who speaks ill of his employer has a death wish. He will be fired. I need to keep my job, which is a very good job."

"Castano," Vanderbilt said in his New Jersey-Sicilian voice, "I swear to you on my oath that you will not be fired because of me. Anything you say to me will not be repeated to another living soul."

Castano crossed himself. "Okay," he said. "I must be nuts to believe you but I do, so here's my Hail Mary pass. Your father has a girlfriend here for the weekend and so does your Uncle Harry. They have many girlfriends. Their girlfriends get younger every year and none of them last very long. The girlfriends get five-star restaurant dinners and jewelry and trips to the Caribbean and Paris and then they're gone. If you ask me, but this is none of my business, none whatsoever.... but if you were to ask for my opinion, your inheritance—if you're waiting for one—is seeping away like water through sand, but what do I know?

"Anyway I have to stay within call until 11 p.m. and by then, believe me, you'll be on your lonesome because your relatives will be very drunk or will have disappeared into their bedrooms with their girlfriends, or both, and you will be left with a choice between late-night TV or Shannay's family in the Bronx or my family and me. I'm sure Shannay would love to take you home to her family dinner but I can tell you that the Line 4 Local to the Bronx at that time of night is not a safe ride and nor is the Express, but I don't think the Express even runs that late. After every holiday, every long weekend, I expect Shannay to report in dead. So if you'd like to give the Castanos a try, get Shannay to call me before she leaves and you can come to Penn Station with me. Your father won't even notice you've gone and I'll take you across the river to a New Jersey Thanksgiving I promise you'll never forget. And this year, this November, we'll be giving special thanks for the election."

A Catholic president! Who could have believed it would happen? *Deo gratias.*"

"Castano, whether or not I take advantage of that generous invitation, I won't forget it."

Shannay was waiting for him when the elevator doors opened on the penthouse floor. "Oh my," she said. "Look at you." She tested the muscles of his upper arms with her thumbs, pressing and pinching, the way she might test melons in a market.

"You think I look good?"

"You turning into one of those TV ads for gym equipment. You sho' ain't that frightened little boy anymore."

"I sho' ain't."

"Get on with you," she said, laughing and slapping his backside. "I got to warn you about something, Master Gwynne."

"I think Castano already warned me."

"About the bimbos, you mean?"

"Is that what they are?"

"Hamptons bimbos, bimbos with manicures and pedicures and Saks Fifth Avenue glad rags and enough gold to weigh 'em down and drown 'em if they ever fall off their boyfriends' yachts. They have gold-digger plans to match their gold chokers, but still bimbos. That about the full reach of your daddy's and your uncle's tastes, Master Gwynne, 'cept I haven't mentioned they also like fake eyelashes, big hair, big boobs, and very small flat backsides."

"Shannay," Vanderbilt laughed, "what a wicked satirist you are."

"Master Gwynne," Shannay said. "Don't you go trying out those big words on me. Don't you go Dryden on me, now."

The dining room table and the sideboard were magnificent with arrangements of gourds in various autumnal colors and contorted shapes. There were stunning swathes of leaves—crimson, dark tangerine, bright yellow—and fresh oranges studded with cloves and a massive centerpiece of pomegranates, cranberries, and glossy magnolia leaves. The whole penthouse smelled of sage and rosemary and thyme. Shannay played fifth wheel to the caterer's team in the kitchen and was expected to stay there. The family and guests were waited on exclusively by black waiters and black wine-stewards dressed in tuxes with starched white shirts and black bow-ties.

"Well," Vanderbilt's father said. "I've been pleasantly surprised by the report from the school. Seems there's a chance that Dryden can make a man out of you after all. This is your Uncle Harry, by the way, my older brother. He's the one who got everything except this penthouse when our father died, so they'd never have let him marry a crazy Frenchwoman, chateau or not, lucky man."

"Pleased to meet you, Uncle Harry." Vanderbilt braced himself for the crunch of his finger bones but found Uncle Harry's handshake moist and slack.

"This family has never believed in dispersal of assets to siblings," Vanderbilt's father explained. "Oldest son gets all, or almost all. It's a way to keep the family holdings intact."

"I let you use our house in the Hamptons whenever you want," Uncle Harry said.

"You do. And you never let me forget who owns it. And this is your cousin Billy, son, and eventually you'll have to grovel to him when you want to use the house in the Hamptons."

"Running part of the family business now," Billy said. "Plus racehorse breeding on the side."

"Pleased to meet you, Billy." Billy's handshake was firm and aggressive.

"So," Billy said in such a way that Vanderbilt instantly knew Billy was privy to the blue dress and to every excessive devotional practice of his mother. "Made any friends at Dryden?"

"Had to turn down a Thanksgiving invitation from the Cabots," Vanderbilt said nonchalantly. "And another one from the royal House of Saud. But family comes first, right?"

His father, his uncle and his cousin all paused. They all looked at him. "Which Cabot?" Billy asked.

"Well, I don't know," Vanderbilt said vaguely. "His father teaches at Harvard and consults for the State Department. Or at least, he did before the election. Which Cabot would that be? I don't know much about the family."

This statement seemed to have much the same effect on Vanderbilt's closest relatives as the Vanderbilt limousine had had on Dryden. "So," Uncle Harry said. "Nephew of Henry Cabot Lodge Jr.? Or second cousin? Or son of a second cousin? Either way, that Nixon-Cabot Lodge ticket lost us the election, dammit. Those Boston Brahmins are too well-mannered to know how to fight to win."

"Too well-bred to take off their kid gloves," Billy said. "Might as well go up against the Kennedy mafia with a butter knife."

"Just the same," Vanderbilt's father said. "Useful contact. Don't underestimate its value. Rumor is that Kennedy will tap Cabot Lodge Jr. for an ambassadorship. JFK's got to watch his own back and his own back door, after all. He can't afford to have the Cabots ganging up against him in Boston, especially not after he whipped Cabot Lodge Jr.'s ass twice, first for his senate seat and then for the White House. So. An invitation to the Cabots, huh, even though we're not quite sure which family offshoot that is. Excellent. Excellent. You should accept. For Christmas, you should accept. I knew the school would straighten you out if anything could."

The caterer's steward appeared with a tray of champagne flutes and smoked oysters. "Exit politics, enter revelry," Vanderbilt's father said. "So now I'd like to introduce my friend Lisette, this gorgeous creature."

"How do you do, Lisette?" Vanderbilt offered his hand. "That's a French name. Are you French?"

"Oh gosh, no. I'm an actress. My agent thought the name would be a good sell." Lisette, who must have been all of twenty and who was indeed gorgeous if one's tastes ran in a certain way, took Vanderbilt's hand in both of hers and stroked her own cheek with it. "You're such a cute little slip of a boy," she said, "you look like a choir boy. You're so adorable, I could just eat you right up."

"I'm dessert," Vanderbilt said archly. "I think you have to work through the cold cuts first."

His father roared with laughter. "Chip off the old block," he said. "Smart as a whip. A lot smarter than your Billy, Harold, wouldn't you say?"

"That wouldn't be hard," Uncle Harry said. "I don't know what's going to happen to the family business after I go. I don't see how I can trust you, Lawrie, even supposing you don't drink too much and play so hard that your lights go out before mine do. Maybe Gwynne can step up to the plate by then? Meanwhile, I'm putting as much as I can into trust funds with managers of my own choosing, because Billy is hopeless. He just doesn't have the killer instinct or any head for management at all, and I don't see his MBA making a difference worth peanuts."

Billy gave both his father and his cousin a thunderous look.

"Speaking of playing too hard," Vanderbilt's father said. "Aren't you going to introduce your current playmate to my son?"

"Forgive me, Gwynne Patrice. Allow me to present my friend, Celise," Uncle Harry said. Celise was not at all in the same gorgeous-creature category as Lisette and yet she gave off the air of someone who thought she was, of someone who had a clear and inflexible sense of what was due to her, of someone who saw herself in a different mirror.

Vanderbilt sensed that any mirror into which Celise looked

took orders from her, though what everyone else saw was what Vanderbilt's mother—*la comtesse*—might have primly described as *une femme pas belle au rabais,* a plain woman available at a discount price. This discrepancy between what others saw and what Celise clearly believed they saw fascinated Vanderbilt.

He had observed the nature of entitlement up close at Dryden and was becoming finely attuned to its gradations. Celise's air of what was rightfully hers was not remotely like Cabot's or like that of the scions of Middle-Eastern potentates who were all so many generations deep in inherited privilege that they were not even faintly aware of its existence or of how it affected their behavior and their views. The sheer oblivion of the entitled, their sheer level of ignorance about other life forms, Vanderbilt was thinking, made these people charming and generous and well-mannered in an impeccably understated way. His own mother, for instance, who was—objectively speaking—financially close to desperation, kept to a code of courteous *noblesse oblige* that was centuries deep in her DNA.

For Celise, however—so Vanderbilt sensed—entitlement was a matter of the will. *I may not be able to prove my pedigree and you may not believe I belong,* **but I do,** *and if you do not accept that fact you will come to regret it.*

Vanderbilt thought of McVie who was also driven by pure will, but McVie knew in his bones that the game was unalterably rigged. *I wasn't born with a Dryden future* was the thudding refrain of each beat of McVie's pumping heart and his running shoes, *but I've earned it. Nevertheless, I know I'll never be accepted by your kind and I don't care. I don't want to belong.*

Celise *did* want to belong. She was going to belong

Here surely was an interesting subject for exploration, for a term paper perhaps. **A Comparative History of Privilege:** *A study of impoverished inheritors of ancient titles versus inheritors of wealth* *at least two centuries old versus Nouveau Riche.* He imagined how Father JG might lay out on the classroom table a set of portraits by Hans Holbein or by his followers, portraits of Erasmus, Cardinal Wolsey, Pope Leo X, Henry VIII, Thomas More, Thomas Cromwell, Katherine of Aragon, Anne Boleyn, Elizabeth I. Discuss low-born versus high-born, he might say. Discuss differences in education, achievements, wealth, death and manner of death. Discuss executions, especially the manner of execution and its meaning (burning at the stake, beheading, dismemberment, rotting head on a pike). Discuss how birth-rank and wealth affect who is commissioned to paint the portrait. Discuss how the portrait painter himself dictates history. Discuss how the sitter's view of himself or herself affects the portrait painter.

Unbidden, a sudden sickening memory flashed before Vanderbilt's eyes. He saw a pompous little boy in a chateau courtyard and a wild girl with matted hair dropping from a tree. *Fat cat,* she accused. *Gros richard…*

"But not anymore," he protested.

"Not any more what?" his father said.

"Uh, sorry, I was thinking aloud." Vanderbilt had to go and stand at the French windows and look out over the park, such a dizzy moment of loss and disorientation overcame him.

"Thinking about what?" his father demanded.

"Oh, nothing really. Dryden, the Cabots, my school room in France…"

Someone put a hand on his arm and stood so close he recoiled. It was Celise. "Forgive me," she murmured. "I don't mean to take liberties, but you look as though you need comfort."

"Thank you, but you're mistaken," Vanderbilt said politely.

Celise stepped closer and put her hand on his arm again, her fingers applying pressure. She put her lips close against his ear and whispered something which he did not quite catch but her grip sent a low electrical buzz from his wrist to his shoulder. There was something faintly menacing about this, all the more so because her touch purported to be tentative.

"I'm sorry," he said, "I didn't quite—" but even as he spoke, he took note of a curious segue in her manner. She was fluid. She had quicksilver costume changes. She became timid and shy. She touched his cheek fleetingly but this time with a nervous air of trespass.

"Forgive me. I didn't mean to offend," she said again, softly. He had a weird sense of being directed on a stage, of being cast in a play whose script he did not know, but then she raised her eyes to meet his. She had a way of maintaining intense eye contact for a disconcertingly long stretch of time, a habit that seemed to mesmerize Uncle Harry and make him jealous.

"Gwynne Patrice," his uncle said sharply. "You are monopolizing Celise and that is very bad form."

"Oh, Harry," Celise said. "It's so sweet of you to be so possessive."

"You'll have to make allowances for my nephew," Uncle Harry said. "He's half French and half Catholic and his mother is full-time French-Catholic neurotic, but we don't hold it against him, especially since the half-French part is also part-Royal."

"My goodness," Celise said. "Can I hug the part-royal part?"

"I don't let that part hang out," Vanderbilt said, dead-pan. "Are you an actress like Lisette?"

"Oh, she's an actress all right," his father laughed.

"I believe my mother had French ancestry," Celise said demurely. "Or perhaps merely fantasized that she did. She had old Louisiana French connections. I'm pleased to meet you, Gwynne Patrice. Neither your father nor your uncle has remotely done you justice."

"Celise!" Uncle Harry warned.

Celise turned in close to Vanderbilt's uncle and nuzzled him. "I'm just being nice to your relatives," she murmured. She bit Uncle Harry on the neck and drew blood.

"Excuse us," Uncle Harry said. "Don't hold up dinner on our account. We left something in our room and we may be detained."

"Last year," Shannay informed Vanderbilt in the kitchen when he snuck out for a break in the horse-talk, stock-market speculation, predictions of doom in the wake of the election, and the general unbearable tedium of the dinner-table conversation, "Celise was your father's girlfriend. She knows what she's after, that one. I have to make their beds and change their sheets, you know, so there's not much I miss. She's a widow, or so she claims, but there are plenty of rumors. No one knows where she came from. She just popped up like a mushroom at Upper East Side parties and fundraisers and at the opera, of course. I know most of the house-keepers between East 42nd and East 96th. Even if only half of what I hear about her is true, it would scorch your ears and rot your socks."

"Is she hoping to marry Uncle Harry?"

"Last year, she was hoping to marry your father but divorce was out of the question, he told her, on account of the kind of Catholic your mother is. I heard him tell her that. So this year she's pitching for your uncle, who's not a Catholic and whose ex-wife is already married to someone else. Good luck with that, is what I'd say. He's the mistress kind, not the re-marrying kind, and anyway he's got a son and heir. So she'll strike out there."

6.

Vanderbilt could not bear the thought of Christmas on Fifth Avenue so when Cabot offered again, he accepted. Christmas in Boston, Christmas on Commonwealth Avenue in the Back Bay: this sounded far more attractive than his father's penthouse, but he needed to call Shannay to apologize and explain.

"Don' need to explain to me," Shannay said. "You think I'd put up with your father if anywhere else paid enough? Besides, now he's planning to stay in the Hamptons which means I can leave earlier for the Bronx.

"But I've got to tell you something, Master Gwynne. Those Goldberg people, I like them, and you are not treating them right. I go visit once a week. I have afternoon tea with them. They make me feel like a lady. Madame Goldberg, she doesn't know what to think. She says you don't answer her letters. She says she has information that will break your heart but she can't reach you."

Vanderbilt wanted nothing to do with information that would break his heart. He had space-walked into a parallel universe and he was not going to leave it. The mere thought of stepping into nothingness again—of free-falling in an intergalactic nowhere where there was zero chance of not being an alien—this caused him a nausea so extreme that he would have to pause and lean against a wall or hang onto a stair rail in order not to lose his balance and fall.

"I don't know what Madame Goldberg means about her letters," he lied to Shannay. "It must be a postal problem."

Christmas with the Cabots in December 1960 was both sumptuous and restrained, as warm and gregarious as it was well-mannered and refined. There were many Cabots with many young children underfoot. The children were exquisitely dressed and were immaculately well-behaved and polite. The house smelled of fresh evergreens. There were pine-bough garlands and mistletoe thickly draped across mantels and twined around staircase banisters. There were Renaissance angels on sideboards. There were many candles in high carved candlesticks and in silver candelabra.

"Your house reminds me of my mother's chateau," Vanderbilt said. "You have some beautiful Louis XV pieces."

"You have to say that to my mother at dinner," Cabot said. "Please. She'll be delighted."

"I promise."

"I have an idea. We should go to the Loire Valley instead of Florence this summer," Cabot suggested, suddenly inspired. "I'll ask my parents. You could travel with us and we can all visit your chateau. Maybe your father will join us?"

"That's..." Vanderbilt's panic was so sudden and extreme that he could not draw breath. A hot pain shot up his spine. "My mother," he said carefully, "is... well, she's reclusive."

"Oh, I forgot." Cabot thumped his forehead with the palm of his hand. "I think your father said something to mine. I'd forgotten. She's a bit... the Emily Dickinson kind, right?"

"Something like that."

"Thoughtless and careless of me, Vanderbilt. I'm sorry. Forgive me?"

"Of course. Can I ask you something, Cabot?"

"Anything."

"What do you think of McVie?"

"I admire him. He's pulling himself up by the bootstraps. Between the two of you, we are going to win the cross-country crown. That's what Dryden does. Gives boys like McVie a shot at grabbing the gold ring."

"Where exactly is Somerville?" Vanderbilt asked.

"Other side of the Charles. North of Cambridge."

"How would we get there?"

"What do you mean?"

"I told him I'd be in Boston for Christmas and he invited me to drop in. Why don't we go meet him tomorrow?"

Cabot stared as though Vanderbilt had suggested they step in front of a subway train. "Well, you know," he said, "oil and water don't mix and you can't make them mix."

"What does that mean?"

"He's just not our sort, that's all."

"You said you admired him."

"I do. But that doesn't mean... I've never been to Somerville is what I mean. It's not the kind of place where Cabots go."

In the spring term of 1961, Cabot cajoled Vanderbilt into a role in Dryden's annual stage production, always part of the graduation ceremonies. "We're very Shakespearean," Cabot said. "It's always a hoot, men playing the female parts in drag. This year we're doing Oscar Wilde's *The Importance of Being Ernest* and we want you to play Ernest, who is really Jack, or also Jack, because you're so good at accents. It's all about multiple identities and social masks."

"I know," Vanderbilt said. "What part will you play?"

"I'll be Algernon. McVie has agreed, under duress, to play Gwendolyn. After all, you two spend hours playing chess so we figured you might as well play at getting married. And I've tricked Benson into playing Lady Bracknell because he's too stupid to know what that means."

"In that case," Vanderbilt said, "I can't resist."

In April 1961, Cabot received notification of his acceptance at MIT and in May of that year the Dryden graduation production of *The Importance of Being Ernest* went down in the annals of the academy as a sensation.

In the fall semester of 1961, when Cabot was no longer at Dryden but had moved on to MIT and urban Boston, Vanderbilt and McVie became closer, running cross-country every morning, playing chess every weekend. But in November, come Thanksgiving, they went their separate family ways. At Vanderbilt's second Thanksgiving on Fifth Avenue, Lisette had given way to Loulou, Uncle Harry had a Georgie on his arm, and Celise had moved on to cousin Billy.

"We really should see more of each other," she said to Vanderbilt, leaning toward him.

"In what way?" he asked.

"In whatever way you would like," she said demurely.

Later, he said to Shannay: "She'll say whatever she thinks you want her to say. She'll let anyone pull her strings."

"That one," Shannay told him, "is pulling her own strings, and everyone else's strings too. One day she'll pull the wrong string and choke her own neck in her very own noose, but plenty folks gonna get throttled along the way before that."

7.

Dawn by dawn, neck and neck, month by month, year by year, McVie and Vanderbilt stayed at the head of the pack on the cross-country run. Day by day, after the run, they were inches apart in the showers. They rarely spoke to each other but Vanderbilt knew there were electromagnetic currents that surged and sparked across the gap between their bodies.

They met only once a week for chess, but they played for hours. McVie almost always won. "I play over Thanksgiving and Christmas and summers too," he explained. "You ever play with anyone else?"

"No one to play with," Vanderbilt said. "I get rusty."

"I've got my parish priest," McVie said. "And Brother Damian too. I never win. Maybe you should spend Thanksgiving and Christmas with us."

Vanderbilt sighed. "I'm locked in. Thanksgiving with my father in New York, which is hell. Christmas with the Cabots, which is heaven."

"You didn't accept my invitation to visit while you were in Boston last Christmas or the one before," McVie said. "Any particular reason?"

"I did want to visit. I tried."

"How did you try?"

"I asked Cabot how to get to Somerville, but he didn't

know how."

"Hah!" McVie said. "That's quite funny. Checkmate, by the way."

By November 1962, at Thanksgiving, Celise was flashing a huge diamond engagement ring, present of William George Cornelius Vanderbilt. "Billy and I are planning a lavish wedding," Celise told Vanderbilt. "I would love to invite your friends the Cabots. Could you let them know?'

"Of course," Vanderbilt said politely. "Though, you know, I don't often see Cabot any more. He's at MIT now."

"But you're still in touch with his family, right? Have they invited you for Christmas again?"

"They have, yes."

"I'll send them an invitation," Celise said.

Vanderbilt spent Christmas with the Cabots in Boston. As always he felt charmed by the family warmth, especially by Cabot's mother.

"Gwynne," she said, late on Christmas night after the traditional rum-soaked plum pudding, "do tell me about your own mother. She must miss you. She must be lonely."

Vanderbilt searched her face for any hint of irony but there was none. He said carefully, "I don't come from a happy family like yours, Mrs. Cabot. I just...I can't talk about it. Even thinking about it makes me feel depressed. I'm sorry."

"You poor boy," Mrs. Cabot said. "I shouldn't have asked."

"You know, Mrs. Cabot," Vanderbilt said, "sometimes I feel like a stone-age man staring at the Massachusetts Turnpike, or like a man on the moon. I would not even have known what 'happy family' meant except that now I've had the privilege of being part of two of them: your family, and the family of my mother's gardener in France."

345

"Tell me about the family of your mother's gardener," Mrs. Cabot said, but the room suddenly tilted and Vanderbilt felt dizzy.

"I can't talk about that either," he managed to say.

"All happy families are alike," Mrs. Cabot said, "but every unhappy family is unhappy in its own way."

"Tolstoy," Vanderbilt said. "Yes, I know. Actually I have an even smaller statistical knowledge of unhappy families. Only my own."

"Dear boy," Mrs. Cabot said. "I do know a little about all this. Your father is, shall we say, not cut out of the best paternal cloth. The Vanderbilts never were. To be blunt, and if you'll forgive me, they were vulgar upstarts who became obscenely rich and the only strand of the family that developed any taste or any signs of civilized behavior or any awareness of art and literature and culture was George Washington Vanderbilt, grandson of that thug, Cornelius, who made the fortune. George Washington Vanderbilt would be your second or third cousin, or some such thing, I suppose. He was the one who designed that chateau in North Carolina and had it built. He married Edith Stuyvesant. That couple were charming and had good taste and their daughter Cornelia married Lord Cecil and so the line became socially acceptable on both sides of the Atlantic, though not for long. Lord Cecil was, shall we say diplomatically, a particular kind of Englishman, and Cornelia left him after only ten years. The British father, not generous by nature, hung on to the Vanderbilt fortune and the two sons. The Cabots have always considered Biltmore *un peu de trop,* but George Washington Vanderbilt was a literary man of culture and taste. He was a voracious reader, and his library at Biltmore is quite extraordinary. More than ten thousand books and they say he read every one."

"I can understand that," Vanderbilt said. "I had a tutor in France who gave me a passion for books."

"That makes you an honorary Cabot. We are so very fond of

you, you know." Cabot's mother touched Vanderbilt affectionately on the shoulder. "You'll always have a home away from home with us."

"Mrs. Cabot, can I ask you a question?"

"Of course, dear boy."

"Since Cabot left Dryden, my closest friend is a boy named McVie. You saw him in the graduation play. He played Gwendolyn."

"Oh yes, I remember. You were all so brilliantly and wickedly funny."

"McVie lives in Somerville and I promised I'd visit him this weekend. Could you tell me how to get there?"

"My goodness!" Mrs. Cabot said. "Well, that's not a question I was expecting. Probably you can get there on the subway, but I've never taken the subway myself so I'm not much help there. I'd certainly be happy to have our chauffeur take you and bring you back. What time would you like to go?"

When the Cabot limousine pulled up outside McVie & Sons, Butchers, in Union Square, Somerville, the commotion was considerable. Neighborhood children pressed up close to the tinted windows, noses and fingertips leaving smudged prints on the glass. Before the chauffeur even reached the rear passenger door to open it, Vanderbilt had already let himself out, an action that did not meet with the driver's approval.

"I'm looking for Patrick McVie," Vanderbilt said to the kids. "Is this his father's shop?"

"Good God, what have you done?" McVie stared in disbelief from the door of the shop.

"I came to visit," Vanderbilt said. "You said you wanted me to."

"Tell the driver to take off before the kids scratch the car or let down the tires. You'll have us hauled up for damages."

"But how will I get back to the Cabots?"

"I'll take you back on the subway. Come inside, you maniac. Upstairs. We live over the shop."

"Can I see your cold storage room first?"

"My father's working in there."

"Can I watch?" Vanderbilt begged.

8.

The summer of 1963 could have been the dreariest summer of Vanderbilt's life but turned out otherwise. The Cabots went to Italy in June, but Vanderbilt had been invited to spend July and August with them in Hyannisport on Cape Cod, not far from the Kennedy compound. He knew instinctively that his summer clothing and his summer loafers would not pass muster in such company. He knew that unless he mentioned Cabots and Kennedys to his father, no clothing allowance would be forthcoming. He was too angry and disgusted to play this card.

He had rather hoped he would be invited to spend the summer months above the butcher's shop in Somerville, Mass., but in the last week of the spring semester, when he ventured to raise this possibility, McVie said: "Things are rough for my Dad right now. I have to work for him all summer."

"I'll be happy to work for him too," Vanderbilt offered.

"My Dad can't afford you."

"I don't need to be paid. I'll do it for pleasure."

"My Dad is too proud to agree to that," McVie said. "And we don't have room for you above the shop. I share my room with two younger brothers."

And so Vanderbilt faced three months on Fifth Avenue. This turned out better than expected. His father spent the time in the Hamptons and did not invite his son. His son was relieved. He dined in the kitchen with Shannay. He spent his mornings exploring the inexhaustible pleasures of Central Park and his afternoons in art museums or libraries. He wanted to attend concerts and opera in the evenings but his father left no money for fripperies such as that. He was, therefore, inordinately proud of himself for obtaining positions as a volunteer usher at Carnegie Hall and at the Metropolitan Opera and the New York Philharmonic. In between usher duties, he heard splendid free performances three nights a week.

In the third week in August, Shannay startled Vanderbilt by saying: "Honey chile, I am going to leave you on your own for six days. I've packaged all your meals in the freezer. I've left thawing and heating instructions for each one."

"Where are you going?" Vanderbilt asked.

"I'm going to Washington, D.C. I'll be staying with friends."

"I didn't know you had friends in D.C."

"I have family all over," she said. "My mother was born in South Carolina, my father in Georgia."

"Are you going to visit the White House and the Capitol? Or what?"

Shannay regarded him levelly for several minutes. "You've been watching the news with me every night. What do you think I'm going to do?"

"I don't know. What are you going to do?"

"What is going to happen in D.C. this week, Master Gwynne? Do you sleep through the television news or what?"

"I don't pay close attention. I daydream, I suppose. Oh...! You mean that march? The black Communist?"

"I mean the Reverend Martin Luther King, yes. I am joining his march for justice."

Vanderbilt was shocked. "Shannay! You can't be serious. That's the criminal Communist rabble."

"You think demonstrating for the right of black folks to vote and to be able to use public bathrooms is Communist, do you, Gwynne Patrice? Is that your idea of democracy? Is that what you believe?"

"*Everyone* knows that Martin Luther King is a Communist."

"Everyone knows that, do they?"

"Well, yes... Everyone does."

"That's what they teach you at Dryden, is it? You are not so different from your father, Gwynne Patrice."

Though he would not otherwise have done so, Vanderbilt watched every televised moment of the March on Washington, the largest demonstration in American history, all 250,000 people, black and white, from all over the country, converging on the Mall and moving as one surging convulsive mass from the Washington Monument to the Lincoln Memorial. He watched and listened to Martin Luther King's speech. *I have a dream....* He was stirred, he was stricken, he was conflicted, he felt accused and did not like it.

He watched for Shannay in the crowd but never saw her.

He waited for her return. Six days, seven days, eight. She did not come back. He was reduced to raiding the butler's pantry and scarfing cookies. He opened soup cans and heated them. There were dried beans and pasta but he did not know how to cook.

He asked the concierge if there had been any sign of Shannay.

"You've got to be kidding," the concierge said.

"What do you mean?"

"I mean the building manager informed all the owners about the black housekeepers and black janitors who went AWOL for that march. They all got laid off. The manager told them not to bother coming back."

"What?! Why?"

"What kind of a question is that?"

9.

About a week before Thanksgiving in November 1963, during morning run, McVie asked: "You going to spend the holiday with your father? Or with the Cabots?"

"It's always Thanksgiving on Fifth Avenue, Christmas with the Cabots," Vanderbilt said. "So I'm stuck with my father—except he doesn't have a new housekeeper yet. Our other housekeeper got fired for joining that march on Washington, so I suppose I'll be forced to go to the Hamptons with my father because I know he won't leave me any money for food."

"You want to try Somerville? Flirt with the dangerous underbelly of the urban beast?"

"Are you inviting me?"

"On one condition. You are not to arrive by limo."

"I thought you didn't have room in your house."

"We don't. You and I will have to sleep on the pull-out sofa in the living room."

"I accept," Vanderbilt said.

It was a Friday, six days before Thanksgiving. Abruptly, in early afternoon, classes were canceled. Vanderbilt passed McVie in a hallway. "What's going on?" he asked.

"The president's been shot and killed," McVie said. "In Dallas."

All through Friday night, all Saturday and Sunday and Monday, the entire school, masters and students, sat numb and sleepless and owl-eyed in the assembly hall watching TV, mostly silent, sometimes weeping, sometimes holding each other. They watched Jackie Kennedy in her blood-stained pink suit, they watched LBJ being sworn in, they watched Jack Ruby shoot Lee Harvey Oswald dead on live TV, they watched the lying-in-state of the flag-draped coffin in the Capitol rotunda (exactly where Abraham Lincoln had lain in state slightly less than a century before), they watched the hundreds of thousands who lined up in the rain throughout the night to file by the coffin, they watched the funeral procession, they watched the riderless horse pulling the caisson, they heard the slow solemn beat of the drum corps, they watched three-year-old John Junior salute his father's remains.

Dryden boys who had never wept in public before, and never intended to, held each other and wept.

No limo came for McVie and Vanderbilt. They took the college shuttle into Springfield and from there they took the bus to Boston. "I've never been on a bus before," Vanderbilt admitted.

"Jesus," McVie said.

"It's fantastic. We're so high up."

"That's one way of looking at it," McVie said.

"We can see the tops of cars. We can see into them. Look at that!"

"What? A truck driver feeling up his girlfriend? Or his truck-stop whore? Big deal."

"Why are you angry with me?"

"I'm not angry with you," McVie said. "I'm just angry. And depressed. And... and desolate. About the country, about my future, about everything. Aren't you?"

"I don't think I feel anything," Vanderbilt said.

They were silent for the next two hours until the bus entered the traffic tangle of the western edge of greater Boston. "We'll get off in Harvard Square," McVie said, "and take another bus from there. It's not far, but there's no telling how long it will take. Depends on traffic."

"Can I ask you something?"

"Only if it's not about the assassination and not about growing up Irish Catholic in Boston and not about being depressed."

"Tell me about Brother Damian."

"If it hadn't been for Brother Damien and our games of chess, I'd probably be behind bars by now instead of at Dryden. But I'm less and less sure that the bargain I made was a good one."

"Don't you like Dryden?"

"Do you?"

"Well.... yes. I didn't expect to, but I do."

"That's because you're part of the tribe. I'm not and I'll never be admitted. What scares me now is I'm turning myself into an outcaste in my own tribe. I have no idea how to prepare you for the McVie family circus."

"I know I'm going to feel at home with your family. My best friend in France was a butcher."

"Yeah, I remember. You told me."

"And you didn't believe me, but Ti-Christophe was an artist with a boning knife. He taught me. My happiest memories in France were in the cold room at the butcher's."

"And did the butcher accept you as part of the tribe?"

"Ahh..." Vanderbilt experienced a shock of enlightenment. "No. He didn't. I think his son hated me. In fact, his son hacked my best friend to death."

"What!?"

"Ignore that. Strike that. I didn't mean to say that."

"You've got the shivers."

"No, I don't. But the butcher and the butcher's son.... You're

354

right. I was not allowed to change tribes."

"Exactly. It's against everyone's rules."

At the family gathering for Thanksgiving dinner, which was as noisy and convivial and violently argumentative as it was full of shared communal weeping and sorrow, McVie's mother startled Vanderbilt by enveloping him in a welcoming hug and then stepping back, slightly shocked with herself, a hand over her mouth. "I shouldn't have done that," she said. "I shouldn't take liberties." She wiped her hands on her apron. "Oh dear, now you've got breadcrumbs on your shirt. I hope I haven't offended you."

Vanderbilt hugged her back. "You haven't offended me, Mrs. McVie. I'll take six of those hugs if you've got some to spare."

"My goodness," she said. "You're not what I was expecting. Not at all what I was expecting. I can see why Pat won't shut up about you."

"Ma!" McVie said, mortified.

"So," McVie's father said. "What's in this for you, huh? Brownie points? Upper crust slumming it in Somerville? I understand you're half-Catholic, so I guess this'll be worth a decade off in Purgatory, if that still matters."

"Dad!" McVie covered his face with his hands. "Is it so difficult to be hospitable to my best friend?"

"Oh, *hospitable*!" McVie's father said. "You lost me already in the big-word department, son. *Best friend*? That's a laugh. Use the sense God gave you, why don't you? If you can't see when you're being pinned on his chest as a virtue medal, then you don't know brisket from rump."

Vanderbilt decided not to try to explain that he had worked in a butcher's shop, that he had been taught how to cut up a side of beef, that he did know brisket from rump.

"Knock it off, Dad," McVie said. "Can't you leave this alone?

Mom, would you like us to leave?"

"Don't be silly," McVie's mother said. "Donal, please. Do you have to prove every time that you're Bog Irish?" To her son and to Vanderbilt and to the guests who were priests and to the rest of the family, she offered extenuating circumstances. "He's already been into the Bushmills, I'm afraid. It's Thanksgiving, after all. And we're in mourning for the president. I hope you'll cut him some slack."

"Mrs. McVie," Vanderbilt said, "he's behaving better than my father would. I'm not offended."

"Your heart's in the right place," offered Brother Damian, the chess-playing teacher from the Marist school.

"*Deo gratias,*" said Father Augustine, the parish priest. "Shall we ask God's blessing on this family and on this nation and especially on the family of our dearly beloved President Kennedy?"

"Amen," everyone said.

"If something is troubling you, son," Father Augustine murmured to Vanderbilt over the dark turkey thighs and roasted sweet potatoes and stuffing, "you could come to confession this weekend."

"Thank you, Father. I will think about that."

"How long since you have been to confession?"

"A long time, Father."

"Apart from this terrible national sorrow in which we all share, I sense that something further, something beyond that, something far beyond that and far more personal, is troubling you. Is there something?"

"So many things, Father, I wouldn't know where to start."

10.

From January onwards, rafts of college acceptance letters began arriving at Dryden. Vanderbilt and McVie were both accepted at Harvard and they ran an extra few miles in celebration. They ran neck and neck in a kind of unspoken pact, neither ever forging ahead.

"Harvard!" McVie kept saying every few miles, between gasps, as though it were an encrypted word he had just pulled from a fortune cookie. He was still trying to translate it.

"Not bad for two misfits," Vanderbilt said.

"Please. You're not a misfit. You're with your own tribe. Your father's on the Board of Trustees."

"And my father thinks of me as an embarrassing alien whom he'd like to disown."

"The way my father thinks of me," McVie said.

"But we do belong to our own tribe of each other, don't we? "

"The misfit tribe?"

"The book-loving tribe. The lapsed-Catholic tribe, still hooked on the ritual and the magic, still nostalgic, the ones who never touch their rosaries but will never be able to throw them out. The cross-country runners. The chess players. Aren't we a tribe?"

"Pathetically small tribe," McVie grunted. "Not much of a prognosis for survival."

"So what? Chess every Sunday when we're at Harvard?" Vanderbilt asked.

"Chess every Sunday," McVie agreed. "And how about chess tonight?"

"Are we going to play to a draw?"

"No way," McVie said. "We both play our best. That's what got us into Harvard, after all. Being best at whatever we tackle is all that we outcasts have."

They were still playing, illegally, after lights out, at midnight. They hid in the library and played by flashlight. McVie won. "We're going to have to sleep on the floor," Vanderbilt said. "Between the stacks. The dorms will be locked."

"Worth it," McVie said.

"Worth it," Vanderbilt agreed. "But next game, you are going to lose."

That same week, another letter arrived by Priority Post. Vanderbilt had to sign for it, which he did automatically before he saw where the letter was from. He had assumed it would be from Harvard, but it was from the Goldbergs in New York. He immediately ran five miles of the cross-country trail, alone, the letter inside his sweat shirt, burning his chest. The trail was two feet deep under powdery snow, fresh fallen, and he kicked up a snow-fog as he ran. The letter smoldered like a radioactive chip.

He got to Latin class late.

"What the hell?!!" McVie whispered, shocked. "What happened to you?"

"Nothing. I just needed to run, that's all."

"Why?"

"Can't tell you."

"You look as though you've been hit by a truck."

"Feel like it too."

McVie was alarmed. "You look as though you've seen a ghost."

"I'm trying not to see a ghost."

"What?"

"Ignore me. Ignore anything I say. I'm not in a normal state of mind, I'm not responsible for anything I say. Okay, so I'm in Purgatory at present and I don't want to talk about it. Leave me alone, okay?"

"Okay."

"Thanks."

Vanderbilt sat in his room and stared at the mountains. He knew the letter would contain bad news. He knew it would be intelligence from St Gilles, about Grand Loup, about Cap, about fallout from the death of Ti-Christophe, about the chateau, about his mother, about any or all of the above. He knew the knowledge would suck him back through a wind tunnel to a time and a place he could not manage, to other tribal spaces to which he had never, and would never, fully belong. He had spent too many years straddling different worlds—the chateau, the gardener's cottage, Ti-Christophe's cutting room—like a man with his feet in two different boats. He had spent too much time climbing out of windows, climbing into windows, trying to remember which voice he should use or which one would come out of his mouth. It was exhausting and dangerous. He felt that he was on the lip of a mud slide and had to grip the arms of his desk chair because the sense of vertigo was so intense.

He did not open the letter. He added it—unopened—to the shoebox where all the other letters were.

Often at night that bottom drawer glowed like a phosphorescent eel. Sometimes it undulated out of its recess and coiled its way through the black room. When it touched his pillow he would wake with a cry and turn on the light and leave it on until morning.

That night—the night of the Priority Post letter from New

York—he tossed and turned and could not sleep until he fell down the steps under the stone bridge and passed out. He could hear fighting. He could see corpses strung up in the trees like Chinese lanterns, lit up by their own red blood. Also strung up were sides of beef, forequarters, hindquarters, necks and shanks. All the bodies and parts of bodies were impaled on steel hooks that slid back and forth on overhead tracks. Vanderbilt himself was shunted at high speed between the bloody remains of Ti-Christophe and a calf he had known personally as Jacqui Jouet on the chateau farm. He had patted this calf as a newborn. He had held the milk bottle in its guzzling mouth. Jacqui Jouet's huge mournful eyes reproached him.

All the hooks squealed on their rails and Vanderbilt felt like a shuttlecock being bounced against carcasses and bodies. He could see the fleshy husk of Grand Loup. He could see Cap. He bounced against them and off them. He covered his eyes. He yanked himself off his hook, losing at least half of his neck which fountained blood. He ran. He kept running and running until he collapsed. At dawn, he found himself half-frozen on the snow-covered grounds in the Dryden woods. He was wrapped in his dormitory quilt.

Winter crawled away, slowly, a beaten dog in ferocious denial. Ice storms, more snow, freezing rain, dirty slush in the streets, black ice on morning pavements, broken hips, sliding cars, fender-benders. But inevitably, surely more slowly than last year or the year before, snow crept away from tree trunks like a tide going out. Crocuses and hyacinths appeared. Coats and boots were crammed into basement storage. Spring flaunted herself.

In the last week of May, both the school and the village of Dryden braced for an annual onslaught. Hundreds of parents, grandparents, siblings and girlfriends were expected. Graduation ceremonies, in elaborate detail, were choreographed. Every inn and Bed and Breakfast in western Massachusetts was booked out. Vanderbilt received word that he was to report to the headmaster's office.

"Vanderbilt," the headmaster said. "Needless to say, we are very proud of you. We always expect to send our boys to Harvard or Yale or MIT. Your father will be here a day in advance of graduation ceremonies for the Board of Trustees dinner. He has sent word that he will meet you on campus on Wednesday at 5 pm for cocktails in the Trustees lounge before the dinner. You may bring a friend. Whom would you like to bring?"

"McVie, sir."

"Ahh," the headmaster said. There was a long pause. "Do you think that's entirely suitable?"

"Why would it not be, sir? He's my best friend and we are both accepted into Harvard."

"Quite right," the headmaster said. "Why would it not be?"

Both McVie and Cabot—though the latter was now a senior at MIT—were invited to the Board of Trustees dinner with the headmaster. The parents of Cabot and McVie were also invited. It was an elegant catered affair. Mrs. McVie gave Vanderbilt a hug. "I'm so nervous," she said. "I've never been to anything so grand." She pulled at her dress. "I ordered it from the Sear's catalogue," she said, "and it's the most expensive outfit I've ever owned since my wedding dress, but I'm not sure it's quite right."

"Mrs. McVie, you look beautiful," Vanderbilt assured her. "Let me introduce you to Mrs. Cabot."

Mrs. Cabot was warm and polite. "You must be very proud of your son," she said.

"Yes, I am. Though, to be truthful, his father would have been happier for him to take over the family business."

"All fathers want that," Mrs. Cabot said. "It's natural, isn't it?

My husband wanted my son to teach Classics but my son chose to be a physicist instead. I wonder, do any parents understand their sons?"

"I'm sure we don't understand ours," Mrs. McVie said. "We don't even understand half the words he uses."

"It's the same with us," Mrs. Cabot sighed. "I have no idea what is meant by *muons* and *quarks*."

"Well, son," Vanderbilt's father said, "I'd be happier if you were planning an MBA at Harvard, but hobnobbing with the Cabots is a promising sign. I've invited Cabot Junior to stay with us in June."

"The Cabots go to Italy in June," Vanderbilt said, "and actually I was planning to spend the summer in Boston."

"Fine, fine. Wherever you want. I'll mostly be in the Hamptons with Julia. But I expect you to spend June with us in New York. And Cabot Junior will be our guest. He's not going to Florence because he's got an interview at Columbia. Any objections?"

"No, sir."

"That's settled then. I'll take both of you back with me in the limo. And now the Cabots will owe us, you understand? They'll be indebted. It's important to know the value of mutual obligations. You scratch my back, I'll scratch yours. It's simply the way things are done."

Scrolls and mortarboards in hand, McVie and Vanderbilt decided not to join the nostalgic hoards climbing up to the Rock. They met in the gym where they stripped themselves of the alien plumage of academic gowns and hoods.

"Let's run," Vanderbilt said.

"Yes, let's run. They'll notice we've gone missing, you know."

"I doubt it. But so what if they do? "

362

"I mean your father will. The headmaster will. My own parents have left already," McVie admitted. "My mother said people were staring at her dress and her shoes. My father said they could all go fuck off."

Vanderbilt laughed. "I'll second that."

"Got something to tell you," McVie said. "Don't get angry."

"What? What is it?"

"I'm not going to Harvard. I've sent my letter of non-acceptance."

"What!? You can't do that! Nobody turns down Harvard."

"I've done it."

"So where are you going?"

"Union Square, Somerville."

"What do you mean?"

"Things are tough for my father right now. All the able-bodied men are getting drafted for Vietnam so the cost of labor goes up. He needs help with the family business."

"I can help. We can help. You won a full-tuition scholarship, for God's sake."

"Yeah. Sounds good. But we still can't afford Harvard. Freshman year, you're not allowed to live off-campus, so there's the room-and-board fee, the cost of text books, the athletics fee, the student activities fee. Anyway, I've had it up to here with being the grateful leper."

"McVie, McVie, don't do this to yourself. There's your future *with* Harvard and your future *without* Harvard and there's an abyss in between. For God's sake, you've been accepted. You can manage this. What about student loans?

"They have to be paid back," McVie reminded. "Not something I can saddle the family with. But we can meet on Sundays for chess, right?"

There was one thing that Vanderbilt did do on the morning of the drive back to New York, following Dryden graduation. He opened the radioactive bottom drawer of his dresser and he lifted the lid from the radioactive box. He took out Myriam Goldberg's paintings of Grand Loup and Cap, though he left them wrapped in silk. He could not bear to look at them but he could not leave them untended before he put the rest of his possessions in storage over the summer. He could not move into his Harvard dorm until September and he was not going to cart everything back and forth to New York. He put the paintings of Grand Loup and Cap, protected by a stiff cardboard folder, in his duffel bag. He changed his mind several times about the rest of the radioactive box but eventually added it, taped shut, to one of the boxes marked for storage.

"Hope you don't mind, Vanderbilt," Cabot said as the passengers spaced themselves in the cavernous kid-leather cabin of the limousine. "I've got this interview and your father offered..."

"I couldn't be happier. What's the interview for?"

"Columbia. Graduate school. Nuclear Physics."

"Already? But you don't graduate from MIT until next year."

Cabot sighed. "Interview process starts this far ahead. It's exhausting. At least you and I will have a year's overlap in Boston. You still running cross-country?"

"Every morning."

"I'm down to a couple of days a week. Never enough time. I'm always pulling all-nighters in the labs. But next year we could do some runs together along the Charles. Sunday mornings, say?"

"Deal," Vanderbilt said. "But I always assumed you'd stay on at MIT for your doctorate."

"Oh, I will if I can. First choice. But it's not like getting into Dryden because your father's on the board. I've applied to five places, which makes me feel reasonably safe. Plenty of students are applying to ten."

"A lot simpler in our day," Vanderbilt's father said.

"Your father's a Harvard professor, for God's sake," Vanderbilt said. "Won't that—?"

Cabot laughed. "Not anymore. Unless of course we're talking about the Business School."

"Anyway, you don't need your father's help. You're brilliant. You'll be accepted wherever you've applied."

"Ah, Vanderbilt," Cabot said. "You're so good for my ego. And so naive."

"You know what's fascinating, son, listening to the two of you?" Vanderbilt's father commented. "You don't sound like an effeminate Frenchie anymore or like a New Yorker either. You sound like a Boston Brahmin. You sound exactly like Cabot. In fact, you sound as choppy as our recently departed JFK. Which means Dryden was a damn good investment."

Vanderbilt winced.

"Tough luck, Vanderbilt," Cabot grinned. "Didn't mean to do you that much harm."

Later, in the Fifth Avenue apartment, in the bedroom he would share with his guest, Vanderbilt told Cabot: "I'm quoting someone from memory, maybe George Bernard Shaw, maybe not, and I probably haven't got this exactly right. *Parents are the last people who should have children.* I don't know the etiquette for apologizing for my father."

Cabot laughed. "Don't you know that's a parent's first duty? To embarrass their children?"

"You can make light of it because your parents are perfect."

"Actually," Cabot said, "they're not. My father thinks I've let him down. But I have to admit they're not too bad."

"As for mine," Vanderbilt said, "I can't believe I'm related to either of them."

BOOK IV
THE GOLDBERG VARIATIONS

1.

The winter of November-December 1963 was a harsh one in the sprawling river system of the Loire and its capillary feeder streams—the Cher, the Indre, the Vienne—all of them flowing west past splendid chateaux and vineyards toward Nantes and St. Nazaire and the oyster-crusted pylons of the fishing village of Le Croisic at the tip of its crooked westward-pointing finger of rock. Between Le Croisic and the jagged shoreline of Newfoundland there was nothing but ocean, three thousand miles of it. Sometimes debris—fragments of fishing boats from Nova Scotia—washed up against the estuarine mouth of the Loire and eddied about its sandy banks. Throughout the vineyards that winter, the ground was white with frost every morning. Snow came early and did not melt but lay around like scattered ice-cream mounds. Ponds glazed over with translucent wafers that farmers had to shatter so that sheep and goats and cattle and dogs could drink.

Capucine herself split logs—she was adept with an axe—and stacked the wood in the shed at the side of the gardener's cottage. She had a canvas log-carrier with wooden handles and could take ten split pieces of firewood into the kitchen at a time. She fed the cast-iron stove every hour. A *cassoulet* simmered fragrantly in one large pot and chicken broth in another but her prime interest was in keeping the cottage warm. Her father's shivers came and went with the brief unpredictable violence of thunderstorm squalls. After each funnel of turbulence, he lay exhausted. He slept, or at least his daughter hoped the stillness was sleep, prayed it was sleep, though her own heart turned somersaults every time the shuddering stopped and his eyes closed. His heart would falter then rally again and then falter again. Bundled up in quilts—which he would hurl off when his internal furnace steamed off the chills—he lay in front of the stove on the couch.

"You must earth up the vines," he said feverishly. "Light the smudge pots. It's urgent. I'm roasting like a rabbit in here, but the vines will freeze if you don't get out there and work." He tried to sit up. His voice was as rattling and wet as a creek that is flowing through gravel. Cap sat at his side and held his hand and felt for his pulse. Bird in a snare, she thought of his heart, worn out from grief and from beating against his rage at his own fatigue. From time to time he would clutch at his chest and she could almost see the pain. She wanted to run to the chateau or to Marie-Claire's and call the doctor again, but she had done it too often. She would have liked to barricade the physician in the cottage and force him to keep watch but he would only say, as he said each time: "There is nothing to be done. It is not uncommon for a stroke to follow a heart attack. Keep him hydrated and keep him warm. Keep feeding him broth. I am the only doctor in St Gilles and there are many urgent calls on my time."

"The *buttage* around the roots has been done, Papa. The smudge pots are lit every night. Many boys from the village have come to my aid. Father Boniface sent all the altar boys to help. The whole village is praying for you. And for the vines."

"Did you send for Lilith and Ti-Christophe?"

Cap closed her eyes and pressed the back of one hand against her mouth before she could sufficiently steady her voice to answer. "Yes, Papa. I sent for them."

Her father grew agitated, his breathing ragged. "Tell them to come quickly. There isn't much time."

"I told them it was urgent, Papa."

Pierre of the velvet pantaloons and the goats came to the cottage door. "The countess wants to see you," he said. "You are to come to the chateau now."

"Please tell Madame la Comtesse," Cap said, "that I send my regrets but I will not leave my father's side." She closed the door in Pierre's face.

For Cap's father, the knock on the door brought on an extreme gust of the shivers. He pulled his quilts close around him and huddled inside, rocking slightly and moaning, until a sudden inner burst of energy shot him upright and he paced the room, the goose-feather train trailing behind. "Coldest winter ever," he said. "Worse than '44. It's a signal."

"It's your fever, Papa."

"It's a signal. I heard something."

"It was Pierre at the door with a message."

"No. I heard a shot."

"It's just a hunter, Papa. Or a poacher."

"No. On the radio. There was a shot."

"I'll turn the radio off, Papa."

"There was a shot. I heard it. The American president has been shot. Is that my fever?"

"It's not your fever, Papa. It's real. It's a terrible thing."

"Ti-Christophe's *maman,* your *maman,* Ti-Christophe, the American president. We think we've survived but we're never safe. All the omens are bad."

"We make our own omens, Papa. You taught me that. We are here. I'm here and I'm not going to leave. We're safe."

"I used to believe," her father said, his voice raspy and weak, "that we did what we had to do, and the fact that we were doing what we had to do was enough. It should be enough. It should be. But I don't know anymore."

"Even if it isn't enough, Papa, we would still do what we have to do."

Pierre knocked on the cottage door with a letter from *la comtesse*.

Ma chère Melusine: Your loyalty to your father is exemplary. That is precisely why it is so essential that you complete <u>le bac</u> in Tours and go on to the Sorbonne. I know your father would wish it. I understand that you cannot countenance the idea of leaving him alone in this illness (whether it is of the spirit or the body or both, I will not attempt to say) but certainly the disappearance of his son and the death of his unborn grandchild have only added to the struggle of his heart. Your father's health matters as much to me as to you. Therefore, so that you can be free to return to the convent, I will take Monsieur le Jardinier into the chateau as my personal guest. He will have a resident nurse and a resident physician. He will have first-class care.

There is also the matter that the survival of the chateau and its vineyard depends on a manager and full-time viticulteur. I have tentatively hired a new manager and he will need to move into the gardener's cottage as soon as possible. Please visit me in the chateau so that we can discuss procedures for moving your father into my residence here.

Cordialement à toi, ma petite Melusine.
Isabelle, Comtesse de la Vallière Vanderbilt

Capucine spent all night at her father's bedside drafting and redrafting a letter. She gave it to Pierre the next morning.

A Madame la Comtesse de la Vallière Vanderbilt.
Ma très chère Comtesse Isabelle:
My father and I owe you everything and can never adequately repay you. You saved his life when the SS were quartered in the

chateau. You have given me one of the finest possible educations. Everything that I know and treasure about art and literature is due to you.

I hope, therefore, that you will forgive me when I say that the place where my father wishes to spend his final days is this cottage where he was born, the very tenancy of which we owe to your goodwill. I cannot and will not leave him alone here. Much as I love my convent school in Tours, much as my teacher nuns are dear to me, much as I will be forever grateful to you for providing my extraordinary education, I must decline.

I know that your financial concern about the vineyard is a real and serious one, but I can do that work. You do not need to hire anyone else. I can become manager of this estate and would love to do so. With respect, chère Madame la Comtesse, I will not leave my father and I beseech you not to require him to leave this cottage.

Avec un respect et une tendresse qu'on ne peut plus,
Melusine, fille du jardinier

There was a knock on the door in early morning and Capucine expected a return note from Pierre. Instead, her cape covered with frost and a dusting of snow, la comtesse stood there in an overly large and clumsy pair of worn leather boots. "The chauffeur's mechanic lent me his work shoes," she said. "It was kind of him. It is more difficult than I had realized to walk through snow and slush." She surveyed her footwear. "Not very glamorous, are they?"

"Madame la Comtesse, you have never looked more magnificent. But you shouldn't have attempted this walk. It's icy underneath the snow. You could have fallen and broken your hip."

"I once saw a girl," the countess said, "who fell out of an apple tree. She did not know I was watching. I always admired her. I thought that if I could have my life over, I would want to be like her. Not afraid of anything or anyone."

Cap was so astonished and so moved by this declaration that she could not speak.

"I have never been inside the gardener's cottage," the countess said. "Will you invite me in, Melusine?"

"Madame la Comtesse, it is an honor."

"Where is he?"

"Here. In front of the fire. Sleeping."

"I will sit beside him," the countess said. "I will come each day. I will attend to his needs. I will engage one of the village women to sit with him through the night. Melusine, may I speak frankly? I have lost a son. I do not want to lose someone who is as dear to me as a daughter. I understand that I have lost my son because I was so afraid of losing him that I sent him away and he has not forgiven me.

"I know I risk making the same mistake with you, Melusine, but I want you to pass *le bac* at the convent in Tours. I will spend every day in this cottage at your father's side to bring this to pass. I hope you will not deny me this. And if there is any change for the worse in your father's condition, I will send a car for you. We will be with him together."

"Madame la Comtesse...."

"On another small matter," the countess said. "It no longer seems to me at all appropriate for you to address me in such a formal way. You are not my daughter and I am not your mother, but I like to flatter myself that the bond between us is one of affection and is something more than formal. I would like you to think of me as your godmother, *ta marraine*, if that would be acceptable to you."

"*Ma chère marraine,*" Cap said. She thought of asking: *Would you permit me to hug you?* but like the girl who fell out of the ap-

373

ple tree, she acted on impulse first and thought later. She threw her arms around the countess and buried her head against that elegant and formidable shoulder and the countess did not resist.

"I'm not crying," Capucine said.

"Nor am I," the countess replied.

2.

The Mother Superior at the convent in Tours woke Cap at dawn. "Phone call," she said.

It was the countess. "Melusine, I have just changed shifts with the night nurse from the village. I am sending the car for you. You should come quickly. I will stay with him."

Cap had one request for the Mother Superior before the car arrived. Could she place a phone call to New York?

"Madame Goldberg," she said when the call went through. "We think the end is very close for my father. The countess is at his side and I'm leaving for St Gilles as soon as her car arrives. I wish you could be here, but I fear that's not possible now before... before the end."

"We will get the first flight we can," Myriam Goldberg promised.

"And do you think you could get a message to Ti-Loup?"

"I will try. But you know I have tried many times—"

"Yes, I know. But still... It wouldn't be right not to try to pass this message on."

Snow was falling. The cypresses were so weighted down with heavy wet white that the tips of their feathered branches touched the graves. In the churchyard of St Gilles, several inches of snow covered the ground. The boots of the pallbearers sent up icy flurries as they pushed their way through the heavy crystalline mush.

The procession of mourners knew better than to follow in these pressed-down ice-slicked ruts.

"You must hold my arm," Cap told the countess. "I don't want you to fall."

La Comtesse Isabelle de la Vallière Vanderbilt wore black silk and was heavily veiled in black chiffon edged with lace. She pressed one white hand to her heart. She swayed a little and it seemed she might fall or faint.

"Melusine," she murmured. "We were children together, your father and I. He should not have gone first. I have no one left now."

"You have me," Cap said.

"You will leave as you should. As I wish for you to do. My son never responds to my letters. Only your father never thought ill of me."

"I never think ill of you."

"Only you and your father." The countess pulled the black chiffon veil from her head and let it float down to the coffin where it settled like the wings of a dragonfly. "He would smile, Melusine," the countess murmured, "don't you think, to see me in the grave-digger's boots?"

There was a reception back at the chateau and the entire village came. Almost the entire village. Monsieur Monsard, the butcher, and his wife and son did not come. The countess stood at one of her windows and looked out toward the church and the graveyard beyond. Cap brought her a hot mug of mulled wine.

"There were informers," the countess said uncertainly. "We know that. I know many in the village condemned me for having the Germans in the chateau."

"The village knew you had no choice."

"Some in the village resisted, nevertheless. I did not have that kind of courage. Those two people by the table? Who are they?

I think I'm supposed to know them but I can't remember who they are."

"The Goldbergs. They arrived just in time. They flew to Paris and rented a car."

"The art collectors from New York?"

"Yes."

"They claimed they had been here before but I had no memory of them. Was it true?"

"It was true. But they were in hiding."

"When?"

"During the Occupation. My father saved their lives. My mother gave hers. That's why they came back. They wanted to find my parents and thank them."

"They recognized my Modigliani."

"They used to own it."

"Ahh." The countess moved her fingers along her rosary as she always did when disturbed. She did this discreetly, under cover of her black silk sleeves. "So many terrible things we do in ignorance. So much harm. Perhaps I can do a small thing to make amends. I will give the painting back."

3.

The Place Jeanne d'Arc in Chinon, like the narrow streets that lead to it, are still paved with cobbles laid down in the Middle Ages. Above and behind the intimate town-square broods the great crumbling ruin of the Chateau de Chinon, the fortress where Henry II, first of the royal line of the Plantagenets, Count of Anjou and King of England, died in 1189. Below the castle the town slopes precipitously down to the Vienne and the visitor can see across the river to the vineyards beyond.

"We stayed in this lovely little inn when we came back looking for Grand Loup and Lilith," Myriam Goldberg said. "Almost four years ago. Such a short time to thank him in return for all the years he gave us."

"That visit was the first time we had actually seen Chinon," Aaron said. "We were Parisians, you understand. We were completely Parisian. We had no knowledge of the provinces and no interest in them. Not even in the Loire Valley and the chateaux."

"Not even in this town?" Cap reproached. "Where Rabelais was born and where Jeanne d'Arc first met the Dauphin?"

"Not until it became the place where we first met your mother," Myriam said. "Which seems much more significant to us. Still."

They had not actually *seen* Chinon in February 1944 because they came under cover of darkness, first by a night barge down the Loire from Tours and then upriver by rowboat on the Vienne. The

Chinon safe house, they knew, had to be close by, but they had no idea where. In the castle ruins, perhaps?

"I can't think back to any of that without massive anxiety," Myriam said. "Look at my hands." She laid them palms down on the bistro table though this did nothing to still the tremor. "But your mother was so calm, Lilith. So confident. She had this gift. I don't know how, but she could impart a sense of safety. And against all logic, she could make me believe we were safe."

And here you are, the Goldbergs told Cap. A carbon copy. A reincarnation of your mother.

"No, I'm not like her," Cap said. "I'm not calm and not brave, not at all. I've been too afraid to ask but I have to. Did you get word to Ti-Loup?"

"We tried," Myriam said. "I tried two routes. I called Shannay in the Bronx. She used to be housekeeper at the Vanderbilt penthouse. Ti-Loup's father fired her because she joined Martin Luther King's march, but we've stayed in touch. She said it was no use. She'd left messages for Ti-Loup at Fifth Avenue and at his school, but he never returned her calls. I also sent a letter Priority Post to the Dryden school. Ti-Loup would have had to sign for it. But I never heard back."

"I can't understand it," Cap said. "I just can't. He disappeared when Ti-Christophe disappeared. They both vanished. The last time I saw him, he was looking back through security at Paris airport. He went through the looking-glass. He got vaporized. He doesn't exist."

"Grief is strange," Myriam said. "It's a strange thing. You can't predict, no one can, how you'll handle it."

"Which brings us," Aaron said, "to something we've been planning for a very long time."

4.

The Goldbergs had left it too late to leave Paris. They had watched German troops march down the Champs-Elysées in June 1940. They were aware of the flight of the French government to Bordeaux. They heard General Pétain make his nationwide announcement one week later: "It is with a heavy heart that I tell you today that we must stop fighting." They heard Pétain accede to the abject capitulation of France. They were well aware of the contempt made manifest in Hitler's terms for surrender, which he insisted take place on the very railroad car where the armistice of 1918 had been signed, in the forest of Compiègne, on the eleventh hour of the eleventh day of the eleventh month. They were very familiar with the words carved into the granite monolith which marked that date and that site: *Here ... succumbed the criminal pride of the German empire...vanquished by the free peoples which it tried to enslave.*

They knew that Hitler had the 1918 marker blown up three days later.

The Goldbergs knew all this and yet they did not flee. They were *French*. Their fathers were decorated veterans of the First World War. The Goldbergs had been blind and naive. They were confident that the descendants of the French Revolution would never submit to a German dictator's rants. Besides, they had so many friends—art collectors—whom they believed would

protect them. Those friends did try. For two years, the Goldbergs hid in one of the grand houses on the rue de Varenne in the
seventh arrondissement, but after the round-up of Jews at the Vel
d'Hiver in July 1942....

After that they knew it was too dangerous for their friends, for
the families and children of their friends. Even so, friends hid them
for another eighteen months in a country house outside Etampes,
far from troop-patrolled Paris, in a village so small that it was not
even on most road maps.

But someone informed, and then they were on the move from
day to day, safe house to safe house, passed on from one Resis-
tance escort to another. Their journey from St Gilles to New York
took many months. They had taken the long way round. All the
French Atlantic ports had been closed, either by the Vichy or the
Boche. After the last safe house in France they had gone over the
Pyrenees on foot, then to Portugal by train, then from Lisbon to
Morocco, where they were stalled for a month, then to the Ca-
ribbean and then, and then, from port to port, and at last to New
York. They took any ship that would let them on board.

"We could just as easily have ended up in Shanghai," Aaron said.
"Thousands did and were grateful to get there. Shanghai was the
only port in the world that accepted people without any papers.
But we had papers. Myriam's uncle had sent visas to our friends
in Paris. If we'd gone to Shanghai, we would have taken the first
ship from there to New York. The problem was not getting into
Manhattan. The problem was getting out of France."

The chaos on board the *Espirito Santo* as it left the port of Lisbon
was extreme. There were too many refugees, there was not enough
food. The frail and elderly were dying on deck. Children were
frightened and crying. The crew was sympathetic but frazzled. By

the time the ship reached Jamaica, twenty-eight passengers had died and been buried at sea. It was in Jamaica that Myriam realized she was pregnant. On board ship, after Lisbon, she had simply assumed she was sea-sick. She went into labor in the arrival wharf on the Manhattan Pier in November. A doctor was summoned and a birth certificate was signed. The baby girl was named Lilith. The baby died a week later in Brooklyn.

"My uncle and all my relatives were Orthodox," Myriam said. "My uncle's rabbi decreed that a baby who died after less than 30 days had not really existed and should not be mourned. This was according to Maimonides and the Laws of Mourning in the Mishneh Torah. So there was no funeral and we did not sit *shiva*. It was not permitted for me to speak of my baby. It was not permitted for me to cry. For months I lay in bed all day. I pulled a pillow over my head when I cried. I prayed to die."

"And I urged her to live," Aaron said. "I said first we had to find Grand Loup and Lilith and thank them. After that, she could choose, and I would accept her choice."

The search took many years. Resistance archives were impossible to come by for more than a decade, and even in the sixties people were still secretive in France. No one wanted to talk about what happened. But then, in St Gilles, the Goldbergs recognized Grand Loup. They recognized their own Modigliani painting on the wall of the chateau.

They had a birth certificate for Lilith Goldberg but no death certificate. Lilith Goldberg was born in November 1944. Capucine, daughter of Grand Loup and Lilith, was probably born the same month, same year, but had no birth certificate. This seemed to the Goldbergs a sign as clear as was the burning bush to Moses.

"We never had other children," Myriam said. "That was my form of grieving, you understand? I felt it would be disloyal. Not logical, but trauma and grief aren't logical."

"We think of you as our daughter," Aaron said, "miraculously given back to us. We want to bring you to New York. We believe it is morally right. Your parents did what was morally right though it was against French law at the time, for which your mother was punished by death."

The Goldbergs had friends who were in immigration law. They had consulted these friends. To cover all legal bases, this was what would be required: if she would consent, Cap would be formally adopted as Lilith Goldberg and would be sworn in as a citizen at the American Embassy in Paris.

"I have a cousin at NYU," Myriam said. "I took the liberty of sending her the paper you wrote on the seventeenth-century paintings of Philippe de Champaigne. The one you wrote for the convent school in Tours. My cousin is very impressed and we want to sponsor you as a student in Art History at NYU."

In the cobbled town square in Chinon, Cap felt as though she were falling from a parachute that had not opened.

The countess was unavailable for farewells. She had gone, Pierre reported, to Paris. Nevertheless, on the morning of Cap's departure as Lilith Goldberg, Pierre arrived at the gardener's cottage with two small but exquisitely gift-wrapped boxes.

Inside one, swathed in tissue, was a jeweller's sac of gold mesh. The drawstring tie of silk ribbon was also gold. There was a card of linen parchment in an envelope. In beautiful hand-written script the card said: *Pour te protéger. Ta marreine.*

The gold-mesh sac contained a rosary of lapis-lazuli beads on a silver chain.

Inside the second box, tied with blue ribbon, was a bundle of letters. They all bore New York postmarks dated 1960, were all addressed to Cap, and the handwriting on the envelopes was that of Ti-Loup. The envelopes had never been opened. The deckle parchment card, handwritten, said in approximate translation: *At the time I truly believed that this was best for everyone. I was wrong. I know my son has never forgiven me. I hope you can, Melusine. Ta marreine.*

The Goldbergs reported that Pierre had presented them with the Modigliani as a gift. There was a handwritten card:

Chère Madame, cher Monsieur Goldberg:

I am returning what once belonged to you, something you treasured personally, but also something of great value to the world of art. You are taking from me someone I hold precious. I hope she will return to me some day. Until then, I hope I can learn to be as forgiving and gracious about theft and loss as you have been.

Comtesse Isabelle de la Vallière Vanderbilt.

5.

Lilith Goldberg would not have believed it possible that the human ear could tolerate so much noise at any one point in time. Manhattan caused her auditory pain. She was equally astonished by the eerie fact that she could leave Madison Avenue, speak to the doorman of the Goldbergs' building, pass through the lobby and enter the interior courtyard of hostas and ferns and white impatiens and garden benches where nothing but tranquil silence reigned. There was a beautiful cast-iron Lipchitz sculpture that rose like a bird on the wing—or perhaps like a silken scarf unfurling itself in the breeze—from a cluster of white caladiums, green-veined. The plaque at the base of the statue read: *In tribute to Lilith and Grand Loup. Gift of Myriam and Aaron Goldberg.*

Lilith Goldberg spent hours every day in this courtyard, sometimes reading, sometimes studying, sometimes simply contemplating the sculpture and the lush shade garden. She also spent many hours—sometimes alone, sometimes in the company of Myriam Goldberg—in the Metropolitan Museum of Art, in the Frick, in MOMA, in the Guggenheim. They went to concerts together. Lilith obtained a student card and a library card. She learned—with occasional disconcerting moments of error—to think of herself as Lilith Goldberg.

She had acquired a habit of passing the lapis lazuli beads of the rosary through her fingers, not as an act of faith or belief (both of which now felt to her far beyond reach) but as a meditational habit. The practice evoked all her happiest memories. It was calming. She usually did this in private last thing at night, sometimes on waking in the morning, but once, absent-mindedly, in the interior garden of the Madison Avenue apartments. On this occasion she provoked shock. An elderly gentleman, a co-resident in the building, shared her garden bench.

"That's a curious sight," he said. "A Jewish girl with a rosary."

Lilith Goldberg felt the panic of an imposter caught red-handed.

"I know what it means," the old man said gently. "You were kept in hiding in a convent. You acquired the habit of disguise and now you can't shed it, right?"

"That's true," Lilith said. "I can't shed the habit of disguise."

"My own wife and daughter were hidden by nuns for three years," the old man said. "Until the roundup at the Vélodrome d'Hiver. Then they were sent to Auschwitz and I lost them."

"How did you get out?" Lilith asked.

"I didn't. I was already here. I was sending back every penny I earned to bring them out. I still send money back to that convent. The nuns gave my wife and daughter three years. That's something."

Lilith rested her hand on his frail wrist. "I like to hope that there are more good people than evil people," she said.

"I would like to hope that too," the old man said, "but I don't. I can't. There *are* good people, however, and our duty in life is to be one of them, even though we will be outnumbered. But can I suggest that you should not display your rosary in this building? It will evoke as many bad memories for residents as good ones."

Lilith Goldberg had the luxury of three months of summer—June, July, August—before her classes began at NYU in the fall of 1964. She filled these months with art museums, concerts, theater, with reading, with walking in Central Park, a place which seemed to her its own planet, moving in its own separate galaxy, not really a part of Manhattan at all. She discovered the Ramble, a densely wooded promontory jutting into the lake like a question mark at the core of the park. From the serpentine trails of the Ramble she could neither see nor hear the city, which was as amazing to her as the existence of the tranquil courtyard within the Goldberg building. She wandered under dappled light for hours, in a state of bliss, imagining herself back in the forest surrounding St Gilles.

One day there was an unexpected guest at the Goldbergs when she returned for lunch.

"This is Shannay," Myriam explained. "She used to be the housekeeper for the Vanderbilt penthouse. She knew Madame la Comtesse."

"Years back, years back," Shannay said. "'Can't hardly remember her. So this is Capucine?" Shannay studied Cap intently. "Who never answered any of his letters?"

"Who never got any of his letters," Myriam reminded.

"Such a state he would get into," Shannay said. "Every hour pestering me, wanting to know. *Aren't there any letters for me, Shannay?* He kept the paintings of you and your father on his dresser every night, you know, until he went to Dryden, then he turned into somebody else."

Cap felt dizzy. She needed to sit down. She was not sure she felt equal to hearing anything more.

"In three years," Shannay said, "he hardly ever came back to stay with his pa—can't say I blame him for that—and when he did come back he didn't want to talk about nothing. He didn't want to know nothing. He changed. He turned into a Vanderbilt, I hate to say it, but that is the Gospel truth. And after that march, the March on Washington, which glory be to God I was part of, after that his pa fired me and I haven't seen either of them since.

Never once tried to contact me. Never returned any of my calls, even though I knew him better than either of his parents ever did. I was the one who went to him when he cried in the night. I was the one sang lullabies to him. I was the one took him in his stroller to Central Park. It still hurts, I won't lie to you, that he never once tried to reach me after that march, never returned a single call. He was someone else. He turned into a Vanderbilt."

Cap said carefully and neutrally: "We all change. I probably wouldn't even recognize Ti-Loup if I saw him today."

"You *could* see Master Gwynne today if you wanted to," Shannay said. "That's what I come to tell Myriam. I live back with my family in the Bronx but I know the new housekeeper in the Vanderbilt place. Their kind not going to hire anyone who can afford to live on Manhattan, that's for sure. We have a network, you know. We look out for each other when someone gets fired. So you want to know what I know?"

"I'm not sure," Cap said.

"Gwynne Patrice is here this month with one of his upper-crust Boston friends. His pa already high-tailed it out to the Hamptons with his latest girlfriend. So it's just Gwynne Patrice and the Boston Brahmin and I thought Myriam might want to know. Had no idea I would get to meet the famous Capucine. I just thought Myriam might want to drop by and speak to the boy who used to be Gwynne Patrice."

"But it would be better if you yourself went, Lilith," Myriam said. "Catch him off guard."

"I don't think that would be a good idea."

"Don't you want to know what happened?" Myriam asked.

"I don't think so," Cap said. "Well, don't we already know? He isn't Ti-Loup anymore. And I'm not Capucine. I'm Lilith now."

"I'll tell you one thing," Shannay said. "He brought Myriam's paintings of you and your father back with him. The new housekeeper told me that."

"It's not me, it's a painting of my mother."

"Well it looks like you. He keeps them wrapped in silk in his dresser drawer but he's been looking at them every day and then covering them up again. There's not much anyone can hide from a housekeeper, I can promise you that."

6.

Lilith Goldberg paced up and down Fifth Avenue from the Frick at East 70th to the corner of East 73rd, up and back, up and back. Each time she passed the ornate facade of the building where Ti-Loup was born, she could not muster the courage to push the buzzer on the great wooden doors and speak to the doorman, an act that now seemed to her far more perilous than her first visit to the Chateau de Boissy. At East 72nd, on her tenth circuit, she crossed Fifth and entered the park. She walked down the mall to Bethesda Terrace, crossed the beautiful Bow Bridge to the far side of the lake, and entered the Ramble. She sat on a bench at the lakeshore and watched the ducks.

What is gained if I see him again? she asked herself.

What is lost if I don't? What is lost if I don't even try?

She did not have a clear answer to any of her questions but she did know that the memory that both she and Ti-Loup were avoiding—and would never be able to expunge—was the death of Petit Christophe. Murder *per se* was not the crux of the nightmare. The kernel of what had precipitated Grand Loup's heart attack and stroke and partial paralysis was the disappearance of two bodies, and the key to what troubled Ti-Loup and Cap was that Ti-Christophe's body, before it disappeared, was slashed with far more wounds than were required for killing. His body was gruesomely marked with post-mortem hate. Perhaps concealing that fact from Grand Loup had done more harm than good. Certainly that weighty secret haunted both Ti-Loup and Cap.

There is nothing to lose, Lilith Goldberg decided.

"Which floor?" asked the doorman in the Fifth Avenue building that was next but one to the north-east corner of East 72nd.

"The penthouse," Lilith said.

When the doorman pressed the intercom buzzer, she expected to hear the voice of the new African-American housekeeper or perhaps the vocal New York equivalent of Pierre of the pantaloons.

She heard Ti-Loup. He was doing one of his accents, an unfamiliar one, but she knew his voice. "Who is it?" he asked.

She made her own voice go low. "It's Petit Christophe," she said.

The intercom went dead. "I'm sorry," the doorman said, "but he hasn't buzzed you in."

"That's okay," Lilith said, relieved. "He wasn't expecting me." She had no idea where her own words, her own voice, had come from. They had arrived without forethought or plan, almost without her own awareness. Now she played them back with nervous shock. Well then. Nothing to lose, she thought as she stepped back out onto Fifth Avenue, and I won't have to reproach myself for not trying, though I've just done something very stupid and very cruel and I don't know why. She waited for the lights at the corner of East 72nd. She would return to the Ramble and sit by the lake for as long as it took. She felt light-headed, as though she were drunk. The light seemed to favor, interminably, the taxis and buses heading south on Fifth. Now, finally, the pedestrian light turned green.

"Cap!" someone shouted. And there he was, running from the portico of his building. She did not step into the crossing. She waited. They stood there, inches apart.

"My father died," she said. "Six months ago."

"I was afraid of knowing that," Ti-Loup said.

"He had a heart attack and then a stroke not long after Ti-Christophe.... and he never got well again."

They clutched at each other then. They held each other and wept.

This was Manhattan. Nobody stopped to stare. Nobody even noticed.

"Vanderbilt?" Cabot asked. "Everything okay?"

Cap and Ti-Loup floated up from a very deep and dark place to find themselves alarmingly exposed to hundreds of people on the corner of Fifth Avenue and East 72nd. They blinked, dazed, as miners do when emerging from the shaft.

"You left in such a rush," Cabot said, "I was sure you must have had devastating news. Are you okay?"

"Sure," Vanderbilt said. "I'm fine. Just caught off guard by a visitor from France. Unexpected."

"And who is this gorgeous French woman?" Cabot asked.

"*Ah, monsieur,*" Cap said, "*comme vous êtes gentil! Je m'apelle Lilith Goldberg. Je suis une amie d'enfance.*"

"Translate for me, Vanderbilt. I don't know any French."

"She's a childhood friend," Vanderbilt said. "We grew up in the same village. Her name's... uh... . She told you her name. She does speak English."

"My name's Lilith Goldberg," Cap said.

"Well in that case," Cabot responded, taking Cap's hand with an only slightly sardonic Gallic flourish and kissing her fingers, "what are you doing here in New York, Lilith Goldberg?"

"I'll be a student at NYU in the fall," Lilith said. "Art History. And you are?"

"I'm Cabot. I was at Dryden with Vanderbilt. I gather this is an emotional reunion. I don't know Manhattan well, but I do know that one of the places to celebrate is the Loeb boathouse in the park. Can I treat you both to champagne? I've just had great news myself. I've got advance acceptance at Columbia for my PhD. Mind you, I haven't given my response yet. I'd prefer to stay at MIT if I get the chance."

"Well," Vanderbilt said. "Congratulations, Cabot. That's wonderful news. But perhaps we could celebrate tomorrow? My friend and I haven't seen each other for years and I think perhaps—"

"I've seen the boathouse from the Ramble," Lilith said. "It looks so beautiful. I've never been there but I'd love to."

"Settled then," Cabot said. "Vanderbilt, you can have your private reunion tomorrow."

"When I left," Lilith explained, "after my father's funeral, your mother gave me the letters you'd sent in those first few weeks. I have finally read them, four years later."

"I don't think I can remember the boy who wrote them," Vanderbilt said.

"I can. But he isn't you."

"It's not that I've forgotten anyone or anything or that St Gilles doesn't matter. It's more like—"

"You don't need to explain."

"It's like jumping from a plane with no parachute. I feel absolute terror. I don't dare go back there, not even inside my head."

"It's okay, Ti-Loup. It's okay. This is how I remember you, the first time you climbed out your window and came into our kitchen. I was roasting rabbits, remember? And that's how I remember you: scared."

"I told you," he said. "I am not that boy."

"I am not that girl either," Lilith replied. She was calm and quiet. She pushed her chair, very slightly, away from the bar.

"You don't know me," Vanderbilt said.

393

"You don't know me either. Cabot asked me out, by the way. We are having dinner tonight before the concert at Lincoln Center."

7.

Every week, after term began, Lilith Goldberg wrote to *la comtesse* and she received a reply every week.

Ma chère marraine, Lilith wrote. *I am on cloud nine. The Met's collection of seventeenth and eighteenth-century French paintings and furniture is extraordinary. I spend hours there every week. I like to imagine you there beside me. Then we would have a glass of wine somewhere nearby and discuss the paintings, especially Philippe de Champaigne's The Annunciation. It was done at the request of the mother of Louis XIV, for her private chapel. I will never forget that moment when I first heard from you the story of the mother of Louis XIV.... I spend hours in front of that painting.*

I have seen Gwynne Patrice. He avoids contact with his father as much as possible. He has not forgotten us. He is deeply troubled, but he sends his love.

"There's a phone call for you," Myriam Goldberg said. "From Boston."

The call was from Cabot. "I can't get you out of my mind," he said.

"How did you get this phone number?"

"From the Vanderbilt housekeeper, who gave me the number of the former housekeeper, Shannay, who gave me this number...I had to pester them. It took quite a while."

"Ah." Lilith wanted to ask if Ti-Loup was okay but she did not know how to ask. What would she call him?

"I've been going on and on about you," Cabot told her. "And my mother said, *For God's sake, call her.* So I just gulped down a shot of whiskey and now I'm calling. Can I invite you up here for a weekend? To stay with us?"

"That's... You take me completely by surprise. I don't know what to say."

"Say yes."

"But..."

"My mother was over the moon when she found out the girl turning me into an insomniac was studying seventeenth-century French painting. And my father said *A girl I can talk to? Bring her here.* So it will be a crushing disappointment to the whole family if you don't visit. And of course we'll invite Vanderbilt too. My parents have kind of adopted him and we've always had him spend Christmas here. Will you come?"

"That's... well... I'd love to."

"Mind you," Cabot said, "I haven't told my parents your last name. But you're not really Jewish, are you? Vanderbilt said you weren't."

Lilith could see her own breath floating in front of her mouth like a cobweb. She could scarcely get air into her lungs. "Vanderbilt is wrong," she said. "I'm really Jewish. Perhaps it would be better if I don't come."

"Don't say that!" Cabot pleaded. "Don't hang up. That was idiotic of me. It doesn't matter what you are, and it won't matter to my parents either. Please come."

"Ah you sure?"

"I'm so sure that if you don't come, I think my parents might sue me."

"All right. I'll take the Greyhound."

"Good grief, you mustn't do that. Greyhound buses are horrible. My parents use a car service. A driver will pick you up and deliver you right to our house."

Cabot was waiting outside the carved oak doors of the mansion on Commonwealth Avenue. He kissed her and took her overnight bag. "You must tell my mother all about Philippe de Champaigne," he said. "I haven't read up on art since I had to do it at Dryden but I've been cramming on the French Baroque for the last few weeks. That's why my parents are already crazy about you. My mother wants to take you to the Boston Museum of Fine Arts and the Isabella Gardner."

"Am I allowed to tell her my last name?" Lilith asked.

"That was an unbelievably stupid thing for me to say," Cabot responded. "I have no idea why I did that. Nobody cares about that sort of thing anymore."

"Some people do," Lilith assured him.

"Well, we don't. The Cabots don't."

"Your house is so beautiful," Lilith told Mrs. Cabot. "And your furniture." She trailed her fingers across a mahogany sideboard, English, eighteenth century. "I'm more knowledgeable about French baroque, but this is lovely."

"Tell me about Vanderbilt's mother," Mrs. Cabot said.

"Ah... She's... she's my godmother. I am extremely fond of her." Lilith wondered if she should say *Are you wondering how a French countess came to be godmother to a Jewish child?*

"I gather she has some extraordinary antiques in her chateau. And some valuable paintings, though we had to pry that information from Vanderbilt on his visits."

"He never cared for life in the chateau. But his mother's collection is superb. She inherited most of it. It was because of her and because of her chateau that I fell in love with the French baroque."

"Tomorrow," Mrs. Cabot said, "I want to take you to the Isabella Gardner Museum, an extraordinary place. And tomorrow evening we will have a big Cabot family dinner. We've invited Vanderbilt because it's far too long since we've seen him. And I've also invited some friends who are art curators. I think you'll enjoy them."

The Cabot dining room reminded Cap of the chateau. The table, set with silver candelabra and the finest china, had places for twelve, though there was a separate table in the kitchen for the children. There seemed to be a lot of Cabots—married older siblings—as well as close family friends connected to the world of art museums and the Boston Symphony. The dinner was catered. The chef, in starched linen top hat with fresh-baked pouf, appeared in the dining room briefly to offer and describe the *amuse bouche* and to announce the menu to come. There was even a Pierre, though not in pantaloons. Cap hardly dared look at Ti-Loup, seated opposite, but their eyes met and a shared vision of the velvet knickers hovered between them, blurred at the edges and vanishing into blue nothing just as the candle flames did. They bit on their smiles and studied their linen napkins.

They did not know what they should call each other in alien company.

They did not even know how to think about each other.

"So. Vanderbilt," Mr. Cabot said. "I know my son has told you that I always wished he would take the courses you are taking. But, alas, we can't live our children's lives for them. How's 'Introduction to Philosophy' going?"

"I love it, sir. I'm hoping to take a course with you next year."

"And you, Lilith," Mrs. Cabot said. "What are your career plans after Art History at NYU?"

Lilith was hesitant. "Well, I always used to assume Paris and the Louvre. But perhaps Sotheby's now. I have a connection."

"Oh my dear," Mrs. Cabot said. "You mustn't think New York is the center of the cultural world. We have extraordinary opportunities here in Boston: the Museum of Fine Arts, the Isabella Gardner, the Fogg at Harvard."

"And heaven knows," Mr. Cabot said, "even MIT, for all its blinkers, has an Alexander Calder and some other unconventional art. I suppose we have to learn to accept it. People didn't know what to make of Picasso once. You might be able to induce my son to show you what physicists think of as art."

Cabot Junior tapped his wine glass with a spoon. "I would like to propose a toast," he said, "to Lilith Goldberg. I will take it upon myself to be her cultural guide to Boston."

"I'll drink to that," his father said.

Glasses were clinked, wine sipped. Cap smiled at Cabot and he blew her a kiss. She was afraid to look at Ti-Loup, but he raised his glass high. "To Lilith Goldberg," he said rather loudly. "May she conquer Boston."

After dinner, as people were murmuring thanks and farewells in the hallway, Lilith and Vanderbilt exchanged a very decorous and very formal French parting, not touching, but kissing the air three times, left, right, left, not quite touching each other's cheeks. On the final kiss, Ti-Loup whispered close to her ear: "Cap the Conqueror. All hail," and then he embraced Mrs. Cabot warmly at the door, shook Mr. Cabot's hand and left without looking back.

Cabot handed Lilith a folded slip of paper as they went upstairs to separate bedrooms. "Vanderbilt asked me to give you this. It's the phone number in his dorm room at Harvard. He asked if you'd call him in the morning. I refuse to be jealous because you're more like brother and sister, right?"

"More or less," Lilith said. "We grew up in the same house."

"But I thought *he* showed a flash of jealousy," Cabot noted. "Not the, you know, romantic or sexual kind. I guess everyone feels possessive about childhood friends. Vanderbilt and I were best friends at Dryden, his first year, my last. And after I left for MIT, I caught myself feeling jealous about his new best friend, McVie. Childish, isn't it? And yet it still bugs me when he spends Thanksgiving with the McVies instead of with us."

"I don't know McVie. I don't know about any of Ti... of Vanderbilt's friends from Dryden. We drifted apart after he left France. Lost contact."

"It happens. Well. Goodnight. Sleep well."

"Goodnight, Cabot. This has been a beautiful day. Thank you." She stood on tiptoe to kiss him on the cheek but the gesture turned suddenly into fiercely passionate clinch and Lilith could scarcely breathe for the wild movement of Cabot's tongue inside her mouth.

She did not dislike the sensation.

When they separated and stood inches apart in the upstairs hall, their breathing ragged, unspoken possibilities hovered.

Cabot closed his hand over the brass doorknob of his own bedroom. "We could," he said softly. "If you wished."

Lilith hesitated at the guest room door, opposite. "My father died recently... I just don't feel ready for anything much."

"I'm such a rash idiot," Cabot said, "as my father always points out. Fools rushing in, etc. I hope you won't hold it against me."

"I don't hold anything against you," Lilith said. "See you in the morning. Good night."

8.

The next morning, a Sunday, Gwynne Vanderbilt met Lilith Goldberg at the subway station in Harvard Square. He waited for her outside the turnstiles by the flower sellers and newspaper stands. Instinctively they embraced and stood holding each other in that murky underground space.

"Cap," he said. "Can I call you Cap?"

"Only in private. Cap's unauthorized. Lilith Goldberg is legal. Can I call you Ti-Loup?"

"Only in private. And nothing *but* Ti-Loup in private."

He took her through the glut of traffic in the Square and led her into the tranquil green space of Harvard Yard. "It's beautiful," Cap said. "It's like the chateau courtyard. It's like the enclosed garden in the Goldbergs' building."

"Yes. I love it. I love being here." He pointed out landmarks: Widener Library, the picture-postcard white steeple of Memorial Church, his own freshman dorm. "You still like taking long walks?"

"I walk more than an hour every day in Central Park."

"Okay, where we're going is a twenty-minute, maybe thirty-minute walk."

"Where are we going?"

"To Mass at St. Ann's church in Somerville."

"You're kidding."

"I'm not. You willing to come with me to Mass?"

"Not wild about it."

"I know. Who would have thought? But I have to. I go to confession because I have to talk to someone about... you know. I have terrible dreams. I'm covered in blood and I wake up and my sheets are drenched with sweat."

"I have nightmares too."

"I stopped having them while I was at Dryden. I was someone else there. It was like living on a different planet. But now it's all coming back. I can't deal with it."

"We should never have left the bodies," Cap said.

"We should have stopped them," Ti-Loup said. "I should have run between them."

"Then *you* would have been killed."

"And Ti-Christophe would still be alive."

"You and Ti-Christophe would both be dead, and Papa would still be dead. You know what I really can't make sense of? My father was dying and you didn't even write. He loved you like a son, Ti-Loup, and you couldn't even write."

"That's why I go to confession. That's just one of the reasons. There's something wrong with me. There's always been something wrong with me."

"There's not. There's never been anything wrong with you. But why didn't you write?"

"I don't know. I don't know. Sheer panic. Guilt. Too afraid of anything that might suck me back to that day... Too afraid of becoming *that boy* again. Saying I'm sorry won't mean anything, but I'm sorry. We're in Somerville now. It's a pretty rough area. Gangs, Irish Mafia, Mack the Knife. But no one will do anything violent on a Sunday. Everyone's Boston Irish and Catholic and they all go to St Ann's. And here we are."

St Ann's was a great red brick hulk of Romanesque Revival with a blocky tower on one side surmounted by a squat copper spire.

"Well," Cap said. "It's not St Gilles, is it?"

"Not twelfth century, not stone. Not the sort of thing that matters to my mother."

"To me too," Cap said. "Architectural beauty. All kinds of beauty. They matter."

"This *church* matters to me," Ti-Loup said. "It's where my best friend from Dryden was baptized and where he received his First Communion."

"And St Gilles? Where we received our First Communion?"

"I hated it. I knew what everyone was thinking. No one at St Ann's knows I ever had to wear a blue dress or climb out my window every night. I'm guessing you can understand the difference. At St Ann's you'll meet my best friend from Dryden."

"Your next best friend after Cabot."

"My *best* friend, after Cabot moved on. His name is Patrick McVie. His father owns a butcher shop. McVie is going to remind you of Ti-Christophe and we're going to have lunch with his family after Mass. Unless that would be too blue-collar for your taste."

"I'm the gardener's daughter, remember? My brother was a butcher's apprentice."

"Before you crossed over. But I think you and the McVies will get along."

The dining room in the McVie's living quarters, which were above the butcher's, was small and crowded. There were eighteen people, counting the children underfoot, as well as the priest from St Ann's and Brother Damian from McVie's Marist school. The meal was not exactly lunch. It was a heavy dinner, the main Sunday meal, with a cauldron of Irish stew (beef, heavy with gravy, carrots, lentils, dollops of red wine) and a deep bowl of mashed potatoes.

Guests ladled their own servings and found a space at the table.

Ti-Loup made official introductions. "This is Lilith Goldberg," he said. "But don't be fooled by her name. I don't want to go into it, but we received our First Communion together in the church of St Gilles in France. I have a photograph to prove it."

"So do I," Cap said.

She was seated between Ti-Loup and Patrick McVie.

"So, Lilith," Patrick McVie's father said. "I'm confused. My son tells me your brother was a butcher."

"A butcher's apprentice, yes sir. And an excellent one."

"And he taught young Vanderbilt here."

"Yes, sir. He did."

"And Vanderbilt is damn good. I've watched him and I have to admit it. It don't make sense for some blue-blood aristo who's French to boot, but he wants to work in my shop."

"You'd be lucky to have him, sir."

"My opinion too. But I didn't expect my son to meet a master butcher at Dryden."

"I'll put you in a taxi," Ti-Loup said.

"Don't be ridiculous. I'll take the subway. Let's walk back to Harvard Square."

"Do you have to go back to the Cabots?"

"Well, yes. I'm their guest for the weekend. They think the world of you."

"Tell me, and don't lie. Did you sleep with Cabot last night?"

"With Simon? No."

"With *Simon!* So that's how it is. Did he ask you to?'

"Not exactly."

"Are you going to sleep with him?"

Cap stared at him. "You know, Ti-Loup, you've always been your own worst enemy."

404

9.

Lilith Goldberg was invited to the Cabots for Thanksgiving Dinner but she explained—with all due gratitude and thanks—that she was already committed to the Goldbergs. Vanderbilt was invited by both the Cabots and the Goldbergs but he had already accepted an invitation from the McVies.

At the Goldbergs, Lilith met the adult nieces and nephews of Myriam and Aaron. The two nephews, married, considered themselves Orthodox and lived in Brooklyn, and thus Myriam's Thanksgiving dinner, of necessity, was strictly kosher. The niece, Naomi, considered herself ex-Orthodox and more-or-less secular though she still kept the High Holy Days. She lived in Manhattan.

"You're like our phantom cousin," Naomi told Cap. "We've heard about your mother all our lives. In fact, I work for the Lilith Foundation."

"What's the Lilith Foundation?"

"You mean my aunt hasn't told you? That's so Aunt Myriam. The Lilith Foundation paid to bring you here, paid for the legal work, pays for your tuition at NYU. And my job is to keep the torch lit. We have information networks. We sponsor refugees from wherever in the world there's a need. It's all in homage to your mother."

"You've never told me," Lilith accused.

"It's not about *telling*," Myriam said. "We're just doing what your mother and father did."

"How do you find the people—?"

"There are networks. Human Rights networks. There are safe houses. Exactly the way there were in France during the war. Vietnam, Cambodia, the Middle East, Eastern Europe, the new African nations, it works the same way. Word of mouth. These are the people you can trust; these are the people you can't. Word gets out. From survivors, from prisons, from families whose members have disappeared. There are ways to collect evidence and get it out to the press. Buying and selling art is one of those ways."

"I'd like to do that," Lilith said.

"Your mother would be pleased. Grand Loup would be proud of you. I have a Sotheby's connection if you're willing to travel to places not considered entirely safe."

One week after Thanksgiving, Ti-Loup called Cap, distraught. "McVie has been drafted," he said. "He's being shipped off to Vietnam."

"Why is he being drafted?"

"Because he lost his student deferment. Because he couldn't afford to go to Harvard."

"He said he didn't want to go to Harvard."

"He did and he didn't. Either way, his family couldn't manage it. That's the way the draft works. I can't bear it."

"Do you want me to come up to Boston?"

"There's no room at the McVies."

"I can stay with the Cabots. Simon said I'd be welcome any time."

"Oh. Right. Well then, by all means stay with Simon."

"Ti-Loup, I'm thinking about *us*. Shouldn't we be together with McVie before he's shipped out?"

"Yes. Yes, you're right. But how will you get here?"

"By Greyhound."

"I'll meet you at the terminal then."

"At least," McVie said, raising his beer in the McVie dining room above the butcher's shop, "I'll get my last Christmas on US soil before I leave. Fort Bragg, North Carolina. Never been in the South."

"But they'll let you come home for Christmas, won't they?" his mother asked.

"I'm not sure. Twenty-four-hour leave, maybe."

"You will come back to us," his mother said. "From Vietnam, I mean. I know it. I'll pray every day, I'll burn a candle at St Ann's every day, and God will keep you safe."

"And when you come back," his father said, "I will kill the fatted calf and roast it whole."

"And while you're gone," Ti-Loup said, "I'll take your place in the butcher's shop. I'll work here every weekend."

Patrick McVie did fly home to Boston for Christmas 1964. Ti-Loup and Cap—she stayed with the Cabots—joined the family for the Somerville celebration. "It's a new recipe," Mrs. McVie said. "I slow-roasted the turkey all night. It's so tender it's falling off the bone."

"The Viet Cong make tunnels under the rice paddies," McVie's little brother said. "They told us about that at school. The tunnels are booby-trapped, so don't go down there, Pat."

"Hey," McVie said, tousling his little brother's hair, "even the potato famine couldn't kill off the Irish. We're in Boston till kingdom come."

"They shot President Kennedy," his little brother said mournfully.

Before dawn on a Friday in February 1965, Cap was shocked awake in New York by a phone call from Boston. "He's been killed," Ti-Loup said. "McVie has been killed."

"Dear God. Oh, Ti-Loup, no. Oh no! That's so horrible."

"Once I finish my freshman year, I'm moving off campus. I'll move into his room. I'll work for his father. I'm going to drop out of Harvard."

"He wouldn't want you to do that," Cap said.

"That's what Brother Damian says. But I'm responsible for two deaths that should never have happened."

"You're not responsible for either of those deaths."

"I am. You're not listening. I'm ashamed of being me. I have to find a way to atone. I can't face my nights anymore."

10.

Someone touched Cap on the shoulder. She was working at her carrel, deep in the stacks of the Art History library at NYU. "Ti-Loup! You almost gave me a heart attack. What are you doing here?"

"I have to talk to you."

"How did you find me?"

"I called NYU, got transferred to Art History, they said you'd be in the library. I asked the librarian."

"You've dropped out," Cap accused. "You shouldn't have. People make bad decisions when they're in shock."

"I haven't made *any* decisions. I'm not capable. I've come from the Port Authority Terminal. I just arrived. I took the overnight Greyhound."

"Oh, Ti-Loup." He looked ravaged. His hands were trembling. There were dark circles under his eyes. Cap held out her arms and he clung to her, his mouth against her shoulder. He made no sound but she could feel the seismic shuddering of his body.

"I haven't slept since I heard," he said. "I think I'm out of my mind."

"You need rest. You need sleep. I'm taking you home."

"I don't have a home."

"I'm taking you to *my* home. Madison Avenue."

"With those people? The ones who stayed in the safe house?"

"Yes."

"No," Ti-Loup said. "No. I can't do that. I can't talk to strangers. I can't be with anyone who knew Ti-Christophe."

He was feverish. He was shivering. He was shaking violently.

"I'm taking you to Emergency," Cap decided.

"No. I'm taking the bus back to Boston."

"That's crazy. You just arrived! Ti-Loup, you're in shock." She tried to hold him. "I'm going to take care of you," she promised, but he pushed her away and hailed a cab. *Penn Station*, she heard him tell the driver, and before she could even jam the door with her foot, with her arm, with anything, the taxi had pulled into traffic.

"Follow that cab," she told the next driver.

She was so close behind him that she could almost clutch his jacket, but trying to reach the Port Authority bus terminal via the underground walkways from Penn Station was like being caught in a cement-mixer's drum: the grinding noise, the buffeting, the thumping of other bodies, everyone rushing, everyone impatient, the booming echo chamber of rolling steel in the Penn Station cave. Cap put her hands over her ears to shut out the assault and in those seconds several people and several pieces of baggage pushed into the space ahead of her and she lost sight of Ti-Loup.

There was a flash of light—probably someone's camera, probably someone storing a farewell image of someone else—but for a dizzying second Cap was flare-blind and saw the countess, saw an elegant woman in a hazy fluorescent swirl, saw Aéroport de Paris. In vivid color and slow motion she saw Ti-Loup disappearing through sliding glass doors, half turning back to wave as the shutter clicked and the forked jag of the flashbulb moved like lightening. "Excuse me, excuse me," she said, slightly frantic, weaving between bodies and cases. She raced down the rabbit hole from the train platforms to the bus departure gates. The tunnel kept getting longer. Ti-Loup seemed very far ahead. He was not pausing or turning back and she had to run faster. "Sorry, sorry, I'm late, I'm late," she told those she bumped into as she passed.

"It's not the end of the world if you miss the bus," someone called. "There's always the next one."

She reached for the back of Ti-Loup's jacket and grabbed it. "Are you trying to lose me?" she gasped, out of breath.

"Let go of me," he said vehemently. "I hate goodbyes."

"Then let's not say goodbye. I'll come with you."

"And where will you stay?"

"I could stay with the Cabots."

"No!"

"Why not?"

"You know why not."

"Simon doesn't even live with his parents anymore. It's his *parents* I'd stay with."

"*Simon*. So you keep up with where Cabot is living, do you?"

"Ti-Loup, how can you be like this?"

"You know Cabot's mother is match-making. You know she's picked you out."

"And you know no one's ever been able to tell me what to do."

"You invade everything. No space of mine is off-limits to you. The chateau. The Cabots. The butcher shop."

"Why are you angry with me? What are you so angry about?"

"About everything. I'm angry about everything. I'm angry that McVie got drafted. I'm angry that he's dead. I'm furious that he's dead. I'm furious with God. I'm furious with anyone who makes excuses for God. I'm furious that Cabots and Vanderbilts never get drafted."

"Then you should join the Resistance."

"Yes. No. I don't know." Ti-Loup slumped against a pillar in the underground space and sank to the tiled floor. Lilith sat on the floor beside him. They leaned into each other. "McVie's parents hate all that anti-war stuff but now they're like boats without a rudder. They don't know what they think. They're just stunned and I'm angry that the only thing I can do to help is work in the butcher shop on Saturdays."

"That's not nothing. That will mean a lot to the McVies."

"You know," Ti-Loup said, following an entirely different thought-path, "I have trouble believing that people simply cease to exist." He snapped his fingers. "Just like that. I don't see how that's possible."

"I don't either," Cap said. "And they don't. Papa and Ti-Christophe are always with me."

"I can't tell if McVie's father wants my help, which he needs, or if he hates having me in the shop because I'm not his son. Sometimes I think he hates me as much as Michel Monsard and his father hated Ti-Christophe and me. They are flying McVie home in a body bag. He's nineteen years old."

"It's horrible."

"I don't sleep anymore," Ti-Loup said. "I can't sleep." His eyes were not still. They were like the eyes of a fly, watching all directions at once. He blinked rapidly. "I don't think I'll ever sleep again."

Cap wrapped her arms around him. "Ti-Loup." She could feel his heart thumping against hers. She willed calmness into him.

"I have to talk to someone," Ti-Loup said.

"You can talk to me every night. I'll call you."

"I'm not in my dorm room in the evenings. I work in the library then."

"So what time suits?" But Cap's words were drowned by the racket of buses revving and braking, the surge of passengers embarking and disembarking, the thump and scrape of luggage. Ti-Loup sprinted to the boarding area and swung himself up into the bus. "You can call *me*," Cap cried. "Whatever time suits. You've got the Goldbergs' number."

Ti-Loup either did not hear or affected not to. Already the bus was moving and she could not see him through the dark tinted glass. She tried to keep up as the sleek metal animal leaped out of the parking bay. She was walking fast, swerving for other buses, swerving for people hefting cases. The terminal was an obstacle course. Drivers were yelling at her. She was stumbling through forbidden zones. At the exit she stood watching and waving until the Greyhound was nothing but a silver smudge against the point where the parallel sides of Eighth Avenue met. Ti-Loup had reached the vanishing point. Cap felt bereft.

She tried calling his dorm room several evenings in a row: at suppertime, earlier in the evening, last thing at night. She tried early morning calls. She left messages. Her calls were not returned. She tried calling the McVies' number on weekends. Mrs. McVie was always warm and gracious. "I'll tell him you called," she would say. "You know we are all of us having trouble since Pat... since he didn't come back."

"I'm so sorry, Mrs. McVie."

"Thank you, dear. We pray for his soul every day. We pray for our own. We pray that we'll be able to bear it."

"And Vanderbilt? Is he okay?"

"Managing as well as any of us, I think. Which isn't very well. He asked us to call him Pat because that's part of his real name which was Gwynne Patrice. He said he always hated the Gwynne, and Patrice would be Patrick in Boston. He was *our* Pat's best friend so I do try to call him Patrick, but it's, you know... it's not easy. My husband can't do it."

If Mr. McVie answered Cap's call, he hung up immediately. He did not do this quietly. Cap felt as though a door had been banged in her face. Sometimes Mr. McVie barked: "Leave us alone, why don't you?"

Myriam found Cap silently weeping and fingering her rosary in the inner courtyard of the building on Madison. She put her arm around Cap's shoulders.

"It doesn't make any sense," Cap said.

"Death and loss never make sense, and nor does grief."

"But how can he shut out the one person who knows him better than anyone else and the one most wanting to comfort him?"

"There is no predicting how anyone will be affected," Myriam said. "No predicting what anyone will do. No predicting how you yourself will act when you feel as though your heart has been ripped out."

"My heart *has* been ripped out. Several times."

"Mine too," Myriam said. "But you find you can go on living."

Cap immersed herself obsessively in her courses at NYU. This involved many hours in the Metropolitan Museum of Art. It seemed to her that one could never sit long enough in front of a painting. There was always some new and astonishing detail of brushwork or perspective to be observed, though from time to time she would be embarrassed by a security guard politely tapping her on the shoulder. "Miss, it's closing time." How could that be? she would wonder. Surely she had barely arrived? For this reason, one of her courses —"Painters on Painting"—was particularly reassuring, especially Vincent van Gogh's letters to his brother. *I would gladly give ten years of my life,* Van Gogh wrote to Theo, *to be able to sit for fourteen days in front of Rembrandt's "The Jewish Bride" with barely a crust of dry bread to eat.*

Cap understood.

It was a source of torment to her that she herself had no talent for drawing or painting. Her only talent was for *looking at paintings*, for *touching* furniture.

"That is not an insignificant gift," Myriam Goldberg reassured her. "It is the gift of the collector and conservator. If it were not for us, many of the greatest achievements of the greatest artists would be lost or destroyed."

"But you paint also," Cap pointed out.

"A minor talent. My gift for acquiring and conserving is more important to the collective memory and the collective conscience, I like to think. If you could paint, Cap, how would you paint Ti-Loup?"

Cap thought about this. She began to dream about painting Ti-Loup, but in her dreams she worked all night then woke to find the canvas blank. In one dream, she found a sixteenth-century French painting on her easel, a brilliant forgery. She had never seen the original, which hung in the National Gallery in London, but she had seen a print of "St Gilles and the Hind." The label assigned to the painter by art historians was simply the Master of St Gilles.

St Gilles. Was the village named for him? Or had he lived there?

Cap had seen two paintings by the Master of St Gilles in the Musée des Beaux Arts in Tours but she had not seen "St Gilles and the Hind." In her dream, the original was luminous and enlarged. There was the kneeling French king and there in the background was the village of St Gilles and the chateau. There, in the middle foreground, near the right edge of the painting, was the rocky mass inside of which the safe house was hidden. There was the secret entrance beneath the stone bridge. There was St Gilles himself—though clearly Grand Loup had been the sitter—cradling the wounded hind, an arrow shot by one of the king's archers projecting from its flank. The hind was dying in the arms of Grand Loup. The arrow had also pierced the hand of the saint as he stroked and calmed and sought to protect the terrified animal.

You have wounded me also, Grand Loup seemed to say. *And just as deeply.*

"Lilith," Myriam Goldberg said, "Simon Cabot is here to see you."

""I thought I might find Vanderbilt here," Simon explained. "That's why I came."

"I haven't had contact for weeks," Cap said. "He won't return calls."

"He's not here in New York?"

"He did come down, but he went back again almost immediately."

"Apparently he's moved off campus and I haven't been able to reach him. I don't know what's happening."

"Nor do I."

"To be honest, I'm lying about why I came down," Cabot said. "Or partly lying. I'm seriously worried about Vanderbilt, but it was also my excuse to see you. Can we go somewhere private? For dinner and drinks?"

"There's a bistro a block away," Cap said.

Cabot reached across the table and rested his large hand over Cap's. She had a visual image of the hand of St Gilles above the slash in the dying hind's flank. She felt comforted. She made no attempt to move her hand away from his.

"I thought McVie might know where Vanderbilt is," Cabot said. "I know McVie lives in Somerville somewhere. I called Dryden and got his home phone number but when I tried it an operator said the number had been disconnected. I tried the phone book and called every McVie in Somerville but not one was the right one and not one was helpful."

"McVie was killed," Cap said. "In Vietnam."

"Dear God! Why don't I know about that? Why wasn't it in the

Alumni newsletter?"

"It was very recent. But how many Dryden alumni get drafted? Who'd be keeping track?"

"Jesus!" Cabot said, shocked by sudden knowledge. "Our kind never get drafted." He added, a tad defensively, "But we do have distinguished officers in the Marines. Alumni, I mean. Dryden has a sterling service record."

"Ti-Loup is devastated."

"Who?"

"Vanderbilt. Ti-Loup is his childhood nickname. He's working in the butcher shop on weekends to make amends. At least to try."

"Butcher shop?"

"McVie's father has a butcher shop in Somerville."

"Good God! I had no idea. I mean, I knew they lived in Somerville but I guess I assumed... Actually I never gave a thought to what they did."

"McVie used to work for the family business and now Vanderbilt has taken his place. If he's moved off campus, I suspect that's where he's living now. He must have moved in with the McVies."

"Then we should rescue him," Cabot said.

"I don't think he'd see it that way. I don't think he'd appreciate that view of the McVies. But I *would* like to see him. Talk to him."

"Then come up to Boston for the weekend. You can stay with my family. I drove down and I'll take you back with me."

"All right."

"Or you could stay with me. I have my own apartment now in Cambridge. A stone's throw from MIT."

"Yes, you told me."

"Would you stay with me?"

"I'll think about that," Cap said.

"Can I ask you something personal, Lilith?"

"I can't promise I'll answer."

417

"You and Vanderbilt...? Is there something between you?"

"There's our entire childhood between us. There's France. There's language and culture. There's the village we grew up in. There's our first communion. There's seven years, every day, with our Jesuit tutor. There's the chateau and the gardener's cottage, there's my father and his mother... There's everything."

"Wait a minute. First communion? Jesuit tutor? So you're not really Jewish after all?"

"No, I'm really not. I hope you won't ask me to explain. It's too complicated."

"Okay, I won't ask. But all that... childhood, first communion, France, etcetera, it's stiff competition. But apart from all that? I mean... you know... is there something between you *now?* Between you and Vanderbilt?"

Cap sighed and studied her hands. "I honestly don't know. I can't answer that even for myself."

"But he matters to you."

"Of course he matters to me."

"Too much for anyone else to matter?"

"I don't know."

"I'm staying at a hotel in Greenwich Village tonight. Would you come for an after-dinner drink?"

"I think.... yes, I think I would, Simon."

11.

Cabot's studio apartment off Central Square, tenth floor, had a view not only of the Charles River and of MIT itself but also of the splendid gold dome of the State House crowning Beacon Hill across the river. Below Beacon Hill, the Boston Common spread itself out like a softly lumpy green quilt. Cap could see the swans and the swan boats on the pond.

"That's where the British troops were mustered," Cabot said. "The Redcoats. 1775. Marched from there to Concord to silence the shot heard round the world."

"Your ancestors marched? Or fired the shot?"

"Good God, neither. My great-great-great-whatevers were still living in Salem then and were far too busy making a fortune in shipping to get involved in the Revolution. They didn't even move to Boston till the ruckus was well and truly over. They weren't about to risk the family wealth by getting embroiled in a war."

"But if they were in shipping, their ships must have taken sides. Redcoats or rebels?"

"Neither. They were privateers. They shipped opium, slaves, and rum. Why do you think the family is so devoted to benefaction of the arts and of all that is charitable and good? It's about atoning for family sins."

"Does your mother think that?"

"We all think it. We all know it. Every wealthy family has skeletons in the closet. We're not about to give it all away but we do want to buy salvation. Ever asked Vanderbilt how the family got its money?"

"Oh, Vanderbilt knows very well. He'd like to divest."

"Divesting's a bit extreme. Better use of accumulated wealth can be made."

"Ah Simon. You are so refreshingly uncomplicated."

"I have a feeling that's not a compliment."

"It was meant as a compliment."

"But you are addicted to complicated people."

"Am I?" Lilith thought about this. "I think I haven't known many uncomplicated people. I don't know if it's a European thing or a Catholic thing, but it's not an American thing. I envy Americans."

"You shouldn't. We're manic. We never feel we've got to where we should have got. We can't rest. We can't stop."

"Direct opposite of people like me. We're lost."

"That's not the impression you give. Complicated, yes, which makes you compelling. But not lost. You're like my mother and my father. Lord of all you survey."

Lilith was astonished. "My own mother and my own father," she said, "knew that life could be snuffed out in an instant. My father used to say: *You can never see around the next curve. So you live that way. You don't want to be ashamed of your final act and you never know what is going to be that last act.*"

"That's a daunting credo. I prefer not even to think about the next curve. Just go at it, that's my motto, no matter what's waiting out of sight. Speaking of which, are we going to Somerville today?"

"Ah. Speaking of which," Lilith sighed, "would you mind if I went alone? I mean, I've been there before. I've met the McVies. And I just think it would be better if I talk to Ti.... talk to Vanderbilt alone until I can get a sense of..."

"Of whether he's cracked up or is just depressed."

"Yes. If it must be put so bluntly."

"As long as we have dinner with my parents tonight," Cabot said. "As long as you bring Vanderbilt along, no matter what state he's in."

"I'll try. About bringing him, I mean. I don't feel very hopeful on that score, but I will certainly join you and your parents for dinner."

The butcher's shop in Somerville smelled exactly like *La Boucherie Monsard*.

"What are you doing here?" Ti-Loup demanded. He had a cleaver in his right hand and it descended like a guillotine blade on the massive oak block, splintering a shank bone of veal.

Cap closed her eyes and breathed deeply. "This smells like Petit Christophe," she said in French.

The woman who had ordered veal looked nervous. "Maybe I'll come back later," she said. "If you could have the shank packaged and labeled?"

Ti-Loup heard nothing, not the woman's voice, not the jangling bell as the shop door opened and closed on Union Square. "Ti-Loup? *Tu vas bien?*" Cap was not conscious of speaking in French. She *smelled* in French.

"I don't know what you're saying," Ti-Loup said in English, his gaze hostile and blank.

"Yes, it is very disturbing," Brother Damian agreed. "Pat McVie's parents find it disturbing. I believe it's a stage of shock and guilt. I believe it will pass. The thing is, you see, he doesn't want to be a Vanderbilt. He holds himself accountable."

"What can we do?"

"Wait," Brother Damian said. "I am in a certain amount of trouble with my own order for discussing Vietnam issues—all points of view—with students in the Marist school where I teach. These are serious life-and-death issues for my students, patriotism vs. those who are used as cannon fodder. They know they can be drafted any day. It's a race issue and a class issue, they can see that. I've involved Patrick in coming to discussion groups at the school."

"Patrick?"

"Vanderbilt. He asked to be introduced as Patrick McVie. He's trying to be the lost son."

"This sounds frightening. It sounds dangerous."

"Yes, it is. I'm not trained as a pastoral counselor but he trusts me and he won't talk to anyone else. He does have suicidal thoughts."

"Why won't he talk to *me*? He knows he can trust me."

"He isn't sure of that."

"How can he not be sure?"

"He knows you're in touch with his mother. He knows you're in touch with the Cabots. That bothers him. He's... well, for the time being, he's paranoid, I think."

"Shouldn't we...? Shouldn't he be...?" Cap was casting about for a way to ask if Ti-Loup should be hospitalized. "Tell him," she said, but could not think of a comfort formula sufficiently potent. "Tell him that whenever he's ready to talk to me again, I'll be waiting and I'll serve roasted rabbits."

Cabot called Lilith several nights a week, late, sometimes very late, sometimes after midnight from his MIT lab. She had her own phone line at the Goldbergs. One weekend a month, she would explain that she was going to Boston or that she was staying with a friend in Greenwich Village.

"Can we hope," Aaron Goldberg asked, "that you are seeing Ti-Loup?"

"I wish you wouldn't ask me that question."

"We won't ask," Myriam Goldberg said, "but we won't give up hope, and you shouldn't either, Lilith."

"I'm finding hope cruel," Lilith said. "I think it's saner to turn the page and move on."

"You may be right," Myriam said. "But sometimes waiting after all hope is gone is worth the wait. After all, that's how we found Grand Loup and you."

"But while one is waiting?"

"That is the difficult part," Myriam conceded. "You do what you have to do to survive and function. And Simon Cabot is a very nice young man."

12.

Sometimes, when Lilith answered the phone late at night, the caller did not speak. When that happened, she did not say "Simon?"

She waited. Sometimes a minute would pass.

"Is that you, Ti-Loup?" she would ask if more than a minute passed.

Then the caller would hang up.

In early spring, March '68, two months before she expected to graduate from NYU, Lilith Goldberg sensed a dark shadow above the page of the book she was studying. She was ensconced in her carrel in the library.

"Simon!" she said. "You startled me."

"I'm not Cabot."

"Ti-Loup! Dear God!"

"You were expecting Cabot."

"You nearly gave me a heart attack."

"That's my role. The Black Reaper."

"Oh for God's sake, stop it, Ti-Loup. Don't be so tiresome and so self-pitying."

"Is that how you see me?"

"No. Yes. I don't know. You're not the only one who's faced death and loss. How does it help to push everyone away?"

"You want me to leave?"

"No, I don't. I want you to snap out of it."

"Brother Damian said you promised that when I was ready to talk, you'd serve roast rabbits."

"Ah…" Wisps of wood smoke seemed to rise from the library stacks. "I will. I will. But a bit of notice in advance would have helped. In Manhattan, you can't pick up skinned rabbit at the deli. Probably not even at the butcher's shop in Somerville."

A ghost of a smile flickered across Ti-Loup's face. "True," he admitted. He turned and paced up and down the narrow passageway between the library stacks. "You think I'm not trying, but I am. I'm trying to snap out of it. I'm trying to make restitution. I'm working with inner-city kids. I tutor them. I take them on cross-country runs."

"That is such good news, Ti-Loup."

"I came to ask something. Will you come to my graduation in May? I don't have anyone else."

"So you *will* graduate! You didn't drop out. Thank God. But won't McVie's parents be there?"

"I can't ask that. It's too cruel. It should be their son in cap and gown."

"Surely Brother Damian will be there?"

"He feels he can't. He feels it would be disloyal. Will you come?"

"Of course I'll come. Will you come to mine at NYU?"

"Will Cabot be there?"

"Well, yes. The whole Cabot family. And the Goldbergs. And your mother."

"My mother?"

"You know, Ti-Loup, your mother and I write to each other every week."

"Then I won't be there."

"Do you have any idea, Ti-Loup, of how much you've hurt her?"

"Does she have any idea of how much she hurt me?"

"Yes, she does. She gave me all your letters, unopened. I told you that. She said she thought it was for the best when she did it but now she knew she was wrong. She would do anything to undo the past."

"No, she wouldn't. She would never have let me work as a butcher in St Gilles. I couldn't bear to have either of my parents at my graduation. They would poison it. You can come or not come as you choose. There won't be anyone else."

"I'll come. But I'll be devastated if you don't come to mine."

"You'll survive. You'll always survive. You're tough as nails."

Legend has it that since the first graduation ceremony in 1642 it has never rained on a Harvard Commencement, always held outdoors in Harvard Yard. Even God wouldn't dare to mar the day, the myth goes. In fact, in more than three centuries, it *has* rained a handful of times, but on the day of Ti-Loup's graduation the sun was hot and bright and the grass and the trees in the Yard were lushly green and the graceful white spire on Memorial Church was almost blinding. Even so there was a subdued note to the celebration and many of the students wore black armbands. The assassinations of Martin Luther King and Robert Kennedy were horrifyingly recent and the speakers made somber reference to those events.

"You know," Ti-Loup confessed, mortar-board and scroll in hand, "on the day King was killed, I went into Mem Church to pray. I'd never been inside before. It was half full of faculty and students. Later I went to St Ann's. There were scores of people weeping and praying. Why does no one recognize a martyr till he's martyred? King was condemned in sermons in that church. We believed he was a Communist stirring up racial warfare. Everyone did."

"Not everyone. The Goldbergs joined his march on Washington in '63."

"Did they?" Ti-Loup twisted his graduation scroll as though it were a knot he was tying. "So did Shannay. My father fired her."

"I wonder if the Goldbergs ever told her that they were there too."

"I've never done one worthwhile thing in my life," Ti-Loup said.

"That is a stupid thing to say."

"I'm thinking of becoming a priest."

"What?" Cap closed her eyes. She saw Father Boniface raising the chalice in the church of St Gilles. She saw the back of Monsieur Monsard's turkey neck. She heard Ti-Christophe's footsteps leaving the nave. She saw the countess and her waif of a son as she and her father passed them in the aisle. She saw the boy's eyes, his blue shift. She remembered that his eyes and her eyes met for a second. She remembered that his were frightened and that she had made her own face turn grotesque. Perhaps she had poked out her tongue.

If I hadn't been so heedlessly cruel and bossy, she wondered, would he ever have climbed out his window?

When? When do you plan to turn celibate? she thought of asking him. Do you want to become Father JG whom you mocked, whom you so often mocked?

She said, "My father never thought very highly of priests. He suspected some of collaboration. They only have to answer to the bishop, he said. We have to answer to God."

"And your own graduation?" Ti-Loup asked, as though their conversation had been moving on a different track altogether. "How was that?"

"Subdued," Cap said carefully. "Like here. Black armbands."

"And your personal guests? What about them?"

427

"There was one painful absence. It's hard to forgive you, but I do."

"And my mother? What did she say?"

"She said she was glad her investment in a Jesuit tutor and a convent school in Tours had not gone astray. She said she was proud of me."

"Did she ask about me?"

"Obliquely. She was afraid to ask. People try not to expose their wounds, Ti-Loup, as you yourself know very well."

"I don't believe my mother has any."

"You have massive blind spots, Ti-Loup, like everyone else. Like almost everyone else. I think the only person I've ever known who had no blind spots at all was my father. But maybe my view of him is my own blind spot."

"It's not. When I was a child and I prayed *Our Father, who art in heaven,* it was your father's face I saw. Still do.'

"Then why didn't you...? Why? Your mother and I were at his bedside when he died. The Goldbergs came over for the funeral but you didn't even call or write."

"Don't," Ti-Loup said. "Don't. For some sins there's no absolution."

Cap sighed. "I told your mother you hadn't forgiven any of us, that she wasn't the only one. You avoided us all, I said. You cut everyone off. I didn't tell her I'd be here today. I just told her you'd forbidden your father to come. I thought that would be some sort of comfort."

"And Cabot?"

"The Cabots were wonderful and so were the Goldbergs. They threw a party for me. You're just going to have to learn to share, Ti-Loup. Unfortunately, from my point of view, the guest of honor never showed up at the party. But I have some significant pieces of news. The first is that I've legally changed my name, with the Goldbergs' blessing. Lilith belongs to my mother and me, but I

428

also need a name that belongs to papa and Ti-Christophe. I'm Lilith Jardine now. Legally."

"Lilith Jardine."

"Like the sound of it?"

"Not as much as the sound of Cap. But Lilith Jardine is as beautiful and difficult and alarming as when she first dropped out of our apple tree."

"*Our* apple tree. Papa's and mine."

"My point exactly. Lilith Jardine. She who must not be contradicted."

"The second thing is my graduation present to you. I've signed up for Harvard Summer School and I'm moving to Boston. Mrs. Cabot, bless her, has arranged internships for me at the Fogg and the Boston Museum of Fine Arts. Minimal intern's pay but I can afford a studio apartment."

"That's my graduation present?"

"You don't like it?"

"Oh, I love being indebted to the Cabots."

Cap batted her forehead with the palms of her hands, exasperated. "You are as spiky as prickly-pear cactus, and yet the Cabots love you, Ti-Loup."

"Easy for them."

"Why is it easy for them when you treat them so badly and so rudely?"

"That would take a lengthy paper on the history of privilege and on why some of us would like to divest ourselves of that history."

"There's a course on that topic, or something like it, in the Summer School catalogue. It's called *The Sociology of Power.* I signed us both up for it. It'll be like being back together with Father JG."

"Paradise regained," Ti-Loup said.

"Cynicism's inappropriate for someone who plans to

take orders."

"You actually signed me up without asking?"

"There weren't many spaces left, so I thought I should. You're free to withdraw."

"You haven't changed. Still Joan of Arc bullying the Dauphin."

"You haven't changed either," Cap said.

13.

The summer-school course on "The Sociology of Power" was held in a building facing onto Harvard Yard. It was an old building and smelled of crumbling brick, pigeon droppings and stale student. A bourgeois attitude toward laundry was out of fashion in 1968, as were overly clean feet, which did not match the funky hand-made sandals. Because desks in the amphitheater rose in curved and stepped ranks—like pairs of brows around the steep central aisle—the students were inclined to take short cuts. They used the serried rows as climbing monkeys might and they scrambled over one another to reach an unoccupied seat.

Each intensive seven-week seminar met daily, either for three hours in the morning or three hours in the afternoon. In June '68, the first classes were convened a mere twenty days after Sirhan Sirhan blew Bobby Kennedy's skull into shards, and scarcely two weeks after RFK was laid to rest in Arlington alongside the grave of his brother. This grisly event seemed in no way to cloud the sunny enthusiasm of the Summer-School Director who made his way from class to class with the same uplifting words. The Harvard Crimson quoted him front page center. "Harvard Summer School is mainly about fun," he said. (*He means sex and pot*, students sniggered.) "We have a long history of testimonials," the Director said, "from students who swear that summer school was the best part of their Harvard years." (*Not all of them remember any of it too clearly,* students joked.) Of course, the Director added, intense intellectual focus was integral to the experience. "I do not mean by fun," he said, "that you won't exercise brainpower to the Nth degree." What he promised was that the mental buzz would be fun: classes and study by day, parties by night.

Summer school students from years past were freely quoted by the *Crimson.* We can't begin to tell you, they said, how much sex happens at night. It's so intense. Those summer-school friendships last for life.

In the lecture hall, Lilith was rudely whacked on the head by a cloth drawstring bag that was heavy with books. Drawstring green sacks, visible on campus by the hundreds, were the only acceptable mode for humping texts from one class to the next. A briefcase was unacceptable. It might suggest a banker or a lawyer or some other lower form of moral life, whereas a Harvard green bag in that particular summer was a potent signifier of virtue. The student stepping over Lilith was effusive with apology. "Terribly sorry," he said. "Didn't mean to be so clumsy. Just had an over-whelming desire to sit next to you and this was the only way I could get in. D'you mind?"

Lilith rubbed the back of her head gingerly. "It will cost you," she said drily.

"Exactly what I was hoping. Can I take you to lunch after this?"

"No, you can't," Vanderbilt interjected, leaning forward from the seat on Lilith's far side. "What are you, a freelance lecher?"

Lilith laid a gentling hand on Vanderbilt's forearm. "I was only joking when I said it would cost you," she told the book-bag man.

"That's a pity," he said. "What's your name?"

"Lilith Jardine. What's yours?"

"Rumpelstiltskin. Find out my real name and I'll take you to

432

dinner at the Ritz. I'll treat you *both* to dinner at the Ritz, you and your keeper."

"We don't eat at places like the Ritz," Vanderbilt said. "On principle."

"What's your guard dog's name?" Rumpelstiltskin asked.

"My name is Patrick McVie. Does behaving like a lout come naturally to you? Or do you have to work at it?"

"Hey, look, you're right. I apologize. I'm behaving like an asshole. Happens when I'm nervous. I've had girlfriends turn straw into gold who swear I can turn gold into shit." Rumpelstiltskin leaned across Lilith and extended his right hand. "Shake on it?" His smile was beatific, his manner warm.

Patrick McVie paused for three seconds then extended his hand. "Okay. Shake. Sorry to be so prickly."

The professor entered the room then, and to get attention he clapped his hands twice, very loudly. Even so, the din of chatter did not stop instantly but faded in a slow diminuendo, during which McVie murmured against Lilith's ear: *Oozing charm from every pore, he oiled his way across the floor.* She turned to him, startled. "Rumpelstiltskin," he whispered. "Not the professor."

The professor was moderately famous and had appeared on national television to discuss the assassination epidemic (JFK, Malcolm X, Martin Luther King, Robert Kennedy). His hair was pulled back in a ponytail and he wore jeans and a Harvard T-shirt. A peace symbol made of soldered nails hung from a leather cord around his neck. "Much as I regret having to disagree publicly with the Harvard Summer School Director," he said, "this course will not be about fun, unless we are talking about the ways in which the powerful have fun on the backs of those they exploit, on the backs of those who are sent into combat to preserve the privileges of power."

That was his opening salvo.

He quoted Marcuse's *One-Dimensional Man: The people recognize themselves in their commodities; they find their soul in their automobile, hi-fi set, split-level home, kitchen equipment.* He quoted Norman O. Brown's *Love's Body: I am what is mine.... The boundaries of our property are extended by mixing our persons with things, and this is the essence of the labor process.*

"Since they are on the reading list," the professor said, "I trust you have already read both books. If not, stay up all night and make sure you have read them by tomorrow. Herbert Marcuse himself will speak to this class next week. He will be open to debate and discussion."

Someone called out from the third row: "Are Marcuse and Brown in political and philosophical agreement?"

"For the most part, yes," the professor said. "They are personal friends. There are some points on which they disagree. So." He cast his eyes over the class. "Are you your things? Your commodities? Or are you something other than your things? Do you believe you have a soul? Can your soul express itself independently of your desire to hang onto your things?"

"Doesn't that depend, sir, on what we consider *our things?*" another student called out. "I mean, 'having fun in summer school' or having a mini-fridge in my dorm room is not one of my *things* or I wouldn't have signed up for your course. Shifting gears in our political culture so that we change leaders by ballot box and not by assassin's bullet, that's one of my *things*. It's not tangible though. It's not a commodity."

"Are you claiming," the professor asked, "that your Harvard degree will not function as a commodity? That you will not exchange it in the marketplace for your future income level, for instance? For where you will live? For whether you or your future sons will be drafted? For whether you will live in the safe or unsafe areas of a city?"

"Does that mean, sir," the challenger parried, "that you and Marcuse and Brown hold all things equivalent? Are you saying there is no moral gradation between a new refrigerator and a passion for social justice?"

There was a great clamor of support and dissent from the class. Amid the hubbub, McVie (astonishing Lilith) stood and demanded in a loud and clear voice: "I have to ask, sir, if Marcuse or Brown ever had to take an ax to a chicken's head? Did they ever go hungry? Did they ever get drafted? Do they have the faintest idea of what *things* might mean to people who have don't have many things?"

"The peasant speaks!" someone else in the class called out.

"The so-called peasant has a valid point," the professor said. "Do Marcuse and Brown speak only, and obliviously, for the middle class? For the upper middle class and above?"

"*Can* the peasant speak? Can he ever speak?" Rumpelstiltskin was standing now. "Does the peasant have words in which to speak? Or can only the *ex-peasant* parrot the words of Marcuse? Can he only speak when he has swapped his farm overalls for a Harvard green bag?" Rumpelstiltskin did not shout, yet his voice was crisp and clear above the din. He required a response as his due and yet he did not come across as aggressive. He had an air of charming disdain. "Isn't this romantic agrarianism?" he asked. "Tolstoy pretending to be a serf. Gandhi sufficiently propped up by wealthy donors to sit at a spinning wheel and turn out homespun. Is this moral bullshit or isn't it? I'm laying bets that the faux-peasant is a guilt-ridden private-school type, wealthy as Croesus."

McVie was still standing. He looked stunned, like a boy caught red-handed in an apple tree.

Lilith could not take her eyes off Rumpelstiltskin. She wanted to throw something at him but she was also mesmerized by him. He caught her eye and held it. He had the most intense and un-

435

nerving gaze she had ever been skewered by. He smiled slightly and raised one eyebrow, implying sardonic collusion.

She turned away and reached for McVie's hand and tugged him back down to his seat. "That was superb," she whispered.

"Well," the professor said. "Class warfare breaks out! It is not the intention of this course to be a political confessional or a public-shaming event in the manner of Madame Mao's Red Guards, so I won't ask our two provocateurs to identify themselves or their backgrounds."

There was a drumming, as of kettledrums, of palms of hands against desks, a traditional academic sound of either fierce agreement or of protest.

"I do, however," the professor continued, "hope to shake you all out of complacency. I hope to rattle your received and mostly unexamined preconceptions. And if I were to make an informed guess, by way of purposely flustering you, let me suggest that Speaker Number One is of genuine peasant stock and has had experience of being socially excluded by the elite. He is legitimately angry. I would say that Speaker Number Two is projecting. He is projecting vehemently. He doth, in fact, protest far too much it seems to me. He sounds like one of Madame Mao's Red Guards desperate to prove how fiercely revolutionary he is and how very untainted he is by the counter-revolutionary strains of the bourgeoisie. So I will hazard a guess that he is actually from of a wealthy and privileged background, feels not the slightest impulse to apologize for this, but feels he can readily detect what he thinks of as the Tolstoy syndrome in someone else. This syndrome infuriates him, particularly, I suspect, because his ancestors profited from the 'romantic agrarianism' he so disdainfully mentions, which is to say from the labor of the happy peasant."

"Talk about hypocrisy," Rumpelstiltskin murmured in Lilith's right ear. "The professor's family has huge land holdings in Virginia. Ancestors were big slave owners. My family happens to know his."

Lilith raised one quizzical eyebrow. Does that mean, her eyebrow suggested, that your ancestors also owned slaves?

"Naturally." Rumpelstiltskin answered her unspoken question. "It takes one to know one. Southerners, I mean. Prof's a Southerner who shed his accent as fast as he could."

A black student, one of only two in the class, stood in the top back tier and spoke calmly and clearly. "I would like to congratulate you, sir, on your intention to shake the class out of complacency. Speaking of the sociology of power, can I ask you to comment on the statement of the Director of the Summer School, as reported in the Harvard Crimson, that there is no racial tension whatsoever at Harvard. What there is, he said, is a universal concern about race relations. I would very much appreciate your gloss on this, sir."

Absolutely every member of the class swiveled to observe the back row, *up in the gods,* where the tall student seemed almost to butt his head against the ceiling.

"You have touched the nerve center of the issue," the professor said. "Intentions are liberal, I think we all believe that. We all ascribe to that. And yet this overwhelmingly white class, without exception, is looking at you as though you had batwings and were covered in scales."

"I'm glad you noticed that, sir," the black student said. "Your honesty is very refreshing. I'm from Atlanta, Morehouse College, a black college as you are all well aware. In Georgia, we're never in any doubt about our status. White folks don't like black folks and they'll tell you straight to your face. Here everyone at summer school makes nice, but with the whole class still staring up at me I can hear what they're thinking. *Oh, he can talk! Oh, he can think!"*

The only other black student in the class, several rows further forward, now felt empowered to speak up. "White students are polite to me on campus," he said, "but not off campus. In the subway, they look the other way. It's Harvard and privilege, not me, that gets the respect."

"I cannot dispute that," the professor said. "The problem is—and this problem is the gorilla in the room—the problem is that knowledge itself is never innocent. It expresses the interests of those who own it and make you pay for it. Harvard, for instance. The fact that we have only two black students in this class, for instance. Your professors, for instance. Me, for instance. I have tenure. I can risk speaking out. Think about it. Argue about it. May it cause you insomniac nights for the next seven weeks and many hours of arguments in the watering holes of Harvard Square."

"Want to join us for lunch?" Lilith asked.

"Depends," Rumpelstiltskin said. "Depends on McVie here. Are we in a state of war or a state of truce?"

"*Knowledge itself is never innocent,*" McVie repeated. "I'm more than willing to discuss that and I'm eager to hear your views on 'romantic agrarianism.'"

"That hit home, didn't it? I could see you were stung."

"Whose book were you parroting?"

Rumpelstiltskin smiled like a cat gentling the mouse between its paws. "We can discuss this all afternoon."

"No we can't," McVie said. "I've got a class."

"Ahh." Rumpelstiltskin seemed to stretch out comfortably into a notional space. "Lilith," he said. "I hope you're free for the whole afternoon. To extend the discussion, I mean."

"Afraid not. I have an internship at the Fogg. I'm due there from two until five."

"Damn. I've struck out. I'm desolate. But I know the perfect place for a quick lunch and political fist-fight. And we'll just have to meet there again at six to continue debate. It's a basement pub on Dunster Street. I hope that won't be stooping too low for you, McVie?"

All three were seated on high bar stools watching the feet that passed the basement windows of the Dunster Street pub.

"So, McTolstoy, why do I have the feeling I've seen you before?" Rumpelstiltskin asked.

"I have no idea," McVie said. "I know I've never seen you before today."

"Is your name really McVie?"

"Is yours really Rumpelstiltskin?"

"Where do you come from?"

"Somerville, Mass. Boston Irish. I work as a butcher."

"Why do I find that unlikely?" Rumpelstiltskin demanded.

"Perhaps because you have a very ignorant notion of the Boston Irish and of butchers. I'm not the only butcher to get into Harvard. What about you?"

"Oh, I'm from all over. Father in the military, always on the move. What are your views on Vietnam?"

"What are you? CIA?"

"Hah! Just curious, given we are taking the same course. I'm assuming we both think Vietnam was a mistake. First Kennedy's mistake and now Johnson's. You can take it from me I'm against the draft."

"I don't know if Vietnam was a mistake or not," McVie said. "But I do know the burden is not equally shared, and nor are the deaths, but they should be."

"In that case, why don't you enlist?"

"I've been asking myself that same question. Why don't you?"

"For sound historical reasons," Rumpelstiltskin said. "Allow me to cite the Hundred Flowers Rebellion, 1956, Mao Tse-Tung spouting classical Qin dynasty precepts, *Let a hundred flowers bloom, and a hundred schools of thought contend.* You have to hand it to Mao, he was a genius, a devious and diabolically clever Machiavelli, Asian version. Understood the Mandarin intelligentsia and their soft Achilles' heel. So he invites them, welcomes them, bowing low and sounding the gongs. *Come to the banquet prepared in your honor. Share your critical views of the party regime.* And they did, poor suckers, after which he promptly shoveled them off by the thousand to labor camps. *I have enticed the snakes out of their caves,* he said. And that's why I won't enlist, and nor should you. There are better uses for people with brains than having their brains blown out by the Vietcong."

"A provocative argument," McVie admitted. "I need to think about my answer."

Lilith was studying Rumpelstiltskin's hands. They had a life of their own, the fingers playing silent jazz perhaps, touching flatware, balancing a teaspoon on one thumb. His eyes, however, did not shift focus and she herself was the scrutinized object. She sensed this and refused to acknowledge the fact until she observed an awkward self-consciousness in his fingers. They stilled themselves. The watcher realized he was being watched, being monitored closely. Only then did she raise her eyes to meet his. She returned his stare levelly. She would not blink. This seemed to excite him. She could see the slow lazy curve of his smile, a shark's smile.

"You have an encyclopedic range of knowledge," she said. "It's quite impressive."

"I read avidly," he shrugged. "Anything that takes my fancy really, and a wide range of subjects do take my fancy. Also, pure genetic good luck, I happen to have a photographic memory." He leaned toward her in a way that implied established intimacy. "I'm attracted to others who read a lot and think in unconventional ways." His hand brushed hers and Lilith leaned slightly away. "Like McTolstoy here. I want to hear his views on more equitable combat deaths and on wider democratic enlistment."

Lilith telegraphed caution to McVie. *He thinks he has enticed the snakes out of their caves,* her eyes warned.

"So McTolstoy, how about some mental chess on the pros and cons of the draft?"

"I'll take you on, but not right now. I have to get to my afternoon class." McVie kissed Lilith on the lips and gathered up his green bag and books. "I'm not sure where you stand, Mr. Rumpelstiltskin, or even if you know or care where you stand, or if you just like holding court and playing games, but even so you are a formidable thinker and worth a duel."

"What's his afternoon class?" Rumpelstiltskin asked.

"St Augustine, the Just War, and Liberation Theology."

"Jesus! The Latin-American guerrilla priests, Helder Camara and all that? A genuine imitation Tolstoy!"

"You're well informed on Latin America. Are you an imitation cynic or a real one?" Lilith wanted to know.

"Hey, Lucifer!" someone called. Two young men, beer tankards in hand, stopped by their bar stools. "Saw you in class today," one of them said to Lilith. "Watch out for Lucifer here. He's slippery. Some of us think he's CIA."

"Nah. Thinks he's Don Juan," the other student warned, mock seriously. "Keeps notches on his bed post. Watch that he doesn't slip something into your drink."

Rumpelstiltskin waved them off. "I hope you two don't have an afternoon class. You're drunk already. Shoo!" To Lilith he said, "Private game. We swore to augment each other's sexual reputation. Means nothing, alas." He summoned the bartender. "Don't serve them again. They're over the limit."

"So," Lilith said. "Your name is Lucifer. It suits you. You owe me dinner at the Ritz but I'm not interested in claiming the prize."

"Lucifer's not my real name. Just my *nom de guerre*. I've got a small business on the side to pay for school and I run my business under that name. "

"McVie and I don't usually socialize with business types. But if their minds are sufficiently interesting, we make exceptions."

"Ah. So I have a sufficiently interesting mind."

"Let's just say you make the first cut. You get to try out."

When Lilith left the pub on Dunster Street, crossed Harvard Yard, and entered the courtyard of the Fogg Art Museum, she passed under the elaborate carved architrave on Quincy Street and stepped back four centuries in time. She entered an Italian Renaissance courtyard with travertine arches, replica of the facade of a sixteenth-century church in Montepulciano. She might have been entering the central court of a Tuscan palazzo. She could imagine Castiglioni himself stepping out of a gallery, out of one of the galleries, *The Book of the Courtier* under his arm. Nothing of the din of Harvard Square traffic could be heard. The Fogg was a wonder.

Lilith paused in front of the polychrome wooden statue of Our Lady of Sorrows, twelfth century, in the courtyard. The virgin was missing one forearm and one foot and much of the blue of her gown had faded or peeled away, but her gilded coronet was in place and her face was still flesh-toned and gentle, her eyes sad. This was not the virgin with squirming infant but a mother whose son had been taken and brutally killed.

Lilith inclined her head and touched in respect the iron rod where a left foot had once been attached. She was due to report in the curator's office for the kind of drudge work required of an intern, but first she had to yield to temptation and give herself over to Poussin's *Holy Family*, early seventeenth century, French. This was a compulsion. This was why she would have been happy to kiss the feet of Mrs. Cabot who had arranged the connection with the Fogg.

If you gaze at Poussin too long, Lilith thought, you could drown in primary color, especially in his yellows and his reds.

"He painted for Richelieu and the pope and the Barbarini," someone said. His lips were touching her ear. "What does that tell you?"

"Are you stalking me, Lucifer?" Lilith asked, startled.

"What do his patrons tell you about the sociology of power?"

Lilith stared at the painting again. "I would say that color mattered more to him than politics. But of course you are right. Knowledge is never innocent and nor is art. Painters paint what their patrons pay them for. What are you doing here?"

"I followed you."

"I don't like to be tailed. What are you? Are you CIA? Did your friends hit the nail on the head?"

"I'm afraid my two drunken friends were nearer the mark when they mentioned Don Juan but I'm impeccably well behaved on all occasions, a consummate gentleman, strict Southern training. You won't ever have to fear unwanted advances. I'm a true romantic. *See how she leans her cheek upon her hand. O! that I were a glove upon that hand.*"

"Oh please!" Lilith said. "If you ever stalk me again, you can forget lunches or dinners or anything else on Dunster Street."

"I thought I made the first cut on account of my interesting mind."

"You did. But you just got dropped."

"I'll back off," Lucifer said. "I promise. Just don't cut me from the try-outs. It would break my heart."

"A lot of people have to live with broken hearts," Lilith said.

Lilith's internship duties were somewhat less thrilling than she had hoped. Her duties involved mailing letters to potential donors, answering mail from existing donors and members, sending out press releases, coordinating with other Harvard fund-raising activities, sending out brochures of upcoming exhibitions to alumni, typing, checking files, licking stamps. That was the dull mechanical part. On the other hand, she was required to keep up with any new scholarly findings on the provenance of the permanent collection. That was pure enjoyment. That was when Lucifer's comment about Cardinal Richelieu as one of Poussin's patrons sparked a research detour. That was how she discovered Richelieu had tastes that were less than devout. In 1635, when Poussin had already ensconced himself in Rome, he was summoned back to Paris by the French king's cardinal to paint a series of scenes devoted to Bacchus, Pan, and Silenus. These were not for Notre Dame or the king or the Louvre. They were for Richelieu's private chateau in Poitou. The paintings were bawdy. They were high-class porn, as dense with naked bodies and breasts and thighs and buttocks as with Poussin's gorgeous reds and yellows and cobalt blues.

"Simon!" Lilith was in the Fogg, lost in Poussin. "Do you have to shock me like this?"

"Only way I can be sure you won't disappear before I track you down. How come you've been avoiding me since you moved to Boston?"

"I haven't been avoiding you. There's been no time. I have a class, I have library time, I have this internship, I have another internship at the MFA."

"Not convincing. Why haven't you called? Has this got something to do with Vanderbilt?"

"Sort of."

"And then there's the fact," Cabot said, "that apparently you are no longer Lilith Goldberg. Don't you think some explanation is in order?"

"Yes," Lilith said. "It is. I've behaved badly. I should have called you. The Goldbergs are my adoptive parents. With their blessing, I've reverted to my French name. Not sure your family will find a Catholic name any less disturbing than a Jewish one."

"My parents don't care what your name is but they do care about you. And about us. You could move into my apartment, you know. I want you to."

"That's... that's a lovely invitation, Simon."

"But?"

"Hard to explain to someone who's generations deep in belonging. Moving in, moving out, changing worlds... it takes more energy than you could know." How was it possible to explain? From gardener's cottage to chateau, from France to New York, from New York to Boston, from Jesuit tutor and convent nuns to NYU and Harvard... "I feel I need time to settle in."

"At least I know I'll always be able to find you here," Cabot said. "What's the painting you've been staring at?"

"Poussin's *Holy Family.* Isn't it amazing?"

"Hmm. If you say so. What am I supposed to be seeing?"

"Look at the incredible red of the Virgin's gown. A century earlier, and he could have been burned at the stake for that color. The Virgin as scarlet woman? Color was everything to Poussin. Pigment was God, God was in paint."

"Actually," Cabot said, "If God exists, he exists as an elegant equation. I'm going to require my mother to send a formal written dinner invitation to you and Vanderbilt, both. As long as he's there too, he can't get jealous. You can discuss God and Poussin with my parents."

14.

The day was full of light and lilacs and Cap brushed the soft-petalled cones with her fingers as she passed. Summer in Cambridge was glorious and she expected the afternoon's march to Fenway Park to be as festive as village weddings in St Gilles. Perhaps dancing would break out. Perhaps the police would accept flowers in their lapels. The sun was shining, the war would end, swords would be beaten into ploughshares. It was the dawning of the age of enlightenment.

"I feel so happy to be alive," she told Ti-Loup exuberantly, and then checked herself. It seemed to her that Ti-Loup carried McVie on his shoulders like a heavy backpack that he could not set down. He moved inside a rain cloud that would not lift. "Sorry," she said. "That was flippant. But we are marching for *him*. For McVie. *In memoriam*. We are marching for an end to the war."

"I'm not sure I'll go on the march. There'll be police barricades. TV cameras. I don't want to show up on the evening news."

"We'll be two little dots in the crowd."

"Not if they zoom in for close-ups. I don't want to have to deal with my father's disdain and outrage. Or with my mother's sense of being shamed."

"Why would you have to deal with it when you refuse even to see either one?"

"I'd know what they were thinking."

Cap was startled. On some level, she thought, he is still the boy from the chateau (fearful) and the boy from Dryden (a snob.) Certain social codes still constrain him. She said tartly: "You mean you can't see yourself as part of the huddled masses. It's not something a Vanderbilt or a Dryden grad would do."

"It's not something a McVie would do. I'm much more worried about McVie's parents. If they see me on TV, they'll think I'm saying their son's death was pointless."

"But you're not. You're saying the opposite."

"I'm not sure they'll see it that way."

"So what are you saying? You don't think this war should stop?"

"I do want it to stop. The McVies want it to stop. They're just not comfortable with this sort of protest and nor am I."

"Don't you want the war to stop before McVie's younger brothers get drafted?"

"Of course I do. I suppose you're right. I should be there."

"So I'll meet you on the Common then, before the march?"

"I suppose." Ti-Loup sounded moodily uncertain. "I hope the McVies don't see me on TV."

There was a seafood hole-in-the-wall in Somerville where they met after Friday-evening mass. "You didn't show up," Cap accused. "You missed a historical moment in Fenway Park. You missed Pete Seeger. You missed Gene McCarthy. You missed something extraordinary. You never intended to march."

"I didn't know if I would or if I wouldn't," Ti-Loup said. "'At the last minute, I couldn't."

A platter of pan-fried fish arrived and they ate in silence. "Someone's offered me a ride down to New York this weekend," Cap ventured. "I want to see the Goldbergs and your mother. I miss them. I'll stay with the Goldbergs.'

"Is your ride with Cabot?"

447

"No, it's not. Simon is as allergic to marching with the rabble as you are. Cabots don't join street protests any more than Vanderbilts do."

"So who is giving you a ride?"

"No one who matters. Just someone planning to join the anti-war sit-in in Central Park."

"Not that jerk Rumpelstiltskin, I hope."

"Actually, yes. His name's Lucifer. He offered at Fenway Park and since you weren't there... I accepted purely because I want to see...."

"Right," Ti-Loup said bitterly. "And we can be sure Rumpelstiltskin's motive is anti-war pure."

15.

The fall of 1968 was all in a rush with the richness of red and gold and new workloads. Ti-Loup and Cap were both taking two grad-school courses as well as working full-time. Ti-Loup had a heavy teaching schedule as an adjunct, four courses at three different institutions. Adjuncts are the serfs of the academic world and Ti-Loup was on subsistence-level pay. He spent his waking hours either in front of a class or traveling from one institution to another. He introduced himself to his students as Patrick McVie, though his pay checks came under his legal name. Since college administrations pay about as much attention to adjuncts as to ants, no one noticed the difference. On Saturdays, he worked as a butcher.

Lilith Jardine took on a full-time position at the Boston Museum of Fine Arts, also at an income level that was excessively modest. She put in ten extra hours per week as an unpaid intern at the Fogg because it was a pleasure she could not bear to give up.

The Cabots invited both Lilith and Vanderbilt for Christmas dinner. Vanderbilt had already accepted an invitation from the McVies who indicated that Lilith was also welcome.

"I would feel like an intruder," she said. "I only met McVie once and they are all still in mourning. I just think I'd make them uncomfortable."

"So," Vanderbilt said. "You don't want to spend Christmas with me."

"You know I want to spend Christmas with you. This would be simple if we went to the Cabots."

"I can't do that. You could turn the Cabots down."

"I can't do that without an explanation they would understand. And I can't leave your mother alone. She's invited me too. So what I've decided is this. I'll come to Christmas Eve mass at St Ann's with you, then I'll take the overnight Greyhound to Manhattan. I'll sleep on the bus and get there in time to have Christmas dinner with your mother. That's something the Cabots will understand."

"Melusine!" the countess said. "What a joy it is to see you again."

"*Ma marreine.*" The two women embraced in formal French style, three times, though lips really touched cheeks. Really touched. They held each other.

"I am not weeping," the countess said, wiping her cheeks. "I have an allergic reaction to the dust in the heating ducts. I must tell you, Melusine, I did not at all like that brash American who drove you down here in the summer."

"I don't like him either, and I don't trust him. I apologize for foisting him on you."

"I'm glad I was able to bundle him off so quickly with my vulgar young relative-by-marriage. Now we will have a proper French Christmas. Foie Gras and sauterne. Christmas simply isn't Christmas without *foie gras*. Tell me, do you see my son ever?"

"I went to midnight Mass with him last night. He had your rosary—the pearls and the jade—in his pocket. I watched him pass the beads through his fingers."

"He goes to Mass?"

"Every week."

"Then he is in God's hands. That is enough. Will you excuse me?" Although the sound was muffled with towels, Cap could hear stifled weeping from the bathroom.

16.

There were two days in 1969 that Cap was forever after to think of as the Days of Extreme and Catastrophic Weather. One was in late January, mid-winter, the day of the blizzard; the other was in June, high summer, hurricane season, a day of torrential rain and gale-force winds.

On the day of the blizzard there were radio alerts throughout Cambridge and Boston. All places of business were dismissing employees early. All classes were cancelled. The plows were out, but most roads except for the Massachusetts Turnpike were close to impassable. Taxis and cars were buried under snow drifts and tow trucks were unable to reach them. Some subway lines were still running but all trains were delayed. Anyone who had cross-country skis, snow shoes, sleds or toboggans used them on the streets. Temporary shelters were being set up in churches and schools. Power was out in huge swathes of the city and many phone lines were down, and yet Cap's phone rang in her office at the museum.

"I'm still on campus at Harvard," Ti-Loup said. "My class has been canceled. Can you get home?"

"The Green Line's not running," Cap said. "But I'm planning to walk to Park Street and take the Red Line from there. I've heard the Red Line's still running."

"In that case, I'll wait for you at Harvard Square. Bottom of the subway stairs."

"It's going to take me a while to get there."

"I'll wait. I've got something important to tell you."

This was the way Cap remembered it. When they came above ground at the subway stop in Harvard Square, all the traffic was stalled. The whole world seemed astonishingly silent below its thick blanket of white. The snow in Harvard Yard was almost up to their knees. They pushed through it and their boots made a kind of surf with white powder rising in graceful arcs on each side like cresting waves. Cap laughed. "Sort of like crossing the White Sea, not the Red," she said. "The Parting of the Snowy Swell. Poussin painted the other one, the Israelites and the Egyptians, but I don't know what he'd do with all this white."

"I've enlisted," Ti-Loup announced abruptly. "Infantry. I leave for Fort Bragg next week."

It could have been the blowing snow. It could have been the tea-cup of the Yard, always an echo chamber with its red brick buildings huddling close and hovering like anxious parents. It could have been an auditory and optical illusion that Memorial Church sighed and inclined its spire in shock and sorrow. For whatever reason, Cap was snow-blind and snow-deaf. She could not see Ti-Loup. All she heard was a muffled reverberation, not intelligible.

"I couldn't hear you," she said. "What did you say?"

There was another day, the day of the exchanges, not marked in any calendar or diary but occurring somewhere between the two extreme-weather days. This was the day of White Magic, the day of relics and talismanic objects, the day when the anguished know they have reached the end of the line, the day they accept sorcery as the last best hope even as they are incapable of belief. This day replayed itself so endlessly and in so many surreal forms in dreams and nightmares, that Cap was never quite certain where it had taken place.

"Have you told your mother?" Cap asked.

"No. I don't intend to. You have my permission to tell her only after I'm shipped out."

"This is senseless," Cap said. "This is utterly senseless. How is this going to help the McVies? If you're killed, it will be just one more weight for them to bear. The guilt will crush them."

"It will prove to them that they're not alone," Ti-Loup said. "It will comfort them. Their son had a friend who was willing to die for him."

Cap found herself pummeling his chest. "What about me?" she demanded. "Who's going to comfort me?"

"I'm sure Cabot will step into the breach."

"How dare you! How dare you! This is a stupid kind of suicide, completely useless. You want to get yourself killed. You do, don't you? Will that bring back McVie or Ti-Christophe?"

"Their blood won't be on my hands. I can't live with their blood on my hands."

Cap pounded his chest. "You fucking narcissist! This is so senseless. You want your blood on *my* hands, on McVie's parents' hands. If you're killed or wounded, I'll never forgive you. And if you live I'll never speak to you again."

They must have gone back to Cap's studio apartment for ongoing battle and drinks because she did remember yanking open the drawer of her dresser with such force that it smashed its brake moldings and crashed to the floor. There was a shimmery spill of trinkets and photographs, among them the rosary of lapis-lazuli beads on a silver thread. Cap threw the beads at Ti-Loup. "Throttle yourself with these," she shouted. "They might keep you alive, but if they do, I still won't ever speak to you again, you selfish self-preoccupied self-destructive blue-dress boy who wets himself."

In the hollow aftermath of her curse, she could not stop trembling. Ti-Loup wrapped the rosary around his wrist and stood looking out the window at the city.

"I didn't mean that," Cap said.

"You know what *will* keep me safe?" Ti-Loup said. "*These* will." He reached under his shirt and pulled up a ball chain with two dog tags attached. "And if they don't, they'll make sense of what I'm doing. McVie's parents had copies of his dog-tags made from the one the military sent back. You know, they leave one on the body for identification and send the other one back to the family. I promised them that this time, both tags will come back, and if they don't… then at least they will know that his death has been honored." And then Ti-Loup reached into a pocket. He extracted a delicate tracery of pearls and jade. He did not throw the rosary at Cap. He pulled her angry hands toward him and cupped them and spilled the beads into them. "Keep these in memory of me," he said.

In the eyes of the military, Cap had no standing as next-of-kin, and on the day of notification, in hurricane season, most of the power lines and phone lines along the entire east coast were down. Flooding was widespread. Bridges were swept away.

Even so, even though the phone call from the countess did not reach her until two days later, Cap knew the moment when it happened. She was in the courtyard of the Fogg and nobody else was in sight but she felt a blow on the back of her head. She lurched forward. She managed to steady herself. She knew. Her legs would not hold. She huddled down on the slate courtyard slabs, her back against the stone wall.

The Ice Age had already set in.

"You're shivering," someone said. "It must be a fever."

Someone brought a shawl and covered her. Mrs. Cabot was

454

called and arrived with a limousine. Certain things Cap remembered: the beautiful Cabot bedroom on Commonwealth Avenue; Simon sitting on the edge of her bed, holding her hand; Mrs. Cabot arranging a month's leave from the museum; McVie's mother visiting and weeping.

She remembered the phone conversation with the countess. "Melusine," the countess said, but then could not speak.

"I already know, *ma marreine*. I already know. I don't have any details, but I know."

"A letter was delivered," the countess said, or tried to say. "Hand-delivered. Two officers."

Cap remembered that first she made a decision to return to work and to return to her own apartment but found she could not sleep there. The pressure of emptiness was too great, the absence too dark a presence. She felt crowded and jostled. Memories flew up like starlings from whatever she touched.

Perhaps she managed a few more weeks at the museum. Those weeks were foggy. Halfway through a task she would be unable to remember why she was doing it. She decided to return to New York, and the Goldbergs came for her and tended her in their apartment for days, maybe for weeks? She was not sure for how long. Mostly she sat in the tranquil courtyard of their building except for when, daily, she visited the penthouse on Fifth Avenue.

The concierge shook his head sadly. "The countess never leaves the building," he said. "I'll call the housekeeper and let her know you are on your way up."

The countess was wearing black. She seemed smaller each day. Our Lady of Sorrows, Cap thought. Two centuries back, she had been painted by Philippe de Champagne, a mother in mourning who had endured for years the mockery of the court, who had waited too long for the son that history snatched from her. The countess held in her hands and on her lap a letter which she would not let go. It was embossed and on ivory parchment. *Missing in Action,* it said.

BOOK V
DAYBORO

1.

During an Ice Age, life-forms do continue to exist though they mutate. They adapt. They become something other than what they once were. If they don't adapt, they die—they die out—and mass extinctions occur. The evidence for expunged forms of primordial life is known from fossils in Arctic and Antarctic ice cores, as well as in rock formations that were once part of the ocean floor. Trilobites, for instance, the first marine arthropods, more or less had the planet to themselves in the Early Cambrian period, many millions of years ago, but were utterly wiped out, effaced, in the Permian period, first of the Ice Ages, also millions of years ago. Yet the exoskeletal remains of trilobites are everywhere, *everywhere*, found by the hundreds, by the thousands, found by paleontologists with rock hammers and found by children clambering over rocky shores.

During the Pleistocene Era, when the last great Ice Age gouged its savage glacial invasion of lush temperate regions, the dinosaurs and the wooly mammoths ceased to be, but more modest life forms survived. They changed in appearance and habitat and habit, but they survived.

So it had been with the Goldbergs, who survived tectonic upheaval and a cataclysm that was a hair's breadth away from mass extinction.

So it was with Lilith Jardine who survived displacement and

erasure of kin.

After Ti-Loup's vanishing in Vietnam, after the Cabots and Simon had sustained her for the first week, she had returned to her own apartment and folded herself into pupal form, compact, minimalist, eclipsed. She pleated her arms and legs inside the cocoon of her blankets. Mrs. Cabot arranged her leave from the museum. Cap unplugged her phone. She did not collect mail from her box in the lobby. She did not open her door. She went into a dormant phase. When she ate, which was infrequently and sparely, she worked her way through the canned food stored in her pantry. She drank water.

And then, perhaps because all the canned food was gone, perhaps because September branches were tapping against her window and the brilliant reds and golds sent a signal, sent some sort of quickening current through her veins, then her body emerged from its chrysalis. She crawled out of her bedroom. She called the Cabots, she accepted their dinner invitation, she attended a concert with Simon. She called the Goldbergs, she accepted an invitation to stay with them until she found a Manhattan apartment. She moved back to New York. She obtained a position at Sotheby's—in Appraisals and Valuations—working by day, taking M.A. courses by night, increasing her expertise in the painting and furniture of the French Baroque. She read voraciously. She left no spaces in her waking day for the intrusion of non-work-related thought.

Her training and duties involved, first and foremost, verification of the authenticity of a work. She became a detective. She developed an instinct for the subtle cues and clues to forgeries and erroneous attributions, though she also learned that experts can be brilliantly fooled. She was trained to provide fair-market assessments for collectors, for buyers and sellers. She calculated tax write-offs for charitable donations to museums and insurance valuations for loans or thefts. She discovered that a huge part of the global traffic in art, even the legal part, was secret. Sotheby's (and Bonhams and Christie's) were required to be and were lavishly rewarded for being, in a sense, high-class pimps for connoisseurs and collectors. Their task was to connect sellers who wished to sell anonymously with private buyers who wanted their acquisitions kept untracked. The paintings and antiques so traded never appeared in catalogues or auction lots, and it was rare for sellers actually to meet the buyers, but when Lilith was the go-between, she did see the art that changed hands.

She would have been willing to live on bread and water for that privilege alone. She did render that privilege—the act of seeing the works that changed owners so clandestinely—as a benefit and a donation to the Lilith Foundation.

She began to travel to places where art was privately bought and sold for fabulous prices and where lives were worth nothing. In covert meetings, via covert word-of-mouth networks, she gathered photographs and eye-witness testimony from the underside of cities where wealthy collectors lived. Few could bear to look at the photographs or read the accounts she was given. For newspapers, even those with major international clout, the images were too disturbing to publish. Departments of State and of national security (in numerous countries, including her own) saw them as a risk to delicate diplomatic balancing acts and confiscated the evidence when they could. Lilith developed ingenious methods of smuggling: slipping her photographs between glued tourist postcards; interleafing eye-witness accounts between the pages of paperback thrillers or even between the sheets of documentation on the provenance of certain works of art. All evidence which got past dragnets and obstacles went into an archive. There it was kept for a future when perhaps such horrors would no longer be possible or where generations yet to come might read missing chapters of family history.

Lilith had her own studio apartment on the upper west side and from her windows she could see the massy crowns of trees in Central Park. She would sit in the dark and watch the night sky and run a string of pearls and jade through her fingers. She thought of these beads as trilobites, the exoskeletal remains of Ti-Loup. She would picture her own lapis-lazuli beads floating in a rice paddy somewhere, or buried in a mush of blood and mud, or wrapped like a tourniquet on the wrist-bone of Ti-Loup in a shallow grave, or perhaps worn as a dazzling trophy round the neck of some village woman or little girl. She always hoped it might be a little girl. She began to embellish that hope. She began to imagine a life for that little girl.

Although she considered the idea utterly irrational and absurd, she knew she did believe, on some embarrassingly atavistic level, that both rosaries (the lapis lazuli-and-silver, the pearls-and-jade) had totemic power. She could see the little girl making her way to Saigon, the rosary under her T-shirt always hidden. The little girl would also have in her possession two other secret treasures, two sets of dog tags removed from bones she had stumbled upon while foraging for rice in a paddy long after the harvest. She would have been fearful of theft before she could exchange her finds for food. She would seek refuge in a bombed-out convent. She would be taken in by nuns and given shelter and food and an education. One day, one year, she would trace down the meaning of the beads and the dog tags. She would find the Vanderbilts and the McVies. She would find Lilith. She would even find Cap.

One day, Cap and that little girl would meet. Cap visualized the meeting in 1001 different places and different ways. The fantasy gave her peace. She would fall asleep inventing new chapters and the little girl would be waiting for her in dreams.

Often Simon Cabot visited from Boston and Lilith's spirit would lift like a small bird in an updraft of pleasure. This took her by surprise every time. She did not expect felicity to last and she was sure some penalty would follow. They would dine at an excellent restaurant of Simon's choosing, go to a concert or the theater, and then he would stay for the night. His visits made her almost happy.

"We could live together," he would murmur into her pillow.

"I know. I know we could, I know that. Some day. But not yet. I'd be no good for you yet. I'm no good to anyone right now."

"Why don't you let me be the judge of that?"

"Because you aren't in a position to know how lost I am. You see my functioning mask. Behind that, there's nothing. I don't feel anything at all. I'm in deep freeze."

"Let me thaw you out."

"I can't give up Sotheby's. It makes functioning possible."

"Sotheby's has an office in Boston now."

"I travel too much," she said. "And I can't give up the Lilith Foundation either. When I'm doing that work I travel to places... well, you know, it's never certain that I'll come back. I've been detained at borders. I've had my passport confiscated for days at a time."

"I have uncles and cousins in the foreign service and the State Department," Simon reminded. "We would always get you out. Of course it goes without saying that we... my family... we wish you wouldn't do this kind of thing. Not because we don't admire your courage, but it's a grey zone, isn't it? a legal and political shadow zone ..."

"Yes. You see? I'm not a good bet for a Cabot."

"Cabots have never resisted dangerous bets. All my money's on you. And I'll wait."

During the Ice Age, the countess found it harder to adapt. She would not, could not, leave the Vanderbilt penthouse, the interior of which had been refashioned to resemble the Chateau de Boissy. The countess sat in her salon in such a way that she could always see the Philippe de Champaigne painting in her marble foyer. Her eyes rested not on the Virgin, nor on the sorrowful queen, nor on her vigorous squirming firstborn, Louis XIV, who was about to grab scepter and crown from the Virgin's hands. She gazed at the infant Duc d'Orleans in his blue smock, frail little wisp of a royal baby brother. She was waiting for him to look at her, to step out of the painting. The embossed letter from military headquarters was always either under her pillow or in her hands.

"I don't know how to pray for him, Melusine," she would say. "I don't know if I should pray for his life or for his soul."

Sometimes the countess ate the food the housekeeper brought on a tray, but more and more often she did not. Sometimes she drank water or tea, more often not. From time to time, she had to be hospitalized. She was on anti-depressants. Lilith sat with her for at least an hour every evening when she could, when she was not traveling. Sometimes the countess would blink rapidly as though waking from sleep. "You should not be here," she would say. "You have your own life. Go away."

"You sat with my father," Lilith said, "when he was dying."

"I'm not dying," the countess said.

"Good."

"But I'd like to. I just have to know what happened first. They are talking about POW exchanges now. Bones are being returned. That's what I'm waiting for."

Lilith wondered if her own mother had clung to life, waiting for news.

"If my own mother were still alive," she said. "If I had ever known my own mother, this is what I would want to do while she was waiting for news. I would have wanted to stay with her."

Sometimes the Goldbergs visited. Sometimes the countess recognized them, sometimes not. "You remind me of a painting," she said once, quite suddenly, to Myriam. "Not the kind I collect. Someone modern. Someone Jewish, I think. Can't remember the name."

"Modigliani, perhaps?"

"Yes, that's it. I picked it up for a song but I'm not sure what happened to it."

"You returned it to us," Myriam said. "Would you like to see it again?"

"No. No. I never thought much of it. It's not the kind of thing I collect."

From time to time, because she had stopped eating and drinking, the countess was hospitalized. At such times, her estranged husband would return from the Hamptons or from Europe and take up residence again on Fifth Avenue, often accompanied by his nephew and his nephew's wife. The family lawyers would be summoned. It was the opinion of the lawyers, of the estranged husband and his nephew and the nephew's wife, that the countess—for her own self-protection and wellbeing—should be committed.

This opinion surfaced on the society page of the *New York Post*. The Vanderbilt nephew was quoted. "My aunt is no longer capable of taking care of herself," he said. "But that is only one part of the problem. The penthouse belongs to my uncle and since my cousin was tragically lost in Vietnam, it will eventually belong to me. But it is a deteriorating asset. My uncle is a generous man and his marriage-separation contract permits my aunt to live there for as long as she is capable of taking care of the property and of herself. She is no longer capable of either."

The brief article in the *New York Post*, shown to the countess by a nurse in her hospital ward, had the effect of an adrenaline shot. The countess rallied, ate, drank, returned to Fifth Avenue, hired a new housekeeper and a chef, hosted a dinner party or two. Then, sadly, she began to sink back into an agoraphobic and anorexic state. The cycle continued for several years until the ice caps began to melt and the dawn of a new era—interglacial in geological terms—shot the first warm rays of its sunrise through the gloom.

The thaw began when Lilith Jardine added the name of the countess to a mailing list. Lilith herself had been added to that same list by Mrs. McVie. When Lilith received her own first copy of the *MIA-POW Newsletter*—edited by the families of missing and captured soldiers—she also received a brief handwritten note. *Never give up hope*, it said. *We pray for Vanderbilt every night, as well as for the soul of our son. I remember you fondly and pray for you. Sincerely, Vivien McVie.*

At first apathetically, and then avidly, the countess began to read the anguished testimonials and letters. She wrote to other families. For the first time in her life, she was writing to the wives of peach farmers in Georgia whose husbands or sons had never come home, to coal miners in West Virginia who had sent their boys to war, to the sons of missing fathers in Minnesota, to women in Utah who did not know if they were widows or not.

Sometimes she was so eager to receive their letters in response to her own that she would take the elevator down to the lobby. She would open her own mailbox. She would chat briefly with the concierge. When the letter from Decatur, Georgia arrived in August 1976, she was at first unable to read it because of the trembling in her hands, the fog in her eyes. She sat with the unread letter in her lap and gazed out the window at nothing. She did not know how many hours passed before she could focus, before her mind could translate the fog of words, and even then her mind skimmed and skipped and she had to read the letter three times before she could take it in.

Dear Mrs. Vanderbilt,

I saw an article about Vietnam MIA's that are still unaccounted for. There were photographs of the missing and one was your son, Gwynne Patrice Vanderbilt, officially declared MIA, presumed dead, in July 1969. I recognized him from the photograph. I wanted to tell you that I was in the same platoon, the same squad, as your son, though we were always confused about his name....

Hours passed before the countess was capable of making a phone call. She had to leave a message on the answering machine. "Melusine," she said, her voice trembling. "Gwynne Patrice is alive."

A discreet announcement appeared in the *New York Times*. There was to be a thanksgiving mass in St Patrick's Cathedral, a private service of gratitude to the Virgin for the miraculous preservation of the life of the Vanderbilt heir. The countess intended that her expression of gratitude be public but that the mass itself would be private. Unfortunately, the words "Vanderbilt heir" predictably caught the attention of the *New York Post* and other tabloids. Journalists took note and to their astonishment the heir's mother, caught off guard and innocent of the ways of the press, was initially willing to take phone calls. She was exuberant. As proof of a miracle, she read them parts of a letter she had received from a fellow member of her son's platoon, and these extracts were quoted in the *Post* and were reproduced *ad infinitum* in newspapers across the city and across the country and around the world. *I wanted to let you know that your son might not have died in Vietnam, that he might have left there in a fishing boat...He may have drowned or he may be still alive, and if he didn't return home there's a chance he's living in Australia and doesn't remember who he is...*

That particular extract showed up in the *Sydney Morning Her-*

ald and the Melbourne *Age*.

The heir's mother was reported to be in a highly excitable state.

The heir's father was located, with some difficulty, at a resort in Switzerland where he was staying with a young female companion. He was asked to comment and was rather more subdued than his wife. "No one could be happier," he said, "if it should turn out that my son is alive, but we have to face the fact that the chances are remote, the evidence slight. My wife has a history of extreme emotional fragility and turbulence. The news that our son was Missing in Action in Vietnam devastated her. It is not surprising that she will grasp at any straw of hope with all the desperate intensity that has been the sad signature of her life. I ask the press to treat her gently. The last thing I want is for her to fall back into an abyss of depression that requires hospitalization again. Or even, God forbid, that it might be necessary to have her committed."

There were some reports that the letter from Decatur was a hoax.

On radio talk shows, at least eighteen people, scattered across the country, confessed that they had been offered money by a person unknown to write to the countess and to pose as a fellow member of her son's platoon. Those who confessed to the fraudulent letters for pay came from ten different states. Since the countess declined to display the precious original letter, there was no hard evidence that a letter with a Decatur GA postmark existed. Further investigation revealed that the *confessional* letters were hoaxes and that the tabloids had paid for them.

Because of these contradictory and tantalizing titbits, the tabloids buzzed and several hundred people—most of them total strangers to the Vanderbilt family—attended the Mass at St Patrick's. A number of journalists, mainly from the tabloids but also a stringer from *Vogue*, attended too.

The Goldbergs attended, as did former Vanderbilt housekeeper

Shannay and Castano the chauffeur. The Vanderbilt father, still in Switzerland, did not attend, but Celise Vanderbilt, the wife of his nephew did. The nephew himself, cousin of the possibly still-living heir, did not attend.

Lilith Jardine attended the thanksgiving mass and sat with the countess. She kept one hand in the pocket of her jacket and fingered the pearl and jade beads. She had never let the countess know they were in her possession or that she had given her own rosary in exchange. She was not sure what the countess might feel about this. She was not sure how she herself felt about anything. She did not, in fact, feel anything much at all. She was thankful that the countess was vibrant again but the degree of that vibrancy disturbed her. She feared a crash.

"You remember, *ma marreine*," she said gently, "how he would never answer our letters? If he is alive, even if he does not have amnesia, he does not want to be found."

"It does not matter," the countess assured her. "All that matters is that the Virgin has given me a sign. He did not die in Vietnam. I do not need him to come back. I do not even need him to make contact. It is enough that he is alive and that is something I *know* in here." She placed her right hand over her heart.

Lilith hoped that this benign mood of the countess would not flutter. She hoped it would build a nest and stay still. She asked herself: do I believe he is alive? She could feel nothing but doubt. She also asked herself: if he is alive, is that enough? Almost enough, she thought. But if she were still able to pray she would have added a rider: May he be at peace with himself.

After the Mass, Celise Vanderbilt embraced the countess on the cathedral steps. Photographers captured the moment. "What we must do," Celise told them, "is expend every possible effort to track the heir down. The happiness of Lady Isabelle depends on it. I can promise you, we will find him."

"Melusine," the countess whispered, "do not let that woman touch me again."

A cathedral usher thrust a small deckle-edged ivory envelope into Lilith's hands. Inside was a card with a gold-leaf border and embossed gilt lettering.

Celise Vanderbilt

is pleased to invite you to a small private reception at the
Waldorf-Astoria
immediately following the Mass at St Patrick's Cathedral
to celebrate the survival of
Gwynne Patrice de la Vallière Vanderbilt

The countess was also handed an invitation. Before she opened it, she brushed the swarm of photographers away with an irritable and imperious sweep of her arm. *As flies to wanton boys*, Lilith could not help thinking, *are we to the tabloids; they squash us for their sport.*

"Ignore them," the countess said. "They have more ink than we have blood." She swayed a little with shock when she read the card. "Such audacity, Melusine," she said, trembling. "Such vulgarity."

"Tacky," Lilith said. "I think that's the right word. Nevertheless, should we go? Perhaps we should. There will be supercilious comment in the *New York Post* if we don't."

"Also if we do," the countess said. "I would not want to be in the same room as anyone who reads the *New York Post*." She hailed a cab. "I'm going home."

"I think I'll go to the reception," Lilith said, "just to keep an ear to the ground."

At the Waldorf-Astoria, in the private room reserved for the reception, Lilith saw TV cameras and tabloid stringers chatting each other up. Celise greeted her effusively inside a halo of flashbulbs going off like the Fourth of July. "I've known the heir since he was fourteen," Celise told the cameras. She spoke softly, implying intimacy. "I thought of him as a sweet little brother. When he was a boarder at prep school, he used to spend the holidays with us, Thanksgiving, Christmas, birthdays." Leaning close to Lilith's ear, she murmured: "He was refusing to read or answer his mother's letters back then."

"Really?"

"Should I tell them that?" Celise whispered.

Lilith smiled. "I'm sure there's no stopping you."

Something in her tone caused Celise to pause, if only briefly. "Allow me to introduce Lilith Jardine," she told the cameras. "She's an appraisal expert with Sotheby's." She dropped her voice. "I probably shouldn't tell you this but her father was the gardener for the Vanderbilt chateau in France. The countess took her in as a childhood playmate for the heir whom we now hope is alive and well. Isn't that an interesting journey? From the bean patch to the baroque?"

This was, in point of fact, the very headline used by the *Post* above the front page photograph of Mrs. Celise Vanderbilt with the childhood friend of the long-lost heir. *From Bean Patch to Baroque,* the caption read.

Lilith sought, as politely as possible, to extricate herself from Celise and from the housefly-eyes of the cameras. Someone tapped her on the shoulder and offered escape, pulling her through an exit door. "Thank God," she said. "I was having trouble breathing in there." She leaned back against the hallway wall, her eyes closed. "You have no idea how much I wanted to get away."

"You have no idea how much I wanted to get you away."

Lilith opened her eyes. "I don't believe this. What on earth are you doing here, Lucifer? Were you in the church?"

"No. I was here, organizing this little event for Celise."

"How do you know her?"

"Don't you remember? Summer '68. You introduced us. Or rater, you introduced me to the countess and the countess introduced me to her niece."

"She's not a niece."

"I did already know that McVie was Vanderbilt, by the way, before I even drove you to New York. Give me some credit. And we three did take a summer course together. I'd like to flatter myself you couldn't forget."

"It's not high on my memory list, but I do remember you stood me up at the Oyster Bar."

"Greatest mistake of my life."

"I doubt that."

"These days," Lucifer said, "we have clients in common, you and I. Some of your sellers and buyers invest with me. Didn't you know?"

"I didn't," Lilith said. "But don't take it personally. I'm interested only in art, not the art business."

"Sotheby's *is* the art business."

"True. But I work in appraisals not auctions or sales. I see a lot of extraordinary paintings and that's all that interests me."

Lucifer laughed. "Who are you kidding? I know exactly what you're actually doing. I have connections, you should know."

"Really? Why should I know?"

"Because, like McVie, or Vanderbilt McVie, you blunder into things you don't understand. You can set off an avalanche of damage without the faintest idea of what you've done."

"Fortunately the world has straight arrows like you to protect it."

"You want some inside information on that letter from Georgia? The former member of Vanderbilt's platoon is covering his ass. He got himself into Walter Reed because of a car crash, driving while drunk, not because of injuries in Vietnam. He was well paid for the letter. Way too convenient that the sole eye-witness account to the fishing-boat fantasy died before the sob story was invented. You can't seriously believe this ludicrous shipwreck-amnesia theory."

"I can't. No. But I'm happy the countess believes."

"Wants to believe."

"Yes, wants to believe."

"And so do you."

"Wrong as usual, Lucifer."

"Not my name anymore. And you can't fool me. I know you, Lilith."

"You do not know me, Lucifer. You never have. Not even remotely."

"If I were a betting man—and actually I am a betting man—but I only make bets that I can't lose. If I were a *normal* betting man, I'd bet that if McVie-Vanderbilt is actually alive and well somewhere on the planet—and I concede he might be, because he was the kind who'd turn into a deserter as soon as the going got rough—I bet that the minute he sends you some signal, you'll go running. And here's another bet, and this is the kind I *do* usually make because I have certain sources of information not available to all and sundry. If you keep on going the way you're going, you are not going to die in your bed or on American soil. This jaunting around the world as an art appraiser is not invisible, you know. You're playing with fire."

"Thank you, Lucifer, for that warning. I'll keep it in mind."

2.

Simon Cabot showed up in Lilith's office at Sotheby's waving a gilt-embossed card. *Celise Vanderbilt is pleased to invite you....* "What does this mean?"

"She sent you an invitation too?"

"No. It was mailed to my parents but it isn't even postmarked until the day of the event. I mean, it's an invitation to something that's already taken place. What does it mean?"

"It means Celise Vanderbilt would love to make your family aware of her social status."

"I mean *this. To celebrate the survival of....* Is Vanderbilt alive?"

Lilith sighed. "We don't know. It seems there's a chance, but it's remote. Someone from Vanderbilt's platoon sent the countess a letter but it might be a hoax."

"How long have you known about this chance?"

"We don't know anything really."

"Why didn't you call me?"

"There was nothing reliable to tell."

"Who is this Celise person? Is she Vanderbilt's aunt?"

"No blood relation. She's married to his cousin. "

"Is she the one who used to be his father's mistress?"

"She's the one. Then she was his uncle's mistress, then she married the uncle's son. The uncle's dead now."

Cabot laughed. "That woman knows what she's doing. If the

473

uncle's dead, then when Vanderbilt's father dies, the cousin will be the heir. He's not going to want Vanderbilt found alive and nor is his wife. This reception is about staking her claim. Staking it publicly."

"She has nothing to worry about. If Vanderbilt is alive, he's not going to want to be found."

"The question is, Do *you* want to find him alive?"

"I don't know. The last time we saw each other I was furious with him for enlisting. I said things that should never be said. Things that can't be unsaid. I'd be ashamed to see him again."

"He won't feel the same way."

"Oh, you don't know Vanderbilt. Although you should. When he cuts ties, he cuts them absolutely and permanently. Don't you remember?"

"So where does this leave us?" Cabot wanted to know. "*Us*. Does this make any difference to us?"

"I think it might," Lilith said. "Yes, I think it might. I hope I'll stop having nightmares about how he died. I would like to believe he's alive somewhere, and happy, and doesn't want to be found. I think perhaps I'll begin to feel free."

"In that case, why don't you come up to Boston for the weekend? My mother asked me to ask you. She's hoping for an intimate family dinner on Saturday night."

"I accept."

"I think Commonwealth Avenue is the most beautiful street in Boston," Lilith said. She was gazing from the Cabot windows onto the wide grassy median strip with its graceful trees, its civic statues, its footpaths, its joggers and dog-walkers and its elegant elderly Bostonian Bluebloods moving in slow and stately fashion with the aid of canes.

"Why don't you come back to the Fogg?" Mrs. Cabot asked.

"Oh, you know I love the Fogg. But I have to do what I'm

doing with the Lilith Foundation and that requires an art-auction house with a global reach. I know you don't approve of what I'm doing but it's my way of feeling that my parents are close to me."

"My primary concern is utterly selfish," Mrs. Cabot said. "I hope to have grandchildren and I don't want my son to be hurt. I don't want him to pine away because he keeps hoping. And that's what is happening, you know. Of course, we loved Vanderbilt too, so I understand. If he's alive, if he's found, can I ask how you feel about him?"

"Honestly, even for myself, I can't unravel my feelings for him. We were children together. We grew up on the same estate. We had the same tutor, the same classroom, day after day for seven years. We more or less shared the same mother (who was his) and the same father (who was mine) and the same older brother (mine) whom we both adored."

"Where is your brother?"

"He died. Vanderbilt and I watched him die. I think we never recovered. I think we never learned how to live separate lives. At least, I didn't."

"Let me show you something," Mrs. Cabot said. "It's in my own study. It's quite a small painting."

Lilith studied the pastoral scene: a pale almost bleached sky, a horizon of trees turning gold, village houses with violet shadows, in the foreground the stubble of harvested fields.

"Is it a Monet?" she asked.

"It is not a Monet, but it *was* painted in his garden at Giverny. It is by Lilla Cabot Perry who spent ten summers at the turn of the century in Giverny. She became a close friend of Monet. In fact, she was his first and fiercest champion in this country. She introduced the Impressionists to these shores. Some of her work is in the Fogg."

"I do remember them. But you know, since my main interests

are centuries earlier—"

"I know. There's a reason I'm telling you this. Lilla's father was a Cabot and a distinguished Boston surgeon. Her mother was a Lowell. Her parents were ardent abolitionists and they hid runaway slaves before and during the Civil War. In the Cabot family, we prefer orthodoxy and decorum, I won't pretend otherwise. But the family has also had members who broke the law for reasons of conscience. We have embraced them. I wish you wouldn't do what you are doing, but I admire you for it."

"Thank you," Lilith said.

"Lilla Cabot Perry and Henry James were children together," Mrs. Cabot said. "Quite close when they were young. In the long run, it didn't turn out to mean much. Lilla Cabot married Thomas Perry, one of Henry James's best friends, and was very happy."

3.

Shortly after Vanderbilt's hypothetical and epistolary resurrection, Lilith and Simon Cabot began to share two weekends per month. On the first weekend, Simon flew to New York. On the third weekend, Lilith flew north. They left clothing and underwear and toiletries in each other's apartments. When Simon was not living in his lab at MIT (a practice which he vehemently denied but of which he was frequently accused), he was globe-trotting. He presented conference papers from Berkeley to Beijing. Lilith's presence was requested for art appraisals in Europe, the Middle East, Africa, Asia. There were compensations for this manic and dangerously jetlagged life. Their weekend trysts were sexually electric.

Lilith loved working for Sotheby's though she grew increasingly nervous each time she linked an appraisal to the gathering of politically dangerous data. Her store of dark knowledge—of the horrific things that human beings are capable of inflicting on other human beings—was growing inexorably and invading her dreams. She found she could not always accept assignments. Each year she made fewer side trips. She had to counter her sense of dread with transfusions of optimism and a belief that there were some moments in time and some places where horror could not intrude.

Every year, she spent Thanksgiving in New York (midday dinner with the Goldbergs; evening supper with the countess) and

Christmas with the Cabots in Boston. Over time, she and Simon adjusted their schedules. They traveled together. They took the countess out to dinner every week. When she averted her gaze from humankind's worst behaviors, Cap herself felt serene. On weeknights, when she was alone, she would sit in the dark and gaze up at the night sky. The pearl rosary passed through her fingers. At each jade meditation point she thought of the little girl in Vietnam who might be fingering lapis lazuli beads.

Ti-Loup and Ti-Christophe and her father had all faded into something like the afterglow of a sunset. Only happy memories came back: Ti-Loup climbing out of the chateau window and climbing back in; Ti-Christophe demonstrating the channels where the boning knife could slip; Papa presiding over roasted rabbit; Father JG explaining the Field of the Cloth of Gold; a shared First Communion.

And then lightning struck.

In October 1994, a few days before Halloween, Lawrence Gwynne Vanderbilt died of a heart attack. In coitus. There was a brief tactful obituary in the *New York Times*. There was much more titillating detail on the front page of the *New York Post*.

The countess called. "Do you think we should try to find Gwynne Patrice, Melusine? He inherits everything now."

"Even if we could find him, I don't think he would be interested, *ma marraine*."

"But if he doesn't remember? Don't you think we should make some effort to let him know? Maybe there will be people who recognize him, who can tell him who he is."

"If it matters to you," Cap said carefully, but even as she said it she felt anxiety, "if it matters to you, you could ask your lawyer to contact the press in Australia. He could place notices in the newspapers." Cap saw that a storm was lashing the trees in Central Park. A fusillade of October leaves strafed her windows and rattled like hail. She felt under sudden attack. She feared what a non-response to a newsprint advertisement might do to the countess's state of mind. She feared what a response—an actual response—might do to her own state of mind.

One week later, the countess called again, this time in extreme distress. "Melusine, can you come quickly?" She sounded distraught. "I don't know what to do. Come quickly.'

"I'll come as soon as I can," Cap promised, but the countess had called her at work and it was late afternoon and rush hour and Cap was in her Greenwich Village office. On the clogged streets of Manhattan, buses were impossible in the late afternoon. So were cabs. At such times, it was faster to walk but the distance was fifty blocks, more than two miles, and Cap was tired and was wearing heels. She took the subway but the platforms were thick with commuters and the first train was packed so tightly that cramming herself into a car was not even possible. She managed to squeeze into the third train and got off at Lexington and East 68th. By the time she reached the corner of Fifth and East72nd, almost an hour had passed.

The doorman in the building on Fifth Avenue beckoned urgently. "There's been a bit of a scene, Ms Jardine," he said. "I had to call an ambulance but the countess refused to leave her apartment so they gave her a sedative. I had security escort the other lady out of the building."

"What other lady?"

"The other Mrs. Vanderbilt. She was here. It seems she has a key to the apartment and when the countess came back from her afternoon visit to the Frick, the other Mrs. Vanderbilt was in her rooms. I blame myself, but I don't know how she got to the elevators without my seeing her. I remember I had to sign for a package and she must have slipped in then. I'll call up and tell the countess you are here, but she'll still be sedated."

Cap had her own key, but she knocked first. The door opened all of two inches, the length of the interior chain. "*Ma marraine? C'est moi, Melusine.*'

"*J'arrive,*" the countess said, her voice slurred. She was slow and clumsy in unhooking the chain, but in spite of the sedative, she trembled violently. Cap locked the door and refastened the chain. She held the frail woman in her arms. She was taller now than the countess and above the other woman's head she saw them both in the great baroque mirror and saw also the painting that she had first seen as a child in the chateau.

"What happened?" she asked.

"That woman was opening the drawers in my desk. She says I have until the end of December to move out. The family lawyers will serve notice this week."

"How did she get a key?"

"My husband always had a key. He was the legal owner. And now the nephew is the legal owner and he has the key."

"I'll have the locks changed tomorrow," Cap assured her. "She won't be able to do that again. And the lawyers can't make you leave. You have a legal separation agreement. You can stay here for as long as you live."

They had moved into the salon and the countess sank into her cushioned chair. "But you see," she said sadly, "he left me no income at all. While he was alive, he paid the condominium fee and the utilities. That has stopped. I will have to sell some more paintings. I will have to try to sell the chateau."

"We can challenge your husband's nephew legally," Cap said. "I'll talk to a lawyer. If you have a legal right to stay here for as long as you live, then the necessary financial provisions must be made. Don't upset yourself. I'll look after this. Let me make you some tea."

"I think I'll have cognac," the countess said.

480

In January 1995, the Vanderbilt family lawyers sued the countess for refusing to have her son declared dead. "I will not declare him dead," the countess said firmly, "because he is not. He is living. I have proof. I have a letter from someone who was in his platoon. He did not die in Vietnam and he did not drown." But the letter was missing from her desk. "I had it in one of the secret drawers," she told Cap. "That woman has stolen it."

"I made a photocopy," Cap said, "when you first showed it to me. I'll give it to your lawyers. Don't worry."

4.

In October 1995, Cap found a message on her answering machine. *Lilith, can you call me? It's urgent. I have news that may change your life.* The voice was that of Myriam Goldberg.

A week had passed before Cap received the message. She had been in London, bringing together a seller and a buyer whose transaction was to be kept beneath the art market's radar. When she returned to New York, she listened to all her messages and returned Myriam's call first. "What is it?" she asked.

"A package has arrived for you. It's addressed to Lilith Jardine, in care of Aaron & Myriam Goldberg. You need to come and see it as soon as you can."

"Where's it from?"

"It's about the size of a chocolate box and it's plastered with Australian stamps. There's no sender's name or address."

Cap sat in the courtyard of the Goldberg's building for some time before she could summon the courage to take the elevator to the sixth floor, and then she sat in one of their armchairs for a much longer time, the package in her lap, before she had the courage to open it. She let her eyes rest on the Modigliani painting on the Goldberg's wall.

"Years after we have lost them, things that belong to us do find their way back," Myriam said. "If we wait long enough. And sometimes people come back too."

On the back of the package was a hand-inked warning: *To be opened only by addressee. Otherwise to be destroyed.*

"Would you have done that?" Cap asked. "If you'd lost track of me?"

"I don't think so. No, I couldn't have done that. Imagine if someone had destroyed the Modigliani? But I would never have opened your package. I would have kept it in a safe deposit box."

"I think," Lilith said, "if you don't mind, I'd like to be sitting alone in your courtyard when I open this."

The parcel, the size of a chocolate box, was wrapped in coarse brown paper cross-tied with string. In the upper right quadrant there were several wildly colorful Australian stamps. One bore the stars of the Southern Cross on a cobalt field. Another showed a soft-furred aquatic animal against dark green water. The creature somewhat resembled a beaver but had a broad duck-billed mouth.

There was no return address on the package and the postmark was blurred and unclear.

Lilith pulled off the string and the brown paper. Inside was a cardboard box, *Cadbury's Old Gold Chocolates,* stuffed with tissue. The tissue was white and was scrunched into translucent layers that shivered like eggshells after the baby birds have hatched. At the heart of the nest was a cluster of beads, vividly blue, cobalt blue, strung on a silver chain. Lilith gathered the beads in her right hand and pressed them against her lips.

A woman sitting on another bench in the courtyard looked up, startled. "Are you all right?"

Lilith nodded and gave a reassuring flick of her hand.

"Well, if you're sure," the woman said uncertainly, and walked back into the lobby of the building.

Lilith had no idea how long she sat there but once the low-voltage courtyard lights came on and the sky turned dark, she thought to examine the chocolate box more closely. Under all the layers of tissue was a two-page letter, sealed in an envelope, handwritten. She knew the writing. There was no salutation, no greeting.

I don't know if this will ever reach you. I don't know where you live, which name you are using, or even if you are still alive. I don't know if the Goldbergs still live at this address but it's the only safe place I dare send because there's something I know the Goldbergs understand. They know that when you disappear from your life in order to save your life, it's essential to leave no trace. I am counting on them, and on you.

The last time I saw you, you were right about me and you were right to be angry. Expiatory suicide is exactly what I had in mind, but expiation never comes cheap and easy. I thought my past had been severed from my now as absolutely as a cleaver slices shoulder from rib. Quite literally, I had no past. It had been erased. Or perhaps I myself had erased it. Yesterday was the horizon of my memory. Beyond that, there was nothing.

My sense of smell and my hands remembered things before my brain did. I remembered the smell of fresh-slaughtered meat. Didn't know where I was or how I got there, but I worked on cattle stations and loved the life. Found out I was in the Northern Territory of Australia. On the cattle stations they kill and hang and cut their own steers and my hands remembered what to do with a boning knife.

So why am I making contact (possibly making contact?) after all these years? I'm told it's been years, but my sense of time has gone haywire. Bits and pieces come back and float away. It's like putting a jigsaw together, except the pieces won't stay where I put them. And recently, I've been rattled. I'm spooked. Suddenly people with cameras keep showing up at the local pub and asking questions about a man who doesn't exist. I'm supposed to remem-

ber him. I think I used to be him. Why and how are they asking these questions here? The pub owner and the local people don't like strangers any more than I do and they won't answer nosy questions or give me away. But I was tricked into an interview with TV cameras. I don't know where and how this interview is going to be used.

And then you began to show up in dreams. You beckon and disappear. When I follow, I'm under a bridge and you've vanished and what I see is Ti-Christophe's body. I wake in a sweat and I'm afraid to go back to sleep. Not all the dreams are nightmares. In one, you float out of an apple tree. Another time, you are roasting rabbits and when I wake I can smell them.

What came back next were names, the names on the dog tags that were too dangerous to keep, so dangerous the villagers had to destroy them. Vanderbilt and McVie. I remembered what they meant. And I remembered that I had a son and I remembered his name. I remembered Grand Loup and Father JG. Fragment by fragment, other things came back. Simon Cabot. The Modigliani painting. The Goldbergs, whose address came back in a dream. I mean that quite literally. I saw the envelopes they sent to Dryden, the ones I never opened. I will not tell you what my name is now, and the ones by which you have known me mean nothing here.

I will pretend that you want to see me and so I am sending directions.

You should fly to Brisbane, Australia. At the airport, you should rent a car and a road map and drive to Dayboro, up on the slopes of the Great Dividing Range, in a loop of the North Pine River. It will remind you of the valley of the Vienne, except for alfalfa pasture instead of vineyards and sheep and cattle instead of goats and chateaux. Dayboro is even smaller than St Gilles, though it has more churches, three churches, built not of stone but of wood. They won't last beyond the next bush fire. Each church is smaller

485

than *Grand Loup's* cottage.

There is no other way to get here except by road, some of it unpaved, much of it steep with hairpin turns. From Samford Village, on the north-west edge of Brisbane, you should take the Mount Samson Road and after thirty minutes of climbing you'll reach Dayboro. Where the Mount Samson Road ends—in a T-junction with Lacey's Creek Road—you will be facing the Dayboro Pub. It's a sprawling wooden colonial building with a wide front veranda. A massive Moreton Bay fig tree shades the veranda like a green umbrella, more than welcome under the Queensland sun. Prepare for more heat and humidity than you have ever known.

You should ask at the bar inside for the Man from Nowhere, the one who's a butcher and breeds cattle. The pub owner's a friend and he knows I'm rattled by strangers asking questions. He'll be suspicious. He'll check you out. You should say only, "He's expecting me," and you should show by way of proof the rosary (this one, the lapis-lazuli one, which by rights should be on the floor of the South China sea, and would be, except for a chain of miracles in which neither of us could possibly believe. If you are reading this letter, you will have that rosary in your hands, which could mean that both of us may have to abandon our scorn for the miraculous.)

After you've told the pub owner that I'm expecting you, you should order a beer (you should ask for whatever's on tap; you will blow my cover forever if you order wine) and you should sit at one of the tables on the veranda, under the Moreton Bay fig, until I join you. Bring no one with you and don't bring a camera. If you do, the pub owner will warn me and I won't show up. Whatever you do, say nothing about your past or mine.

To be honest, I don't know if I hope you'll get this or not. I don't know if I hope you'll show up in Dayboro or not. If you knew the grief I feel at casting your rosary into the unreliable currents of the postal service.... Sometimes I hope you'll get it, sometimes I hope I'm unshackling my past once and for all. Most of the time I know I am tossing a precious relic into the ocean of time and praying that it will come back to me.

Who could possibly have believed I would become so superstitious? Not me.

How Father JG would be amused!

The letter was unsigned.

5.

At Brisbane airport, the man at the Budget Car rental desk traced out the route with a red felt marker on the map. "After Samford Village," he explained to Lilith, "you will be climbing through rainforest country. D'Aguilar Range. Foothill spur of our Great Divide. Not the Rockies, but we think it's impressive. Third-longest mountain range in the world, as a matter of fact. Hugs the east coast for more than 2000 miles, northern tip of Queensland to the Grampians, west of Melbourne."

"And I'll be surrounded by jungle?"

"I wish. Used to be. Once upon a time this was all rainforest, all Queensland east of the mountains, including where we're standing now. When I was a kid, the road you'll be taking was a green tunnel, canopy thick as a roof. Sunlight was always green." The Budget rental manager sighed. "Now? The rainforest shrinks every week. Cleared for subdivisions and for farming. Sheep, dairy cattle, beef, pineapples. But what can you do? The city spreads, the population grows, people have to be housed and fed. My dad had one of the earliest farms and I grew up there. Rainforest used to press right up against our house."

"Can you show me your farm on this map?" Lilith asked.

"Right here." The man made a small X. "You'll pass it ten minutes after Samford Village, twenty minutes before you get to Dayboro."

"Do you go back often?"

"Can't bear to. Breaks my heart. Some bloody developer from Melbourne bought two hundred hectares, demolished the houses and the farms. It's a yuppie village now, all swimming pools and driveways and lawns. Still"—he smiled bravely—"they can't ruin the D'Aguilar Range or the lakes or the Pine River Valley. And the developers haven't got to Dayboro yet. Gorgeous country. You'll find it will be love at first sight. Stop at one of the lookout points and you can see all the way to Moreton Bay."

"Which means I'll be seeing the Pacific?"

"You will. Yes. You'll be seeing what Captain Cook saw in 1770, except in reverse."

"Are you sure you expect me to bring this car back to the airport?"

"Yeah. I've got your credit card imprint, don't I? But do I expect you to tell me you've bought some land and that you'll be coming back as soon as you can? That won't surprise me. Happens all the time, especially when Americans visit. They get embarrassingly excited. It's the frontier, they tell me. It's the last frontier, it's virgin forest. You'd think they'd seen Adam and Eve at the Dayboro Pub."

"So you're Cap," the publican said, emerging from the shadowy interior of the bar and crossing the wide veranda.

"How do you know my name?"

"That's what the butcher bloke calls you." He placed a large mug of pale golden ale on the wooden table, not very delicately, sloshing the beer on the table and on his customer's lap. "Hey, Sean!" he called back into the bar. "You can go now. All clear."

He went inside and came back with a tea towel and wiped the spill off the table. "Sorry about that," he said.

"I have never seen such an enormous tree in my life," Cap told him with awe, looking up into the vast spreading boughs and the dark leaf ceiling.

"Yeah. Moreton Bay fig. Native to our neck of the woods."

"It doesn't just cover your veranda, it covers your whole building. Your pub's a tree house."

"Yeah. Keeps us cool. Some newspaper bloke measured the crown, edge to edge, and reckons she's 45 meters."

"What's that in feet?"

"Gee, I dunno. Roughly multiply by three is the rule, I reckon."

"So about 140 feet?"

"Whatever. If you say so. And she's 50 meters tall, that tree is. She's a lot older than the pub, which has been here since before Adam, and she's messed up our foundations and our plumbing more than once. She's a bit of a bitch. One day her roots will just topple us over or swallow us up. So. Cap. Pleased to meetcha. I'm Brendan O'Sullivan." He extended a damp and not entirely clean beery hand. "Since you're a fellow Mick, drink's on the house."

"Thank you for the drink. What did you say I was?"

"Another Mick. Aren't ya?"

"I don't know what a Mick is."

"The rosary. Catholic, aren't ya?"

"Oh. Yes. Well, sort of. Baptized and confirmed, but I don't, you know... I'm not exactly—"

"Enough said. Bet I've stayed away from confession longer than you have, even though Father Pat comes here for a drink or three every day. But once a Mick always a Mick, hey? Where're you from? Well, obviously America. You sound American. Where'd your family come from?"

"Oh. From all over."

"So how do you know the butcher, our mystery man?"

"It's a long story," Cap said.

"All his stories are long," Brendan O'Sullivan said, "but we don't know if any of them are true. We do know he did his stint in

Vietnam and came back with a scar on his face and a gimpy leg but he won't talk about that. He won't talk about what he did when he first came back. He just showed up one day out of nowhere. Claims he's worked every cattle station from Darwin to here and back and I believe him. He knows beer and he knows beef and he's a genuine Aussie and a regular Queenslander, so we let him set up camp here even though we suspect he might have been born in Darwin. The thing is, we don't like foreigners here, and by foreigners I mean anyone who isn't born and bred in Queensland, so we don't often let foreigners put down stakes in our neck of the woods. And we don't even much like having foreigners visit, so count yourself lucky that he's vouched for you."

"I am counting myself lucky. Is it always this hot and steamy?"

Brendan O'Sullivan laughed. "You call this hot and steamy? It's only October, for God's sake. Better not stick around for January."

Cap pointed to a road sign with arrow, not far away. There was a dog-leg turn just beyond it. "That long low building at the turn? The billboard says *Dayboro Butchery*. Does my friend work there?"

"Used to. For a couple of years. That's when we decided he was okay. That's why we let him settle in. It's our regional abattoir, that place. After his steers have been hung, he still does the halving and quartering and cutting there but he's planning on building his own cold storage place on his farm. He's working on it. I tell ya, he's the Beethoven of butchers, not that we're into Beethoven round here, but he is. Into Beethoven, I mean. He has pretty strange tastes for a butcher. I sent Sean for him, by the way, after you flashed the holy beads. He doesn't have a phone. He'll be on his way but it'll be a bit of a wait."

The main street of Dayboro was not very long and not very busy. From the veranda railing where she sat sipping her ale, Cap watched several battered cars pass. She saw a small truck laden with crates marked "pineapples" and "bananas" head down the mountain road toward the city. She watched a milk truck pass. Looking uphill toward the blue and purple mountains, she saw the sky filling up with low dark cloud. She thought she could actually see rain falling like sheer veils on the top of the range.

"Is it going to rain here soon?" she asked Brendan O'Sullivan.

"Nah. Further up the mountain, yeah, but not here. Not before January. We're not high enough. And not before 4 p.m. ever."

"Why not before 4 p.m.?"

"Well, you know, that's the way summer thunderstorms are."

Cap watched an extremely battered pick-up truck chug up the main street and park in front of the pub. It was, approximately, blood-red in color, but large sections had been blow-torched and were of no determinate color at all. Two Australian cattle dogs leapt out of the back of the pick-up and bounded up the wooden steps to the veranda.

"Here he is," Brendan O'Sullivan said. "And here come Bluey and Bligh. Never in my lifetime known a dog drink rum the way Bligh does. Hey, fellas! Now you stop jumping all over this lady here, she's a friend of Ty-Lew's."

"Ti-Loup?" Cap repeated, startled.

"Yeah. That's what we call him. What do you call him?"

"Ah... I call him the Man from Nowhere."

"Yeah. So do we. Don't you know his real name?"

"I've never been sure what his real name is."

"His real name's Christy McLew but we Aussies shorten every word we can. You know, *brekkie* for breakfast, *cuppa* for a cup of tea. After a week we called him Ty McLew then we shortened him to Ty-Lew. Quicker to say."

6.

Perhaps because two boisterous dogs were jumping all over her, perhaps because of the shimmering humid haze, perhaps because of the dark shadow of the Moreton Bay fig, Cap could see nothing but a column of light mounting the steps of the pub and moving toward her. She was blinded. She saw only a shape with bright edges.

"Obviously my dogs love you," said the voice from out of the glare. "You haven't changed, Cap." The voice sounded exactly like that of Brendan O'Sullivan. "The first time I ever saw you, I threatened I'd sic the chateau dogs onto you and you laughed at me and said *The dogs love me*. You haven't changed."

"You have," Cap said. Her eyes began to adjust. She saw the dark outline of a man and then, gradually, his features, his body shape, which was that of a tanned and muscled athlete. She saw the long welt that ran down one side of his face and his neck. "I don't recognize you."

"Yeah, well," he shrugged. "The limp. Bad leg break. Never mended right. Changes my walk. And this thing." He touched the scar on his face. "Plus it's been twenty-six years. *Mais quand même je m'appelle encore Ti-Loup. Comment tu vas, Cap?*"

For some time, she could not speak. It was like being caught in a tunnel with gale-force winds blowing from the four corners of the earth and from every point in between: joy, anger, fury, resent-

493

ment, gratitude, sobbing relief. At last she was able to say, very civilly, very politely, though not without a catch in her voice, *"Je vais bien, merci. Comme vous êtes gentil."*

"Tu sais bien que je ne suis pas du tout gentil."

"C'est vrai. Vous n'êtes pas du tout gentil." She gulped at her ale and looked out into the street. In French, she recognized him, and he was not a kind person, not at all. "You don't give a damn about anyone but yourself."

"C'est ça que tu crois?"

"Yes, I do believe that."

"If you knew how much you don't know," he said. "*Comme tu es impitoyable et brutale.*"

"You're asking for pity?"

"No. Not asking for anything. Not expecting. Just commenting." They studied their glasses of ale. They studied the scarred wooden top of the table with its gouges and stains. "On the other hand," Ti-Loup said. "You came. You're here."

Cap traced a jagged roadmap on the tabletop, no doubt carved by a knife-wielding drunk, with the tip of her index finger. "Your eyes are the same," she said. "Nothing else is the same."

"My dogs seem to love you even more than they love me. That's the same."

"Bluey and Bligh, Brendan said."

"Ah. Well. Those are their public names. Their private names, their real names—and they do know their real names—are Ti-Christophe and Grand Loup. There's more and more I remember. At least, I think I do." He reached across the table and lifted her left hand. "No wedding ring? I've been imagining you as Mrs. Simon Cabot with two children in high school. No?"

"No. But Simon and I are together. We don't have children. And you?"

"There was a woman who kept me alive in Vietnam. We had a

son. They both drowned in the South China Sea. Our boats sailed into a typhoon."

"I'm so sorry, Ti-Loup. We knew about the shipwreck. Your mother got a letter from someone who was in your platoon."

"No one who was in my platoon has the faintest idea of what happened."

"One of them does," Cap said. "How many people were picked up by that passing ship when your boat sank?"

"Don't know. Can't remember anything much about that except my son's arms around my neck letting go. I hung onto a piece of the boat, that's what saved me. Or so I was told. Ran into someone on a cattle station a few years back who'd been on the ship that picked me up. Told me I was hypothermic for twelve hours."

"What does that mean exactly?"

"Violent shivering, agitation, confusion. Apparently they had to strap me into the bed because I kept lunging for my son. Ship's doctor said the amnesia might be permanent."

"And was it? Is it?"

"I don't know, do I? I don't know what I don't remember. That's the problem."

"Some gaps I can fill in for you," Cap said. "From the letter that was written to your mother."

"When was this letter written?"

"Twenty years ago, well almost, in 1976. The ship that picked you up took you to Manila. At least one survivor was flown back to the States and met someone from your platoon in Walter Reed. The name of the guy in your platoon was Ben Wheeler from Decatur, Georgia."

Ti-Loup frowned and shook his head. "I don't remember him. Maybe if I saw a photograph of my platoon, I think, bit by bit, maybe I could remember. But all that... you know. It's just darkness. I can't look there."

495

"I made a photocopy of the letter Ben Wheeler sent to your mother. Her lawyer has one copy but I made another one for you." She reached into her shoulder bag and extracted an envelope. It was sealed. "In case you ever feel ready to read it," she said.

"My mother's lawyer? So I'm being hunted. That's how you tracked me down?"

"I didn't track you down. I came here because you wrote to me and sent directions."

"I wrote to you because I've been tracked down. People have shown up asking Brendan about an American Vietnam vet."

"Brendan thinks you're a genuine Aussie."

"I am," Ti-Loup said.

"Brendan suspects you might have been born in Darwin but he doesn't hold it against you."

Ti-Loup laughed. "Who could have imagined our lives? Who could even believe them?"

"So what does Brendan tell the people asking about the American vet?"

"He tells them the only time I've been out of the country was Vietnam."

"Does everyone believe you? Does anyone guess who you are?'"

"Round here no one cares who I am. What counts is what kind of farmer you are."

"Your father died."

"So I was informed in front of a camera crew."

"You've inherited everything."

"So they told me. I'm not interested."

"Your mother thought you should know. She placed notices in some Australian papers."

"So that's what brought the bloodsuckers out. Brendan says serious money's being thrown around. He was offered one thousand in cash just to tell where I lived. Anyway, I was tricked, but not by Brendan, and not by anyone I know in this town. I'm out there somewhere, though, on some con-man's video, and who knows how it's going to be used?"

"Who was the informer?"

"No one knows, and everyone has closed ranks to protect me. The thing is, no one can come up the road from Brisbane without Brendan seeing and he knows every car that belongs and the ones that don't."

"So how did that camera crew get past him?"

"That's the worry. They told him I was expecting them. They said they were doing a documentary on humanely raised beef and Brendan knows they can't shut me up on that subject in the pub. So he believed them. People trust one another round here. Which is why I now require some secret sign. Like the rosary."

Cap reached into her pocket and let the cobalt beads trail across her fingers.

"They make me think of my son," Ti-Loup said. "His name was Thanh. It's the word for the color of the sky, which is the bluest of blues in Vietnam—not quite the color of those beads, but close."

"Let me give them back to you. Or should I keep them and give you back your mother's pearls and jade?"

"No. You keep the pearls. It was your beads that kept me safe. I admit I would like them back."

"How did you manage to keep them? I mean, in combat? And when your boat went under?"

"They were always around my neck. Always. You'd be surprised how many guys wear good-luck charms under their combat gear. I never let go of your rosary. It was always around my neck. My son's arms were around my neck too but he let go and I couldn't hang on to him." For a long time he stared up the steep road and studied the blue and purple range.

He avoided Cap's eyes.

"What was your wife's name?"

"My son's mother. Her name was Lan. It is the name of a flower, lovely as *une capucine*."

"Do nasturtiums grow in Vietnam?"

"They do, as a matter of fact, though *lan* is the word for an orchid."

"The ship that picked you up..."

"They were looking for shot-down pilots and we got lucky. So you and Simon Cabot live together?"

"Not exactly. Well, yes, more or less. I keep my apartment in Manhattan and he keeps his in Cambridge, but we're together as often...Yes. We do. We've been together a long time." "So does that mean you won't stay overnight in my farmhouse?" Cap turned her ale glass in very precise circles within a large arc. "When I say my farmhouse," Ti-Loup added nervously, "I mean the new one. I built it myself. When I first bought the property there was just a shack, no bigger than Grand Loup's cottage. It was an abandoned dairy farm with the roof falling in and I picked it up for a song. Well, actually, for no cash at all. Bartered cutting up a steer with the manager of the bank in Samford Village."

Cap kept her eyes on the surface of the table. There were two pockmarks, two indentations, and they were the grave eyes of Mrs. Cabot. *Lilla Cabot married Henry James's best friend,* her eyes said, *and she was happy.*

Ti-Loup rushed the silence with talk. "My address is Old Cream Truck Road. Don't you love it? It's a dead end, sadly, in all senses. The dairy farmers are going bankrupt because of mergers and mass-produced milk. Multinationals own the land and the herds. So now it's pineapples and bananas and avocados around here, and very small-scale beef amateurs like me. Subsistence farming is what it is. I'm bounded on three sides by the North Pine River and I have forty hectares, two horses, two dogs, ten steers, two calves, three cows, and I rent a bull when I need one. I've built my own house beside the original shack. My house has a deep veranda on all sides.'

"Does it have a loft?"

"Would you stay if it did?"

"What do you think, Ti-Loup?"

"It has a loft."

7.

Cap was awakened by birdcalls. She was on a mattress on the wooden floor of a loft and the other side of the mattress was empty. She could smell coffee. There were steep wooden stairs leading down to the kitchen. There was a heavy cast-iron wood-fired stove built into an alcove, and a pot of coffee simmered on top. There were several cracked ceramic mugs on a shelf so she chose one and poured herself a very dark drink, almost tar. Both the kitchen and the living room had pairs of French windows, floor to ceiling, all flung wide open to the veranda, which meant that the house appeared to be a minor extension of the great outdoors, a sheltered cove between trees. There were two wicker chairs on the porch though both sagged and had conspicuous gaps in the weave. She sat in one, the hot mug in her hands, and felt the seat give a little and then settle around her, cradling and conforming to her thighs.

There was no sign of Ti-Loup.

The steamy heat of the previous afternoon had given way to benign morning air, not exactly cool—she was certainly comfortable being naked—but pleasantly damp on her skin. The sun was rising and the dew-wet grass was steaming with cottony ribbons that stretched for the sky but wavered as they rose and then faltered and vanished into nothingness. The air was noisy with birdcalls, some melodic, some raucous, not one remotely familiar. A flock of strident parrots, their bodies gaudily red and emerald green, their heads cobalt, their beaks orange, took off from the creek like a clamor of flapping canvases by Poussin. The light, the sounds, the colors, the fragrances: none of it seemed possible to Cap outside the Garden of Eden or the imagination of a painter.

She could smell wet cow, she could hear bellowing (cows or calves?), she could smell the thick rich muck of manure and mud.

From the porch she had a view of lush pasture sloping down to the creek flats. She could see the snake of the river looping the shack on three sides, glinting silver and gold where the sun touched it. She could see mist rising like smoke through the trees which clustered at the edges of the pasture and along the curve of water. She could smell eucalyptus. Part of the sky—the part directly over the river—was so low with cloud that the trees on the bank were shrouded with scarves of chiffon. Everywhere else the sky was clear and intensely blue.

In a corner between one of the porch posts and the ceiling, she saw an enormous cobweb and at its hub a dark spider, the largest she had ever seen. The morning sun lit up every filament of hair on its eight menacing legs. She could see its eyes and they were watching her. She edged her chair further from the post.

First she heard the dogs and then she saw Ti-Loup emerging from the clump of eucalypts to her right. He walked awkwardly, partly because of his limp, partly because of the large floppy rubber boots he was wearing. The dogs reached her first and slobbered all over her. Ti-Loup grinned. "Now that is a beautiful sight," he said.

"It's incredible. It's even more beautiful than St Gilles and my father's cottage and the vineyards along the Vienne and I thought I'd never see anything more beautiful than that."

"I meant you sitting naked on my porch," he said, "with my dogs licking your feet. I see you got coffee."

"I didn't hear you leave."

"Didn't want to wake you. You were deep asleep but my day starts at 5 a.m. Animals are a lot more demanding than vines and beans."

"Where have you been?"

"Had to check one of my pumps. I've rigged up my own irrigation system from the river, very amateur needless to say, but the bloody pump keeps seizing up and breaking down."

"You know how to build and fix pumps now?"

"Oh you have no idea how many things I've learned since I last saw you. But now that I'm seeing you, why don't we go back to the loft?"

"So," Ti-Loup said, when they were both sitting—not entirely naked—on the broken-down wicker chairs. "Think you could live here?"

"Oh, Ti-Loup, you know I was born to be a gardener. I was never happier than helping Papa in the vineyard or tending the vegetables with Ti-Christophe."

"So is that a yes?"

"Don't rush me, Ti-Loup. And can I ask about the spider up there?"

"That's a Huntsman. Completely harmless. In Australia, the smaller the spider, the more deadly. Besides, an eight-foot carpet snake lives under the porch. He looks after the spiders. Also the rats and the mice."

"An eight-foot carpet snake? Underneath us?"

"Harmless. There's another one in the bedroom closet. Sleeps on top of the sheets. I think Ti-Christophe would be proud of me, don't you?"

"Ti-Christophe never met a snake."

"No, I mean the farm. I call it Christopher Farm. It's self-sufficient, which is a fancy word for subsistence living. I fish my own river, I eat my own beef, I have one dairy cow for my milk, and I grow my own vegetables and fruit. For the rest, I make enough money by selling and cutting my own steers and working for the Dayboro butcher. You think Grand Loup and Ti-Christophe would approve?"

"They would love it. Ti-Christophe might feel apprehensive about the spiders and snakes."

"No, he wouldn't, there was nothing could make him flinch. He knew he'd be ganged up on when, you know— But he went."

There was a long silence, very long, while a violent movie replayed itself soundlessly behind their closed eyes.

"I can never forgive myself," Ti-Loup said. "I watched it happen. I did nothing."

"I think we have to stop punishing ourselves."

"That's what I'm trying to do. We could do it together. You could help if you stayed here. Don't you want to? "

"Yes," Cap admitted. "And no. I can't give up my whole world for a farm. I fell in love with other things too, especially paintings, especially fine cabinetry, especially anything made in France before 1800."

"I blame my mother for that. You crossed over."

"Not as thoroughly as you did. Me, I want to keep a foot in both worlds. But you. Look at you. You live in a loft and you're a butcher."

"I'm a local joke as a butcher because this is supposed to be dairy land, it's been dairy for the last hundred years. Brendan O'Sullivan grew up on this farm and his father went broke and killed himself and the bank took over the farm and Brendan had to go work in the pub. He owns the pub now and his off-sider, his son Sean, helps me out two days a week. See that shack on the slope above the house? Built in 1900 by Brendan's grandfather. That's where I lived for the first ten years. Couldn't knock it down."

503

Cap smiled. "It looks like the gardener's cottage." She felt as though she were falling backwards through time and space, the countess in blue silk watching her from the grand staircase in the chateau. *So you like beautiful things...* "You keep a foot in both worlds too," she said. "This house, especially the veranda ...Louis XIV's cabinet-makers couldn't have done it better." She kneeled to stroke the highly polished veranda floor. "This is so beautiful."

"Queensland silky oak. The posts are Queensland red cedar."

"When did you learn to do this?"

"Bartered beef cuts for lessons from local craftsmen."

"Your woodwork would bring tears of pleasure to your mother's eyes."

"The wood came from my own land. See all the trees along the river? And on the other side of it? I planted them. We're bringing the rainforest back. Let me show you." He led her along narrow trails between the trees, the dogs mad with delight and constantly chasing scrub turkeys. There was an understory of ferns and small palms, but the crowns of the tallest trees were almost touching overhead. "Another ten years," Ti-Loup said, "and the canopy will be restored. There'll be a thick green ceiling up there and I'll be making my own rain."

"What do you mean?"

"A rainforest's a living greenhouse. Humid air rises, can't escape through the canopy, condenses, falls as rain in the late afternoon and evening. Repeats the cycle every day in the hot wet season."

Cap tried to remember the timid boy in the blue dress, afraid of making his mother sad. Then he became Ti-Loup who wanted to be a butcher. Then he became Vanderbilt and a Dryden snob, and then he became McVie who died in combat in Vietnam. And now he had become an Australian version of Ti-Christophe and the kind of artisan whose work his mother used to collect for the chateau.

"I plan to build my herd up to twenty-five but no higher," he said. "Natural pasture, humane slaughtering, permaculture, lots of different terms but basically they all mean the same thing. Small is beautiful. No mass transport, no brutal road trains with cattle crammed in like sardines, no feed lots alongside abattoirs to fatten the animals up before slaughter, no force-feeding to cause kidney stress and pain. My little herd is grass-fed. They roam free in my paddocks. It's a farming revolution and I'm part of it. I love what I'm doing. I want you to love it too."

Cap paced up and down the weathered porch. She even passed close to the Huntsman spider who was definitely watching her and she barely flinched. She was debating what she should say next. The words felt cobwebby. There was threat at their core. She said as neutrally as possible: "I love what I'm doing too, Ti-Loup. I work for Sotheby's. I'm an appraiser."

"They have a branch in Sydney," he said. "You could transfer from New York."

"They have a small office, I think, but that's all. They sponsor occasional auctions. They send someone out from London. Or from New York."

"Couldn't that someone be you?"

"Maybe. But it's not just Sotheby's. There's something else I do and I can only do it when I'm traveling for a global auction house. It's more or less what my parents did. You could say I work for the Resistance. I rescue people."

"From where?"

"From wherever people need to be rescued."

"But where are you doing this?"

"Middle East, most often. Sometimes Africa. Asia. I get evidence out when I can. I arrange escape routes if I can."

"What kind of escape routes?'

"The kind that got the Goldbergs out of France."

"Aren't you afraid?"

"All the time. This isn't something I do every day, you understand. Or even every month. Maybe every two or three months. Rest of the time, I'm just doing regular appraisals."

"Are you watched?"

"Probably. I've been detained. I'm always nervous at points of entry and exit, but I got into Brisbane with no hassle. When I showed my passport, the guy said *No worries, mate,* and I couldn't help laughing. Why did he call me *mate?*"

"Because *she'll be right, mate,* that's the rule in Australia. That's why I'm staying here. I was scared my whole life until I thought I was drowning. I thought I *had* drowned and I had to find my son because he was there too, in the place where drowned people go. And then somehow, apparently, I got to Darwin and nothing can ever scare me again. I've already been to the worst places anyone can go."

Cap thought about this. "There are, actually, worse things," she said. "People can be broken in such ways that they can never be put back together again. I've seen photographs. That's why I can't stop what I'm doing. I owe my parents."

"Let's take a run with the dogs," Ti-Loup said.

They found the small herd in the lower paddock beside the creek. The dogs went crazy. "I've rented a bull for two weeks," Ti-Loup explained. "You can see he's sniffing up Dido. We'd better get out of here and leave them to it. Hey, boys!" he called to the dogs.

"How did you learn to do all this?" Cap asked.

"Trial and error. By making a fool of myself more times than any idiot should. Worked my way from Darwin to here on cattle stations. Saved enough to buy my own cattle. Learned the best breeds for this climate, learned which breeds are tick-resistant and which aren't. Best breed for here are Aussie-bred Brahmans. Next

506

best are French Charolais. There's enough Loire Valley chauvinism in me to own three French cows."

"Father JG would be impressed with your diligence."

Ti-Loup laughed. "Somehow I doubt that. But he'd be pleased with my library which is many times bigger than my herd. It's in storage crates at the pub at present. I still have my Cicero—well, not my original copy, naturally, which never even got to Vietnam, but I buy mail-order books through the Dayboro Post Office. I still read Cicero. And Augustine."

"We are so weird, Ti-Loup. Do you realize that? We are so not normal."

"We've never been normal. So why couldn't we start up a new kind of abnormal? Couldn't you combine Sotheby's and your rescue work with living on a small cattle farm?"

"Couldn't you run a small cattle farm in New York State?"

"Never. I'd be trapped in Vanderbilt air. I wouldn't be able to breathe. And it wouldn't just be the family, it would be the name."

"You could change your name."

"I've changed my name several times and yet a TV crew had their cameras right here and asked if I knew that my Vanderbilt father had died. I can run to the end of the world but I still can't hide. All my mother's damn fault. How dare she advertise in Australian papers?"

"I'm afraid that's my fault. I suggested it because your mother felt you should know that you inherited everything."

"I don't want it."

"Then let your mother know you're alive and sign everything over to her."

"And what would the press and the lawyers do with that? First I'd have to prove who I was and I don't even have a starting point. I don't have sufficient ID to get a copy of my own birth certificate, not that I'd want to. I don't have a passport. I don't have a driver's license."

"How can you drive your truck without a license?"

"Farm country. Nobody checks stuff like that out here. Nobody cares. I don't have a telephone. I live so far off the beaten track that anyone who finds me is lost. I live by barter and cash. I don't have any ID whatsoever."

"What about the title to your farm? That must be a legal document."

"The title is actually in Brendan's name. Suits both of us. If I die first, the place is already his. If he dies first, then Sean owns this when I go."

"What about your two sets of dog tags?"

"They were radioactive to the village that kept me alive. If the VC found the tags, everyone would've been torched. I don't know what they did with them, but believe me, both Vanderbilt and McVie are dead and gone. "

"McVie's mother sends me a card every year. She writes that she prays for the soul of McVie and she prays for your safe return."

Ti-Loup was so startled and so moved by this that he could not speak.

"Your mother arranged a Thanksgiving Mass at St. Patrick's. Mrs. McVie saw something in the paper and she wrote that she gave thanks at St Ann's."

Ti-Loup threw sticks for his dogs to retrieve, a game that kept him occupied for ten minutes. Without looking at Cap, he asked when the mass had been held.

"Twenty years ago, almost. When your mother got the letter that said you might be alive. There was a ripple in the press at the time but it soon fizzled out. No one would remember it now."

"Is my mother all right?"

"She wasn't. For a long time, she wasn't. She nearly went under. But after that letter came she was fine."

"Thanks be to God." Ti-Loup crossed himself. "Old habit," he said, embarrassed. "But it was such a lead weight, you have no idea, being the one who made her sad. There was nothing I could do to shift it. Nothing. It crushed the life out of me."

"I remember. But it wasn't your fault. It wasn't you who made her sad."

"Yes it was. Don't you remember what happened when she found out I was working for a butcher? I was promptly sent into exile."

"It wasn't *you*. It was because she knew that the village and the whole Vanderbilt family would mock her. And mock *you*. She couldn't bear it."

"Better to make *my* life miserable, right?"

"What a narcissist you are. She was afraid for you. She was aware of much more than we were. She suddenly saw the Monsards for what they were and she was afraid for all of us. She was afraid they would kill you, kill us, kill Papa, because of what we knew."

"She didn't know what we knew."

"She didn't know everything we knew, not then. But the Monsards visited her and made veiled threats and her intuition told her the rest. And she was right. I'm still afraid of the Monsards. Your mother is still afraid of them too."

"You said she's fine now."

"She *was* fine, until your father died. Her situation's been precarious again since that, but I think I've got things straightened out with the help of a lawyer."

The dogs came bounding up from the pasture and threw themselves at Cap. "Want some cattle-farm training?" Ti-Loup asked.

Cap stared at him. "That's abrupt. Is this an apprenticeship test? Or just change of dangerous subject?"

"This paddock's for the cows the bull's not interested in at pres-

509

ent. I have to inspect them for ticks. Constant battle. They've had their annual shots, but this is rainforest country and that means ticks. The Brahmans are bred tick-resistant, but my Charolais are always at risk. Here's what we're looking for." He pulled tight a section of the soft moleskin hide of a cow, behind one ear. "See?" He pointed to a glossy dark blister about the size of a pea. "She's already engorged, this tick. Tick fever is a problem." He pulled from the pocket of his overalls a small bottle filled with kerosene and a pair of tweezers. He extracted the tick, dropped it into the fluid and screwed the cap on. "Tick one off the list," he said.

After dark, Ti-Loup and Cap dragged the mattress out onto the porch and lay there looking up at the Southern Cross. "I don't have a telephone," Ti-Loup said, "but I do have a good sound system. Let's listen to Bach."

A light breeze rustled the gum trees. One of the horses whinnied and the dogs pricked their ears and made soft sounds then subsided again until the music filled the house and the porch and the pasture. "Cello Suite No. 1," Ti-Loup said. "Look at the dogs." Bluey and Bligh nestled themselves into the mattress and draped themselves across Ti-Loup's legs. They appeared utterly relaxed and contented. "For cattle dogs," Ti-Loup said, "they have very sophisticated tastes."

"I don't know how I can leave," Cap said.

"So don't leave."

"But I don't see how I can stay."

"What did you mean," Ti-Loup asked over breakfast on the veranda, "when you said my mother's situation is precarious?"

"Your father left her no money to live on, not even enough to pay the utilities or the condominium fee."

"She'll get everything that would have gone to me."

"No, she won't. The terms of your father's will won't allow it. She can stay in the penthouse for as long as she lives but she has no income at all so the family lawyers are trying to have her evicted. If you don't show up to claim your inheritance then everything goes to your cousin, but he's dead, so everything will go to Celise. I don't see how that can stand up legally since she remarried, but she kept the Vanderbilt name and she can afford the best legal team money can buy and she's very determined."

"Who'd Celise marry this time around?"

"She married Lucifer. Can you believe it?"

"Hah. I can. They deserve each other."

"I've hired a lawyer to keep the jackals at bay and I'm privately paying your mother's bills, but I've made sure she doesn't know that. The lawyer tells her he's worked things out."

"Cap! I can't let you do that. My mother has other resources. She has the chateau."

"It's a ruin. After Papa died there was no one to manage it. She's trying to sell it."

"She has the paintings and antiques. She has jewelry."

"She's been selling them."

"There has to be something that can be done."

"There is. You could produce proof of your identity and proof that you are alive. You would have to claim your inheritance and then sign it over to your mother."

"I have to think about that," Ti-Loup said. "I have to walk when I'm thinking. Boys!" The dogs leaped off the veranda and followed him into the thick stand of trees along the river. Cap heard the dogs giving little yaps of pleasure as they ran. They were gone for three hours.

"I can't do it," Ti-Loup said. They were lying on the mattress in the loft, looking up through the skylight at the stars. "I know it sounds simple but I can't. Once the lawyers know I'm alive and where I am, the press will know, and I'll have the world crawling all over this place. It's unthinkable."

"I don't believe you're world-famous Ti-Loup. It's even possible you overrate the importance of the Vanderbilt name. Things will be horrible for a month or so and then the press will lose interest. No one will remember."

"That's longer than I could handle. You know the gutter press would track down that pathetic little boy who used to wear a blue dress and they'd blast photographs from every front page and on TV. There's no sewer they won't crawl into."

"Would anyone in Dayboro care?"

Ti-Loup stared at her. "*I'd* care. I've escaped. But you want to sic my past onto me again. It's like a succubus. It would be unbearable if anyone in Daboro knew about all that. There'd be jokes behind my back in the pub. After a few drinks, they wouldn't be able to resist."

"It's okay," Cap said. "Let's drop this. The lawyer and I can manage things. I'll make sure your mother is okay. And I'll ask Sotheby's for a transfer to Sydney."

"Will they announce that?"

"I can ask them not to. *Currently traveling on private appraisals,* is what they'll say. But I can't lie to Simon or your mother about where I'll be. I couldn't do that."

"If you tell them you've found me, I can promise you I won't be here when you get back."

Cap felt her heart lurch. "You're trying to do what you always do," she accused. "You're going to vanish again. But I won't let you."

"Hush," he murmured into her ear. "I didn't mean it. You won't drown," and they thrashed about and held each other as though

512

they were indeed floundering through deeper and deeper water, as though only their ferocious grasp on the moment could keep them alive.

On the veranda, they lay in the warm dark with Bach's cello suites and stared at the Milky Way.

"What is that star there?" Cap asked.

"That's Alpha Centauri. It's a pointer star. There are two of them. Draw a line between them and keep going and you've reached the Southern Cross."

"The Southern Cross is stunning. Why haven't I ever noticed it before?"

"Can't be seen north of the equator."

"*The fault, Ti-Loup, lies not in our stars but in ourselves.*"

"I can see Father JG frowning," Ti-Loup said. "I can hear him saying *Inappropriate, Mademoiselle Melusine.*"

"I would never have believed I'd miss him so much. And the chateau and St Gilles. And Papa and Ti-Christophe."

"Ti-Christophe and Grand Loup are here," Ti-Loup said, stroking his dogs.

8.

There was a send-off for Cap in the pub. Everybody in Dayboro came. Ty-Lew shouted drinks all round. "She's coming back," he promised. "And by the way, you can call her Cap instead of Lilith. It's her family nickname since she was a kid. She's coming back and she's coming to stay."

"Sort of," Cap explained. "I'll be working in Sydney but I'll be coming up every weekend."

"How did you two meet?" someone asked.

"Oh, you know these American women," Ty-Lew said, "the way they backpack around the world. Opal fields, cattle stations, the Outback. We met decades ago. Didn't expect to connect again."

"Here's to the lovers," someone said, and much beer was consumed.

"I wish I could drive you to the airport," Ti-Loup murmured. "But what if I'm stopped? No license. Safer if Sean drives us."

"I have to return the car anyway," Cap said. "And this isn't cut and dried yet, you know. I have to see if Sotheby's will agree. And I have some appraisal trips already set up for next month. They're also Lilith Foundation trips. I have a crucial one in London and another one in Shanghai."

"Crucial. Meaning what?"

"Meaning I hope to get access to a billionaire art collector of a brutal regime."

"You're not going to keep doing this, are you? After you transfer to Sydney?"

Cap thought of saying: *You sound like Simon and Mrs. Cabot.*

"I'll have to think about that," she said. "But I don't really think I can stop."

In November 1995, Cap obtained a transfer to Sotheby's in Sydney for a year. The New York house agreed to be vague about location. Traveling on private appraisals was their formulaic response to all inquiries.

"Traveling out of the country for a *year?*" Simon said when she told him. "Traveling where?"

"Sotheby's promised the clients they wouldn't say."

"So how do we stay in contact?"

Cap studied the New York skyline beyond her apartment window. "We can't," she said.

"Is this what I think it is about? Is this your way of breaking up?"

"Yes," she confessed.

"But why?"

"Not because I don't love you. And not because we haven't been happy together. And not because I don't adore your family, because I do. But I'm a vagabond. I'm not cut out to be a Cabot and you should be free to find someone who is. You're too nice to free yourself so I'm thrusting freedom upon you."

"I'm not going to accept this," Simon said.

"That's why I'm not giving you a choice."

The meeting in London was not quite what Cap thought it would be. The encounter was full of covert threat and menace and it seemed unlikely that she would be invited to the palace in Zimbabwe. In Shanghai, she learned that Chinese officials who sensed the wind turning had multiple ways and means of getting their paintings and capital out of the country before they fell from the

Party's grace. They squirrelled away assets anywhere from Hong Kong to Switzerland to the Caymans. The defector let her know, subtly, that since she was now in possession of sensitive information she would do well to ensure that her lips were forever sealed.

Sotheby's is scrupulous about client privacy, she assured him. She flew from Shanghai to Sydney. The stunning beauty of Sydney overwhelmed her. She found a small studio apartment in Balmain and could see the harbor from her windows. She had an office in the heart of the city. She did not need a car. She could go wherever she needed to go on foot or by train or by harbor ferries. She fell in love with the Opera House. She loved Circular Quay. She loved taking the ferry to Manly. She felt as animated and elated as she had felt on the first day she stepped inside the chateau. She had passed through some invisible membrane and entered a hitherto unimaginably beautiful new world.

She was astonished to find how many collectors in Australia owned or wished to buy paintings and antiques from the era of the French baroque. She was abashed to learn of the extent of such collections on display in art galleries and museums. She discovered Aboriginal art. She felt awed and excited. All this she did as Lilith Jardine.

On Friday evenings, she flew to Brisbane and rented a car. She drove to Dayboro and slept in a loft with Ti-Loup. She became Cap, the gardener's daughter, the woman who loved to bury her hands in rich soil.

"Now I'm the one secretly escaping," she told Ti-Loup. "Climbing out of my Sotheby's window on Friday nights. Climbing back in on Monday mornings."

"Do you ever wonder," Ti-Loup asked one night, "what Michel Monsard and his father did with the bodies?"

Cap flinched. "I try not to."

516

Once a week, from Sydney, Cap spoke by telephone to the countess. She never said where she was calling from. The countess said that all was well. The lawyer had worked something out. However, she said, the Vanderbilt lawyers claimed the letter from Decatur, Georgia—or, rather, the photocopy of that letter—was a cut-and-paste fraud. They were still suing her. The trial was due to begin sometime early in '96 but the lawyer whom Cap had hired had assured the countess there was nothing the Vanderbilts could do. They could not evict her because all penthouse expenses were now being paid.

"Where are you, Melusine?" the countess would ask. "When are you coming back?"

"When you need me, *ma marraine*," Cap replied. "Whenever you need me. But until then, I'm on the road."

She called the Goldbergs from time to time and gave them the telephone number of the Dayboro pub. "If something urgent comes up," she said, "call this number and say you have a message for Cap. Don't forget to allow for the time difference. Day is night. If you wake Brendan O'Sullivan in the middle of the night, he's going to be surly. And you must promise that you do not give this number to another living soul."

One Monday, due to weather-delayed flights, Lilith Jardine was late getting back to her Sydney office. The receptionist at Sotheby's told her: "Your cousin from America was here this morning. He wanted to know where you were."

"My cousin?"

"The one who collects Aboriginal art. He's here to buy and he wanted to see you. I told him you left town every weekend. I asked him to leave a number but he said he'd call back."

"Which cousin?" Lilith asked. "What was his name?"

"He didn't leave one."

No one called back that week. Cap took particular precautions the following weekend. She rented a car, drove north to Newcastle, left the car at the airport and flew to Brisbane from there. She decided to say nothing to Ti-Loup. She did not want to spook him or trigger nightmares. She was confident she could cover her traces. On Monday morning she told the Sotheby's receptionist: "I don't have an American cousin. Bu there's a man in New York who's been stalking me. I may need a restraining order. Can I ask you to divulge nothing whatsoever about me?"

"Oh my God!" the receptionist said. "Of course. That's awful. I told him nothing. The only thing I said was that Europcar picked you up at the office every Friday and took you to the airport but we didn't know where you went. You asked me to reserve those cars for you. I'm sorry if I told them something I shouldn't have."

"Please don't tell him anything else. You didn't give him my Sydney address or phone number, did you?"

"Of course not," the receptionist said, shocked. "We never give out information like that."

In early March 1996, on a Sunday, Brendan was awakened by a phone call. It was five o'clock in the morning. "Jesus, Mary and Joseph!" he said. "Who the hell is this?"

"This is Myriam Goldberg in New York. I apologize if I got the time zones wrong. Can you ask Cap to call me? Tell her it's urgent."

When Cap called back, Myriam told her: "The *New York Post* has announced that the Vanderbilt claimant will appear in court next week."

"What on earth does that mean?"

"We don't know. No one knows. The countess is in quite a state."

"I'll book a flight immediately," Cap said. "I'll fly tomorrow if I can. I'll be there."

To Ti-Loup she said: "I think we finally know why that TV

crew tricked you. I think I know how that video will be used."

When the video was shown in court in Lower Manhattan, Cap was in the balcony and the countess was at her side. As the camera panned down towards the loop of the river and the pasture and the cattle and the house with its loft and its wide veranda, Cap had a profound and disturbing sense of violation. The serpent had slithered into Eden. *You cannot keep any secrets from me*, the serpent hissed. *I know everything. I will track you down and exhibit you to the world.*

Cap knew Ti-Loup in all his incarnations. She felt her godmother's shock like an earth tremor moving along the balcony seats. The countess gripped Cap by the wrist and her grasp was fierce. "It is Gwynne Patrice," she whispered. "He has changed, but I know him.'

When her own name was mentioned by the interviewer, the countess gave a small stifled cry and slumped against Cap just as the claimant and his horse jumped the fence. "I am so cold," she whispered to Cap. "It's freezing in here. I have never felt so cold in my life.

She lost consciousness then.

Cap had to summon an officer of the court and an ambulance was called. Reporters with microphones were jostling the stretcher at the ambulance doors and one of them jabbed a mike in the patient's face. The paramedics pushed him aside and a policeman grabbed him.

"She's had a stroke," the paramedic told Cap in the back of the van. "I think we'll make it, but you know there's always damage. We won't know for a few days how much."

The countess was discharged several days later, her body paralyzed on the right side. She could speak but only with difficulty. It took intimacy and intuition to translate what she said.

Cap placed a phone call to the Dayboro pub. "Get Ti-Loup to call this number," she said.

"We're in a war zone now," Brendan told her. "That video made news here. The place is crawling with reporters and TV crews, but so far we've managed to bamboozle them. We've sent them to the Black Stump and back. But I tell ya, I dunno what to make of this, Cap. He's always seemed true blue Aussie to me. He isn't really one of those fat cats, is he?"

"He really isn't," Cap said.

When Ti-Loup called the Fifth Avenue apartment, Cap told him: "Your mother had a stroke when she saw the video in court. I've hired nurses for round-the-clock shifts but I'm not going to leave her. I'll come back when I can."

"I'm under siege," Ti-Loup said. "The place is crawling with reporters. I'm going underground."

"What do you mean?"

"Got a safe house."

"Where? Where will you be?"

"I'll leave breadcrumbs," he said. "You'll find me."

Most of the time, Cap sat at her godmother's bedside and held her unresponsive right hand. She kept the penthouse filled with the music of the French baroque. She read aloud from both Molière and Racine. Sometimes, when she was reading Molière, she thought she saw a half-smile on the left side of her godmother's lips.

One day, in her strangled way, the countess sought to make something clear to Cap. *I would like to be buried in St Gilles,* she said.

"You are not dying," Cap said. "But if and when you do, I'll take you back to St Gilles."

The end came suddenly. Someone entered the bedroom and Cap turned to speak to the nurse, but it was not the nurse. It was

Celise. "How the hell did you get in here?" Cap demanded.

"I've brought flowers," Celise said. "I only came to see how poor dear Isabelle is doing." She leaned over the countess and kissed her forehead. The countess flinched violently.

Cap called down to the doorman and security arrived within minutes. Celise was escorted from the room.

Cap pressed her godmother's good hand against her own cheek. "*Ma marraine*," she said. "Gwynne Patrice is alive and well. I have seen him. He sends you his love and he wanted me to give you this."

She took both of her godmother's hands, the live one and the dead one, and cupped them between her own. With her left hand, she held that frail cradle of flesh and bone together and she took the pearl and jade rosary from her pocket. She let the rosary fall like slow water into those trembling palms. With her good hand, the countess pressed the rosary against her lips. *I knew it,* she tried to say. *I knew it.*

She died smiling with the pearls pressed to her lips.

In the cavernous church in St Gilles, a handful of villagers gathered. Marie-Claire was there with her husband, who still did not remember who he was. Father Boniface had long since passed on and a new young priest chanted the service for the burial of the dead. The Goldbergs had accompanied Cap on the flight that took the coffin on its last trip home. The night before the funeral Cap had the coffin draped and displayed in state, as it were, in the grand salon of the chateau, now stark and empty of furniture. With Marie-Claire and the Goldbergs, she kept the last watch.

Within the medieval stone church, the chant of the priest reverberated back from the high Gothic vaults: *Requiem aeternam dona eis, Domine, et lux perpetua luceat eis. Requiescat in pace. Amen.*

Eternal rest grant unto her, O Lord, and let perpetual light shine upon her. May she rest in peace. Amen.

9.

Cap and Ti-Loup lay in the loft looking up through the skylight at the stars, surrounded by Bach's cello suites.

"I was afraid you wouldn't be here when I got back," Cap said. "When you said you were going underground, what did you mean?"

"I meant exactly what I said. When I lived in the shack, I dug out a cellar. It's under the back porch and I used it as my cold storage room. I can lift a whole section of porch floor and disappear."

"How big is it?"

"Not very big. Big enough to hide in for a few hours if I see a reporter or a camera. The problem is the dogs. They'll give me away."

"They'll follow the bread crumbs."

"I still have to work that part out."

"Can I see your safe house?"

"I'll show you tomorrow."

"You can't hide very long in a hole in the ground."

"The Goldbergs did. It's bigger than the space in your mother's laundry van."

"I was holding your mother's hand when she died," Cap told him. "I gave her own rosary back to her, the pearls and jade. I told her you'd sent it. She died smiling."

"I'm glad you did that."

"Your mother and I were holding Papa's hands when he died," Cap said. "No one should die alone. There should always be someone holding your hand when you die."

"Or you should have Bach," Ti-Loup said. "I would happily die with Bach's cello suites in my ears."

"We spent the night before the funeral in the chateau, in the grand salon. It was strange to be back there, all those memories, all those ghosts. It's a ruin. I wanted to spend the next night in the gardener's cottage, in the loft, but the ladder has rotted away."

"None of that seems real to me," Ti-Loup said. "It's like a fairy tale told to children, full of ogres and magic, signifying nothing."

"I wonder if Father JG is still alive," Cap said.

"Is La Boucherie Monsard still there?"

"The shop and the sign are still there. I don't know if the Monsards are still there. I couldn't bear to go in or even ask. They didn't come to the funeral, I'm glad to say."

"Did you go to the safe house?"

"No. I asked the Goldbergs if they wanted to, but they said no, definitely not. They've sold their Manhattan apartment, by the way. They're moving to Florida this summer, a retirement village, Beth Shalom."

"Time to switch from Bach's sorrow to Beethoven's Ninth," Ti-Loup said. He filled the house with melodic jubilation and they lay quietly on the mattress in the loft and gazed up at Alpha Centauri.

"Whatever this is about," Brendan said, "the Aussie tabloids are smelling blood. They've turned into piranhas. We can send 'em off to Woop-Woop and Bunyah till kingdom come, but they still circle back. It's the limp and the scar. You're not easy to hide, Ty-Lew. And another thing: people are being offered serious money. So far, no one's cracked, but I don't know how long it might be."

"This will pass," Cap said. "Next week they'll find a body in

Watson's Bay or there'll be a juicy divorce. But until it passes, I suggest we hide Ti-Loup in plain sight in my unit in Sydney. Sean, can you manage the farm and the herd while we're gone? Can you play dumb with reporters?"

"I can play dumb with anyone," Sean said. "And I can manage the herd and the farm."

"I don't want to hide in Sydney," Ti-Loup protested. "And I'm not leaving my dogs."

"We can take the dogs with us," Cap said.

"I'd rather take off for the back-of-beyond, Alice Springs or Channel Country or Tennant Creek or Katherine. I've worked all those cattle stations. No one asks questions or ever asks for ID, and if any reporters show up from Sydney or Melbourne, they'll be led on a wild goose chase."

"Please," Cap begged. "You'll be invisible in Sydney and the harbor is one block from my apartment. We can be together until this blows over and you can take the dogs running along the foreshore every day. We don't want anything, we're not challenging anything, so why would the Vanderbilt lawyers even bother? They'll forget we exist."

Six months in Sydney seemed interminable to Ti-Loup. He called Brendan from Sydney every day. "Sean's doing okay," Brendan assured him. "Four calves. Two heifers, two bullocks. Sean will look after the castrating. Of course, with you not here to do the butchering, the Brisbane orders are falling behind. Customers notice the difference."

When Cap received a very strange FedEx envelope in early October, Ti-Loup made up his mind. "I'm going back to the farm," he said. "I think it's blown over. And if it hasn't, then I'll leave the dogs at the pub and disappear into my safe house until the cameras give up. They won't get any copy out of me."

"Someone anonymous," Cap said, "has sent me round-trip air

tickets to New York and reservations at the Grand Hyatt next door to Grand Central. Sent to my Sotheby's office with no explanation. It's probably a collector working under the radar, it's probably Zimbabwe or Shanghai, but the trip coincides with the wrapping-up of the trial, so who knows?"

"Who cares?" Ti-Loup said. "Just don't be gone long. And come back."

"I promise," Cap said.

BOOK VI
IDENTITY: A MELODRAMA
IN MULTIPLE ACTS

1.

In espionage, as in con games, there are unwritten rules, though both spies and con men have always felt free to break them. Nevertheless, ironically, they are stunned and outraged when others transgress. They are always taken by surprise. They never see penalties coming.

Marlowe, who never saw penalties coming, is reading the *New York Times* over breakfast. *Oh, for the cold war when life was simpler,* he reads, *when spies and spy catchers played by unwritten rules as formal as the structure of a sonnet.* The piece is by foreign correspondent Tim Weiner, who won the Pulitzer for his book on the CIA.

"I see the Vanderbilt fraud is no longer front page news," Celise says. She is across the table, nibbling at toast. She has another section of the *Times*—the Arts section—tucked under her plate.

The lives of today's spies are more like free verse, Tim Weiner writes, *famously defined by Robert Frost as playing tennis without a net.*

Marlowe reads that the Foreign Intelligence Service of the former USSR is accusing the US of entrapment, of breaking the rules by giving a visa to Vladimir Galkin and then arresting him as soon as he arrived. Galkin is a former KGB spook who had nutted out certain Pentagon secrets—Star Wars defense-system stuff—and squirreled them off to Moscow, as the FBI very well knew when they gave him a post-Cold-War visa. They were waiting when he stepped onto American soil. Entrapment! Russia is outraged. The Americans, they say, have breached the code of behavior of espionage and Russia is ready to retaliate against current and former agents of the CIA. There was a time, the Russians say, when the unwritten rules were followed. If an American agent was caught in the act in Moscow, he lost diplomatic immunity and was expelled. He was not arrested and shipped to the Gulag.

But now? Honor among thieves is no more. Let the ensnarers beware!

"Have you noticed?" Celise asks.

"Sorry. Noticed what?"

"The Vanderbilt affair has practically dropped out of sight, but this scuttlebutt from the butcher in France will ratchet things up."

"What scuttlebutt?"

"The Fox News interview from that French village, St Gilles. Didn't you see it? The butcher's son? He's got evidence, photographs, of a murder. Remember all that talk about the gardener's son and the butcher's daughter?"

"Not really."

"You should have paid closer attention to the trial. It was supposedly an honor killing because the butcher's daughter was pregnant, or else the gardener's son fled out of fear. Well. That was the theory in 1960 when the gardener's son disappeared. Now it seems *he* was a killer and he's still alive. Alive and well in *Australia*.

"Yes?"

"Turns out someone else disappeared, same time, no one knew why. He didn't live in St Gilles. He worked in a factory in Tours and he was a friend of the butcher's son. The butcher and his son found the body in the woods, and took a photograph, but when they went back to retrieve the body it had gone. They were too afraid of the chateau to report the murder. But now that the gardener and the countess are dead, the butcher's son will swear under oath that the gardener's son was the killer. And he recognizes the Vanderbilt fraud as the gardener's son."

Marlowe watches her face. "How much did Fox pay him for this statement?'

"The gardener's daughter was an accomplice," Celise says.

"To what?"

"She helped cover up the murder and get her brother out France. I'm just telling you what the butcher's son swears. This'll bring the story back to page one. Funny that right now you have to hunt the back pages for clues."

"Funny," Marlowe agrees. But true. Like a spent skyrocket, the trial has smoldered its way through the paper from headlines to demoted back sections like Travel or Art. Minor revelations—especially from France, especially from the village of St Gilles, especially from cattle stations in Queensland—are still being ferreted out and filed by Pulitzer chasers but readers are losing interest. That could change suddenly, he knows. There will be meteoric spikes and plummeting dips in mass fixations, it always happens.

"Your absence at the MOMA fundraiser was noticed," Celise says. She extends the folded paper to show him a photograph. "If you keep abandoning me at gala events, you'll set tongues wagging. Do you see who I'm with?" Marlowe makes an indecipherable sound. "Gianni Versace," Celise says. "He's invited me—well, us—to visit him at his South Beach mansion. I accepted, but I told him I wasn't sure we could count on you. I told him you'd been rather preoccupied lately. But it's against the rules, you know, not to show up when we're sponsors and on the fundraising board."

Marlowe thinks of saying: Breaking the rules has never bothered you much.

"Are you listening to me?" Celise asks.

"Gianni Versace," Marlowe says, playing back her words in his head. "You've been invited." All the chickens do come home to roost, he thinks, watching her watching him. Eventually. "He's invested with me, did you know?"

"I didn't, but he mentioned it, and of course I wasn't surprised. He asked if there was anything to these rumors he keeps hearing, securities investigations, possible irregularities, that sort of thing. I told him of course not. Jealous rival firms, I said. They propagate smears. But Gianni said he was thinking of pulling some of his money out anyway, spreading the risk."

"Always sensible to spread the risk," Marlowe says smoothly. "But Versace has nothing to complain about. I've given him higher returns than he can possibly get anywhere else."

"That's why I thought it was diplomatic to accept. Good for both of us, don't you think? And if I can coax him into hosting a fundraiser gala at his mansion, well... Should I go? Without you, I mean, if you can't spare the time?"

"Why not?" Survival rule number one for spies as for con men is *Don't tip your hand. Keep your cards close to your chest.*

Rule number two: *Find your target's Achilles heel.*

"You promise you won't sulk if you see photos of me and Gianni and some of his guests—I mean the famous ones who *aren't* gay—in Vanity Fair?"

"When are you thinking of going?"

"Gianni suggested this weekend. Will that be alright?"

Marlowe reaches across the table and takes her hand. He raises it to his lips and kisses her fingers. "I will bury myself in work while you're gone. Go and raise tons of money and tons of attention, my dear."

Marlowe knows that the place to start is with the Boykins of North Carolina. If his wife's first husband had been Tom Boykin, a grounds-man on the Biltmore Estate, then Marlowe knows very well that there will be many other Boykins—both closely and distantly related to Tom—who are still living in Asheville NC and in Buncombe County and indeed throughout the Carolinas. There will be black Boykins and white Boykins. That is the way it is in the South. Everyone has slaves in the family tree and the descendants of slaves still carry the name of the master (who was, after all, often enough, the biological patriarch.)

Marlowe flies to Asheville, North Carolina. He will start with the white Boykins and he will start with the Biltmore Estate, which has always kept meticulous records on employees as well as remarkably detailed financial accounts. Thus he is able to follow a trail to the Auto Body Repair shop of Jeremiah Boykin in the township of Sandy Mush, north-west of Asheville and close to the Tennessee line.

"Tom's my brother," Jeremiah Boykin says. "Was." There is an odd echo to his voice which booms out from under a car in his workshop and bounces back from the workshop walls. He lies on his back and Marlowe can see only his legs which project crab-like on the concrete floor. The feet begin crab-walking and Jeremiah Boykin rolls himself out from under. His flat wooden platform has swiveling corner castors and as his whole torso becomes visible he executes a couple of full-circle spins, perhaps just for the fun of it, perhaps because he needs the momentum to push himself up. He takes a few seconds to regain balance and leans against the side of the car. "Back then, when Tom was alive, I was working on Biltmore too, as a blacksmith. Making iron cartwheels with tourists watching. They like to keep the Old World alive at Biltmore. But after what happened to Tom, I quit."

"What exactly happened to your brother?"

"Tractor accident, they said. Personally, I believe she bumped him off."

"Celise, you mean?"

"Celise? Who's Celise?"

"Tom's wife. Your brother was her first husband."

"Yeah? Well she wasn't Celise back then. She was Alice Brownwell. Her mother was Hallie, one of the Biltmore maids."

"And you think Alice Brownwell killed your brother?"

"Not something I'd ever be able to prove and anyway she wouldn't have dirtied her own hands. But she had this way with men, you know? Strange, really, because she wasn't good-looking, but there was something…. She seemed dangerous, and that turns some guys on. They trotted after her with their tongues hanging out. Tom sure did. He would have died for her. Well, he did die for her."

"How did they meet?"

"On the estate. We all grew up in Biltmore Village and we all worked on the estate. Our father was in charge of machinery, landscape machinery—you know, mowers, tractors, back hoes—and we lived in a cottage just outside the grounds, close to the gatehouse. The whole village was close to the gatehouse."

"And who lived in the village?"

"Everyone. Gardeners, plumbers, electricians, housemaids. Biltmore Village was built for staff and for tourists. Built by the Vanderbilts. By them and for them. Ever been there?'

"Not for years. But yes, often actually, when I was young. My family's connected."

"With upstairs or downstairs?"

"Both."

"Well then, you should know. We all lived in each other's pockets. We were all a stone's throw from the gatehouse. We were always on call."

"And everyone in the village worked at the chateau?"

"No, not everyone. Some worked as staff in the guest houses and hotels in Biltmore Village. There were droves of tourists, you know, famous people, New Yorkers, aristocrats from Europe, movie stars. Hallie, Alice's mother, was a chateau maid not a guest-house maid and she made sure you knew it. It wasn't a picnic, being a Biltmore maid. It wasn't easy work, cleaning and dusting and scrubbing and polishing the silver every single day before the next day's tourists arrived. My mother was a Biltmore maid but she lived in the village, not in the chateau like Alice's mother. My mother worked long hours and came home dead tired, but she did see a lot of famous people and heard plenty of gossip."

" What kind of gossip?

"Well, you know, hundreds of rooms and thousands of acres, a lot of hanky-panky could happen. We weren't supposed to so-cialize with visitors. If you got caught, you got fired, but there are always ways and means. Hallie set her cap at anyone who might be her ticket out of domestic service. No one knew who Alice's fa-ther was, there were so many candidates. But Hallie told Alice her father was a lord or a prince or some such thing. The details kept changing. Sometimes he came from New York, sometimes London or Paris. No matter how many times Hallie contradicted herself, Alice believed her every time. Hallie was smart enough never to name a name because she had sworn, she said, not to betray a gen-tleman and because she got money every month for staying silent.

"Alice always believed she was a cut above everyone else. She might have been a plain Jane, but she knew in her bones she was entitled. Our daddy knew that was bullshit. Alice's father was an ax man, a lumber man, one of the Biltmore forestry crew. Daddy saw him and Hallie going at it in the sawmill, mid-winter, and he figured out nine months from there. Aren't no guests at Bilt-more in mid-winter. But what do you know? Alice's daddy got conveniently killed by a tree that fell the wrong way so he wasn't around to contradict. Our daddy didn't go around telling anyone what he saw. If you wanted to keep your job, you kept your mouth shut. Alice believed what she wanted to believe and Tom believed Alice. Wanted to, anyway. Our daddy tried to tell him, 'Tom, you are marrying bad blood,' he might as well have tried chatting up a tornado. Tom acted like the Angel Gabriel had bowed down to him when Alice said yes."

"How old were Tom and Alice when they married?"

"Alice was sixteen, Tom was twenty. By twenty-one he was dead. Summer is when the tourists and wealthy guests arrive in swarms and Tom didn't make it much past that first summer. Like mother, like daughter. Alice was cheating before and after the wedding and everyone knew except Tom. His body wasn't cold in the grave before she took off for New York."

"Didn't that raise eyebrows?"

"Oh it sure did. Most of us put two and two together."

"What about the local police? Weren't they suspicious?"

"They sure were. They also knew their jobs depended on not making waves. They questioned everyone. Alice was serving High Tea to tourists when Tom was killed."

"So why do you think she's responsible for the... you know... the accident?"

"I saw her with one of the mechanics in the machine shop a few days before. He was just a kid. You know that age when it's exciting to have sex on a workbench with the smell of machine oil in the air? I wasn't the only one who saw. One of the other blacksmiths whispered to me, *If I were you, I'd warn Tom there's a raven on his shoulder.* But what could I do? Plenty of friends had already told Tom she was cheating and he wouldn't believe them."

"So you think this kid in the machine shop...?"

"My bet is that he did something to the brakes on the tractor, favor for favor, but all the dumb kid got out of it was he got him-self killed when Tom's tractor crashed into his. A week later, Alice ran off to New York because of a one-night stand with a movie star who'd been a guest. We heard he wasn't thrilled to be chased all the way back to the Big Apple and he sent her packing. But can you believe she sued him for seducing a minor? There was an out-of-court settlement, is what we heard. She wouldn't sell her story to the tabloids if he set her up in the style to which she believed she was entitled. Anyway, that's what we heard. She was Alice Boykin when she left here. Well, Alice Brownwell Boykin, but everyone knew the last names wouldn't stick. They'd wash off in the shower. She was still Alice to everyone here. So now she's Celise, gone fancy. I'm willing to bet she landed on her feet and found another sugar daddy very fast. What's your interest, anyway? Are you writing a book?"

"I'm the last of her sugar-daddies," Marlowe says. "Third husband. And I think I may be writing a book."

"Holy shit! Good luck with that. I'll lay bets you won't be her last mark. If I were you, I'd watch my back."

"I am watching my back," Marlowe says.

"Do you know who her second husband was?"

"He was a Vanderbilt," Marlowe says. "And he died in the saddle. Literally. Horse racing accident."

"Surprise, surprise."

"Where's Hallie now?"

"Dead and buried."

"Natural causes?" Marlowe asks.

"We all thought so. No one raised any questions at the time. You might want to talk to Sally-Lee Stapleton. She lives in Ashville. She knew my sister-in-law from way back when they were both kids and Tom's wife was still Alice Brownwell, daughter of a Biltmore maid."

536

2.

Sally-Lee Stapleton lives in a modest brick bungalow in Asheville. "Funny thing," she says. "We were both born in the servants' quarters, Alice and me. We had nice rooms. We both had a free education, a good one, and I've never stopped being grateful to the Vanderbilts for that. It wasn't just us white kids. The Vanderbilts were the first family in the South to educate the children of their black domestics. They built schools for them on the estate. But Alice.... she never knew for sure who her father was."

Sally-Lee proffers for examination a framed photograph—two women, two girl children—that stands on the sideboard. "This is us," she says. "These are our mothers. I think we were four or five when that was taken. She destroyed my mother's life, Alice did, and mine too for a while and yet I owe her everything. That's what I think, looking back. I can still see her with her hand on her hip by the time we were thirteen, I can still hear her: *Just because this is the way things are doesn't mean they have to stay this way. We could be Vanderbilts, Sally-Lee. We could be whatever we want.*

"And she was right," Sally-Lee says. "If my mom hadn't been fired, if we hadn't been turned out of the estate, I would never have gone to Community College in Charlotte. I would never have come back to Asheville to teach. I would never have met Anson, my husband. I wouldn't have three children and one grandchild so far. I've had a good life. I've been lucky. That's not what Alice intended but I owe her for that just the same."

"When your mothers were maids and you were children together...?"

"The rest of us kids called her Alice the Malice," Sally-Lee says. "Not to her face, of course. We all knew better than to mess with Alice."

"What would happen if you did?"

"Things would go missing, not valuable things but things that mattered. For example, one Christmas my mother gave me a crystal necklace I'd been hankering for ever since I saw it in the Sears' catalogue. Every night, I used to wrap it up in a handkerchief and put it in the top drawer of my dresser. When Alice came to play, I showed her where I kept it. Every morning I'd take it out and put in on. One morning it wasn't there. Of course at first I kept asking myself: Did I put it away last night? Did I take it off before my shower? Did I leave it in the bathroom? Did the clasp break when I was mopping the floor? Anyway, I never found it again.

"Another thing that disappeared was a Bill Haley record that I played to death. Never knew what happened to it. Alice was always so sweet about these things. She'd help you look. And so you trusted her, you'd confide things to her in total confidence and they'd come back like boomerangs to smack you in the face. After a while—but it's hard to believe, looking back, how long it took—we all put two and two together. We all became scared of her. Dead scared. Things stolen from guests might show up in your room, under your mattress, in your dresser drawer. The Biltmore manager would get an anonymous tip. People got fired. They just vanished like your private keepsakes did. One day you'd see a fellow servant—a friend—at the staff meeting, next day they were gone, no trace of them left behind."

"Is that what happened to you?"

"No. It was different, the way we got kicked out. In one of my stupid stages of thinking how sweet Alice was—it was after she helped me search for my Bill Haley record—I told her I was worried sick about my mother. I told her my mother was depressed and that I'd begun to find bottles of whisky under her mattress. The estate manager got an anonymous note. They found whisky bottles in my mother's bedroom and she was fired, which was probably the best thing that ever have happened to my mom and me. Alice and I were sixteen when that happened.

"There was a movie star visiting Biltmore at the time. I'll call him Jason because we shouldn't speak ill of the dead. I can tell you that Jason seduced just about everyone in skirts while he was there. Alice got pregnant, but the pregnancy magically disappeared before anyone noticed except me. She married Tom Boykin pretty quick after that, but the rumor was Alice had paid someone to take photographs of her and Jason in bed and someone sent them to Tom. In my mind, there's no question that the person who sent him the pictures was Alice herself. Of course she waited until after the wedding.

"She could spin rumors and float them out like dandelion puffs. Poor Tom, he was suckered from the git-go. Supposed to be a tractor accident killed him, but I think he killed himself after he found out about the baby and the abortion and the Kodak porn. Alice took off for New York and I don't know what happened to her after that and have never wanted to know."

3.

In a Holiday Inn in Asheville, North Carolina, Marlowe lies on the queen-size bed, propped up by pillows. He takes from his briefcase a folder that is labeled in black felt marker, his own handwriting, or rather hand printing, rather clumsy, all block letters, upper case: **CV FILE**

More than a week has passed since he printed off the contents of the file, since he had a contact—a hacker—decode the keystrokes of his wife's password and decrypt the file. For reasons only partially clear to him, partially obscure, he has not yet read it in detail. He has skimmed it. As soon as he realized he had been out-played and out-conned, that he was married to a Master of the Game more cunning than anyone else he had known, he was overcome by an onslaught of anxiety so intense that he had to hide the folder from himself. He jammed it into his briefcase and hid his briefcase in the safe in his office, the lavishly furnished shadow office for his shadow investment company. He alone had the combination for that safe. He had seen enough. He knew she knew.

He knows that she knows. She knows his fortune is smoke and mirrors and she is making plans to jump ship. She will take him down before she jumps. Already she has initiated leaks to the tabloids and the SEC.

It is checkmate. Parachute time.

Well, two can play that game. He is a master player himself, but first he needs to study the board. He needs to know all the pieces that are still in play and where they are.

The legal-size manila folder feels radioactive. He sets it down again, quickly, on the quilt on the unoccupied side of the bed, and goes to the mini-bar to pour himself a Scotch. The bottles are tiny so he adds a second one to his glass and from the ice bucket scoops a few cubes. At the window he takes several quick gulps to calm himself. The window has a gloomy view of the parking lot. He pulls the drapes closed. They are lined with canvas, thick and heavy and off-white, the drapes themselves the color of dirty sand erratically crisscrossed with black rectangles that interlock with red squares. They are hideous but they do shut out the light. Even though he has asked for a smoke-free room, the drapes stink of stale cigarettes.

It is not so easy, he thinks, to erase evidence of earlier regimes.

Fortified and calmed by the Scotch and by the murk of the room, he returns to the bed, switches on the bedside lamp, and picks up the folder.

It is full of letterhead correspondence that dates back to the time of paper and typescript and priority registered mail, has later been scanned and encrypted, and now—through hacker archeology—has been returned to paper again. Marlowe does not doubt that the original hard-copy correspondence has been destroyed. He feels like Schliemann excavating the ancient city of Troy, or like Howard Carter discovering King Tut's tomb. It is not easy, he thinks, to dig up the past but it is even harder to erase every trace.

His memory, like a spooked horse bolting between the shafts, returns to Dryden (one of his prep schools) and to Harvard, to Shelley and Keats. He feels like a traveler from an antique land who stumbles, in the middle of the desert of his life, on two humongous legs of stone and an inscription:

My name is OZYMANDIAS, King of Kings.
Look on my works ye Mighty, and despair!
Nothing beside remains. Round the decay
Of that Colossal Wreck, boundless and bare,
The lone and level sands stretch far away.

He feels like some addled watcher of the skies when a distant galaxy, older than time, swims into the telescope's eye. He feels *like stout Cortez, when with eagle eyes / He stared at the Pacific.... Silent upon a peak in Darien.*

Silent upon his queen-size Holiday Inn bed, Marlowe leafs through pages. The file contains hundreds of items, mostly correspondence, sometimes invoices, sometimes receipts or photocopies of checks, the earliest dating from 1976. All the correspondence was originally on letterhead paper—well, perhaps not the most recent communications, which may have been born in binary codes—and the letterhead is either that of Celise Vanderbilt (with assorted office addresses and assorted honorary titles) or that of a legal firm with offices in Washington, Baltimore, and New York: Willson Williams & Walter, Attorneys at Law. Marlowe is familiar with the firm, which is well known for its high-priced and highly successful defense of celebrities charged with criminal violence. It is rumored—and certainly widely known in intelligence circles—that the firm will make discreet arrangements at arm's length for clients whose needs might put them at risk of such charges. It is public knowledge that the firm has rendered exemplary service to such demonized groups as the Mafia. The missives from Celise far outnumber those from the attorneys. Marlowe skims through the pages, all communications from Celise being pared to essentials, all responses legally careful.

November 5, 1976
To: Stanley Willson
Willson, Williams, &Walter, Attorneys at Law

Dear Stanley:
I enclose a clipping from the New York Post re: letter sent to the Vanderbilt countess. Could signal brewing of a fraudulent claim or something more serious. If the son is indeed alive it is crucial that he be located. Please undertake all necessary research in Australia, in France, among Vietnam vets. Your expense account will be unlimited. Please report only to me, and do so often.
Sincerely, CV

June 8, 1977
Dear Ms. Vanderbilt:
We have examined the passenger and crew lists of every Australian naval vessel leaving the Philippines shortly before or after the Fall of Saigon. None had any former combatants on board. We found anecdotal evidence of unidentified Americans who left a ship in Darwin, but on a cost-benefit analysis, we recommend that you accept the probable conclusion that the Vanderbilt heir drowned in the South China Sea.
We enclose an itemized list of expenses incurred in this search.
Yours sincerely,
Stanley Willson, Attorney at Law

June 15, 1977
Dear Stanley:
Your expenses seem extraordinarily high but I'm sure they are warranted.... Darwin anecdotal evidence could be important.

Please spare no expense in recruiting informants. You should have eyes and ears on every cattle ranch between Darwin and Australian cities to the south and east. Let no stone be unturned along these routes, no drunken gossip unrecorded.

Should you find a possible candidate for the heir, I trust you will proceed with all due discretion as instructed, especially with regard to the subcontracting of necessary tasks. No residual evidence should remain.

Yours sincerely, CV

Marlowe added another mini-bottle of Scotch to his glass and skipped a few sheets of paper, a few years. He settled on February 1978 when Billy Vanderbilt, his predecessor as husband of Celise, was killed. He found an expense account entry for $50,000 and brief letter.

February 20, 1978
Dear Stanley:
Thank you for prompt dispatch and absolute discretion.
Yours sincerely, CV

February 26, 1978
Dear Ms Vanderbilt:
I regret to inform you that a groom in the Vanderbilt stables is proving difficult. It may be necessary to have him charged with criminal negligence. Then again, such action may incite further police investigation and be counter-productive. Either route involves risk. It is our legal experience that payment for silence never ends with the first demand. I await your instructions.

Yours sincerely,
Stanley Willson

March 3, 1978

Dear Stanley:

Charges should be laid, unless and until other more definitive (and entirely discreet) means can be found. Meanwhile I require you to draw up a pre-nuptial agreement for my impending remarriage. I can assure you there will be no shortage of funds.

Sincerely, CV

June 15, 1978

Dear Stanley:

The pre-nuptial agreement is entirely satisfactory. Thank you. Now that new and unlimited funds are at my disposal, please focus close investigative attention as follows:

a) Doormen, delivery men, etc at Penthouse

b) LJ, so called; investigate questionable political activity

c) Goldbergs, art collectors and donors; close ties with LJ; sponsors of questionable political activity

d) Find informants in village of St Gilles in Loire Valley; pay them well.

Yours sincerely, CV

Marlowe flipped through pages of expenses paid to delivery men who took packages to the Fifth Avenue penthouse and to the Goldbergs' building on Madison Avenue. It was clear that attempts to bribe both doormen had failed. Nevertheless, there were detailed plans of the arrangement of rooms in the penthouse, and also photographs (photocopies of photographs) of the interiors of the rooms, of paintings, of antique furniture, of *armoires*, of *fauteuilles*, of *prie-dieux*. There were numerous invoices and dis-

bursements to cattlemen and drovers and truck drivers in Outback Australia, to the families of Vietnam Vets all over the country, to small business owners and farmers and vineyard owners in
St Gilles and all along the valleys of the Vienne and the Loire.

Marlowe skipped through pages of documentation on Sotheby's private art deals, on Lilith's collection of evidence on the
side, on her border detentions, on her Cabot liaisons, on her
movements between Boston and New York. He skipped all the
way to the death of Lawrence Gwynne Vanderbilt in October 1994.

November 1, 1994
  Dear Stanley:
  *You will appreciate the increased urgency in the search since
the death of the patriarch. Please redouble your efforts.*
  Sincerely, CV

And then, many pages and documents later:

October 15, 1995
  Dear Stanley,
  Subscription to **Natural Farming in Queensland** *innovative and
brilliant. Spare no expense on camera crew and script. The video should
be professional and polished. We will use it in court.*
  Sincerely, CV

November 5, 1995
  Dear Stanley:
  *Whatever you paid the informant at Sotheby's in Sydney was
worth the cost. The eagle has landed. We have proof of contact
between claimant and bait in Australia.*
  Sincerely, CV

There were several extremely large disbursements of funds in late '95 and early '96, most to Australia, some to France. And then…

March1, 1996

Dear Stanley,

Please schedule claimant video to be shown in court next week. Place teaser announcements in New York Post. *On other matters: It may be time to move on to a new funding source. I have intimations that the current supply may be shaky. Can you investigate further? You should by-pass the SEC. Waste of time. You could sell snake oil and the Brooklyn Bridge to the SEC. Go direct to clients, take them to dinner, keep tally of those who have already withdrawn their winnings and those who have not, keep tally of duration of time between investment deposit and withdrawal.*

Sincerely, CV

September20, 1996

Dear Stanley,

Excellent work tracking movements in Australia. Once date of final week of trial can be estimated, arrange delivery to Sotheby's office of round-trip tickets from Sydney to New York and make hotel reservations to ensure that bait attends trial. Canvass possible buyers and sellers of information re political activities of bait. Encourage competition and bid prices up. Arrange terminal incident to benefit of highest bidder.

Sincerely, CV

October30, 1996

Dear Stanley,

Jury verdict a great success and buys time. Video of French butcher will buy more time. Trial by media (cold-case murder; subversive politics) will gut and delay appeal of claimant case, but it will not eliminate risk. We have perhaps opened a can of worms: unintended consequences, more tenacious investigative journalists than we bargained for, hordes of them. Now that we have done all the leg work, they are riding our coat-tails. Once they get DNA, game's over, and sooner or later someone will. We are looking at a ticking time bomb which must be defused. In duplicate.

I trust you to make arrangements that will be as discreet and untraceable as they are final.

Sincerely, CV

November 5, 1996

Dear Stanley,

Investigation into current funding source confirms suspicions. Vaporization and vanishing point imminent. Generate media melodrama on scope of fraud, but begin arrangements for quiet terminal exit. According to unconfirmed reports, etc., disgraced financier suicidal, etc. A substantial sum has been deposited to your account to cover cost of arrangements.

Sincerely, CV

On the final page of the folder labeled CV, labeled by Marlowe himself in black-felt marker, there is nothing but a black-and-white photocopy of Tenniel's illustration of the Cheshire Cat from *Alice's Adventures in Wonderland*. Above it, there is a handwritten dedication:

To Lucifer: It's been a great game and I've enjoyed every minute. You're not a Master Player, but you're good. Congratulations on tracking me down, but I'm afraid it's too late. Love, Celise.

Marlowe stares at the image.

I tried to warn you, the Cheshire Cat grins. *Remember?*

Its eyes gleam in the dark. *You are finished, you know*, the cat says, *but your stage exit will be as graceful and mysterious as mine.* Starting with the tip of its tail, the Cheshire Cat begins to disappear until only its grin is left. *You thought you were the cat's meow*, the grin says, *but you were wrong. You are not a Master of the Game, but only a second-rate player. Be nervous*, the grin says as it vanishes.

Marlowe is nervous.

But two can play this game, he thinks. He knows it is too late to save his kingdom of smoke. The die is cast, the vault empty, but he can take Celise down before he goes and he can save Lilith. One day, perhaps, Lilith will thank him. As to Vanderbilt or McVie or whoever he really is, there Marlowe is indifferent, but it's clear that Celise herself is convinced that McLew is the real McCoy, the real Vanderbilt thing, and Celise doesn't leave any loose ends.

One day, perhaps, Lilith will understand what Marlowe has done for her, done for them, what he has given up.

He begins drafting and sending out from his laptop anonymous tips to contacts who will pass the message on. He knows the tabloids and Fox News will gorge on these snippets as alligators gorge on rotten meat.

Unconfirmed rumors suggest police in North Carolina are reinvestigating cold case. Reported Biltmore accident may have been murder...

Did Celise Vanderbilt hire hit men...?

Real truth about society hostess Celise Vanderbilt: mother was promiscuous Biltmore housemaid, father an unknown one-

549

night stand...

Unconfirmed sources reveal that a trove of incriminating correspondence between Celise Vanderbilt and her lawyers has been made available to the press by a reliable anonymous source...

Legal firm working for Celise Vanderbilt notorious for mafia connections...

Marlowe pours himself one last mini-bottle of Scotch and then sleeps. He dreams of tomorrow's headlines. He dreams of the late-breaking news on Fox and is falling asleep with a smile on his face when his bedside telephone rings. "Package delivery for you," the receptionist on the front desk says.

Marlowe is about to say that not a living soul knows where he is and then he realizes.

"Give me a few minutes," he says. "I'll be down to pick it up."

"I'm sending it up to your room," the receptionist says.

Marlowe stuffs his laptop and folder into his overnight bag and heads for the parking lot. He guns his rented car and leaves Asheville behind him, but November snow and black ice have slicked the roads. He is nervous. He brakes going into a curve but brakes cautiously, and although he understands instantly that the brake lines have been cut he steers into a snowbank as deep and soft as a feather pillow.

The last thing he sees before the police and the ambulance arrive is the explosion at the Holiday Inn and the smile of the Cheshire Cat.

EPILOGUE

On the five-hour flight across the country from New York, Cap is fixated on the front page of the *New York Post* which leers at her from the seat pocket of the woman beside her. *Unsolved murder from 1960 ... Fraudulent claimant may be killer ... Female accomplice ... subversive activity ... Interpol alerted ... Arrests expected in Australia ...*

Cap has decided what she will do. At Los Angeles, she will make a phone call to Marie-Claire in St Gilles and she will call the Mother Superior at the convent in Tours. She will ask them to contact the police. She will offer sworn testimony that she witnessed a bloody knife-fight in the woods of St Gilles in 1960. The fight was over Chantal Monsard, the butcher's daughter. Cap saw her own brother kill his rival from Tours and she saw Michel Monsard, son of the butcher, kill her brother. When she returned with her father, the bodies had disappeared. She will ask that the gendarmerie from Tours interrogate the Monsard family and search for evidence of skeletal remains in the woods and in the butcher's establishment. If bones are found, DNA can identify the dead. I witnessed the murder of my own brother, she will say, and I will swear to that under oath.

Cap calculates the time-zone change in France. She will not be able to make the call from Los Angeles because in France it will be somewhere between midnight and dawn. She will have to wait until Sydney.

She does not dare leave the LAX transit lounge in spite of the long weary wait—four hours—and in spite of being on East Coast body-clock time. If she has to go through security again, the risk of being detained on some pretext is too high. Nervously, she scans the magazine and newspaper stands in the transit lounge. The front pages of two tabloids display the same stabbed body of Olivier, the same headlines. Cap watches as various people, their wheeled carry-on baggage parked at their ankles, pick up the papers and thumb through them and put them back. Their eyes have the glazed airport look of all travelers with long layovers. They are bored. They glance at corpse and "claimant" and turn the page. This is old news. If you have seen an image of one stabbed body, you have seen them all.

She moves to her gate for the flight to Sydney. She is subjected to Fox News, hardwired into every airport-lounge ceiling.

"We have late-breaking news," an announcer says. "There has been a surprising twist, an astounding U-turn, in the Vanderbilt case." The screen image splits: announcer on the left half, Celise Vanderbilt on the right. Cap is riveted. "A trove of legal documents and photographs has been anonymously delivered to this channel. It seems that society hostess Celise Vanderbilt has been paying a high-priced legal firm to disseminate false information to the press. The firm of Willson Williams and Walter is notorious for its service to organized crime. The documents suggest that Ms Vanderbilt may have bribed and murdered her way into the highest social circles... The firm's legal correspondence has been subpoenaed. Police investigations are underway and Ms Vanderbilt has gone into hiding."

What a difference a five-hour flight can make! Cap marvels, traveling from dread to delirious disbelief at the speed of a penthouse elevator whose cable has snapped. Down, down, down, she drops into peaceful exhausted sleep and has to be shaken awake when her flight is called. Before she sinks back into sleep on the fifteen-hour flight to Sydney she wonders: but how was it found, the evidence that damned Celise? Who turned it in?

At Sydney airport, after clearing customs and immigration, she calls the Dayboro pub. She has to leave a message on the answering machine. "Brendan, it's Cap. I'm in Sydney. I haven't even got to the domestic terminal yet, but I'll take the first flight to Brisbane and rent a car. You can expect me in a few more hours. Get a message out to Ti-Loup that I'm on my way. And tell him, there's nothing to worry about. It's all over except for the shouting and the party. No one is going to bother him again.'

Cap parks under the green awning of the Moreton Bay fig. She takes the veranda steps two at a time. At several tables on the veranda, farmhands are having lunch and Cap waves to them and they wave back. In the murk of the bar she can see a few shapes huddled over their beers, four men at the pool table. She can barely see Brendan behind the bar. She is still sunblind, but she says to him: "Come out from behind there, Brendan, so I can hug you. Did you get my message? Is he on his way?"

"Cap," Brendan says. "Cap, I have something to tell you. I have a letter for you. But have a drink first. Drink's on the house."

"Is he on his way?"

"You better read the letter."

The letter, addressed simply to *Cap* in Ti-Loup's handwriting, is in a sealed envelope.

"Before you read it, Cap... You gotta understand the place has been swarming with reporters, cameras, telescope lenses, tabloids throwing money around. He couldn't stand it, Cap. He just couldn't stand it. He's gone."

"Gone where?"

"Who knows? Any place where he can't be found."

"Until when?"

"That's the question, isn't it?" Brendan says.

Cap sits on the veranda of Ti-Loup's house, looking up at the Southern Cross. The night is warm. She can hear the murmuring of the herd down by the river. Somewhere, she knows, perhaps in Queensland, perhaps in the Northern Territory, perhaps somewhere along the Birdsville Track, Ti-Loup is looking up at those stars, those same stars.

The note in the envelope says only:

Dearest Cap, Sorry about this. I'll be back. I hope you will wait for me. Love, Ti-Loup.

She beams a message up to the Southern Cross. She believes it will be ricocheted back to where he is, wherever he is. She imagines him lying in his sleeping bag under the splendid sky. Congratulations, Ti-Loup, she says. You have proved you are not who you are. I will be waiting when you get back.

Bibliography

Annear, Robyn: *The Man Who Lost Himself: The Unbelievable Story of the Tichborne Claimant* (Melbourne, Text Publishing, 2002)

Bhattacharjee, Yudhijit: "The Mind of a Con Man", *New York Times Sunday Magazine*, 26 April 2013

Erdely, Sabrina Rubin: "The Girl Who Conned the Ivy League: How a high school dropout created the ultimate fake ID, scammed her way into Harvard and Columbia, and became the target of a nationwide manhunt", *Rolling Stone*, Issue 1080, June 11, 2009

Henriques, Diana B: *The Wizard of Lies: Bernie Madoff and the Death of Trust* (New York, Times Books/HenryHolt, 2011)

Vanderbilt, Arthur T. II:
Fortune's Children: The Fall of the House of Vanderbilt (New York, HarperCollins/Perennial, 2001, © William Morrow, 1989)

Acknowledgments

A short section of this novel, "On the Czech-Slovak Border," in slightly different form, appeared in Hecate vol 38, nos.1&2 (2012): 207-9, an interdisciplinary feminist journal of literature and ideas, published twice-yearly by University of Queensland.

The image of the Cheshire Cat is taken from Sir John Tenniel's illustrations for the 1865 edition of Lewis Carroll's Alice's Adventures in Wonderland.

I am deeply indebted to Carolyn Taylor Koroloff, my fellow student at high school in Australia. Her intimate knowledge of farming in Queensland (especially of ecological and self-sustaining practices, both in rainforest and in cattle country) has been invaluable to me. I confess to purloining two of her beautiful houses for three of my novels, and also to appropriating the lovely Darling Downs house, self-built, of my husband's nephew Mark Blake. All three houses are at the heart of their own private Edens, surrounded by rolling hills, lush pasture, and rainforest or dense bush. From their verandas and balconies no other sign of human habitation is visible. This is my personal idea of paradise. Ti-Loup's house in Dayboro is a conflation of Carolyn's house near Gatton and Mark's house outside Warwick.

About the Author

Janette Turner Hospital was born and educated in Australia. She grew up on the steamy sub-tropical coast of the north-eastern state of Queensland and began her teaching career in remote tropical high schools. She and her husband, also a Queenslander, moved to the USA in the late 1960s for graduate school. At the time, they had no intention of staying, but since then both Hospitals have taught in universities in Australia, Canada, England, and the United States.

Hospital's first published short story appeared in the Atlantic Monthly (USA) and received an "Atlantic First" citation in 1978. Her first novel, *The Ivory Swing* (set in the village in South India where she and her husband spent a sabbatical in 1977) won the $50,000 Seal First Novel Award in 1982. Since then she has won a number of prizes for her nine novels and four short story collections, and her work has been published in twelve languages. Her novels have appeared in New York Times "Notable Books of the Year" lists, and she has won the Queensland Premier's Literary Award and Australia's Patrick White Award for lifetime literary achievement. A recent short story, "Afterlife of a Stolen Child," was included in Best American Mystery Stories 2015.

Janette Turner Hospital is Carolina Distinguished Professor Emerita at the University of South Carolina and Adjunct Professor of English at the University of Queensland, Australia. She has been Visiting Writer in Residence at MIT, Boston University, Colgate, and Columbia. She spends parts of each year in South Carolina, New York, and Australia.

For more information, visit www.janetteturnerhospital.com

Proof

58418197R00314

Made in the USA
Charleston, SC
09 July 2016